MISS BUSBY INVESTIGATES

DEATH
OF A
PENNILESS
POET

KAREN BAUGH MENUHIN
& ZOE MARKHAM

For Ollie,
Who ought to take a leaf out of Miss Busby's
book and walk the dog a bit more often!
From Zoe.

CHAPTER 1

Cotswolds: May 1922

'Isabelle, have you heard what the police are saying? It's a *travesty*.' Mrs Adeline Fanshawe's voice boomed through the telephone. Miss Busby moved the receiver a little further from her ear.

'Good morning, Adeline. And good morning Mabel,' she replied pointedly into the mouthpiece, knowing the young operator would struggle to resist such an opening. 'I do hope your mother is feeling better?'

A brief silence followed, before, 'Much better, thank you, Miss Busby.'

Adeline *tsked* down the line. Miss Busby had reminded her several times to be sparing with sensitive information imparted over the telephone, lest it make its way round the exchange and through the surrounding villages before she'd hung up. When Adeline was bursting with news, however, she rarely took time to think.

'I haven't heard anything this morning,' Miss Busby went on, glancing at the clock on the mantel piece. It was a little after 10am. 'And I have yet to catch sight of the paperboy.'

At the word "paperboy" a low growl emanated from the sofa facing the fireplace. Nestled amidst the cushions, a solid little Jack Russell, white with black and tan patches, opened one bright eye suspiciously. Paperboys were his least favourite of all boys.

'Isabelle, you really must keep up with the world. Something dreadful has happened, and I will not allow it. Bring your notebook and pencil. Indeed, bring all your detecting paraphernalia. I shall collect you from the village green in ten minutes.'

'But Adeline, I—'

The line went dead. Miss Busby sighed as she replaced the candlestick receiver. She had recently invested in the device on the doctor's advice when one of her neighbours had taken ill. Bloxford was somewhat isolated, particularly in winter, and a telephone could prove a lifeline in time of need. Since its installation, however, it had performed exclusively as a 'news' disseminator for her local, and vocal, most well-informed friend. Although this was the first time that Adeline had mentioned "detecting paraphernalia."

'Well, Barnaby,' she sighed, making her way through to the kitchen, 'I can't think what could have happened, but you had better come along, and I suspect you'll need a snack or two.' Opening the cupboard next to the sink, she took a handful of hard biscuits from the glass jar and stowed them in the pocket of her pale blue cardigan. Paired with a cream blouse and smart navy skirt, she considered herself sufficiently dressed for an outing.

She called for Pudding, her ginger tom, at the back door. It was no surprise when he didn't appear; he had mice to chase and warm spring sunshine to sleep in, and would be perfectly happy in the flower-filled garden until she returned.

Miss Busby, a lady of a suitable age and acutely clever, having taught at the local school, gazed about her comfortable living room: the chintz cushions in place on the sofa, the armchairs before the unlit fireplace in neat order, no dust on shelves or bookcase, and the lattice windows sparkling clean. She gave a satisfied nod.

With the words 'detecting paraphernalia' in mind, she went to the under-stairs cupboard and reached for the bag Inspector McKay had given her the previous December. Made of the most beautiful soft brown leather, it contained a jar of fingerprint powder, a soft shaving brush, a torch, penknife, and her leather-bound notepad and pencils.

The inspector had presented it as a peace offering of sorts, and she felt a flicker of excitement at the prospect of giving it a fresh outing. This was soon tempered by sadness at the thought of how things had ended at Little Minton, and the tragedy of it.

'But I'm getting ahead of myself,' she murmured. 'There is no point fearing the worst, after all.'

A jacket seemed unnecessary, given the warmth of the day and cloudless blue sky. She slipped on her comfortable walking shoes, took Barnaby's tartan lead from the coat stand in the hall and opened the front door onto bright sunshine and the flushed face of young Dennis.

'Good Lord, Dennis, what are you doing here? You gave me a fright.'

'Sorry Miss! I was just about 'ter knock!'

Of all her ex-pupils, Dennis Ogden was among her favourites. Teachers should never have favourites, but retired teachers, she felt, were a different matter.

With his cap at a jaunty angle over curly brown hair, tie askew and Post Office jacket unbuttoned in the warmth of the day, he looked every inch the schoolboy she remembered. All that was missing were the short trousers and muddy knees.

Miss Busby smiled. 'That's quite all right. Good morning, Dennis.'

'Morning Miss! Innit' nice out?'

'It most certainly is,' she agreed, as a blur of determined dog flew past them, making straight for the post van idling in the lane. Barnaby jumped into the open door to take the worn leather seat up front, his tail wagging in excitement.

'Not today I'm afraid,' Miss Busby called to the little dog. 'You will have to come out.' His ears drooped but he didn't move.

She pulled the front door closed behind her and turned to Dennis. 'Well?'

'Eh?'

'If you were about to knock I assume you have a parcel for me?'

He looked down at his empty hands, seeming momentarily surprised. 'Oh, no. I haven't, Miss. Sorry.'

Miss Busby raised an eyebrow.

'But I've got a message for you,' he went on, as if suddenly remembering. 'From Mrs Mary Fellows. She says you're to go over for your lunch today, if you're free. Cook's doing sole, and there might be lemon pudding. And can you bring the dog, she says, because it's Matron's day off.'

'Lovely.' Miss Busby's smile widened. 'Please tell her I would be delighted. Oh,' she added as an afterthought, 'and mention Adeline Fanshawe may be joining us.'

'But I can't. I'm not going back that way Miss! Can't you telephone? I'll be late with the rest of the post!'

'Nonsense, Dennis, it won't take a moment. I believe they have sausages for breakfast on Mondays. If you hurry, I'm sure Mary will find one or two for your trouble.' She politely refrained from adding that no one would notice if he was late; he was late with the post most days, after all.

Once more calling the dog to come out of the van, she strolled up the lane towards the village green. Barnaby caught her up, then raced ahead, gleefully darting along the verge, snuffling through yellow cowslips and burgeoning buttercups with unfettered delight.

Every day was a new adventure for the little dog, and one could do worse, Miss Busby thought, than follow his example. As they crested a small incline and the village green came into view, so too did the gleaming white expanse of Adeline's Rolls Royce.

'Come here, Barnaby,' Miss Busby called as Adeline motored towards them with evident impatience.

'For heaven's sake, Isabelle!' she called through the open window. 'Do come along! Put the dog in the back, I've put the blanket down. There is no time to waste. This is urgent!'

'Well, you might have said as much,' Miss Busby muttered as she settled the dog before climbing in. Adeline yanked the steering wheel to turn the car around, then sped off towards the main road.

'How could I, with that telephone operator listening to every word. You know I can't abide gossip, Isabelle.'

Miss Busby hid a smile with a glance out of the window. Adeline, of course, was no idle gossip, but she was a woman extremely fond of news, and possessed of a natural volume which had a tendency to dispense said news far and wide.

'I was caught by young Dennis,' Miss Busby explained. 'We are invited to lunch at Spring Meadows today. But do tell me, whatever has happened?'

'The most awful thing. A suicide, and worse; an innocent man's life is hanging in the balance!'

Isabelle turned to her in surprise. No stranger to Adeline's flair for the dramatic, she noted her friend looked flushed, her eyes welling as genuine concern washed over her plump features.

'Good gracious, whose?'

'Ezekiel Melnyk's. We must help him, Isabelle. He's such a lovely man.'

'But who has died?'

'His lodger, of course. Do keep up.' Adeline turned to her in disapproval, revving up both the car and her emotions. 'And after what Mrs Harrison told me–'

'Who is Mrs Harrison? Really Adeline, you must calm down and explain,' Miss Busby said. 'And watch the road.'

Adeline took a breath and fixed her eyes on the undulating route ahead. 'I went to Chipping Common to collect my blue and yellow frock from Harrison's Haberdashers first thing this morning. I'd had it taken in, you see, after losing a little winter excess, and it's my favourite. Anyway, Mrs Harrison was most upset. She informed me Sergeant Heaton had just left, having declared that the case was now a murder enquiry. *'The foreign gentleman is firmly in the frame,'* he told her, *'It could not have been anyone but him.'* She was quite distraught, knowing as well as I how gentle Ezekiel's nature is and how absurd the notion that he could be capable of such a thing.'

'So the lodger's suicide is, in fact, now thought to be murder?' Miss Busby was trying to pick the facts from her friend's agitated rambling.

'Yes, of course! The poor man died,' Adeline's tone

was exasperated, 'two days ago! Surely you must have heard.'

'I haven't seen a newspaper–' she tried again.

'You should ask your young friend Miss Wesley at the *Oxford News*, she would have reported it.'

Miss Busby suspected she would do better to ask the paperboy, who had a habit of only appearing when he felt like it. 'But who was this lodger?'

'Gabriel Travis, a poet and bookbinder, and Mr Melnyk's dear friend. He was found dead in his rooms in the attic above the bookshop on Saturday. They say he had shot himself sometime in the night. Sergeant Heaton himself pronounced it suicide the moment the man was found next morning.'

'And this was in the newspaper?'

'I've no idea, Isabelle. I really don't have time to read them.' She sighed dramatically. 'Anyway, I went to Chipping Common on my way home from Oxford the very afternoon after it happened. I fancied a copy of *Whose Body* by Dorothy Sayers, but there is such a buzz about it Blackwell's had sold out. I went into Melnyk's bookshop to see if he had one, and found Ezekiel in absolute tatters. He told me the whole story.'

'And this was two days ago,' Miss Busby stated, trying to gain a clear view of events.

'Yes, and Melnyk's Books is next door to Harrison's Haberdashery. Anyway, the sergeant has somehow got it into his thick skull that it was murder, despite everything pointing to suicide. When I arrived at the haberdashery this morning, I saw the bookshop was locked and dark and the shutters were closed. After talking to Mrs Harrison it was patently obvious that Mr Melnyk had been taken under arrest. I decided something *must* be done, so I made my way to the post office and telephoned you. Isabelle, you must use your skills to save Mr Melnyk!'

'Adeline, I don't *know* Mr Melnyk.' She tried to keep the exasperation from her voice.

Adeline turned to her in surprise. 'Of course you do. Mr Melnyk. Melnyk's Books on Hayle Court Road. Really, Isabelle.'

'Eyes on the road, Adeline. We cannot help your friend unless we arrive in one piece.' Miss Busby thought for a moment. She hadn't visited Chipping Common in some time and tended to use the mobile library nowadays. Her circumstances, whilst far from dire, did lend themselves to caution in the spending department, and Mrs Friedli, the mobile librarian, always carried a good selection of mystery novels. 'Ah, yes,' she suddenly recalled. 'I bought a rather lovely edition of *The Velveteen Rabbit* for the school from Melnyk's Books. A foreign gentleman?' She tilted her head slightly to the side as the image began to take shape. 'Softly spoken. He had an ear trumpet sticking out of his top pocket.'

'That's him,' Adeline confirmed.

'I thought the ear trumpet at odds,' Miss Busby said. 'I never saw him use it, and he spoke quietly. Other deaf people I've met tend to speak more loudly than most.'

'Ezekiel is not like other people,' Adeline pronounced. 'His hearing was damaged in those awful pogroms. He was forced to escape the Crimea amid gunfire and bombs. It's not true deafness, he simply struggles if several people are talking at once.' She waved a hand. 'Oh, Isabelle, he really is a prince among men. He used to help me track down all manner of rare medical tomes for James when he was alive. And he would always have the most wonderful stories,' she expounded, her emotions getting the better of her. 'There's not a thing the man doesn't know. And the languages he can speak – such a gift – he really is a marvel. How someone can come from such horror, with such gentle kindness…' Adeline suddenly choked on a sob.

Miss Busby turned to see her dash tears from her eyes.

'Oh Adeline, I'm so sorry–'

'They will try to hang him.' Her tone hardened as anger flared to replace sorrow. 'For a murder he did not commit.'

'Why didn't you go to the police station this morning?' Miss Busby asked. 'You could have asked them what they had done with Mr Melnyk.'

'Whatever would be the point?' Adeline remarked, incredulous. 'Never mind the indecision – suicide one minute, murder the next! – if the sergeant suspects Ezekiel Melnyk of murdering anyone he's clearly a fool. Fancies himself some sort of Sherlock Holmes, I shouldn't wonder. Probably strutting around the town in a deerstalker as we speak. No, I knew I should call you. I thought we could talk to Ezekiel and you could collect evidence, and—'

'But you think he's been taken away to a police cell.' Miss Busby pointed out, then closed her eyes as they veered around a slow-moving cyclist on the road into Chipping Common

'Yes, well,' Adeline was cavalier about such details, 'we shall break in, or some such. Use your imagination, Isabelle! It's not as if we don't have investigative experience.' She braked suddenly, causing them to shudder to an abrupt halt outside Melnyk's Books. 'Here we are. There is no time to lose!'

CHAPTER 2

Miss Busby peered around her friend to see an old-fashioned bookshop. Stone built in the usual Cotswolds style, it was situated in a quiet backstreet at the end of a row of three shops. A black sign with gold lettering was positioned above a large mullioned window displaying a neat row of leather bound books. An elderly gentleman hunched over a desk was quite apparent through the glass.

'I assume that is Mr Melnyk,' Miss Busby remarked.

'Oh, thank heavens.' Adeline swung open the car door. 'Do hurry along, Isabelle.'

Miss Busby sat for a moment. After their frenetic dash across the Oxfordshire countryside, the chap in question was simply sitting in his shop. She bit back a sigh and disembarked.

Adeline was already marching towards the shop, her bright summer dress – red, yellow and gold in a pattern as vivid and flamboyant as her personality – billowing over her comfortable frame. Silver grey hair curled and set. She cut a determined figure, as she had ever since Isabelle had known her. It was a wonder that the pair had always been such close friends, being rather dissimilar in many ways. *You're like bookends*, Randolf had always said, with a wry smile. *You work best together.*

'Out you come, Barnaby.' Miss Busby opened the back door for the little dog to hop down into the cobbled street. 'And be nice to the man,' she instructed. 'It sounds as if he has quite enough to deal with without you growling at him.'

A small brass bell jingled above the door. Miss Busby entered and was instantly enveloped by the deliciously unique bookshop smell. Paper and leather and must and mould and...*knowledge*. She knew the last was unreasonable, but she felt it all the same. There was no other smell quite like it.

Rows of neatly ordered shelves stood sentry, each section clearly labelled with all recruits standing smartly to attention. Sunlight filtered through the window to spread across the desk and illuminate piles of receipts, books awaiting repair, and the forlorn figure of Mr Ezekiel Melnyk, who was now rising stiffly to his feet to greet them.

'Here's Miss Busby,' Adeline announced. 'Isabelle, this is Ezekiel Melnyk. A most dear old friend.'

Mr Melnyk offered a smile, which failed to lift the melancholy dulling his brown eyes.

'Most delighted to make your acquaintance,' he said with a courteous bow.

Miss Busby spotted the brass ear trumpet tucked in the top pocket of his burgundy jacket. His trousers were a more sombre black, paired with a smartly pressed white shirt and paisley-patterned bow tie. Tufts of fuzzy grey hair – the only part of the man that wasn't perfectly neat and orderly – surrounded a red and gold velvet yarmulke perched on his head.

Murderers came in all shapes and sizes, Miss Busby knew only too well, but one could be forgiven for thinking that such a nicely attired, well-mannered gentleman would be thoroughly incapable of so much as swatting a fly.

'You have the most exceptional shop, Mr Melnyk,' she said. 'I have been remiss in not visiting for some time.'

'You are most kind. Please, sit,' he offered, gesturing to two plain wooden chairs in front of the desk. Both hosted a small pile of books. 'Ah, forgive me,' he said as he realised. 'They will be quite comfortable upon the floor, I am certain.' He moved them almost reverently, allowing the ladies to sit in their place.

Barnaby, previously occupied with the scents hidden within the deep carpeting, trotted over to take a good look at the man.

'Ah, and here is a most unusual customer,' Mr Melnyk remarked. They took a moment to take measure of each other. Neither apparently recognised any threat. Barnaby turned to face Miss Busby and stared pointedly towards her cardigan pocket; eyes bright, one ear up, one down, button nose twitching, tail aloft.

'His name is Barnaby. And if you don't object, Mr Melnyk, I shall give him a biscuit and he will occupy himself quietly on your rug.'

'Yes, of course!' The man's eyes crinkled at the sight of the little dog trotting towards the fireplace with his prize. 'A companion of the most charming kind.'

'He belongs to a friend of mine,' Miss Busby explained. 'She has been unwell, and the sheltered home doesn't permit dogs. But we arrange regular visits.'

'How wonderful. A shared dog! And he is a good dog. Many books are brought to me in need of repair after suffering the teeth of such animals. But now I see it is not the fault of the animals. If biscuits are provided, the taste of books pales in comparison!'

Miss Busby liked the man immediately. He was just her sort of person.

'Gabriel,' he continued, 'would make the needed repairs where he could. I suggest always that customers with canine companions purchase leather bound editions. Harder for the teeth to bite through, you understand.'

'Gabriel was your lodger, Mr Melnyk?' Miss Busby asked gently.

He nodded, reaching for a handkerchief from his pocket.

'Yes, indeed. Mr Gabriel Travis. A poet in heart and soul. That was his daily toil when not repairing books for me. The muse, his "angel" as he would call her, was always with him. Gabriel did not yet find a publisher for his poems, but he never mislaid his faith. And in mending broken books he was working with words – healing them within their bindings, he would say.' Mr Melnyk sniffed and wiped away a tear. 'He was my friend. I can hardly believe he is gone for always.'

Taking his seat behind the desk, he clasped the handkerchief tightly in both hands. 'Please, forgive me,' he said. 'It has been most distressing.'

'Mrs Harrison from the haberdashery told me what happened,' Adeline said sombrely. 'Now, you mustn't worry about a thing. Miss Busby is an accomplished sleuth –' Miss Busby opened her mouth to object, but Adeline gave no quarter '– and there is not a doubt in my mind that she will extricate you from this absurd situation. Murder, indeed. The very notion. And I, of course, shall help. *The law*, as Mr Dickens concurs, *is an ass*,' she concluded.

Mr Melnyk gave a gentle smile. 'I believe that to have been the opinion of Mr Bumble, rather than Mr Dickens, dear lady. But I appreciate the sentiment just the same.' A spark shone in his eyes for just a moment, before the sadness returned.

'Mr Melnyk, I shall be glad to help in any way I can,' Miss Busby assured him, 'but I'm no sleuth, I'm afraid.'

'Nonsense,' Adeline proclaimed. 'You solved the murders at Little Minton.'

The man's eyes widened in surprise.

'I had a great deal of help, Adeline,' Miss Busby pointed out. 'And I'm sure the authorities would have got to the bottom of it all in their own time.'

'*Pfft.*' Adeline expressed her doubt loudly enough to make Barnaby look up from the rug. 'Time is something we do not have. And besides, *I* shall help you. What do you need?'

Miss Busby looked at the bookseller, his expression flickering with something dangerously akin to hope. She held back a sigh. 'Perhaps a pot of coffee, to start?' she suggested, feeling things were becoming a little overwrought. 'If that's agreeable, Mr Melnyk?'

'Coffee, yes, of course.' He rose to his feet, but Miss Busby held up a hand.

'Mrs Fanshawe will arrange it.' She shot Adeline a pointed look before returning her attention to the bookseller. 'You and I, Mr Melnyk, perhaps ought to start at the beginning.' Delving into her bag, Miss Busby retrieved her notebook and pencil, and began by writing the date on a fresh page.

Adeline dithered. Clearly thrilled that Miss Busby was now on the case, she was markedly less pleased at being sent off to prepare refreshments. Indecision flickered, before she concluded she was still up on the deal and strode off to muster supplies.

'It was some time over the night of Friday, or in the smallest hours of the morning of Saturday,' Ezekiel began, 'that Gabriel…Gabriel Travis…' his voice wavered, 'my lodger and most dear friend, was shot to death in his rooms, in the attic above my flat.'

Adeline could be heard rummaging in the little kitchenette in the alcove at the back of the shop as Miss

Busby respectfully took notes. 'How awful for you,' she said softly, before gently pressing, 'Do you recall the precise time you heard the shot?'

'I did not hear any shot.' He shook his head sadly, sunlight catching the faded gold embroidery on his yarmulke.

Miss Busby raised a brow. 'Oh? But your hearing seems – if you'll forgive me – remarkably good, Mr Melnyk. I notice you haven't once reached for your ear trumpet.'

'I can read lips just as I read the written word,' he explained. 'But yes, although my ears are a little broken, they still function. When many people speak in the shop at once it is hard for me. When only one or two, it is not too severe a problem.' Miss Busby recalled Adeline had explained as much. 'That is to say, I am able to have heard the gunshot. It is a puzzle to the police sergeant, who I am sorry to say regards me with utmost suspicion, that I did not. But it cannot be helped. I have always been the strong sleeper. I heard nothing.'

'Didn't your neighbours hear it?' Adeline called from the kitchenette. 'Mrs Harrison surely must have done.'

Miss Busby wondered the same. Melnyk's Books stood in a row of three shops and the sound would surely carry.

'I have no neighbours at night, dear lady,' Mr Melnyk called in reply. 'When the shops close it is just myself and…well, now it is just myself.'

'Are there flats in the adjoining shops?' Miss Busby asked.

'Indeed, a flat in each, and the attic rooms above.'

'And the other flats are unoccupied at night?'

He nodded sadly. 'In days now gone, there was noise and laughter, and company in the evenings. Mrs Rose Harrison – she was Mrs Doyle, but has remarried, her shop is now Harrison's Haberdashery…'

Miss Busby smiled. 'How fortuitous, marrying someone whose surname fits so snugly with one's profession.'

'Indeed, and Rose now lives with Mr Harrison, a most pleasant gentleman, just a few streets down. Beside Harrison's there are Mrs Fowler and her son Martin, these are the pharmacists. They have a beautiful home at the top of the hill.' He pointed up the road, where the roof of a large house could be made out. 'All of which is to say,' he went on, 'there was only me, no other, to hear the gunshot at night.'

Miss Busby glanced through the mullioned glass at the little side street tucked away from the bustling town. A garage took up a good chunk of the area opposite, with no other homes nearby. The noise of the engines, machinery, and metal work, she supposed, being a factor. It had been a blacksmith's originally, she seemed to recall, and people would even then have shied away from living nearby. 'And what time do the shops close, Mr Melnyk?' she asked.

'Always 6 o'clock in the evening. Unless on a Thursday, when it will be 7 o'clock. And each night I myself place the bolt on the shop door when I go to bed at 10 o'clock.'

Miss Busby looked up in surprise. Bolting doors, or even locking them, was unusual in the peaceful quiet of the Cotswolds. Especially if one were at home at the time.

'There was great trouble, back in my country,' he explained, seeing her expression. 'It is different, here, but the oldest habit is the most reluctant to die. Bolting the door is such a habit. It makes me feel safe, and I thought it would keep my friend safe also…' He hesitated. 'There is no other entrance to his rooms, you see.'

She nodded in understanding, thinking his experience must be unique in the small market town of Chipping Common. 'And do you open at 9 o'clock each morning?'

'Every day since I am first buying the shop. But not today,' he added, eyes downcast. 'I was rather dismayed and remained here, behind the shutters, in darkness. I am sorry if it caused distress.'

'No, no, nothing I cannot manage,' Adeline called out.

Miss Busby refrained from comment. 'You are not open on Sundays, of course,' she continued.

'No, there are no shops open on Sundays,' he confirmed.

She thought for a moment. 'I do hope you won't think me impertinent, Mr Melnyk–'

'Ezekiel, please,' he insisted. 'And I could never think such an admirable lady impertinent.'

Miss Busby smiled. 'You are most kind. But I wonder, is it…straightforward, for you to open the shop on Saturdays?'

He offered her a smile, reflexively reaching a hand to his yarmulke.

'In my country, it would be unstraightforward. Here, it is not the same. And here is my home now. My friends and neighbours enjoy often to buy their books on Saturdays, and always take Sundays for their day of rest. I think my Lord will be happy for me to ensure they have something good to read on Sundays, and also happy that I rest one full day. I think he will not mind which.'

Miss Busby smiled and nodded. She was beginning to see more and more why Adeline was so fond of the old gentleman.

'Well, if you were the only one around to hear the shot, which in fact you didn't,' Adeline piped up, raising her voice over the whistling of the kettle, 'then how on earth does anyone know *when* Gabriel was shot?'

'Yesterday the police sergeant tells me they have been able to ascertain the time of death as being after 10 o'clock at night, and before 9 o'clock in the morning,' Mr Melnyk explained. 'Although I do not know if this is by scientific discovery or simple common sense, as those are the hours my shop door remains secured.'

Miss Busby noted down the times. 'I think in either case we must suppose that whoever killed your friend would have relied upon your weakened hearing in order not to be discovered,' Miss Busby concluded.

'Yes, it could be so.' Ezekiel sighed.

'Or *she*, let us not forget.' Adeline clattered cups together from the kitchenette.

Mr Melnyk looked towards the back, momentarily horrified.

CHAPTER 3

'The odds, Adeline,' Miss Busby called towards the back of the shop, 'would most strongly—'

'We must keep an open mind, Isabelle.' Adeline loudly overrode her objection. 'And besides, the vast majority of Chipping Common is well acquainted with Mr Melnyk's ear trumpet.'

'Yes, indeed, but such supposition will not help, I am afraid,' Mr Melnyk replied sadly.

Miss Busby's head tilted in enquiry just as Adeline returned to the room with a steaming coffee pot, milk jug, and three cups and saucers precariously balanced on a tin tray.

Mr Melnyk quickly moved a copy of Dickens' 'A Tale of two Cities' just before she plonked the tray down on the plain oak desk.

'One lump or two, Mr Melnyk?'

'No sugar, thank you, dear lady,' he answered. 'And also no milk for me, if you would be so kind.'

'Two please,' Miss Busby said, feeling she needed the boost. 'And milk, thank you.'

With a fortifying sip taken on board, Miss Busby returned to the subject. 'Why will supposition not help, Mr Melnyk?'

'Oh, you will see,' he replied, 'as we go on. It is really the most peculiar thing.' He smiled, sipped his coffee, then frowned once more as he continued. 'It was normal not to encounter Gabriel before lunch. He would write his compositions in the quiet of the mornings, becoming lost in the weaving of his words. But he would often join me for lunch in the shop. It was the time he would share his writings, and I would share new acquisitions in need of rebinding. When he did not come down on Saturday, our busiest day and one he would surely never miss, I went up to see if he perhaps was unwell. The door was closed, which was as usual for him. He is always keeping both doors and windows closed at night during the warmer months, you understand, because of the moths.'

'Ah, yes.' Adeline nodded. 'Absolute terrors. Wreak havoc on one's clothes.'

'It is the books he is thinking of,' Mr Melnyk explained. 'The moths, they enjoy to eat the paper as much as the clothes.'

'It must get awfully hot up there in the summer,' Miss Busby said.

'Yes, dear lady, it becomes stifling in the night time, but the comfort of his beloved books is always more important than his own. And in the daytime he would let in the air,' he explained.

Miss Busby nodded.

'And so, I knocked several times, but he makes no answer. I become concerned, so I go inside, calling his name. The door is not locked, of course, although there is a key. I went inside, as I said, and I…that is to say…' Emotion caught in his voice and he struggled to continue.

'Shall we stop for a moment?' Miss Busby suggested, seeing his distress.

'No, no.' He dabbed his eyes with his handkerchief. 'We must continue. It is no good, after all, to detain a story in the middle.' He took a breath. 'Gabriel was seated at his writing desk, the gun in his right hand, papers clutched tight in his left. He had…slumped across the surface. There was much blood. Too much blood. It had flowed across the papers strewn over the desk and floor beside. His words…his poems. Such a terrible waste. Such a tragedy for him…and for myself also.'

He lowered his head to stare at his hands. Adeline dropped a sugar cube into his coffee in the hope it would help.

'And when the police sergeant saw the scene, it appeared to him as if Mr Travis had shot himself?' Miss Busby asked, hoping a businesslike tone would put them back on track.

'Yes, yes, exactly so.' Mr Melnyk sniffed, then replaced his handkerchief in his pocket. 'But we run ahead. I felt on his neck for a pulse. His wrist, also. I had hoped… but I knew, of course, with so much blood…'

Adeline leaned across, poised to pour him more coffee. Miss Busby put a restraining hand on her arm and gave a gentle shake of the head. He had barely touched the drink as it was.

'I rushed to Fowler's Pharmacy, they have a telephone, you see. I explained the terrible event and that I am needing to talk with the doctor and the hospital. Mrs Fowler thought it quicker in the circumstances to run for the police station. Which I then did.'

'Well, really,' Adeline huffed. 'She might have saved you the trouble.'

'Yes, that does seem perhaps a little unkind,' Miss Busby concurred, taking Mr Melnyk's age into account.

Mr Melnyk shook his head. 'She is a perfectly correct lady. She was thinking only of the fastest path to help. When I reached the station, the sergeant ran back here with me at once. We run up to the top, the sergeant is shocked, but quickly rights himself. He too felt Gabriel's pulse, and confirmed the situation was as it appeared. He then looked at the attic and the shop in much detail. He took many notes, just as you are doing now.' Mr Melnyk nodded to Miss Busby's notebook. 'He asked if I knew any reason Gabriel would take his life in such a manner.'

'And did you?' Miss Busby leaned forward, beginning to find herself absorbed in the story, before she remembered it wasn't a story; it was a life that had been taken.

'Oh, there were very many reasons,' he replied. 'Gabriel was troubled in his soul. He had lost his wife and his daughter. His story is most tragic. But for nine years he lived above my shop and dealt quietly with his pain every day, like – oh, I forget my words when troubled. How do you say, like the Greek philosophers?'

'Stoically,' Adeline supplied.

'Yes! Most stoically. He wrote his poems. He bound the books. He had smiles for everyone. Why he would lose that fight, suddenly, in the middle of the night, I cannot say. I told the sergeant as much, before he left to arrange the ambulance.'

'How terribly sad.' Miss Busby was beginning to feel the same empathy she imagined Adeline was feeling. Mr Melnyk certainly seemed the most peaceful and sympathetic sort of man. 'But what happened to make the sergeant change his mind?'

Adeline *tsked* loudly from her chair, no doubt about to comment on his ineptitude in general. A stern look from Miss Busby reverted her attention to her coffee.

'You know, this is perhaps the worst thing of all,' Mr Melnyk replied. 'I do not know what happened. Gabriel…his body…was examined, as is to be expected in these cases, I am told, and the police sergeant returned late yesterday evening, a constable beside him. I forget the young man's name. They looked at

Gabriel's rooms once more. Nothing had been touched, the sergeant tells me I must leave everything as it is from when he died. I wanted to open the windows and clean the blood at least, but I was not permitted.'

More *tutting* from Adeline ensued.

'They spent time up there together. I was not permitted to be present. Then they go outside to look around for many minutes more. When they return, they tell me Gabriel was murdered, and that his death had only been dressed up as if it were a suicide.'

'The incompetence!' Adeline exclaimed, unable to hold her indignation any longer.

Miss Busby felt a tingling in her spine. A staged suicide? To what end? A humble poet, a gentle bookseller… Her mind began to whirr.

'If the sergeant had only a cursory look initially,' she reasoned, 'and alone, it's perfectly plausible he could have missed an important detail. Chipping Common is hardly known for wickedness, and he probably has little experience of unnatural death.'

'Well, you may say that, Isabelle, but wait until you hear—' Adeline began.

'We are almost there, dear lady,' Mr Melnyk interrupted her gently. 'Miss Busby has a mind a little like my own, I think, and prefers her pages turned in order.'

'Indeed I do.' Miss Busby nodded gratefully to him as she placed her cup and saucer on the desk. The coffee and sugar were beginning to work their magic, and

Mr Melnyk's tale had a much calmer chronology than Adeline's earlier, frantic version. She was beginning to feel on firmer ground as the story took shape.

'They asked many questions, it did not seem they would ever stop. Had I argued with Gabriel? Did he owe money? Had he made some mistake in his work and ruined a rare edition? Each question more unthinkable than the last. What medicines do I keep in my home? Did I know Gabriel owned a gun?'

His voice broke on the last word.

'Did you?' Miss Busby asked softly.

'Yes. That is to say, no. I knew he did not own a gun. Gabriel was a most peaceful man.' He cleared his throat and took a breath. 'I grew dizzy with it. They take my fingers.'

'What?!' Adeline looked aghast.

'Fingerprints, I should think,' Miss Busby suggested.

'Yes, I am sorry, the prints of my fingers. They look at the rooms in my flat. Search my bookshop and make such a great mess of the shelves that I weep. It took me most of the night to return everything in its rightful place. It is because of this, also, I was late to open this morning for the very first time. It added most sincerely to my dismay.' He paused for a sip of coffee and to catch his breath before continuing.

'They take my official papers, tell me I must not leave the town. That I am under suspicion of murder, and an inspector will come with more questions soon. I asked them why they think I would do such a thing.

I told them Gabriel was my friend. But they would not listen.'

'Why wouldn't they listen, do you think, Mr Melnyk?' Miss Busby asked quietly.

'Because I am the only person who could have made this crime. As Mr Conan Doyle himself says, *When you have eliminated all which is impossible then whatever remains, however improbable, must be the truth.* The police sergeant and his constable are in good company in this respect at least.'

Adeline narrowed her eyes in disapproval. Miss Busby feared she was about to make further disparaging deerstalker remarks with reference to Sergeant Heaton, but Mr Melnyk left her no opportunity.

'You see, Miss Busby, friend of my friend, there is not a single mark of forced entry. The lock is undamaged. All the windows intact. The bolt on the shop door still engaged when I opened on Saturday morning. And so the only person who could possibly have shot Gabriel, is myself. And worse than this – the most terrible of all – Gabriel is killed with my very own pistol. So you see, dear lady, in some way I understand why the police think me to blame. If it had not been for myself, Gabriel would still be alive.'

'Nonsense.' Adeline was direct as ever. 'If a man wishes to kill himself, or another, he will find a way. If it hadn't been your gun, it would have been a different gun, and the end result just the same.'

'Perhaps. But also, perhaps not. The poor man's

expression was tortured. I did not keep the weapon safe as I should have done. Its home was inside the cash drawer, right to the back, here in the shop.'

'But you keep the drawer locked, surely?' Miss Busby asked.

'No.' His misery seemed to deepen. 'I am always in the shop in the day, and at night no other can come in. I thought it would be safe. I kept the gun *to* be safe.'

'You must not think of it another moment,' Adeline told him. 'Really. The gun is immaterial. They are two a penny since everyone came back from the war.'

'Who else knew where you kept it, Mr Melnyk?' Miss Busby pressed.

'Gabriel,' he answered glumly, a man defeated. 'Only myself and Gabriel.'

* * *

Some short time later, the two ladies headed toward the broader main street, a busy and bustling place. Miss Busby attached Barnaby's tartan lead lest he take exception to any passersby. The police station was only a short walk away, and with Adeline taking point they reached it in no time, both women deep in thought. They approached the drab red-brick building set behind a high privet hedge in silence. Barnaby wagged his tail and pulled on the lead to snuffle below it. Adeline straightened up, took a breath, and declared it was time to do battle.

Miss Busby paused.

'I ought to wait here with Barnaby,' she said, glad of the excuse not to follow Adeline inside. 'And it's perhaps best if we don't overwhelm the sergeant.'

Adeline huffed, raising an eyebrow in disdain. 'The man has distinctly overwhelmed Ezekiel.'

'Yes, and I do understand your concern for your friend,' Miss Busby agreed, 'but for his sake, Adeline, perhaps it would be just as well to be gentle with the officer? One catches more flies with honey than vinegar, after all.'

As Adeline disappeared inside the building, Miss Busby wished their efforts with the detecting kit hadn't fallen so flat. Following their discussion with Mr Melnyk, Adeline had demanded action, and the trio had climbed the stairs to the attic only to discover that the police sergeant had locked the rooms and taken the key to preserve the scene. Whilst Adeline had been itching to give lock picking a try, a set of lock picks was the one item Miss Busby did not possess.

As much to appear helpful and possibly give a little comfort, Miss Busby had then dusted the shop door handle and the handle of the door to Gabriel's rooms for fingerprints, while Mr Melnyk had looked on forlornly. Both surfaces had been awash with a mixture of prints and could offer no help whatsoever, not to mention the fact they soon realised they had no prints with which to compare them, and had simply got rather carried away.

The singular saving grace was that Mr Melnyk was able to tell them the only fingerprints to be found on the gun had belonged to Travis.

'And you are absolutely sure the bolt on the shop door was still in place when you opened on Saturday?' Miss Busby had asked him no less than three times before they'd left. Each time his answer had been the same:

'I am positive. It was firmly secured as always. Nothing was out of order.'

Miss Busby believed him, because if the man had been guilty he would simply have said the bolt had not been in place. And he surely wouldn't have used his own gun for the act. That was the most baffling thing of all: the two facts that proclaimed his guilt also screamed his innocence.

The station door opened with a loud squeak, pulling Miss Busby from her thoughts. Adeline emerged with a face like thunder. 'An inspector from Oxford is due any moment!' she pronounced, as though the end was next to nigh.

CHAPTER 4

Miss Busby's eyebrows shot up. 'Inspector McKay?'

'Sergeant Heaton refused to say.'

'Why?' Miss Busby asked, although she suspected she could hazard a guess. Adeline could be quite forthright when riled, and she was on a mission to prove the constabulary wrong. Her approach had probably been of the high-handed variety.

'He had the nerve to imply it was none of my concern, as I neither live here, nor was I anywhere near the place on the night in question.'

'Goodness,' Miss Busby muttered, thinking he wasn't far wrong. Although as Adeline was a stalwart member of the local community, the sergeant could have been a little more diplomatic in the circumstances.

'I left a message for the inspector to call you at Lavender Cottage,' Adeline continued.

'Why not have him call you?' Miss Busby objected. 'Mr Melnyk is your acquaintance, after all.' She knew how Inspector McKay, if it was indeed to be him, would react to the news that she was once again taking a "civilian" interest in police matters. The pair had argued the subject at length the previous Christmas.

'Because you have form for this sort of thing, Isabelle. And anyway, I won't be home if we're lunching at Spring Meadows.'

'Neither will I!' Miss Busby retorted. 'And if his arrival is imminent, why not simply wait for him here?'

'We could, but who knows how long he'll be. And I suddenly find myself rather hungry. What are we having, do you know?' Adeline was already marching back towards the white Rolls Royce.

Barnaby tugged her along in Adeline's wake, and Miss Busby gave in to the inevitable. 'I believe it to be sole.'

'Lovely. We can let Mary in on what's happened. Get a wider perspective, now that we know Ezekiel is not in immediate danger of arrest.'

'I doubt he ever was,' Miss Busby reasoned as they climbed into the car. 'It seems all they have is circumstantial evidence.'

'Travis was killed with Ezekiel's own gun, Isabelle,' Adeline protested.

'Yes, but the gun was mercifully free of his prints. Not to mention it was kept in a rather… insecure manner.'

Having been surprised to find a man as gentle and peaceable as Mr Melnyk in possession of a weapon at all, he had explained to Miss Busby and Adeline how he had purchased the gun during the troubles in

Crimea, and been reluctant to part with it after all he'd seen since. *It makes me feel a little safer,* he'd said. *'If such an item can be deemed to make one feel such. And now of course I wish only that I had left it behind.'*

As to why he had kept the gun in the shop, in the cash drawer of all places, he couldn't say. If anyone were to rob him, Adeline had pointed out, they would surely find the cash and the gun both.

'I never feared to be robbed,' he had said mournfully. *'Only to be losing my life. And now my friend's life has been taken and it is me who is to blame.'*

'Anyone could have taken the gun from the cash drawer, at just about any time,' Miss Busby continued. 'Fortunately for Mr Melnyk.'

'Not for Mr Travis,' Adeline added as she steered the Rolls out of town.

'No. Well, the police may suspect all they wish, but I'm quite sure any judge worth his salt would throw a charge like that straight out of court. There's nothing concrete to draw upon.'

'But we can't leave the poor man under suspicion for the rest of his life,' Adeline pointed out. 'And besides, what about the real killer?'

'If, indeed, there is one,' Miss Busby mused. 'I should like to know what made them so certain it wasn't suicide after all. Mr Melnyk implied the man had endured more than his fair share of tragedy.'

'Well, we shall get to the bottom of it after lunch. I haven't had sole in ages!'

The drive back was rather more relaxed. Although Adeline was still irked by the way the sergeant had spoken to her, she brightened as they motored along country lanes in the direction of Little Minton.

Spring sunshine painted the flourishing fields surrounding them a vivid green. The woods beyond Chipping Common displayed a glorious mass of bluebells. The sight of them never failed to cheer Miss Busby. She had walked there many times in her youth, hand in hand with Randolf, admiring snowdrops, bluebells, and daffodils alike. Not to mention the views over the Cotswolds which were your reward should you make it up to the highest point, as the pair of them had on many occasions.

Could she walk that far now, she wondered? Perhaps with Adeline to chivvy her on, and plenty of time taken, she might manage it. Barnaby would adore it. She would have to make the suggestion.

'Isabelle!'

She jumped in her seat, startled. 'Whatever is it?'

'I was asking about the sole. Is it Dover, or lemon?'

'Oh. I was miles away. I'm afraid I don't know.'

Adeline slowed the Rolls as they entered Little Minton and drove on to the newly completed Spring Meadows sheltered housing development. A row of small bungalows spread behind a larger building where residents could mingle, and take meals, all with the safety and security of nursing staff on hand.

It occupied the site of the old woollen mill, set back

from the road, and surrounded by peaceful fields. A large vegetable garden was newly established to the rear, an elderly jersey cow occupied a meadow, and a chicken coop sat in the orchard. The place had been thoughtfully designed to sustain the inhabitants with milk, eggs, and the requisite necessities.

Miss Busby was delighted that two of her friends had secured homes that suited their needs so perfectly. Last Christmas they'd tried to persuade her to join them, but she had felt then, as she did now, that she wasn't ready to give up her beloved cottage, or her independence just yet. Still, it was a comfort to know that when the time came she would have the option.

'Here we are then,' Adeline announced, wrestling the large car through the narrow gates and into the gravelled driveway fronting the handsome main building.

Miss Busby disembarked and released Barnaby. He made straight for the last bungalow of the row, shouldering the green garden gate open and jumping up at the front door with several excited *yips*.

Mary Fellows appeared through the open doorway and made a delighted fuss of the dog. Small in stature, she was almost dwarfed by a long grey dress and heavy cardigan, but her cheeks glowed, as did her eyes.

'Adeline, how lovely to see you. Young Dennis mentioned you might be joining us.' She shut the door behind her and put a steadying hand on the rail that ran along her path.

Miss Busby stepped forward and slipped an arm through Mary's. 'Shall we have some lunch?'

Barnaby dashed ahead as they made their way to the main building. Pale green walls, pastoral paintings, cushioned bench seats, wood floors and tall windows gave an airy aspect to the entrance.

Enid Montgomery was peering through the glass of the closed double doors into the dining room. Smartly dressed in a bright yellow blouse and matching skirt, she remained a handsome woman despite age and illness. A few streaks of auburn still shone amidst the thick white hair swept back from her forehead. She turned and caught sight of the company.

'There's no need to look at me in that manner, Isabelle. I am in no danger of imminent demise, I assure you.' Enid leaned on her stick, seeming a little thinner but as acerbic as ever.

Adeline gave Enid an appreciative nod; the two were rather alike in manner. 'Why are you waiting out here?' she asked.

'I am waiting,' Enid replied in clipped tones, 'for Mr Waterhouse to finish his lunch and leave, and you are waiting with me.'

'Why?' Adeline pressed.

'Because he really is the most—'

'Enid isn't too keen on him,' Mary cut in. 'Which is rather unfortunate as he is *awfully* keen on her.'

Adeline broke into a delighted grin. 'Is he really? We must—'

'No we must not,' Enid hissed. 'Do be quiet, or he'll hear us.'

Miss Busby smiled to herself.

'There, now, he's going,' Enid said, as the gentleman made his way from the table and off down another corridor. 'Come along.'

Barnaby trotted in beside them. The maid, Jilly, looked neat in a new uniform of black dress and white apron. 'Afternoon, ladies.' She greeted the ensemble warmly then scooped up the dog. 'Cook's saved a lovely dish of leftover sausages for you in the kitchen,' she told him, ruffling his ears as she carried him through.

Selecting an empty table overlooking the rose garden, they settled down to the business of the day.

'Did you hear the sale of The Grange has fallen through,' Enid said. Having put her home up for sale before moving to Spring Meadows, she had thought her financial woes at an end when it had apparently sold.

'Oh, how awful, I'm sorry,' Miss Busby said, as Adeline made sympathetic noises. 'It's such a lovely place, I'm sure it'll be snapped up in no time. Is there any sign of a buyer for your cottage yet, Mary?' she asked, eager for news as whoever bought Mary's cottage would be her next-door neighbour but one.

'No word from Chesterton's yet,' Mary replied.

'Oh.' A disappointed silence fell.

'Four sole is it?' Cook appeared in starched white apron over a blue dress, a white mob cap covering her grey curls.

'Yes, thank you.' Enid answered for them all.

Lunch ordered, Adeline launched into the tale of Ezekiel Melnyk and the unfortunate circumstances surrounding the death of his lodger. She culminated with the news of an inspector en route from Oxford and a telephone call expected at Lavender Cottage forthwith.

'Oh, dear Lord,' Mary managed, as Adeline reached her breathless conclusion. 'And so soon after the commotion here in Little Minton, too.'

'Yes,' Miss Busby agreed. 'You wouldn't think it in our backwater, so far removed from the troubles of the city.'

'*There are many evils*, Isabelle,' Enid quoted, '*and there is no worse evil than man*. I shouldn't think it matters a jot where he lives.' Enid leaned forward, her eyes bright with curiosity. 'Are they quite decided, now? It really *is* murder?'

'It seems that way,' Miss Busby answered before Adeline could begin another tirade about dithering police officers.

'There was no note?' Enid pressed. 'Adeline, you mentioned he had papers in his hand?'

'Yes, poems I believe. Ezekiel said they were the fellow's *raison d'etre*. There was no mention of a note. Mind you, I wouldn't put it past that sergeant to have missed it.' Adeline was about to expound but was interrupted by four plates being set on the table before them: green beans, cheesy mash potatoes, and Dover sole lightly scented with garlic and parsley.

Cook looked on expectantly, nodding at the appreciative looks and comments before once more departing as silently as she'd arrived.

'Is there any salt?' Mary called after her hopefully.

'It's already seasoned,' Cook shot back over her shoulder.

Jilly followed with a jug of water and four glasses. 'Now, you know salt is against doctor's orders, Mrs Fellows,' she admonished.

Enid *tsked*. 'Salt, sherry, pastries. All of it is against doctor's orders. Makes one wonder exactly what we're staying alive *for*.'

Adeline tucked into her fish. 'You shall all come to lunch with me one day,' she said. 'Have a day off from doctor's orders. Although, my word, this is extraordinarily good.'

Murmurs of agreement followed.

'A locked-room mystery,' Enid proclaimed, eyes alight as she wiped her mouth delicately with a napkin. 'I believe that is what we have here. Mr Edgar Allen Poe would be thoroughly intrigued. Have you read his *Murders at the Rue Morgue*?'

Miss Busby and Adeline shook their heads.

'I have,' Mary offered. 'It was rather fun, although not one to read before bed. I don't think that's quite what we're looking at here, though.'

Enid tutted. 'Well, clearly our murderer wasn't a—'

'Enid! You mustn't spoil the ending!' Mary interjected.

Enid smiled. 'Very well. Clearly our murderer was

not *of the same ilk* as Mr Poe's – what an imagination the man had – but the bookshop *was* locked from the inside just the same.' She poured herself more water. 'Your Mr Melnyk claims the murder was committed while the only entrance to the premises was locked and bolted – there is no back door, I take it?'

'No,' Adeline confirmed.

Enid nodded. 'And with no-one but himself and the victim inside. If one is dead, ordinarily I should say the fellow remaining must be the killer,' she ignored Adeline's gasp of horror, 'but that clearly isn't the case here.'

Adeline was indignant on Ezekiel's behalf. 'I should think not. I have known him for years, and he is the most perfect gentleman.'

Enid sniffed. 'The devil wears many guises, Adeline, but it cannot have been Mr Melnyk, simply because he would have lied about the bolt on the bookshop door. And I am quite sure he would have acquired a different weapon to boot.'

Miss Busby nodded. 'Yes, I thought the very same.'

'No one would condemn themselves in such a manner, if they were guilty,' Enid continued. 'Unless it were a rather risky double bluff, which… now, I wonder, would that make it the perfect crime?'

'I can *assure* you—'

'Yes, Adeline, we know.' Enid dismissed her with a wave of the hand. 'I do enjoy a puzzle.' She turned to Miss Busby. 'However do you manage to find them, Isabelle?'

Miss Busby affected affront. 'I do not seek out murders to solve, Enid. And besides, Adeline found this one. And the last, now I come to think of it.'

'I wonder if our killer could have hidden in the bookshop after committing the crime,' Enid went on, 'and then made his escape once Mr Melnyk opened the shop and began to go about his business.'

Adeline's face fell as she absorbed the idea. 'However would we find the culprit if that were the case?'

'There's bound to be a clue that will be his undoing. There always is. A thorough search of the bookshop is what is required.' Enid was quite nonchalant.

'It has already been searched,' Adeline replied, more mutedly. 'Mr Melnyk said the sergeant and young constable made a terrible mess of the shop. Isabelle,' she asked, paling, 'does that mean the clue has been destroyed? Are we too late?'

CHAPTER 5

Jilly reappeared to replace their cleared plates with four bowls of lemon sponge pudding, distracting Adeline from further dramatics.

'What makes you think it is not a locked-room sort of mystery?' Miss Busby asked Mary, wondering what her friend had noticed that she had not.

Mary smiled. 'Do you remember when I had that squirrel in the loft? It was years ago now. I had thought it a ghost at first. So silly of me, but it would only ever scurry about at night. And then you had one in your loft too.'

Miss Busby set her spoon down as understanding dawned.

'Oh, Mary, how clever of you. Of course! We'd had the same squirrel,' she explained to the others, 'running through the attics and hiding from each of us in a different loft when we went up to look. And you think our murderer could have done the same?' She looked at Mary.

'It's quite possible,' Mary concurred. 'There were gaps between the attic walls in each cottage, and it may well be the same for your Mr Melnyk. Although, I suppose the sergeant would already have had a thorough look around.'

'I should very much doubt it,' Adeline grumbled. 'I never once thought…but of course, the rooms are locked and we couldn't get in to see. Isabelle,' she said, eyes shining as the full impact of the possibility dawned, 'we must tell the police. It could make all the difference to Ezekiel. They have to listen to us.'

Miss Busby stuck a spoon in her pudding. 'When we've finished, we can go to Lavender Cottage and await the telephone call from the station.'

'Exactly, so do hurry.' Adeline was once again raring to go.

* * *

Some little time later, they were dashing towards Bloxford.

'Mary's a wonder,' Adeline remarked as she wrenched the large car around the tight bends.

'I know, it's quite incredible that she's still with us after such an awful angina attack last year.'

'Hmm?' Adeline leaned forward to peer through the windscreen. 'Oh, yes, but her theory, I mean. About the attic. I can't believe it didn't occur to us. It quite exonerates Ezekiel if there was another point of access.'

Miss Busby paused. 'Yes, it's certainly something to consider.'

Adeline turned to her, eyebrows raised. 'You don't sound convinced.'

'Eyes forward, Adeline,' Miss Busby reminded her. 'It warrants a look, but there is a marked difference between a squirrel slipping through a small gap and a murderer managing the same.'

'I should imagine the shops and your cottages would have been built around a similar time, and presumably using the same methods. There are bound to be gaps between attics, and to my mind it explains the whole affair,' Adeline decided. 'Ezekiel must expect a thorough and sincere apology from the incompetent sergeant who falsely accused him.'

'How did you and Mr Melnyk come to be friends?' Miss Busby sought to divert her. She was quite sure his wasn't a name Adeline had mentioned before, but she was certainly most forthright in the man's defence.

'Oh, it was years ago. James misplaced a medical text, one they no longer printed, and he became terribly upset about it.' Adeline's late husband had been a respected surgeon who had died before he'd had time to enjoy his retirement, or the gleaming Rolls Royce he'd worked so hard for. 'I visited all manner of bookshops at the time trying to find another one for him. London, Oxford, Reading, but no one could help me. I stopped in Chipping Common on the way home for something or other, saw Melnyk's Books, and ducked in. It wasn't long after he'd first opened. He didn't have the book but he moved heaven and earth to find a copy. It took him three months, and it had to be posted from Ireland in the end, but he never gave up. Knows booksellers in all corners of the world, never mind the country. Extremely diligent. James was thrilled, and even dropped in personally to thank him. After that, I found myself going in once in a while, buying the odd thing for myself, or a gift, and we'd chat about this and that. Such a knowledgeable man. Speaks five languages you know. Can you imagine?'

Miss Busby replied that she could not.

'And of course, the things he's been through in the Crimea…well, it puts one to shame for the human race. Sometimes I find myself thinking of him when I am grumbling over some minor inconvenience or other. When I need to give myself a bit of a talking to.'

Miss Busby nodded as they turned into the single-track lane to Bloxford, the hawthorn hedgerow either side thick with blossom.

'To gain a sense of perspective,' she concurred. She found herself having to do the same at times. When you no longer had a loved one to talk matters through with, it was easy for things to become mixed up and grow out of hand in your mind.

'Ah, now look who is here!' Adeline exclaimed, drawing the car to a stop outside Miss Busby's cottage.

Miss Busby did indeed look. A grey Alvis motor car was parked outside Lavender Cottage, and standing beside it was a tall, smartly dressed, red-haired figure. Inspector Alastair McKay glowered towards the Rolls so fiercely that it made Miss Busby's heart sink.

'Inspector! Thank heavens. Now—' Adeline began before she had even fully emerged from the car.

'Mrs Fanshawe.' He stopped her with a stern tone. 'I'm here to speak to Miss Busby.'

'Oh?' Miss Busby asked, stepping around the car and feigning innocence. 'Good afternoon, Inspector.'

'Good afternoon, Miss Busby. Perhaps you can tell me why, once again, you have taken it upon yourself to—'

'It is so nice to see you, again,' she said, smiling up at him. With his immaculate grey suit closely fitting his muscular frame, and his red hair catching the spring sunshine, he really did look every inch the dashing Scot. 'How long has it been, now? Is your mother keeping well?' she asked.

'I…several months, and yes, thank you, she's as well as can be expected.' The inspector's mother, a former teacher like Miss Busby, was in a home in Edinburgh, afflicted with Alzheimer's. 'But I'm really very disappointed,' he went on, 'to hear you have upset Sergeant Heaton at Chipping Common.'

'She has done nothing of the sort,' Adeline objected. '*I* have upset him. And he deserves upsetting for hounding an innocent man.'

'Mrs Fanshawe—'

'And misreading a crime scene.'

'Now, really—'

'And being rude, not only to a dear friend, but also to *me*.' Adeline folded her arms across her substantial chest and raised her eyebrows, as if daring the inspector to excuse the last. Miss Busby smiled as an exasperated expression crossed his face. Despite his irascible temperament, she realised she had rather missed him.

'Shall I put the kettle on, Inspector?' she asked, heading up the front path without waiting for a reply. 'We can sit in the garden. It's such a pleasant afternoon.'

'That won't be necessary, thank you.' The inspector's words were unnaturally loud in the stillness of the lane.

'Oh?' She turned.

'I don't have the time. I'm here to collect Constable Miller from the local station to assist me with the case.'

'You said you'd come to speak to Miss Busby,' Adeline pointed out.

'Yes, there was no reply to my telephone call so I came as a courtesy whilst I'm passing.'

'Well?' she pressed.

The inspector turned pointedly to Miss Busby. 'I understand you've been to see Mr Melnyk at Melnyk's Books this morning. I must stress,' he stated, his Edinburgh accent lending gravitas to the words, 'that the death of Gabriel Travis is being treated as murder. Mr Melnyk is our primary suspect.' He ignored Adeline's dramatic intake of breath. 'As such, I must caution you not to approach the individual for your own safety.'

'Goodness. Well, we are very grateful for your concern, Inspector. Aren't we, Adeline?'

'We certainly are not!' Adeline retorted tartly. 'It is entirely misplaced.'

'Are you sure I can't offer you tea?' Miss Busby pressed.

'No, thank you. I must be getting on.' He pulled car keys from his pocket.

'But, what about the squirrels–?' Adeline demanded.

'Never mind that now, Adeline. Good day, Inspector,' Miss Busby said with a smile. 'It really is lovely to see you again, even if the circumstances are rather unpleasant.'

The inspector hesitated, then nodded in return and stalked to his car.

Having almost dragged a bewildered Adeline into the cottage and shut the door, Miss Busby went through to the kitchen to fill the kettle.

'Why on earth did you let him go?' Adeline finally managed to bluster. 'We ought to have demanded to know what makes him think it's murder, and what possible evidence he can have against Ezekiel. Not to mention telling him about the squirrel in the attic. *Really*, Isabelle!'

'Do have some sense, Adeline. You saw the mood he was in.' Miss Busby opened the back door to the garden and pointed Adeline toward her outdoor set of table and four chairs placed under the mulberry tree. 'He wouldn't have listened to us, and would only have grown more and more annoyed if we'd pressed him. You remember how he was last year, and he doesn't appear to have mellowed in the meantime. Besides, there's a much easier way to find out what we need to know.'

'Is there?'

'Yes.' Miss Busby popped back into the kitchen to warm the pot before spooning in the tea. Once ready, she carried the tray out to join Adeline under the shade of the tree.

'Well, tell me!' Adeline demanded.

'Haven't you worked it out?' She smiled.

'No, Isabelle, I have not.'

'Bobby Miller...' Miss Busby let the name dangle while pouring tea.

'What about him? Oh!' Understanding dawned. 'Of course! If he's being drafted, we can simply ask him for all the details instead of that prickly Scot!'

'Precisely.' Miss Busby nodded.

'But how? He's about to be taken off to Chipping Common.'

'Oh, that's simple enough. I'll ask young Dennis to take a message to him in the morning. I know you want all the answers now, Adeline,' she said, pre-empting her friend's interruption, 'but the inspector has only just arrived. Best to let him find his feet and make his investigations first. Ezekiel doesn't seem to be in any immediate danger, so we needn't rush in like headless chickens. Slow and steady wins the race.'

Adeline thought for several moments, before finally conceding, 'You are right, I suppose.'

'That's not to say that we can't do a little quiet investigating of our own in the meantime,' Miss Busby offered in consolation.

Adeline brightened immediately. 'What do you have in mind?'

'Well, let's see. Lucy is collecting me later this afternoon for dinner at her father's.'

'Ahh. Sir Richard Lannister.' Adeline offered the sort of knowing smile that would immediately put anyone's back up.

'Yes,' Miss Busby replied curtly. 'And–'

'You seem to be seeing rather a lot of the man lately, Isabelle.'

Miss Busby gave her friend a hard stare. 'We enjoy one another's company, Adeline, and have become friends. There's nothing more to it than that, as well you know.'

'Hmm.' Adeline's eyes remained bright with mischief. 'Didn't he take you to the opera last month? *La Traviata. Such* a romantic–'

'Yes, and he invited you too, but you claimed you were busy with Jemima and the boys.'

'Well, two's company, etcetera, but you are certainly getting out and about much more since you met the man last Christmas.' She sat back, as if pleased with her friend's progress. 'Lucy is to be thoroughly commended for thinking to invite you for the festive season, and introducing you to her father. And of course it doesn't hurt that he's comfortably rich, rather dashing for his age, and a widower to boot.'

'Adeline.' Miss Busby's tone was firm. 'That is quite enough. You know I still think of Randolf every day, and I always shall.'

Adeline lowered her eyes and reached to pat her friend's hand in apology. 'I know, and he will never be replaced.'

Miss Busby nodded in graceful acceptance. 'As I was saying,' she continued in businesslike tone, 'Lucy will be collecting me later, and I shall ask her if she's heard anything about Mr Travis' death. If not, she will know who to ask. Her father commands a pack of news-hounds, after all. And I shall ask him too,' she finished with a pointed look.

Adeline didn't press the matter further. 'And what should I do?' she asked. 'Should I go back to Ezekiel and tell him to check the attic?'

Miss Busby shook her head at once. 'We would only land the poor man in trouble if he were found to have gone into Travis' rooms before the police have given permission. And, I wonder…' she trailed off, not sure quite how to phrase her concern delicately.

'Yes?' Adeline prompted.

'Well, I wonder if it might be best, for the moment, not to visit Mr Melnyk alone.'

'Isabelle, you cannot possibly think–'

Miss Busby stirred sugar into the tea. 'No, I don't believe I do, really,' she admitted before Adeline could build up a head of steam, 'but I think under the circumstances caution is the prudent path to take. And it will curry favour with the inspector.'

Adeline made a disparaging noise.

'I know you're angry with the police, but Inspector McKay makes a better ally than adversary. We can still visit Ezekiel together. Perhaps tomorrow.' Miss Busby paused to sip her tea and think for a moment. 'Do you have any dresses, or perhaps skirts, to which you're not particularly attached?'

'Of course not. I only buy the ones I *am* particularly… ahh, I see where this is headed! You think I should pay another visit to Mrs Harrison.' Adeline swiftly caught up. 'Under the guise of more alterations.'

Miss Busby nodded. 'Your chat this morning was somewhat brief, from what you said?'

'Yes, I ran straight off to telephone you once she told me what had happened.'

'Then Harrison's Haberdashery would be a good place to start. Rose Harrison is right next door to the crime scene. You could ask if she saw, or heard, anything of note, and perhaps get all the local…opinion,' she had almost slipped and said *gossip,* 'on the matter. You might pop into Fowler's, too. It was Ezekiel's first port of call after finding the body, after all.'

Adeline nodded. 'Yes, and I need rose water, by the by. It will save me a trip into Oxford. I don't want any good skirts cut up for no good reason, though.' She took a contemplative sip of tea. 'I could ask to be measured for a new summer dress, that would work well on both counts. I can always do with another one. It will take longer, and afford more opportunity for conversation.'

'Perfect.' Miss Busby nodded in approval.

'Should I go now?'

'Oh, you should finish your tea first,' Miss Busby said. 'Let's meet tomorrow morning and compare notes. Perhaps Lily's Tea Rooms at 11?'

Adeline nodded and took a long drink of tea. 'Now,' she said, placing the empty cup on the table and looking about, 'is there cake?'

CHAPTER 6

With Adeline safely dispatched back to Chipping Common, Miss Busby allowed herself a period of quiet tranquillity in her garden. Truly at its best in the spring, the shrubs bordering the orchard were flowering in shades of blue, pink, and yellow, and the scent of early roses and stocks drifted from the flower borders.

Pudding had rather ruined the herb bed under the kitchen window when he'd first arrived, but she'd planted some catmint by the log store, where he now slept contentedly, leaving her rosemary and thyme undisturbed.

'Well, Barnaby, I suppose we ought to make ready,' she said, checking her watch and noting that Lucy was due soon.

The little dog sleeping at her feet didn't move a muscle, still tired no doubt from the morning outing – not to mention the sausages he'd enjoyed for lunch at Spring Meadows.

'Or you can stay with Pud, if you prefer,' she told him. 'It's just that Richard has a new French chef, and I didn't think you'd want to miss your dinner…'

An ear twitched.

Miss Busby smiled.

A short while later, both were ready at the door as Lucy pulled up outside in her bright red Sunbeam sports car. The young woman broke into a smile at the sight of them.

'Hello! Jump in! You don't mind the roof being down, do you? It's such a beautiful day and it would be a shame to waste it.'

Miss Busby wasn't quite sure, although she knew Barnaby would be in his element. Unlike the delightfully scruffy little terrier, however, she didn't want to arrive at Lannister House in a dishevelled state. Lucy, spotting her discomfort, was quick to pull a cream and blue silk scarf from the glovebox.

'Here, wear this. I keep it for just such occasions.'

Miss Busby obliged and tied it under her chin with a grateful smile.

'You're awfully quiet,' Lucy remarked, turning the car in the lane. 'Is everything alright?'

'Oh, yes, thank you,' Miss Busby said. 'It's just been a rather strange day.'

She relayed the curious tale of Mr Melnyk and poor Gabriel Travis, along with their ensuing discussion at Spring Meadows as they drove towards Oxford – Lannister House being on the outskirts of the city.

'I've not heard a peep, but then I don't cover the smaller towns now,' Lucy said. 'Or crimes, for that matter.'

Miss Busby remembered that, having helped her and the inspector solve the mystery of the dead insurance man last year, Lucy had been promoted at the *Oxford News* and was no longer a 'junior'. She had been given a much bigger role within the city itself.

'Culture and events is my beat now. It's all a lot cheerier,' Lucy went on. 'And I can write under my own name of Lannister at last, which is a relief.'

Miss Busby smiled. The young woman had felt the need to write under her mother's maiden name of Wesley last year, to make her mark on her own merit, but was going from strength to strength now.

'I'll ask around in the office, though,' Lucy continued. 'Make sure we're covering it. It sounds fascinating.'

'What have you been working on recently?' Miss Busby asked.

'I was in Oxford over the weekend interviewing Dorothy Sayers. We're doing an article on her. It's good fun, actually. She's a bit of a local hero. One of the first women to gain a degree from Oxford. And of course her novel, *Whose Body?* has just come out, too. Astonishing, really. An inspiration to us all.'

'How wonderful.' Miss Busby smiled. She would have to borrow Adeline's copy. Although rather disappointed Lucy hadn't arrived with the inside scoop on the murder, she was delighted that her young friend was doing so well.

'I've been covering a lot of musical events as well. There's an American jazz band touring the county at the moment, they're great fun. I'm going to hire them and put on a bit of bash next month for Daddy's birthday. They've been rather maudlin affairs since Mummy died. I thought this might liven us all up a little. Will you come?'

Miss Busby wasn't sure jazz was quite her cup of tea, or Richard's for that matter, but the eager look on Lucy's face was hard to resist.

'I didn't know your father liked jazz,' she hedged.

'Neither does he, yet. But he will. It's impossible not to dance to. Anthony says we should give him a proper dancing cane instead of his walking stick. Do say you'll come?'

Miss Busby smiled at the image. 'Yes, of course I will, thank you.' She suspected Richard would need the moral support.

The Sunbeam picked up speed on the main road, and Miss Busby felt something of a thrill at feeling the wind on her face. *Adeline would enjoy this*, she thought, wondering if her friend might consider a sports car should anything happen to the Rolls. Barnaby, held close on her lap lest he get any ideas, was quite beside himself with excitement, nose going nineteen to the dozen, ears flapping wildly in the breeze.

'Tell me more about this Mr Melnyk,' Lucy shouted over the noise of the engine. 'Are you taking the case?'

Miss Busby laughed. 'Let's just say I'm taking an

interest in the case. Adeline is awfully distressed at the thought of her friend in peril, so there is really no choice in the matter. Much to Inspector McKay's dismay, I'm afraid.'

'Oh, when you said an inspector had been called in, I wondered if it would be him.'

Miss Busby snuck a sidelong glance at Lucy's face. Her cheeks may have been flushed from the wind, or it may have been something else…

'Yes, he has already been to Lavender Cottage to warn me off.'

'Just like old times!' Lucy laughed.

The rest of the drive passed without more talk, the noise becoming too much to overcome until they turned off the main road and up the long, winding incline of the driveway to Lannister House.

A beautiful Jacobean manor house, and former wartime convalescent home, it had been bought and renovated by Sir Richard Lannister four years ago. His son, Anthony, had been sent there from the trenches to recover from a blast injury. Richard had said that the family had consequently spent so much time at the manor that the moment it came up for sale it was the obvious choice. *We practically lived there as it was.'*

As the house came into sight, surrounded by beautiful gardens stretching down into woodland and meadows beyond, Miss Busby found herself thinking how different her life would have been if Randolf had lived. He'd been destined to be the next Earl of Bloxford, and she would have enjoyed a life of ease and comfort at his side in similarly stunning surroundings.

She allowed herself the briefest of regrets, before stiffening her upper lip and reminding herself that she managed perfectly well in her cottage, and had made the best of things. Her time as a teacher, whilst initially unexpected, had turned out to be a joy. She was blessed with good friends, a cosy home, and the satisfaction of a life well lived despite the intervention of cruel fate. She was always made welcome at Bloxford Hall when the family were in residence, and it certainly didn't hurt to enjoy being spoiled at Lannister House once in a while either.

She smiled her thanks as the footman – impeccable in blue livery – rushed from the main entrance to open the car door for her. He escorted her to the butler, who took her jacket and showed her through to the court-yard in stately style. Sir Richard sat on his favourite bench beneath an arbour covered in roses.

'Isabelle! How wonderful!' He stood to greet her with the aid of his walking stick, his customary smile warm, blue eyes sparkling. Tall and slightly built, he wore impeccably pressed cream trousers and white shirt. A neat tie in place, his navy blue blazer lay across the back of the bench. With a gallant kiss of her hand, he led her back to sit beside him, hooking the stick over the arm of the bench with practised ease. The arthritis plaguing his joints was growing progressively worse, but some days were still better than others. The scent of the flowers was light and delicate, the bright colours shining against the greens of the kitchen garden beyond.

'Aren't they magnificent?' he said, seeing her look up at the pink, red, and white flowers. 'Pippin, Iceberg, and Pilgrim.'

Miss Busby turned to him, impressed.

'I knew you'd want to know,' he laughed, 'so I asked Hodges. I've been repeating the names to myself all day. They sound like three small terriers, don't you think? I say,' he went on before she could answer, 'I rather like the headgear, is this a new look?'

Momentarily confused, Miss Busby suddenly realised she hadn't taken the scarf from her hair.

'Oh, heavens, what must you think of me!' She removed it as carefully as she could, hoping all was well beneath.

'I should think you've been in the car with Lucy, that's what! Always tearing around with the wind in her hair. Where has she got to, by the way?'

Miss Busby looked around. 'I must have lost her en route through the house. Perhaps she's taken Barnaby to look for rabbits in the spinney. He makes her laugh when he disappears up to his shoulders down the burrows.' The two of them had grown quite fond of each other in recent months, and had several favourite haunts around the grounds. 'Lost friends, absent dogs, and forgotten scarves. I'm beginning to wonder if my mind might be wandering.'

'Nonsense!' he proclaimed. 'You just need a drink, that's all. Sherry?'

'That would be lovely, thank you.'

With staff dispatched for drinks and nibbles, the pair began to chat easily. Time flew as they discussed what they'd been reading, where they'd been, who they'd seen and so forth, before embarking on the true business of the evening: the new style of crossword Richard was trialling in the paper. Trickier than the usual logical offerings, the clues provided by his mystery setter were cryptic and utterly addictive in nature. Both had developed a fondness for them, and enjoyed wrestling with the clues together. They deciphered anagrams, allusions, and quotations companionably, before the sun began to dip, bringing a chill to the courtyard.

'Come on, let's decamp inside.' Richard set his pencil down, only one clue remaining. 'Perhaps we can find my daughter and your dog on our travels.'

The pair were easy to spot, Barnaby fast asleep on the thick sheepskin rug by the fireplace in the library, Lucy on the sofa opposite with her legs tucked under her, nose buried in a book. Elgar drifted through the house from the gramophone on its own table.

'Lucy, you ought to have ordered the fire lit for the dog, you know how he loves it,' Richard admonished, bending to ruffle the little terrier's ears.

'Dawkins would think me quite mad, it's practically summer!' Lucy objected.

'You should have come and sat outside with us, then,

we missed you,' he said, sitting beside her as Miss
Busby took the armchair opposite.

'Oh, I thought you might like a bit of time to
yourselves,' she said, directing what might have been
the slightest hint of a wink towards Miss Busby, who
offered a stern look in response. She wondered if the
girl had been talking to Adeline.

Lucy laughed lightly. 'Miss Busby has uncovered
another murder. Did she tell you?'

'No! Good lord, you are a veritable magnet for them,
Isabelle! Who is it this time?'

CHAPTER 7

Dawkins, Sir Richard's housekeeper, appeared as if by magic and lit the fire, much to Barnaby's delight. The little dog turned around three times on the rug, before settling down contentedly to nap as Miss Busby told Richard the strange tale of the murdered poet.

'Melnyk, hmm. I don't know the name, but I'm quite sure I recall something about Chipping Common… some sort of scandal. Happens a lot in those little towns – all manner of goings-on, but I'm sure there was something about a girl…Oh, Anthony would know. Where is he, Lucy?'

'I haven't seen him.' She shrugged. 'The minute he hears the dinner gong he'll materialise.'

Richard turned to bellow, 'ANTHONY!' over his shoulder, waking the dog and making Miss Busby jump.

'We're acclimatising him to loud noises,' Lucy commented drily.

Richard tutted. 'He's absolutely fine now,' he told Miss Busby. 'He's come on in leaps and bounds this year. I've even put him back to work on the newspaper. Just little bits here and there to start with. Don't want to throw him in at the deep end, but he needs to be ready to take over from me. I can see full retirement glinting on the horizon. Not that I'm doing a great deal now, of course, at my age, but it's still rather hard to let go of it all.'

Miss Busby looked over to Lucy, wondering how the young woman would feel about her brother taking the reins of the newspaper. She'd put so much work into it when Anthony had been sent to the front, as well as when he'd returned so badly injured. Would she feel aggrieved, now that he was recovered? If she did, no hint of it showed on her face.

'Yes, Father?' Anthony appeared in the doorway. A tall young man in his early thirties, he had his father's blue eyes and his sister's dark hair. His skin still had a pallor to it, and he was painfully thin.

'Oh, hallo Miss B,' he said. 'Hallo hound.' He crossed the room and dropped, cross-legged, to the floor beside Barnaby. Ignoring the wary grumble from the dog, he scratched the fur at the base of his spine. Unable to resist, Barnaby rolled onto his back and succumbed to the attention.

'Chipping Common, Anthony. Wasn't there some sort of hullabaloo there a few years back?' Richard asked.

'I shouldn't think so. Fairly quiet sort of place.' Anthony thought for a moment, rubbing the wiry white fur of the dog's chest. 'Oh, but there was that strange business with the girl.'

Miss Busby sat up, looking at him intently. Lucy did the same.

'I thought so! Now, which girl? Do be a bit more specific,' Richard pressed.

'It was years ago, Father,' Anthony said drily. 'And I don't know if you recall, but I have been away in far-flung fields.'

Sir Richard raised his eyebrows.

'Sorry, Pater,' Anthony conceded. 'I'm hungry, that's all. It can make me a little acerbic.'

Lucy's laugh lightened the mood. 'He's right,' she confirmed. 'Heaven help you if you speak to him before he's had breakfast.'

Anthony laughed with her, and nodded. 'You should ask Cameron Spencer,' he continued. 'He was the one who had a thing about the girl, if memory serves. Or perhaps she had a thing about him? Annie, I think her name was. No, Alice? No… Look, I couldn't say. I didn't see that much of the fellow, but when I did, he was always rattling on about her. It's academic, anyway,' he said with a shrug. 'As I recall, she vanished off the face of the earth.'

Miss Busby felt a tingling along her spine.

'Ah, Spencer… local chap from your battalion, wasn't he?' Richard asked. 'Formidable grandmother. Lady Felicity Spencer. It's coming back to me now.'

Anthony nodded. 'Cameron's a decent sort. Lives at

Hayle Court just beyond the high street with his mater, and her mater, Lady Felicity, too. Although the old girl is on her last legs now, by all accounts.'

'Shame.' Richard shook his head. 'Terrifying creature, but rather fun in her day. Unlike her daughter – one of those self-obsessed sorts. Well, there's the chap to ask. Do you still see him, Anthony?'

'Don't see much of anyone these days,' Anthony said with a wry smile. 'Could get him on the telephone, I suppose. Are you on the trail of a story?'

'I think we might be,' Lucy said, with a look to Miss Busby.

'Ah! May need to call you back to active service on this one!' Richard beamed, clearly thrilled at the thought of his son being involved.

'Righto.' Anthony stood and stretched. 'And it's *Sir* Cameron Spencer, not that he's the sort to fuss. He inherited the title when his grandfather died, his own pater having kicked the bucket some years prior. Anyway, how long till dinner? I could eat a horse.'

Some hours later, after a delicious carré d'agneau en croûte d'herbes with fresh mushrooms and asparagus tips, courtesy of Chef Delisle, Miss Busby sat with Lucy in the drawing room while Richard and Anthony enjoyed their cigars and brandy on the terrace.

Chef had insisted the ladies complete their dining experience with a 'digestif', and Miss Busby consequently found herself sipping cautiously at a small glass of calvados.

'The chef is good, isn't he?' Lucy asked, wincing at the strength of the drink. 'I'm so glad Daddy hired him. He's cheered everyone up.'

Miss Busby tilted her head in enquiry.

'Oh, it's around this time of year Mummy fell ill,' Lucy said. 'Daddy often gets maudlin in the late spring, especially around his birthday. It's why I'm planning the party. But this year he's seemed a bit brighter than usual.'

'Well, that's good,' Miss Busby said. Her head was beginning to swim, and she rather wished she hadn't had the sherry earlier. 'That he's brighter, I mean,' she clarified. 'I know when I lost Randolf it was agonising, but time eases the pain. You never stop missing them, but you do come to a point where you can see a way to carry on. It's difficult to explain.'

'No, I understand, I think,' Lucy said. 'Anthony and I were away at boarding school, so it was easier on us. Daddy was always with Mummy, so of course he'd feel it more.'

Miss Busby nodded and gazed into the fire. All manner of shapes danced in the flames. She put the glass down on the side table, thinking she'd probably had quite enough.

'So, what are we going to do about Annie?' Lucy asked.

Richard had expressly forbidden all talk of murder at the dinner table, and it took Miss Busby a moment to place the name.

'Or indeed Alice,' Miss Busby corrected.

'Yes, trust my brother not to remember! It could be something or nothing,' she went on quietly. 'His memory isn't what it was. The blast damaged him rather profoundly.'

'I should imagine so, poor soul.'

'So, what's your plan?'

'What makes you think I have one?'

Lucy smiled. 'Because I've come to know you rather well.'

'Ah, well in that case…' Miss Busby leaned forward in her seat. 'I have already dispatched Adeline back to Chipping Common to search for clues among the shopkeepers in Ezekiel's row.'

'And to check the attics for access routes? Wasn't Mary clever to think of the squirrel!'

'Mary's still sharp as a tack. Such a relief after her horrible fall last year. Adeline and I are to debrief tomorrow at Lily's Tearooms.'

'Just like old times.'

'Yes, and I shall dispatch young Dennis with a note for Bobby Miller in the morning, who will I'm sure be able to answer the burning question: What revealed the death to be murder? Once we have that answer, we shall be able to move forward.'

'Why Bobby? Wouldn't the inspector be a better bet?' Lucy asked.

'As I said, he's already made it quite clear he's not keen on me getting involved. So I thought it best we plough on alone for now.'

'Ah, so you're drafting Bobby to the team.'

'Well, he can be almost as stubborn as the inspector at times. But when you've had someone crying on your knee after a schoolyard bump or a particularly tricky piece of arithmetic, you often find them a little more pliable.'

Lucy laughed. 'I see. And you would then present your findings and thoughts to the inspector a little later on, I suppose?'

Miss Busby narrowed her eyes. Calvados or no, she had long suspected Lucy to be somewhat enamoured of the handsome inspector, even though he hadn't been particularly friendly – far from it, in fact. McKay had thawed towards the end of their initial investigation though, and she hoped he would do the same in this instance.

'I should think so. If he needs help, of course. It may be that he'll have the case sewn up himself before that point.'

Lucy raised her eyebrows, making Miss Busby give a little giggle. She waved a hand in blame towards the glass. The inspector certainly would have struggled to solve the murder at Little Minton without their help, much as he was unlikely to admit it.

'I just think it will be better to arm ourselves with solid facts from the outset this time,' she concluded. Their own behaviour in the Little Minton murder, in fairness, had not always been quite as responsible as she might have liked.

'Well, it sounds as if you have everything in hand,' Lucy said, finishing her drink and getting to her feet. 'I'll go to the office early tomorrow morning and have a root through the files – see what I can find on Chipping Common, Alice or Annie, Gabriel Travis et al. And perhaps you could return the favour if Adeline has unearthed anything of interest?'

'Yes, of course. You are a dear,' Miss Busby said rising to her feet.

'Do you mind if I don't drive you?' Lucy stood too. 'The calvados has gone straight to my head. I'll ring for Fletcher, if you don't mind.'

Miss Busby said that of course she didn't, and thanked her before making her way out to the terrace to say goodnight to Richard.

'Goodnight, Miss B,' Anthony said with an exaggerated bow and a wide grin, then became serious. 'I'm almost certain the girl was called Alice, you know. Although Amelie is a possibility. Anyhow, I'm off to bed, Father. À demain.'

'Goodnight, son.' He patted the young man affectionately on the shoulder as they made their way inside. 'And goodnight, Isabelle.' He took both her hands in his. 'Once again our time together has felt far too short. Are you sure you won't stay a little longer? An extra nightcap, perhaps, just the two of us?'

Miss Busby smiled. 'It's tempting, but I must get back for Pud, and there's a lot to do in the morning.'

'Ah, detecting!' He gave her right hand a peck before

letting go. 'Right you are. I shan't get in your way. Do telephone, though, if there's anything I can do. And if Anthony can be of help, please, let him, will you?'

'I will,' Miss Busby promised.

'Well here is Fletcher.' He waved a hand in the chauffeur's direction. 'Were you headed for bed? Sorry old chap, but the lady must be returned home safe and sound!'

'Yessir, o'course sir, and there's no problem at all, so there isn't.' Fletcher grinned, opening the door to the black Austin Twenty. Miss Busby climbed aboard and nodded her thanks.

Barnaby had pottered out to see what was happening. He growled in ungrateful manner as Fletcher lifted him in.

'I shall see you soon, I hope,' Richard called, closing the door for her and stepping back as Fletcher started the motor.

Miss Busby nodded and waved, feeling her eyes droop as the car made its way along the immaculate gravel of the drive. With the pleasant warmth of good food and good company upon her, she finally solved the last crossword clue that had puzzled them both: hat could be dry (5).

Derby, she thought, as she slowly drifted into a light doze before they had even reached the main road.

CHAPTER 8

Miss Busby cradled a cup of coffee in the front room of Lavender Cottage and resolved never to touch calvados again. Pudding sat on the back of the sofa, lazily washing his paws and, she would have sworn, judging her.

'I was an innocent victim, Pud,' she told him. 'The French are entirely to blame.' She finished the coffee and went to where her notebook sat open on the davenport desk. Picking up her pencil she leaned forward to add last night's findings.

Sir Cameron Spencer – lives at Hayle Court – served with Anthony Lannister. Supposed dalliance (when?) with girl who disappeared from Chipping Common. Named Annie/Alice/Amelie?

It had seemed so intriguing yesterday evening but looked somewhat underwhelming this morning. Young men naturally became smitten with young women. The disappearance had happened several years ago, and as such could have little bearing on current events.

She sighed. As her previous notes were somewhat sparse, she made an effort to flesh them out while waiting for Dennis, hoping it might spark a connection. She reread her entry for Travis:

Gabriel Travis – poet, bookbinder. Shot between 10pm and 9am on Saturday morning at Melnyk's Books, Chipping Common. Weapon was Melnyk's own gun – discovered missing from the cash drawer where it was kept. No family. Tragic history. Suicide suspected to be staged.

She added something Enid had mentioned at Spring Meadows:

Suicide Note?

If someone had gone to all the trouble of staging a suicide, arranging the body just so, with papers and gun in hand, surely a note would have been a natural addition? Particularly as Mr Travis had been known to have suffered tragedy in his life. Unless the murderer hadn't known this, she wondered, in which case they may have been unsure what to write.

She thought for a moment. Whoever killed the poor man must have planned it carefully. They would have had motive, of course, therefore there must be a history between the victim and culprit. Not to mention he would have known where Mr Melnyk kept his gun. He must therefore have known both men reasonably well, which would surely lead one to suppose the culprit would have known more than enough to forge a note.

Next, she checked her details of the two other shops in Ezekiel's row:

Harrison's Haberdashery next door. (Mrs Harrison now remarried, previously Mrs Doyle.)

Fowler's the Pharmacist next door but one. Ezekiel ran there after finding the body, because they had a telephone.

Beneath these, she wrote:

Roof access? Attics in use?

Then, because she had just thought of it and wanted to ask Bobby Miller, she added:

Windows?

Had any been left open, or damaged? Ezekiel had said the bookshop windows were intact, leaving him under suspicion, but what about those of the other two shops?

Next came Ezekiel's entry.

Ezekiel Melnyk. Primary suspect.

Birth place: Crimea.

Hearing: weak

Demeanour: far from murderous

Motive: ?

Owner of the murder weapon

Would surely have unbolted the shop door or staged a break-in if guilty? And found a different weapon.

Had she left anything out? She thought back to what she had learned about detecting last Christmas. One must always consider motive, opportunity, and means. Ezekiel had opportunity, a motive was currently unfathomable, and means were uncomfortably straightforward – it was his own gun, after all.

She sighed again, long and loud this time, unable to

think of anything more to add. The noise woke Pud, who had nodded off in the morning sun streaming through the front window. He slid down from the sofa and came to jump on her lap, purring loudly.

'I don't seem to be getting anywhere at all,' she told him as she rubbed between his ears. 'And Adeline is so worried for her friend, that's what's at the heart of this.'

Pud butted her hand for further rubs, unconcerned for anything other than his own comfort, as was the way of cats.

'Well, I'm sure the inspector will have looked into matters by now, and Bobby can inform us of any news. No reason to lose hope, eh Pud?'

Taking a fresh sheet of notepaper from the desk drawer, she was just beginning her note to Constable Miller when Dennis' bright red post van trundled down the lane, early for once, which caught her off guard. She returned the cat to the comforts of the sofa and dashed outside, almost too late to ambush him.

'Come in for a moment while I finish this,' she said. Barnaby sniffed at his trousers with unprecedented interest.

'Nurse Delaney over the road's got a new dog,' Dennis maundered. 'It was trying to nip me.'

'Yes, well, that will explain Barnaby's interest. Barnaby, *leave*,' Miss Busby said, finishing her note swiftly and handing it over. 'Now, you will see Bobby Miller gets this won't you Dennis?'

'Oh not 'im again Miss.' Dennis rolled his eyes. The pair had never got along in school, and nothing appeared to have changed since.

'He's in Chipping Common at the moment, so you'll–'

'No he isn't.'

'Isn't he?'

'He's at the station in Little Minton. There's a woman in there all angry sayin' Nurse Delaney's new dog tried to bite her too.'

'Oh, dear, is there?'

'Yup.' Dennis nodded earnestly. 'Bobby was in Chipping Common yesterday, told everyone, proud as punch he was, but he musta' annoyed them all, I reckon, an' they sent him right back. Worse luck.'

'Dennis.' Miss Busby's tone was heavy with warning. 'If you don't have anything nice to say…'

'Yes, Miss. Sorry, Miss.' He tried to act chagrined and singularly failed.

Miss Busby couldn't think why Bobby would have returned so soon – surely they hadn't solved the case already? 'Well, this makes things easier for you. You needn't take the note, I shall be in Little Minton myself this morning.'

'Oh, right. Then I suppose I've got 'ter…I mean, that is 'ter say, would you like a lift down there Miss?'

Miss Busby gave a wry smile as she checked her wristwatch. It was only a little after nine thirty. 'That's very kind of you, Dennis, but as it's a nice morning and I have plenty of time, I think Barnaby and I shall enjoy the walk.'

Dennis brightened instantly. 'Very good, Miss. I'll be off then. Thanks, Miss!'

Only pausing to gather her notebook, pencil, and bag, Miss Busby called Barnaby and set off down the lane. There was a slight chill in the air; she glanced down at her grey woollen skirt and pale pink blouse, wondering if she ought to have added a jacket, or a cardigan at least, but the sun was bright and the movement would soon warm her.

'We both ate a little too well yesterday, didn't we?' she asked the dog, turning the bend and leaving Bloxford behind for the narrow, winding lane that led to Little Minton. 'This will do us the world of good.'

Barnaby gave a small *woof*, as if in happy agreement, and bounded off down the road, zigzagging here and there as various scents teased his nose.

Spring flowers dotting the hedgerows lifted Miss Busby's mood. Celandine, cowslips, and violets, among others, making her think of Richard memorising the varieties of his roses just for her. Her smile grew, and she picked up her pace a little, enjoying the fresh air filling her lungs. Fields swathed in fresh green shoots followed the contours of rolling hills and dales. Red kites soared on rising thermals, a lark sang in a meadow and birds trilled in the hedgerows. By the time the pair reached Little Minton, Miss Busby's spirits were flying.

As she had time to spare before meeting Adeline, she made for Little Minton Police Station, where she found Constable Miller standing behind the long wooden counter, head down, absorbed in some papers.

'Good morning, Bobby,' she called brightly. He looked up in surprise, before an expression of determined fortitude crossed his face.

'Miss,' he said, holding up a hand rather than returning her greeting, 'I know just what you're going to ask me but I can't be telling you anything at all about Chipping Common, Mr Travis, or Mr Melnyk. I just can't. It's the inspector's orders.'

Miss Busby raised an eyebrow, and waited.

'Oh, sorry Miss. Good morning, Miss,' he said formally.

'That's better.'

The young man blushed under his neatly combed black hair. 'The thing is, Inspector McKay said as I had to say it right away, or you'd only go getting ideas.'

Miss Busby's eyes narrowed. 'Did he indeed?'

Bobby shifted uncomfortably behind the counter. 'Well, he did Miss, but now I come to think of it, I don't know if I was supposed to tell you that bit, so I'd be much obliged if you didn't mention it to him.'

Feeling initially thwarted, Miss Busby now felt a small surge of fresh determination within, although one look at Bobby's concerned expression reminded her that the last thing she wanted was to land the young constable in hot water.

'He said as how I might be able to go for my sergeant's training, Miss, if I do well on the case,' Bobby explained earnestly.

The inspector, she realised, had outplayed her. She felt a stab of disappointment in herself, which Bobby misinterpreted.

'Please don't be cross with me, Miss. It's not that I don't want to help you, it's just that…I can't.'

Miss Busby leaned across the counter to place a hand on his arm. 'Of course I'm not cross, Bobby,' she told him, not adding that it was the difficult Scot she was annoyed with. 'Quite the opposite. I shall be the second proudest woman in the town when you receive your promotion.'

'Oh, good, I was getting worried! The second proudest, Miss?' He tilted his head.

'After your mother, of course.'

'Oh…' He flushed again. 'Yes, Miss.'

'Well, it's good to see you're still involved with the case. When Dennis said you'd been sent back–'

'I wasn't sent back, Miss! Well, I was, but only to fetch something for the inspector, then I got caught up with a case of a suspected dog bite because Sergeant Brierly can't stand them. Dogs, I mean.'

'Ah, I see. What sort of something for the Inspector?'

'A book.' Bobby stood a little straighter behind the desk. 'We've got a big medical dictionary here. Doctor Andrews gave it to us ages ago, when he retired. The inspector wants to look at it. They don't have one at

Chipping Common, not being as well organised as we are, you see, and here's closer than Oxford to get it from.'

'Really? A medical dictionary…how interesting.'

'Erm, is it?' Realising his mistake, Bobby's eyes widened. 'I mean, it isn't really, Miss. They're used a lot, you see, when there's a murder. There's three of them over at Oxford.'

Miss Busby waited. It was an old teachers' trick: when a pupil was brought to you in disgrace, nine times out of ten all you had to do was stew them in uncomfortable silence for a few moments, and before you knew it…

'It's just because sometimes if the ambulance men don't notice…that is to say…if the doctor spotted… well, it's just always best to check because… Oh, please, Miss. I'll be in ever so much trouble.' He ended rather pathetically, and Miss Busby felt awful.

'Of course you won't, Bobby. I shall leave you to your work, and we'll pretend I was never here.'

Relief washed over his face. 'Thank you Miss!'

'Give my regards to your mother,' she called as she turned to go, confident she'd learned enough from the unwitting constable for now. If McKay had need of a medical dictionary, some unusual symptom in Travis must point directly to murder. Being the fastidious sort, he would want to confirm matters for himself. It was irksome not to know what sort of symptom, but it pointed to a clever murderer all the same. They would need to proceed with caution.

Back outside, she collected Barnaby from the holly hedge he'd stationed himself under in the hope of mice or shrews, and with mind racing, made her way over to Lily's Tea Rooms.

'What can I get you dear?' Maggie Trounce, the waitress, asked.

Miss Busby toyed with the idea of scrambled eggs and salmon. She hadn't eaten anything before leaving the cottage, and the walk had given her an appetite.

'I think…perhaps just a pot of tea,' she said with a sigh, remembering last night's heavy meal.

'Right you are. Back in a jiffy.'

Miss Busby gazed out of the window. Having asked for a table for two, Maggie had seated her at the large bow window overlooking the high street. Bright sunlight fell at the perfect angle to highlight the plush green velvet furnishings of the cosy tea room.

When Maggie returned and placed the polka-dot tea set on the table, white with green spots to match the decor, she left an extra cup and saucer. 'For Mrs Fanshawe when she gets here,' Maggie said and put a printed card with the cake menu on it at the same time. Miss Busby couldn't help but smile.

'How are Milly and the grandchildren?' she asked, having taught Maggie's daughter.

'Oh, they're grand, thank you.' Maggie beamed. 'Aren't you kind to remember? Oh, and here's Mrs Fanshawe now look, nice and early. I knew that cup'd come in handy!'

Miss Busby glanced out of the window to see the large white Rolls Royce executing a complicated manoeuvre in the narrow street. After several attempts at parking at an orderly angle, Adeline gave up, left the motorcar at a jaunty slant, and hurried inside.

CHAPTER 9

'Isabelle,' Adeline gushed, 'you will not believe – oh, good morning Maggie.'

'Good morning! Give me a shout when you've chosen your cakes,' Maggie said, pulling the chair out for Adeline before bustling off.

'You will not believe,' Adeline went on when they were alone, smoothing her smart navy and red dress about her as she sat, 'what I have discovered. I would have telephoned you last night, but I knew you were at Lannister House and I wanted to double check something this morning. Now, let me think where to start.'

'With the disappearing girl?' Miss Busby hazarded a guess.

Adeline's jaw dropped. 'How on earth–?'

'Richard's son, Anthony, was in the same battalion as Cameron Spencer,' Miss Busby replied, reaching into her bag for her notebook, and a hard biscuit for Barnaby who was almost quivering with expectation under the table. 'Sir Cameron Spencer, technically. Although he's awfully young for the title.'

'What on earth has Cameron Spencer, Sir or otherwise, got to do with anything?' Adeline asked.

'Perhaps it's best if you explain first,' Miss Busby said. 'I only received a vague outline of facts – which may indeed not have been facts at all.'

'What?' Adeline asked, clearly baffled.

'Anthony Lannister's memory is not the strongest.'

'Ah. The wounded boy. Well, of course, it can't be helped. But I still don't see… Oh, never mind. Isabelle, I had a long chat with Mrs Harrison and whilst we were talking of the terrible tragedy and the finger of suspicion pointing to dear Ezekiel, she mentioned that this is not the first time mystery has struck Hayle Court Road.'

Miss Busby poured two cups of tea as Adeline sat back, expectant. 'Go on,' she prompted.

'Well…' Adeline popped a sugar cube into her cup and stirred vigorously. 'In 1914, not long before the war broke out, Mrs Harrison took on a sixteen-year-old girl from the workhouse in Cirencester as an apprentice.'

'Good Lord, I thought that place had closed decades ago.' Miss Busby took out her notebook and made a note of the date.

'Yes, well, it has been cleared out entirely and converted into an infirmary now. There's almost nothing left of the original, which doesn't help us a jot. Although they'll probably still hold records. And one or two staff may have remained. We must go this afternoon and speak to the matron.'

'Must we?'

'Yes. We need to find out more about Alice.'

Ahh, Anthony had been right with the name, Miss Busby thought. She would have to tell him.

'Alice Albion lived in the attic above Harrison's Haberdashery, much as Mr Travis lived in the attic above Melnyk's Books. At least, to begin with she did. You'll recall Mrs Harrison was actually Mrs Doyle until she married Mr Harrison two years later. She moved to her new husband's house nearby, leaving the flat vacant. Alice moved into the flat and the attic space became a storeroom.'

Miss Busby felt a frisson of excitement at seeing her notebook fill with new information, before remembering the crux of the matter.

'This is all very interesting, Adeline, but what exactly does it have to do with Gabriel Travis?'

Adeline took a sip of tea. 'I'm coming to that. Do you recall how long Ezekiel said Travis had lodged with him?'

Miss Busby checked her notes. 'Nine years or so.'

'Precisely, meaning he must have moved in around 1914 – which was the same time as Alice.'

'Yes…?' Miss Busby thought the connection somewhat tenuous, but knew better than to interrupt further.

'Now, a year after Mrs Harrison moved out–'

'Which would be 1917?' Miss Busby checked, trying to keep the dates straight in her book.

'Yes. Just before Christmas of 1917, the 21st of December, in fact, Alice quite simply disappeared.'

'Disappeared how?'

'Disappeared, Isabelle! There is only one way to disappear that I know of. One moment she was in the shop, working as usual, the next she was gone. And no one has seen her since.'

'Yes, but did she take her things? Was there any sign of a struggle? That sort of thing.'

'Some of her things were taken, Mrs Harrison said, the sort that could be easily carried – a selection of clothes from her wardrobe, for example, but others were left abandoned. Books, her sewing kit, and suchlike. And there was money taken from the till.'

Adeline finished her tea, poured herself a fresh cup, and cast an eye over the cake menu. Maggie appeared; Florentines and a fresh pot were ordered.

'So she took the money and ran away,' Miss Busby mused. 'I suppose that's always a risk when taking on someone whose background you don't know. Although,' she thought for a moment, 'I wonder why she would have waited three years to do it.'

'Exactly,' Adeline agreed, eyes shining eagerly. 'It doesn't make sense. The girl had a flat to live in, a respectable trade, and a regular wage. And she left the complete sewing kit behind, with which she could have made money wherever she was going. Mrs Harrison even said she'd discussed Alice taking over the business when the time came. She really was awfully fond of the girl, and not being able to have children of her own, she'd fully intended to leave everything in the shop to her.'

'It does seem an odd time to leave. I suppose there could have been any number of reasons, but I suspect there was a young man involved.'

'As Mrs Harrison suspects too, of course. She says Alice was a dear girl who would never have taken the money or left without some nefarious influence at work. By all accounts she was very pretty – which, coupled with her sweet nature, charmed all the local menfolk…'

Adeline left a heavy pause.

'Oh, surely you can't suspect Mr Travis?' Miss Busby's eyebrows rose. 'He would have been old enough to be her grandfather.'

'Father, probably. But *Love makes fools of us all*,' Adeline pointed out as the biscuits arrived.

Miss Busby couldn't help herself. She had two of the crispy biscuits with another cup of tea.

'Yes, but even if he *was* enamoured of her, it was six years ago. And she clearly didn't run away with him, so what possible bearing can it have on his death?'

'Well…' Adeline floundered. 'The pieces still need to be fitted together, but we're edging closer, I'm sure of it. A young girl Gabriel Travis was known to be charmed by–'

'Was he?' Miss Busby pressed. 'Did Mrs Harrison include him explicitly?'

There was an aggrieved pause. 'Not as such, but *all the local menfolk*, Isabelle. A pretty young girl disappeared in curious circumstances right next door to Mr Travis, and now Mr Travis has been murdered–'

'So you are quite sure, now, that it wasn't suicide after all?'

'I am simply working with the information I have been given!'

Miss Busby nodded, and passed along what Bobby had unwittingly told her that morning.

'Of all the times for the Miller boy to take a professional air,' Adeline grumbled, before continuing, 'But it fits, I suppose. Our murderer must be rather clever in almost getting away with it.'

'Yes, that concerns me a little. Whatever it was, it was clearly clever enough to get past the sergeant and the ambulance men in the first instance.'

'*Pfft*,' Adeline huffed. 'The sergeant has a head full of rocks. And clever or not, our murderer will struggle to be a match for you.'

'Oh, come now.' Miss Busby smiled despite herself. 'I do wonder, though,' she reasoned, 'why he didn't forge a suicide note.'

'Ah, Enid's point.'

'Yes. It's rather odd, don't you think?'

'Perhaps he's not the letter writing sort.'

'Yes, perhaps. Although, what about the papers clutched in Travis' hands?'

'Poems, Ezekiel said,' Adeline reminded her.

'Yes, although Ezekiel wouldn't necessarily have seen anything up close – not in the circumstances.'

'Hmm,' Adeline mused. 'If it was a note, it would only muddy the waters further.'

'Yes, it's awfully confusing.' Miss Busby filed the matter away in the back of her mind, to attack when fewer other issues were darting about. 'Where I'm struggling,' she went on, 'is that I simply cannot see who would benefit from the death of Mr Travis.'

'Oh, I suspect some sort of long-held grudge has been satisfied, a former wrong righted. The clever avenger, after all, would do well to wait a few years to keep people off the scent.'

Miss Busby tried but struggled to see the likelihood. And besides, they were on the scent, after all. Perhaps he ought to have waited a few more years. 'Anthony said Cameron Spencer was taken with the girl,' she said. 'He would have been much nearer her own age.'

'Well she clearly didn't run away with him either,' Adeline huffed.

'No. It's all very odd. I wonder if we should talk to Cameron.'

'I doubt we should. The boy's grandmother – Lady Felicity Spencer – passed away in the early hours this morning. They wouldn't welcome visitors today.'

'Oh, how sad.' Miss Busby paused a respectful moment before continuing, 'Ezekiel would know if Travis and the girl had been close. I wonder why he didn't mention her,' she mused.

'That is the other thing I have to tell you. I went to

see Ezekiel straight after I had spoken to Mrs Harrison, to ask him–'

'Adeline, you *didn't*. After all we said?'

'Yes, yes, I know, but I've told you a hundred times there's nothing to fear from the man. Anyway, the shop was closed and he obviously wasn't there. I went to the station and that officious Sergeant Heaton told me Ezekiel had been brought in for questioning.'

'Well, I suppose it's only natural, in the circumstances. Inspector McKay would be bound to want to speak to him.'

'He could have done so at the bookshop. What need was there to drag the poor fellow to the police station?'

'I'm not sure – to have his fingerprints taken, perhaps?'

'Do keep *up*, Isabelle, Ezekiel told us Heaton had already taken his fingers on Sunday evening.'

'Oh, so he did.' There was something about an agitated Adeline, Miss Busby decided, that made it very easy to forget the small details. She found herself reaching for another biscuit.

'What concerns me the most, the Scot's tyrannical policing methods aside, is the fact that when I drove back to Chipping Common this morning the shop was *still* closed and there was no sign of Ezekiel.'

'They wouldn't have kept him in the police cells overnight, surely?'

'I should certainly hope not, but McKay's car was outside the station, and so as not to set the Caledonian cad off on one of his tirades I came directly to you. But we must act, Isabelle. I fear the noose may be tightening around Ezekiel's neck.'

'The metaphorical noose, Adeline,' Miss Busby reminded her.

'A noose is a noose,' Adeline huffed. 'Now, finish your tea and I shall drive us up to Cirencester so we can find out more about this girl, Alice. Are your notes up to date?'

Miss Busby glanced down at her book. 'Yes, I think so, but Adeline, oughtn't we to find Mr Melnyk first?'

'I have never seen the man anywhere other than in his bookshop, Isabelle. I wouldn't have the first idea where to look.'

'You don't suppose he's perhaps tidying up before opening, or lost in sorrow, like yesterday?'

Adeline gave a sigh. 'It's possible, although I can't see why they would have searched the shop a second time. But we are wasting time. Getting to the bottom of this Alice business is, I'm convinced, the fastest route to exonerating him. Now, Cirencester is a fair lick and I need petrol for the Rolls.'

'There's a direct train to Cirencester at noon, dears,' Maggie announced, appearing at the table to clear the plates. 'I couldn't help overhearing.'

'That's very kind of you, Maggie. Maggie's husband works on the railway, Adeline,' Miss Busby explained.

'That's all well and good, but I prefer to travel under my own steam, as it were.'

'Right you are, dear.' Maggie cleared the table good-naturedly, as they settled the bill.

CHAPTER 10

Adeline started the engine and made good use of the horn to clear their exit while Barnaby added a few barks through the back window. They were just leaving the outskirts of Little Minton when Miss Busby had an idea.

'There are two of us, Adeline, and two matters needing attention. I suggest we tackle one each.'

'Divide and conquer, eh?'

Miss Busby nodded. 'I'm concerned that Mr Melnyk may have taken it upon himself to flee, which will only strengthen suspicions further. You need petrol, did you say?'

'Yes, I have been here, there and everywhere this week.'

'Drop me at the garage in Chipping Common. They can fill the Rolls, and you can be on your way.'

'Whilst you look for Ezekiel.' She grasped the plan.

'I will do my best. He told us Sergeant Heaton had taken his papers, so he won't get far. Did you find a chance to talk to Mrs Fowler at the pharmacy yesterday?'

'Ah. No. I was rather sidetracked.' Adeline pushed her foot to the floor as they approached a steep hill.

'Then there's plenty for me to be getting on with while you talk to the staff at the old workhouse. Come to me for dinner this evening if you'd like, and we'll compare notes.

'What are you having?'

Miss Busby smiled. Adeline was never one to take a risk in matters of the stomach.

'I was thinking of Welsh rarebit.'

'With the good stout?'

'Of course.' Miss Busby shot her friend an affronted look. 'Why would I use bad stout?'

'Very well. Oh, I wish we'd thought to get some sandwiches from Lily's to bring with us.'

'There are plenty of cafes in Cirencester,' Miss Busby pointed out, finding herself wishing that she had plumped for the scrambled eggs and salmon after all.

Adeline dropped Miss Busby and Barnaby outside Melnyk's Books. The shutters were still drawn, the door locked, and after knocking several times there remained no sign of Mr Melnyk.

Miss Busby stood in contemplation next to a van very like Dennis's post office one, but this was marked with the words 'Fowler's Pharmacy'. She watched as the Rolls pulled into the garage opposite. The police station was the logical first step, and she made her way down the street towards it until the sight of Inspector McKay's car parked outside gave her pause. Not wanting to draw his ire a mere 24 hours after assuring him she wouldn't go looking for Ezekiel, or worse, to bring any more trouble to the bookseller by mentioning he was missing, she crossed the road and kept walking.

She hadn't gone far when the church bell struck one o'clock and gave her an idea. *Divine inspiration?* she thought, as she strode forward. St Mary's Church stood at the bottom of the hill upon which the majority of the town of Chipping Common rested. Tall trees and shrubs bordering the large graveyard lent heavy shade to the path, making her feel a distinct chill as she approached the door.

'Barnaby, stay,' she ordered, slipping his leash over one of the railings outside.

She pushed the heavy oak door open. Being far larger than the church at Little Minton, it was naturally even colder inside. She shivered a little, and wished she'd thought to bring a jacket after all.

The chill aside, the church was remarkably beautiful. Sunlight radiating through its great stained-glass window cast a breathtaking mosaic of bright colours streaming across the stone altar and tiled floor toward the dark pews.

'Glorious, is it not?'

A ghostly whisper gave Miss Busby quite the start. The vicar had appeared beside her without a sound.

'Oh, I am so sorry! I didn't mean to alarm you,' he said in a hushed tone.

'That's quite alright.' She recovered herself. 'Yes, it's rather stunning.'

'One can lose oneself in its beauty for hours.' He was quite young for a man of the cloth, albeit with receding sandy hair around a high forehead. He had a kindly face though, and his black cassock was clean and smartly pressed.

Miss Busby nodded and looked on, realising that a third individual was also lost in the light. Ezekiel Melnyk sat in one of the front pews, head turned up to gaze at the gleaming window.

'He has been here all morning, poor man,' the vicar said softly, before the door opened with a slow creak behind them.

They turned to see a rather large, dour-looking woman dressed in full mourning garb of stiff black crepe with a heavy skirt skimming the floor. Long, black velvet gloves graced her hands, and a mourning cap draped with a veil completed the look. Miss Busby blinked. She couldn't recall seeing such dramatic mourning attire in years. The woman must be absolutely evaporating, even in the cool of the church.

'Ah, Mrs Spencer, Miss Spencer, I am so deeply sorry for your loss.' The vicar bowed his head reverently.

Miss Busby noticed a second, much younger woman behind the first. Also wearing black, her dress was far simpler, more modern with a fashionable cut befitting her years. She was slim, with delicate features, startling green eyes, and hair as black and silken as her dress. She would have been remarkably pretty were it not for the supercilious sneer on her face. Had she been one of her pupils, Miss Busby thought, she would have suggested she be careful lest the wind change and she stay that way. *But I'm being unfair,* she chided herself. *The young lady has just lost a grandparent, and grief presents itself in many ways.*

'Mama is too distraught to speak,' Miss Spencer announced, her voice high, tone perfectly in keeping with the sneer. 'I shall be giving you instructions for the service.'

'Thank you, Miss Spencer.' If the vicar was surprised, he disguised it perfectly. 'I shall endeavour to live up to Father Godfrey's example. Father Godfrey was the Spencers' family priest,' he explained, turning to Miss Busby, 'he was sadly lost in the war. I shall be—'

'I'm quite sure all and sundry have no interest in our family business, Vicar,' Miss Spencer snapped. Miss Busby was quite taken aback at the young woman's rudeness. And in the house of God, too.

'Forgive me.' The vicar bowed once more, clearly more tolerant, or perhaps simply better used to the ravages of grief. 'Do please come through to the vestry, and we shall discuss the arrangements.' He turned to Miss Busby once more. 'Good day, Mrs…?'

'Miss Busby,' she said.

The older Spencer woman turned slowly to give her a curious look. She had the same green eyes as her daughter; they glinted with something akin to hostility through the black lace veil. Miss Busby, somewhat affronted having never met the woman, wondered why.

Perhaps she should also attribute this to overwhelming grief?

'Good day, Miss Busby.' The vicar nodded, and smiled gently, seemingly trying to ameliorate the unfriendliness of the haughty pair. 'Do enjoy our beloved church, and perhaps we may see you for Sunday service?'

'Thank you, I will try.' Miss Busby remained polite but non-committal, her eyes returning to Mr Melnyk, who hadn't moved an inch despite the voices.

'Ezekiel?' she said softly, taking a seat in the pew behind.

'Oh, dear lady.' He turned and smiled wanly. 'I did not think to see you again so soon. What a most pleasant surprise.' He was dressed as yesterday, although his bow tie seemed a little wearied, as indeed did the rest of him.

'I'm sorry to interrupt your prayer, but Adeline was worried when she saw you weren't in the shop this morning,' she explained in the subdued tone appropriate for God's house.

'Oh, I hope I have not caused pain once more,' he replied. 'I was not expecting her to return so soon, and it has all been so very…' He couldn't seem to find the words, but Miss Busby nodded to show she understood. She glanced about the church, concerned their voices would carry, but the vicar and supercilious Spencers had disappeared into the vestry.

'Not at all, she has raced off anew, determined to clear your name. In the meantime, I wonder if the two of us might have a chat somewhere more private?' she asked.

His smile grew warmer. 'I came here to ask for help, and my Lord has provided. It is as if I have two guardian angels for my very own.'

Miss Busby found herself smiling at the thought, although she couldn't quite picture Adeline with wings and halo.

Mr Melnyk rose to his feet. 'Yes indeed, it will be pleasant to talk. Now all will be well, I am quite sure of it.' He removed his pocket watch, an old-fashioned type on a chain which he kept in his waistcoat pocket. 'But it is lunchtime. I have homemade vegetable soup to warm, and would be most honoured if you would join me?'

Miss Busby, remembering that she hadn't yet eaten anything other than a few Florentines at Lily's Tea Rooms, replied that she would be delighted.

As the pair made their way up the hill, Barnaby darted joyously around their ankles, tail wagging incessantly; new walks had increased tenfold since Adeline's plea for help.

They talked of the beauty of the countryside as they walked, Mr Melnyk expressing his constant delight in his newfound home. 'Was ever a man more fortunate?' he asked, looking across the fields, the sun glinting off the River Glyme in the distance.

When they arrived back at the bookshop, Mr Melnyk opened the shutters, allowing the sunlight to bathe the books inside, and turned the 'Closed' sign over to state 'Open'.

'You didn't feel like opening the shop this morning?' Miss Busby asked.

'I did not see the reason. Who, after all, will buy their books from a man suspected of murdering his closest friend?'

'Suspected, only. You have not been charged?' Miss Busby queried.

'You are quite right. I was questioned most fervently by the Scottish gentleman yesterday. I fear he was disappointed he had to let me go.'

'Oh, I shouldn't worry. He'll get over it. But when Adeline called this morning she got into another …' Miss Busby stopped short of calling it a 'flap', out of respect, but Mr Melnyk understood completely.

'Like the chickens?' he asked, with a mischievous smile.

'Indeed.' She returned the smile. The man was impossible not to like.

'Please, come through.' He directed her to the back of the shop and the little kitchenette where Adeline had made coffee the previous day. Being too small for a range, it was equipped with a white enamel sink, a single tap, two corner cupboards, a red countertop and a small stove perfect for heating water and, indeed, soup.

'I enjoy to cook here more than to eat solitarily in my rooms,' he explained. 'Gabriel would often join me…

But I suppose now my habit will change. Although taking meals in the shop means I do not have to close.' He cast a forlorn eye out at the deserted shop. 'Perhaps not a consideration for just now.'

Miss Busby noted the high window open above the stove. It was narrow, but someone reasonably slim may well be able to crawl through. 'Do all the shops have the same layout?' she asked.

'Yes, I think for the most part,' Mr Melnyk said, pulling two bowls and two spoons from a corner cupboard. 'Although I have no back door, whereas Mrs Harrison is having one that spills onto the alley, for the rubbish bins. I'm afraid I do not have fresh bread to accompany the soup.'

She made a mental note to check with the other shop owners. If one of the small windows had been left ajar, and if there was indeed access via the roof space…

'Oh, not to worry,' she said, realising he'd mistaken her reverie for concern over there being nothing to dip in the soup. 'It's really very kind of you.'

'It is my pleasure.' He stirred the soup, seeming happy to have something to occupy his attention.

'I wonder, Ezekiel, could your little window have been left open on Friday night?'

'Never, dear lady. I am always careful to close it when I lock the shop.'

She had suspected as much. It was awfully high, though, and he wasn't a tall man.

He turned and noticed her expression.

'Mrs Wharton assists me,' he said, pointing to a rather substantial leather bound Edith Wharton novel on the floor. She realised it would make quite the stepping stool.

'How clever!'

'Books can elevate a person always in more ways than one,' he chuckled. 'I believe I have some scraps of ham, somewhere here…yes.' He produced a saucer of cold cuts from stone sheep in the pantry cupboard. 'Your dog will perhaps enjoy such?'

'He will be quite thrilled, thank you.'

Mr Melnyk looked delighted as Barnaby set to work.

CHAPTER 11

'Now, you say you wish to chat?' Mr Melnyk prompted, serving out two small helpings of the soup and inviting Miss Busby to sit at the little round kitchen table with him.

'Thank you.' She took the soup with a graceful smile. 'It smells delicious. And yes, I rather wondered what you could tell me about Alice.'

'Alice?' Mr Melnyk looked up in surprise. 'Alice Albion? Mrs Harrison's girl?'

'Yes, I understand she went missing from the Haberdashery some time ago?'

He nodded, taking a spoonful of soup and considering carefully before answering. 'It is six years now since we lost her. Most terrible. A beautiful girl both inside and out. We searched and searched, thinking an accident befell her, but we find nothing.'

'Was the girl friendly with Mr Travis, do you know?'

'Alice was a friend to everyone.' Mr Melnyk leaned forward eagerly. 'Do you have news of her? We had all supposed, when so long a time passed, that…well, it is unthinkable.'

'Oh, I'm afraid not,' Miss Busby said quickly, feeling terrible for raising his hopes. 'It was simply that her name popped up when Adeline was investigating matters.'

'Ah.' His shoulders dropped, but he managed a smile. 'Mrs Fanshawe is always most thorough.'

'Yes.' Miss Busby refrained from further comment.

'But you cannot think Alice can have returned and hurt Gabriel?' His eyes widened.

Miss Busby tilted her head. Now here was something they hadn't yet considered. 'I simply wondered what you could tell us about the girl. It seemed unusual, two mysteries occurring next door to one another, even several years apart.'

'I can never believe Alice would hurt anyone, ever.' He looked Miss Busby straight in the eyes, his own fierce and determined. 'You must not think it for one moment. She was gentle and kind.'

Miss Busby considered. 'So quite similar to Mr Travis, in fact?'

'Yes, yes, the two were, how do you say – like in the dressmaking? When the material is similar?'

'Cut from the same cloth?'

'Exactly so! Alice had smiles and kindness for everyone.'

'Including Gabriel?' she pressed.

'Of course including Gabriel. The two were friends. She was interested in how he made better the broken books. Sometimes she could help with the fixing. Sewing was a joy they shared – paper or cloth, the work is the same. Delicate, you see?'

'Yes, I suppose it must be. I'd never considered the similarities.'

'Alice always considered. She was like the sunshine,' he went on, 'making things bright and warm even in the darkness.'

Miss Busby was touched by his words. 'How sad that no one found out what happened to her.' She wondered for a moment why, if people had been so charmed by the girl, more hadn't been done at the time to find her.

He nodded, lowering his eyes and taking a spoonful of soup.

'The police investigated her disappearance, I suppose?' Miss Busby pressed.

He wiped his lips with a napkin. 'They had little interest. Alice was grown by then, an adult, and as such she was free to leave should she wish. Mrs Harrison was very much distraught. And when the money was discovered as having vanished also, well, it stained things as bad for Alice. From then...'

Miss Busby nodded in understanding. 'The authorities assumed she had stolen the money and run away.'

'But Alice would never steal. Why should she? She had good money from Mrs Harrison, who would never cheat her. She was happy. She had a good life here. The police, they don't think like this. They see money missing, and they make their assumption. And that is all.'

Miss Busby knew exactly what he meant. Inspector McKay, diligent though he was, was just the sort to assume the very same. *That was the trouble with policemen*, she mused. *They spent so much time among the criminal element, they tended to tar everyone with the same brush.*

She wondered what the inspector had told Mr Melnyk yesterday, after letting him go. Was it something he'd said that had sent the poor man to church to pray for help? She suspected McKay would not have been terribly kind, as was his way, and she didn't want to ask lest she distress Mr Melnyk further. For her own part, she felt it impossible not to feel sorry for the quiet gentlemen, who was obviously suffering greatly.

'What do *you* think happened to her?' she asked softly.

'Dear lady, I cannot say. Just as with Gabriel I do not understand these things. In my country I saw terrible things. Here, I see people with so much, but still sometimes they must take from others. It is hard for me to understand this.'

Miss Busby nodded and turned her attention to her soup for several moments, deep in thought, before asking, 'And you say you looked for Alice, at the time?'

He nodded. His eyes were heavily shadowed, she noticed, and the lines on his face seemed to be more deeply etched; she wondered at the strain all of this must be putting him under. Were their efforts some-how only making things worse for the poor man? They would have to be careful that in trying to help they didn't simply add to his worries.

'As I said, we searched. We looked in the woods, down to the river, but there was never a sign of her. We asked at the railway, the omnibus, even the carters and carriers. She had vanished as if in a puff of smoke, lost to us forever. And our little town is poorer for it ever since. Now we lose Gabriel too. And I wonder, dear lady, what those of us left behind are to make of it all.'

Miss Busby couldn't think of anything encouraging to say, and so, disappointed with herself, set to finishing her soup.

'And when you say *we* searched,' she said, finally setting her spoon aside and delicately wiping her mouth. 'Who exactly do you mean?'

'Myself and Gabriel of course. Mr and Mrs Harrison also. There were others, although the world was at war, so it was older men and ladies, but it was long ago. My memory is not so young.'

Miss Busby nodded. 'Nor mine. But was there perhaps anyone closer to her own age, do you recall?' she asked. 'Young friends of hers?'

Mr Melnyk thought for a moment. 'It was most sad,' he said after a while. 'Her young friends left soon after she came to the town. For the war. It upset her most fiercely at the time. She made friends easier with the gentlemen of her age, than the young ladies.'

Miss Busby could imagine why. Girls of a certain age were not always prepared to welcome others of different backgrounds. And if Alice were as pretty as everyone said, the boys would have been much more likely to look beyond the girl's workhouse upbringing.

'From then,' Mr Melnyk went on, 'she spends her time mostly with us older peoples. We keep her in good cheer, and she comes to know us as friends also. So then she endeavours to keep us in good cheer in turn.'

'I see,' Miss Busby said. 'And the friends who went to war, can you remember who they were?'

'Yes, dear lady,' he replied. 'That I can recall. The young gentleman from Hayle Court was perhaps her greatest companion.'

'Cameron Spencer?' Miss Busby was all ears.

'Sir Cameron Spencer, yes. The same. A most educated and pleasant young man, and I believe, Alice's young heart's first innocent desire.'

'Goodness, was he really?'

'A handsome young man, of course yes, she would enjoy his company. Clever, always with something interesting to say. She learned much from him, her education at the workhouse having been, how should I say, elemental… Although, I think his family was perhaps not so happy that he spent much time with her.'

'Ah. Yes. Something of a gulf in their situations, of course.' Miss Busby wondered if anything had been said to the girl, or perhaps to her adoptive mother, Mrs Harrison.

'But when you are 16, this is not a concern.' Mr Melnyk gave a sad smile.

Miss Busby nodded. She felt a sinking feeling in her stomach. 'And indeed 17, 18, or 19.'

'Yes.' He nodded eagerly. 'Young romantic love sees no boundaries. It is the most beautiful.'

And often the most devastating, Miss Busby thought.

'So Alice confided in you?' she asked.

'In Gabriel, rather. They spoke often of love, as they did of all emotions. In relation to his poems, you understand. They were both dreamers, very akin. There were times I could not help to overhear. Please, do not think ill of me, dear lady. They would talk always in the shop, you understand.'

'Never in Gabriel's rooms?'

Mr Melnyk's eyebrows rose. 'That would have been not appropriate.'

'No, of course.' Miss Busby made a note to tell Adeline. 'I wasn't implying…' She wasn't sure how to phrase what she had, indeed, been implying, but Mr Melnyk waved away the notion amicably.

'Gabriel was to her the father she did not know. And for him, she was the daughter he had lost. He loved her greatly, but was always careful there could never be any concern. He was her protector, you see?'

Miss Busby believed she did. And her heart began to ache just a little more.

'Gabriel's heart broke when she was no longer here,' he went on. 'Another loved one gone. He had resolved never to remarry, after the loss of his family, but I do not think he ever foresaw finding another daughter in that way. It broke him all over again.'

Miss Busby saw tears threatening as Mr Melnyk rose to his feet and busied himself at the sink with the empty bowls. It felt really rather awful to distress him further, but there was one more thing she felt she needed to understand.

'What happened to Mr Travis' family, if I may ask?'

'There was a fire.' Mr Melnyk cleared his throat, his back still turned. 'At his home, in the north of this country, many years ago. Gabriel was at work, and so thankfully spared, but his wife and daughter, I am afraid they burned to death.'

Miss Busby's hand flew to her mouth. 'Good lord, how terrible.'

'Yes. His home destroyed completely. Everything lost.'

'Oh, the poor man. But where was he working?'

'He was manager at a shoe factory. He began there at age 14, as an apprentice, and worked so very hard until he reaches the top.'

'Goodness. He must have done incredibly well. But he never went back to the factory afterwards?'

'Never. Gabriel worked hard, he would say, and for what? Everything he ever earned burned inside his home, and with his family lost he saw his work as the cruellest reason he was separated from them forever.'

'So what did he do?'

'He became most unwell, to start, as you can imagine. Then he began to wander; he said walking gave him peace, and he would find work along the way where he could, using his skills learned in the factory.'

'Ah, so sewing came into it.'

Mr Melnyk nodded. 'He would bind books, mend shoes for people, or saddles for horses, in return for food and a bed for the night. One day he comes to my shop. Finding a set of encyclopaedias in great need, he stays for several weeks, and we find ourselves with much in common.'

Miss Busby nodded in understanding. Their respective tragedies would have given them a unique understanding of one other. 'And so he stayed.'

'And so he stayed,' Mr Melnyk confirmed. 'For nine years and a little more I enjoy his company. And now I am alone once again, and my situation is…not pleasant. But to complain when I have so much is quite unforgivable. There are many who have nothing.'

'Indeed. May I ask how old Gabriel was?'

'Ah, I had not reason to ask him, but he was neither young nor old. Fifty years perhaps. Not more. Now, dear lady.' He straightened and offered a smile. 'May I prepare coffee for you?'

'No, no, I have taken far too much of your time as it is. But I wonder, in the church you mentioned you had gone there to ask for help. Help with what, if you don't mind my asking?'

'Help to manage my sadness, and strength for what

is to come. The good Lord sent you to me, and we have talked, and I have remembered my troubles are nothing to those of many others. The world is one of joy and sadness. We are never alone in this. We must bear the sorrow, and always try to shine a light for others in their darkness.' He offered a smart bow. 'Thank you, dear Miss Busby.'

Miss Busby blushed. She thought if anything she had only caused him further upset, and it was a blessed relief to know this wasn't the case.

'You are very kind, Mr Melnyk.'

'Ezekiel, please to remember.' He smiled, and walked Miss Busby and Barnaby back through the bookshop. She waved to him through the window as they left, and resolved to double her efforts to help him. *And if Inspector McKay doesn't appreciate it, hard luck!* she thought to herself, leaning down to attach Barnaby's lead and walking straight into the very man himself.

CHAPTER 12

'Miss Busby. What are you doing in Chipping Common?' He raised a fiery red eyebrow and glowered at her, as if he knew all too well. 'And right outside Melnyk's Books to boot.'

Miss Busby didn't appreciate his tone, and stood a little straighter. 'I am shopping, Inspector. I need rose water from Fowler's, if that's quite alright with you.' She raised a brow of her own.

Barnaby looked with bright eyes from one to the other before stepping in front of his mistress and emitting a low growl.

'Good dog,' Miss Busby said softly.

'You're headed in the wrong direction,' the inspector pointed out, taking half a step back. Jack Russells, although diminutive, had a well-earned reputation for ankles when the mood took them.

'That is because I have business at the post office first.' She intended to go there to telephone Lucy at the newspaper, but neglected to tell him that.

'And I suppose your vociferous friend is also in town?' He looked up and down the street as if scanning for the white Rolls Royce. 'Book shopping, perhaps?' he growled.

Miss Busby took a breath and mentally counted to ten. She had often told her young charges to do the same when provoked, and reminded herself she had told Adeline the inspector made a better ally than adversary. Whilst he would need to be confronted soon, the pieces weren't yet in place.

'Mrs Fanshawe is currently in Cirencester, but I shall be only too pleased to pass on your regards.'

His eyes narrowed. 'Cirencester, is it? She wouldn't happen to be passing by the old workhouse?'

A smile played at the corner of Miss Busby's lips; they were on the right track!

'I believe she went in search of some lunch. Now, if you'll excuse me, Inspector…'

She marched off, head in the air, Barnaby trotting at her side. Once they reached the end of the street, she turned and saw the inspector going into Melnyk's Books.

'Quickly, Barnaby.' Hurrying across the road, hoping no one was watching lest they think her quite mad. She scurried back in the direction they had come, hunching over a little to peer cautiously across the road and through the window of the bookshop. She was just able to make out Inspector McKay passing something to Ezekiel. As it caught the sun and glinted – it was a key.

'Aha! Come on, boy!'

Baffled, the little dog trotted back with his mistress,

and this time they continued on uninterrupted to the nearby post office, where he happily sat outside munching a hard biscuit.

A plain young woman looked up from a stool behind the counter as the bell over the door tinkled. Mid-twenties, shingled hair and wearing an unflattering brown frock, she didn't stand or greet her customer; indeed she had a rather sullen air about her.

'Good afternoon. I'd like to use the public telephone, if I may?' Miss Busby asked.

'It's in the corner.' The girl nodded to the back of the shop where a candlestick telephone sat on a small counter with a pad of paper and a stubby pencil on a string beside it.

'Thank you.'

The girl nodded again, and went back to reading something hidden in her lap.

Miss Busby bristled. Little wonder, she thought, that Alice hadn't found friends of her own age among the girls of the town if this was an example.

Picking up the receiver, she asked to be connected to the *Oxford News* Office, where she was quickly put through to Lucy.

'Miss Busby, what a nice surprise!'

'Lucy, are you free for a light supper and confab at Lavender Cottage this evening?'

'I can be. That sounds lovely, actually. Chef's been rather over enthusiastic with the rich sauces. It tends to catch up with one.'

Miss Busby noted with approval that Lucy didn't enquire as to why. She suspected the reporter knew all too well the habits of postmistresses and telephone operators.

'Would you mind picking me up from Chipping Common, at your convenience?'

'Not at all. I should think I'll be another hour or so with this article, it needs to go to my editor before I leave. Shall I come for you straight after?'

'Perfect. I'll wait for you outside the Tolsey. There's a bench overlooking the green.'

'Lovely. See you then.'

As Miss Busby paid for the call, noting the young woman's demeanour hadn't improved, she thought to ask, 'Have you worked here long?'

'Since I left school. My mum's the Postmistress.'

'Ah. How nice for you.'

She shrugged.

'So you would have been here when Alice Albion was working at Harrison's?' Miss Busby went on.

Interest flared in the girl's expression for the first time. '*Princess* Alice?'

'Is that what people called her?'

'It's what *we* called her,' she said, disdain turning her plain face into a rather ugly one. 'All the boys fawning over her like she was royalty. And her just a–'

'Geraldine.' A harsh voice snapped from the back as an older lady appeared with an armful of envelopes she deposited on the counter. 'There's a delivery just come in out the back. Off you go and see to it. I do apologise,' she said, turning to Miss Busby with a sickly sweet smile. 'My daughter has been rather tired of late. Is there anything I can help you with, Mrs…?'

'Thank you, no. I believe I have everything I need. Good day to you.'

Miss Busby's feet were beginning to ache as she made her way back to Fowler's Pharmacy. She was rather pleased Adeline hadn't been able to speak to Mrs Fowler yet, as they would perhaps have something to help. 'We've covered quite some ground today, haven't we Barnaby?' She looked down at the little dog, who looked up with cocked ears and a wag of the tail. She took a moment to appreciate her stalwart companion. Jack Russells never seemed to tire. 'You are a good boy,' she said fondly. He gave a little chuffing sound of acknowledgement, and continued trotting jauntily beside her.

Passing Melnyk's, she looked in to wave to Ezekiel, but he was nowhere to be seen. She wondered if he had already gone up to clean Gabriel Travis' rooms, as the key had surely signified he was now free to do so. Perhaps she should offer her assistance. It would be rather a personal task, she concluded, and he would surely appreciate some privacy. Besides, Adeline would want to be involved. Perhaps they could both visit tomorrow and have a look after Ezekiel had had some time alone with his grief.

She peered in at Harrison's window, noting the shop was busy: three women were clustered around the counter. Miss Busby wondered if they were there for alterations, or had come under some pretext to pry into recent events. It was a stark contrast, either way, to the emptiness of Melnyk's.

Reaching the pharmacy on the other side of the Haberdashery, she noted the freshly painted 'and Son' which had been added to the sign above the door. She slipped Barnaby's leash over an old horse hitch bordering the pavement and pushed open the door with some difficulty.

No cheery bell greeted her entrance, and the inside of the shop was somewhat sombre. A deep mahogany counter ran almost the entire length of the back wall, two rows of drawers with brass knobs lining each of the side walls. Glass display shelves above the drawers held ranks of white bottles with colourful labels. Two hard-backed chairs stood in a corner beside a glass-fronted cabinet filled with blue and white ceramic jars. Another display had pre-prepared items such as talc, soap, toilet water and the like.

Adeline's rose water, she remembered, peering at the choice as a rather handsome young man with dark hair and a smart white coat emerged from the rear of the shop.

'Good afternoon.' Miss Busby greeted him with a warm smile. 'Rose water, please. And I wonder, do you have anything for feet?'

'Just a minute please, my mother will serve you. Mother,' he called over his shoulder, then bent down to take two bottles from under the counter. 'She shan't be a moment,' he said, rising lightly back to his feet.

He flicked striking green eyes at her before his trim figure disappeared back through the heavy blue curtain to the rear. Miss Busby did her best to see beyond, but he was quick to sweep the curtain closed behind him.

She waited in the dim interior, taking a seat to rest her feet in the meantime. The shop's front window was tall, but light was blocked by the items displayed within it: bottles of coloured liquid, boxes of this and that, and a number of rather intimidating conical flasks filled almost every inch of the space.

Noting not one but two cast-iron bolts on the back of the shop door – to protect the stronger medications sold within, she supposed – Miss Busby surmised that if anyone had broken into the little row of shops they must have done so at Harrison's Haberdashery.

The curtain was swept aside once more. This time a tall woman with thin grey hair pulled back in a severe bun, with an equally severe expression in her dark eyes, came through. Dressed in a button up navy jacket and matching skirt, she walked stiffly upright, exuding a businesslike manner.

'I am Mrs Fowler. I apologise for the delay,' she said with a nod. 'My son mentioned feet?'

Ah, so the young gentleman was Martin Fowler, Miss Busby thought.

'Oh, how comforting,' Miss Busby said, standing

and crossing to the counter, 'to have your son working alongside you.'

The woman smiled and the severity instantly lifted from her face. 'Yes, I am blessed with Martin. He is a fully qualified pharmacist.' Pride shone in her eyes. 'Not to mention a war hero. There aren't many who can say the same at his age.'

'No, I should imagine not.' Miss Busby's mind raced through the gears. 'And it must be such a relief to have him with you,' she lowered her voice, 'given recent events.'

'The Travis suicide?' Her face reverted back into sharp angles.

'Oh, I had heard it was considered murder.'

The woman scoffed. 'I should very much doubt it. Poor Travis was a depressive. Just the sort to take his own life. Why on earth would anyone want to murder him?'

CHAPTER 13

Miss Busby blinked. She wouldn't have phrased it so bluntly, but from what others had said it did seem perhaps rather accurate all the same. 'Yes, I did wonder.'

Mrs Fowler's eyes narrowed. 'I do not recall seeing you before, are you local?'

Understanding dawned on Miss Busby – there had probably been any number of busybodies in the shop today, looking for titbits of gossip. The pharmacy proprietors had obviously taken her for one such other. She had better think quickly, she decided.

'Not as such. I am Miss Busby, and my usual pharmacy is Little Minton Medicinals, but I have heard you are far better stocked and rather better qualified.'

A smile creased the woman's lips; her frequent changes of expression shifted like light and shade. 'That is Martin's doing. He is at the cutting edge of pharmaceutical science.'

Miss Busby nodded then made a show of looking around the shop. 'So many medicines, it's a wonder you can hold them all. Do you mix them yourselves on the premises?' Miss Busby realised the question was perhaps a little unusual, and so followed it up with, 'In Little Minton we must often wait for a duty pharmacist to mix some of the more potent powders.'

Mrs Fowler nodded. 'We do our own. There is very little need to wait for medications here. Martin has a workspace upstairs, and a storeroom above. He works tirelessly to ensure we are perfectly self-contained.' Delight in the young man's boundless abilities emanated from her in waves. Here, Miss Busby noted, was a woman thrilled with her son's achievements and not at all shy in showing it. 'He prepares the herbs and mixes the compound drugs himself. My son could have been a doctor had he not chosen to carry on the family business.'

'Well, that explains your reputation. And I'm so pleased you don't believe there could possibly be a…' she lowered her voice once more, as if to approach the matter delicately, '…nefarious character in the vicinity.'

Mrs Fowler sniffed. 'Martin fought in the war, as I mentioned. He is decorated for bravery, and would be more than capable of overcoming any such character. Not that I believe for one moment one exists in the locality.'

'How fortunate. I live alone, and have no such comfort as yours, I'm afraid. I have heard Mr Melnyk from the bookshop locks his doors every evening,' Miss Busby continued, raising her eyebrows ostensibly at the rather unusual practice.

'As do we. Although we store valuable items, so one would expect it.'

'Oh, of course. I should imagine you must need to be terribly secure, under the circumstances.'

Mrs Fowler nodded. 'We are a fortress. Locking pins have been added to all our windows. We have even had our rear door bricked up and have only one entrance. Our medicines are quite safe.'

'How very reassuring. But did I not also hear of a young lady going missing several years ago? I have a dear friend in the area, you see,' Miss Busby thought swiftly as Mrs Fowler's expression darkened, 'and I do so worry.'

She made a mental note to say an extra prayer that night to cover the falsehoods. It was all in a noble cause, after all. And besides, Ezekiel was fast becoming a friend.

'The Albion girl?' Mrs Fowler gave a curt laugh. 'Hardly a lady. Stole from her benefactor and ran off to the bright lights, no doubt.'

'Goodness, did she really?'

'Always a risk, I'm afraid, if one takes in a workhouse stray. I warned Mrs Harrison as soon as I heard she had got the idea to take one on.'

'She would have been about the same age as your son, wouldn't she? The girl, I mean,' Miss Busby asked, with as much nonchalance as she could muster.

'Younger,' Mrs Fowler intoned. 'And with no sense at all.'

'I see. And rather friendly with Sir Cameron Spencer, did I hear?'

Suspicion crept into Mrs Fowler's eyes. Miss Busby feared she was pushing her luck.

'You mustn't think me a gossip,' she insisted. 'It's simply not often I have the opportunity to speak to someone so knowledgeable. And my friend here lives alone, as do I. It is always a concern.'

Mrs Fowler thawed somewhat. 'The girl trailed around after Cameron Spencer and his money, yes. Martin and he went to the front together, they fought in the same battalion. They were both young, though Cameron was not quite as mature as Martin. But he was always an intelligent boy, and became the head of an immensely wealthy family. He is now Sir Cameron Spencer, of course. I thought he tolerated the girl's attentions in quite the gentlemanly fashion, actually. Although, I suppose he can afford to be tolerant.'

Miss Busby's head tilted in consideration. 'I hadn't thought of it quite like that.'

'Few do. I have always pushed Martin to achieve more, not that he needs much pushing. I am a firm believer in the value of hard work and ambition.'

Miss Busby smiled and nodded politely.

'Cameron's mother, Mrs Spencer has never had to concern herself with such matters,' Mrs Fowler went on. 'It must be pleasant, not having to work. Although I for one would feel something of a wastrel. Martin and I do wonderful work for the town.

We contribute to the welfare of people here, and are proud to do so.'

'Of course.' Miss Busby nodded almost reverently. 'Mrs Spencer wouldn't have been keen on a girl like Alice spending time with her son, though,' she continued, all consideration.

'Few mothers would, I'm sure. But I had heard from Martin that Alice's interest lay more towards *older* gentlemen, shall we say.' The woman gave a most disapproving shudder. 'He mentioned she was thick as thieves with the depressive.'

'Mr Travis?' Miss Busby asked.

'Yes. He was rather obsessed with her, and she revelled in the attention. The pair wrote poetry together, I believe. Preposterous, and utterly inappropriate. Ought never to have been allowed. Well, the poor girl had no one to teach her values,' Mrs Fowler went on thoughtfully, her tone softening. 'That was not her fault. I should not imagine workhouse masters hold much ambition for their charges.'

'No, I suppose not, but surely Mrs Harrison…?'

'Yes, yes, but by that age it is too late. It was a noble thought, to bring the girl here, but it put decent folk at risk nonetheless. Little Minton, did you say?' she went on, changing tack and catching Miss Busby rather off guard. 'Nasty business of your own there last year, I believe?'

'Yes, I'm afraid so. I suppose nowhere is entirely safe.' Miss Busby sighed.

'Indeed.' Mrs Fowler looked round as the door opened and an elderly gentleman strode inside. She brought her hands together briskly, the time for idle chatter over. 'Now then. Feet? I am unable to bend for an examination, my back is a constraint, I'm afraid. But I may offer a consultation.'

'Thank you, that will be quite sufficient,' Miss Busby agreed. Several minutes later, armed with both Adeline's rose water and a bottle of Dr Scholl's foot powder for herself, she and Barnaby made their way to the structure known as the Tolsey.

The large, timber-framed building supported by thick stone pillars had once been a trading hub for local wool merchants, and was now used as a market hall. It also doubled as a popular meeting point in the centre of the town, offering both shade in the summer and shelter in the winter. The neatly kept area in front of the building was a delight, with primroses growing amid the grass and towering elm trees providing dappled shade from above. With time to spare, Miss Busby sat on the wooden bench and retrieved her notebook and small pencil from her bag. She proceeded to add comments to each of the existing entries whilst everything was still fresh in her mind.

Alice's entry – the most recent, added in Lily's Tea Rooms with Adeline that morning, read:

Alice Albion – came to Chipping Common in 1914 to work for Rose Harrison (previously Doyle)
Lived in attic above shop flat for 2 years

Rose moved out in 1916 having married Mr Harrison, Alice moved into the flat above the shop – attic used henceforth for storage

Alice disappeared just before Christmas 1917 – aged 19 – money missing from the till.

To this she now added:

Police assumed Alice stole the money and ran away. Mr & Mrs H suspected an accident or outside influence. Searched for her with Gabriel and Ezekiel to no avail.

Alice & Gabriel close – substitute father/daughter – relationship mistaken for more by Martin Fowler and mother?

Town opinion on Alice divided – men seemed to revere, women revile, or at least be wary? (Except Rose Harrison.)

Possibly in love with Sir Cameron Spencer?

Miss Busby thought of the demise of the elderly Lady Felicity Spencer just that morning. Another rather strange coincidence. Although given the woman's age it didn't feel quite as sinister. Still, in the interests of diligence, she added:

Cameron Spencer's grandmother – died 3 days after Gabriel Travis.

Beneath this she wrote an entry for Martin Fowler. Having only met the man for a few brief moments, she felt she knew him inside out from his mother's commentary:

Martin Fowler – served with Cameron Spencer in the war – qualified as pharmacist with family business upon return. Rather handsome. Striking eyes. Distrusted Travis?

As she mulled things over, she also added to the notes she'd made regarding the other two shops in Ezekiel's row. Where she had written *Roof access? Attics in use? Windows?* she now added: *Both attics used for storage. Fowler windows secured, as is the pharmacy.*

Which, as she had suspected, left Harrison's as the only possible weak point for access.

She tapped the pencil on the page for a moment, thinking, trying to be sure she hadn't missed anything.

Ezekiel had mentioned Alice's 'young friends', plural, leaving for the war. Was Martin, unbeknownst to his mother, one of these friends? She made a final note just as the sound of hooves ringing out on the road distracted her from her thoughts. Barnaby let forth a concerned growl as the sound grew closer.

'Rag n' bo-ohne! Raaaag n' bone!' came the cry, and Barnaby, unable to contain himself, shot from under the bench and raced full speed for the horse and flat bed cart rounding the bend.

'Oh, dear Lord, Barnaby, *come back*!' Miss Busby shouted, to no avail. She felt sickened, imagining the poor dog trampled under the heavy hooves of the plodding animal, but the rag and bone man – a scrawny specimen – was lightning fast and stooped to grab the terrier and lift him from the ground.

'Thank goodness!' Picking up her bag, she
   hurried over to retrieve the dog and apologise.

'Yours, is he?' The man grinned with a gap-toothed smile. Barnaby looked utterly bemused.

Miss Busby took the dog in her arms and admonished him, before taking a firm grip on the leash and setting him down.

'Of a sort,' she replied. 'Thank you. I'm sorry if he startled your horse.'

'Take more n' that to worry Robbie, here. A good horse he is, aren't ye, old boy.' He ruffled the horse's forelock with gnarled hands.

'He's very handsome,' Miss Busby said.

The old man was dressed in a mismatched assortment of clothes: an oversized worsted jacket, a grey shirt with missing buttons, black trousers pulled too high by leather braces, and sturdy hobnailed boots on his feet.

'Any old iron, then, Miss?' he asked, looking hopeful. 'Or old rags? It's mostly rags round here, and they all go for making quality paper, ye see. Waste not want not, I says,' he proclaimed, gesturing to the old fashioned flat bed cart pulled by Robbie. Piles of grubby and crumpled old clothes were piled over the boards and held in place between the two sides. A tatty flag of sorts, muddied and torn in places, hung from the rear.

'I'm afraid I haven't,' Miss Busby said. 'I don't live here, you see, I'm waiting for my friend… ah, here she is now.' The bright red Sunbeam purred along the lane before crawling warily past the horse and cart to pull up at the side of the road.

'Is everything alright, Miss Busby?' Lucy called through the window, the roof of the sports car firmly in place this time. Her dark brown hair was immaculately tidy, a neat woollen jacket in almost the exact same shade of brown over a crisp white blouse giving her a professional air.

'Quite alright, thank you,' Miss Busby called in return, before bidding the man good day and climbing into the passenger seat of the car.

She couldn't think of a time she had been more grateful to rest her feet.

'Thank you so much, Lucy, I have quite outdone my walking today.'

'You are looking a little weary,' Lucy agreed, smoothing her dark brown skirt before shifting the car into gear.

'I will just close my eyes a moment,' she replied and promptly fell into a light doze all the way back to Bloxford.

CHAPTER 14

'Are you quite sure I can't help?' Lucy asked from the doorway as Miss Busby busied herself in the kitchen. Her doze in the car – mercifully with the top up this time – had refreshed her, and she insisted she could manage. 'It's only really cheese on toast,' she said. 'With a few extras. Would you like to sit out in the garden?'

'Lovely,' Lucy said. 'The early evening sunshine is always my favourite.' She opened the back door and Pudding flew in, startling her and chirruping eagerly.

'Hello,' Lucy said, recovering with a smile. 'Is it your teatime too?'

'Oh, he'd like this,' Miss Busby said, gathering cheese, butter, and cream for the sauce. 'Although neither the sauce nor the stout would be good for him. And Adeline will object strongly if I omit either.'

'Mummy made rarebit sometimes in the winter evenings,' Lucy said. 'When Cook was off-duty. Anthony used to be forever rummaging about for something to eat at all hours. She always added a drop of Daddy's beer, it made it such a treat.'

Miss Busby smiled at the thought of the younger Lannister family enjoying such a simple dish together. There were no airs or graces to Richard, which she considered one of his many merits.

'I'll keep a little of the mix for him before I add the rest. There are some blankets on the sofa, why don't you take them out in case there's a chill while we sit? I'm sure Adeline won't be long. She's been to the old workhouse to root out information about Alice Albion.'

'Oh yes, our mystery girl. I had a rummage through the news archives in the office, too. Shall we wait until Mrs Fanshawe arrives to discuss?'

Miss Busby, realising Lucy would be at a slight disadvantage information-wise, briefly recounted the details Adeline had already shared concerning Alice's history in Chipping Common. Lucy listened as she gathered three tartan blankets, before taking them outside and draping them over the wooden chairs.

Miss Busby donned a white apron to protect her blouse and turned her full attention to their supper. The cheese mixture, thickened with flour and bread, was bubbling nicely; she was just preparing delicate squares of toast as Adeline arrived.

'Isabelle, that smells divine,' she announced loudly as she let herself in and came through to the kitchen.

'Oh, Adeline, you look exhausted,' Miss Busby observed. It was a long drive from Cirencester, and her friend hadn't had the benefit of a restorative nap. 'Lucy is at the table outside with Barnaby and Pud. Go and sit down.'

'I am tired, and rather rumpled.' She tried in vain to smooth creases from her navy and red dress. 'And annoyed that I had a wasted journey.' Adeline trailed outside to nod a greeting to Lucy and plump down onto the wooden chair under the mulberry tree.

'Well, we have all had a long day.' Miss Busby followed her with a tray laden with plates of delicious cheesy rarebit. She placed them on the table and set out napkins and silverware. 'Let's have something to eat and catch our breath for a moment.'

'I adore eating al fresco.' Adeline brightened at the sight of the meal.

They all tucked in, thoroughly enjoying the treat.

'Worcestershire sauce?' Adeline asked, starting on a second square.

'Of course.'

'And Mackeson Stout?'

'Naturally.' Miss Busby smiled as Adeline nodded reverently.

'It's delicious,' Lucy said. 'Anthony will be green with envy when I tell him.'

'Oh, I didn't think,' Miss Busby said. 'He could have joined us. Would you like to telephone him?' she asked, remembering Richard had been keen for him to be involved. 'There's more than enough to go around.'

'That's kind, but he was having one of his off days

when I left this morning. It happens, from time to time, although not as often as it used to.'

'What a shame. But he was right about the girl. Will you thank him for me?'

Lucy nodded as she took another slice.

'Infuriating business.' Adeline's voice grew heavy with frustration once more. 'This Alice girl is the key to it all, I am sure of it, but the staff at the infirmary are all newly employed. There were charges brought against the master and matron of the workhouse, and it was widely believed the majority of the staff were complicit. They got rid of the lot of them.'

'What sort of charges?' Miss Busby asked.

'Punishments a bit too severe, incoming monies not declared – such as sales from rags and scraps – and inmates' property going missing.' Adeline waved a hand in distaste. 'Tawdry business all round.'

'How awful. And Alice was there when this was going on?' Lucy asked.

'I would imagine so. Workhouse records are still held in the infirmary office, and the silly young thing on duty at the desk was easy enough to get past.'

'Adeline!' Concern flashed across Miss Busby's features.

'Verbally, Isabelle. Good Lord.'

'Well, for a moment it sounded as if you'd simply shouldered your way through!'

'I merely mentioned I was trying to track down a relative and needed a moment with the last decade or so.'

'Those records are supposed to be confidential,' Lucy noted, sounding rather impressed. 'They should have asked you for documentation.'

'The girl was barely out of school pinafores,' Adeline replied. 'I could have walked out with armfuls of files had I felt like it.'

'But what did you learn?' Miss Busby was keen to keep things on track.

'That so many paupers were either tiny babies, or the very old and vulnerable. It was rather heartbreaking, to tell the truth. I shall be seeing some of those records in my sleep.' She stared off into the distance for a moment, before coming to. 'I didn't learn anything whatsoever of any use.' She sighed. 'It was all dates of arrival and departure, medical notes, work allocations, disciplinary matters and the like. Alice Albion seems to have been a well-liked girl of good behaviour, hard-working and skilled with a needle.'

'Not the sort you would expect to steal from her mistress and disappear,' Miss Busby mused.

'No, which is precisely why Mrs Harrison chose her, I should imagine. That and the fact the girl's duties were listed as mending the children's uniforms and sewing new ones as required. She'd have been ideal.'

'It must have been a huge responsibility for Mrs Harrison to take on,' Lucy observed. 'Letting someone into her home and business like that. I can't imagine many would do the same.'

'She didn't have a bad word to say about the girl,'

Adeline said. 'Even after the event. Convinced she was led astray by some nefarious influence.'

'I wonder what made her think of taking on the child in the first place,' Miss Busby said. A light breeze ruffled the leaves on the tree sheltering them, a slight chill causing her to reach back and pull the blanket across her shoulders. She was beginning to feel her earlier fatigue returning; the cheese sauce was bringing on a sense of comfort and contentment that tugged at her eyelids.

'I have already told you, Isabelle,' Adeline chided. 'Rose Harrison could not have children of her own.'

'Yes, but many women are in the same position,' Miss Busby pointed out, 'and few would go to such extremes.'

'Mrs Harrison was a volunteer at the workhouse for several years,' Lucy told them. 'She was on the fund-raising committee, too.'

Adeline and Miss Busby both looked up in surprise.

'It was in the old article I found,' Lucy explained.

Miss Busby explained to Adeline that Lucy had searched the news archives on their behalf.

'There wasn't much else of note, I'm afraid,' she confessed. 'There was only one article mentioning Alice's disappearance on record. It seemed the police didn't suspect foul play. Only a small amount of money was missing, and Mrs Harrison didn't want to press charges. It only seemed newsworthy as a cautionary tale to anyone thinking of taking on a ward from the workhouse. It's really rather sad.' She finished her rarebit and wiped her mouth daintily with the napkin.

'Yes, that's the impression I had from talking to Mrs Fowler at the pharmacy in Chipping Common,' Miss Busby said. 'Although she did have some sympathy for the girl. The workhouse can't have been an easy upbringing. And then of course to be uprooted and replanted in such a small town, where not everyone would welcome her with open arms.'

'Mrs Harrison didn't mention any fundraising involvement to me,' Adeline huffed.

'How odd. I wonder…no, it's silly of me.' Miss Busby rubbed her eyes and stifled a yawn.

'What?' Adeline pressed.

'Well, it will sound rather awful.'

'There's only us here,' Adeline pointed out.

Miss Busby darted a look towards Lucy.

Lucy tutted. 'I hope you know me better than that by now.'

'Yes, of course.' Miss Busby sighed. 'You must forgive me, it's been a busy couple of days. I know you'd never print idle conjecture. It's just,' she turned to her friend, 'Adeline you mentioned monies not being declared, and if Rose was directly involved with the finances…'

Adeline's eyebrows shot skywards. 'You think Mrs Harrison was involved? I have to say, Isabelle, I think it most unlikely. She's a very sweet, rather gentle lady, who clearly still misses the girl.'

'Yes, I'm sure.' Miss Busby gave a little shake of her

head, as if to clear it. 'I'm simply thinking aloud, which I should never do until my thoughts are properly corralled. It just seemed a possible link..'

'*Hmmph.*' Adeline remained unconvinced.

'I shall make a warm drink,' Miss Busby declared, forcing herself up from her chair. Barnaby and Pud followed her into the kitchen, lest she open any interesting cupboards.

'Or perhaps a tot of something stronger?' Adeline enquired hopefully.

'Adeline, I am not sending you back out onto the roads awash with sherry.'

'Perhaps we ought to move inside,' Lucy suggested. The sun had set and the evening chill was making its presence felt more keenly.

Miss Busby put a match to the kindling already gathered in the grate. Soon they were seated on the chairs and sofa comfortably around the fire, warm cups of cocoa in hand, quietly collecting their thoughts.

'Why was Alice at the workhouse, do we know?' Miss Busby asked.

'Abandoned by her young unmarried mother according to the records. The usual story,' Adeline replied. 'I cast my eye over a few of the other girls' files and found much the same.'

'Is it possible history could have repeated itself, and Alice found herself in a similar position?' Lucy posed. 'She might have been awfully embarrassed, and run away in shame.'

'Ezekiel did imply she was admired by the young men in the town. But of course they were away at war,' Miss Busby said thoughtfully, then sipped her cocoa.

'The older men weren't,' Adeline answered darkly, her eyes sparking with fresh determination. 'Alice is the key, Isabelle, I'm certain of it. It all makes perfect sense! Gabriel Travis took advantage of the girl, and of course had no means to support her. He refuted her, and she ran away with what she could carry, heavy with shame and heartbreak.' Adeline sat forward on the sofa, warming to her theme. 'Now, six years later, Alice has rebuilt her life, and returned to Chipping Common to exact her revenge. Where is your notebook, Isabelle? You ought to be writing this down!'

Lucy looked thoughtful. 'It may be within the realms of possibility,' she said, putting her cup onto its saucer. 'Assuming there aren't other avenues you're considering relating to motive?'

'None whatsoever!' Adeline confirmed triumphantly. 'Gabriel Travis was penniless and inconsequential. He had no family, and no friends other than Ezekiel.'

'But he was friends with Alice,' Miss Busby objected.

'Exactly my point! Over friendly, I shouldn't wonder.'

Miss Busby thought for a moment. Mrs Fowler's comments supported the notion, although she'd suggested Alice had welcomed the attention from Gabriel Travis. Ezekiel himself had worried they'd suspect Alice had hurt Gabriel, but had dismissed the notion entirely in the same breath. If the girl *had* returned, surely she would remain recognisable, even after six years. Someone would have seen her. Although if she'd come back after dark, and with a good knowledge of Harrison's, and perhaps the attics above…

She opened her mouth to raise the possibility, but the fervour in Adeline's eyes stopped her. Her friend, so determined in defence of the kindly bookseller, would cling onto the notion and doubtless never let go.

Besides, there was a much more likely culprit.

'Ezekiel said Gabriel was like a father to the girl,' she said. 'And he was most emphatic that Alice was kindness personified and would not hurt a fly.'

'Yes, but–' Adeline quibbled.

'And you trust Ezekiel, don't you?' Miss Busby pressed.

'Yes, but–'

'He also said that she was smitten with Cameron Spencer, a notion Mrs Fowler confirmed.'

That took the wind out of Adeline's sails.

'A dashing young soldier would be a much more likely candidate,' Lucy agreed.

'Yes, but he would have been off *soldiering*, that's the whole point.' Adeline rolled her eyes, exasperated with her companions.

'They do get leave,' Lucy pointed out.

Adeline wavered visibly.

'And there was Martin Fowler, too,' Miss Busby added. 'He fought alongside Cameron Spencer at the front, according to his mother. He's rather dashing himself. Enough to turn any young girl's head I shouldn't wonder.'

'That's as may be,' Adeline countered. 'But both of them are worlds apart from Alice's circumstances. *Sir* Cameron Spencer, for goodness' sake. Can you imagine the horror if either boys' families found them fraternising?'

Miss Busby nodded. 'Yes, Ezekiel said as much in Cameron's case. He made no mention of Martin, though. Mrs Fowler did imply that any sort of relationship between the girl and a more reputable family would certainly have caused concern.'

'Young girls tend not to worry so much about that these days,' Lucy added leaning against an embroidered cushion. 'Not where matters of the heart are concerned.'

Miss Busby smiled sadly. Ezekiel had known that, too. The world was difficult for girls of an in-between age to navigate, even at the best of times. Alice would have stood less chance than most. 'Lucy, would Anthony be likely to recall when Cameron was back in Chipping Common on leave? Or is that a stretch, do you think?'

Lucy shrugged. 'I can ask. If not, there will be records. I can check those, if you'd like.'

'Perfect, thank you. And he didn't mention Martin, of course, but I wonder if you could ask about him too? He may remember something helpful. And his leave records too, if possible?'

The young reporter nodded.

'It's such a strange coincidence,' Miss Busby contin-ued, her brain racing ahead as the sweet cocoa worked its magic, 'that Cameron's grandmother should die so soon after all this.'

'Nonsense. Lady Felicity Spencer was not only ancient but had been unwell for some time,' Adeline objected.

'Perhaps, and yet I do wonder… *To lose one may be regarded as a misfortune, to lose two looks like carelessness.*'

'Oh, isn't that Oscar Wilde? He's great fun.' Lucy smiled.

The clock on Miss Busby's mantelpiece struck the hour. Final snippets of information needed to be exchanged and a plan of action reached if they were to get to their beds at a reasonable hour. Standing and clearing the cups and saucers, she told Adeline and Lucy about her chat with Mrs Fowler, the security arrangements at the pharmacy, the disdain for Alice shown by the young girl at the post office, and the tragic tale of Gabriel Travis' family.

Lucy listened intently, and even took some notes of her own, whilst Adeline fidgeted throughout, clearly convinced she had found the culprit and affronted the others couldn't see it. When Miss Busby reported her encounter with Inspector McKay and the key, however, Adeline pounced.

'We must go and search Travis' rooms at once,' she insisted. 'Why didn't you say earlier, Isabelle? Come along.' She rose to her feet, startling Pudding, who had settled on the cushion behind her head. The large ginger cat plummeted down on top of Barnaby, who'd been comfortably wedged beside Adeline. A moment of fur-filled chaos ensued, with much affronted hissing and confused growls and yips. Lucy found herself unable to help for laughing.

A few stern words from Miss Busby quickly settled the contretemps, but Adeline was harder to rein in. It was only when she was reminded of Ezekiel's mournful visit to the church that morning, and the stress events were putting on his own disposition, not to mention the lateness of the hour, that she was persuaded to leave matters until the following day.

'As you were acquainted with Lady Felicity Spencer, perhaps you could pay a visit to the family tomorrow morning?' Miss Busby asked, hoping to divert her attention. 'You could pay your respects, and find details of the funeral. And perhaps, if it seems appropriate, sound them out a little about Alice?'

'To what end? Surely you don't suspect Alice of killing the old woman because she'd disapproved of her grandson's infatuation with her?' Adeline scoffed.

It wasn't a huge leap from suspecting her of killing Gabriel Travis, Miss Busby thought, but refrained from comment.

'Simply to flesh out our picture of things,' she replied. 'If it seems too crass, perhaps you could ask Mrs Harrison? She might know how the Spencer family viewed the girl. Then I can meet you at Melnyk's Books after lunch.'

'Why after lunch? What will you be doing in the morning?' Adeline demanded.

'I have an errand to run,' Miss Busby replied, choosing not to add that she felt rather strongly in need of a rest.

'I'll see what I can find out about home leave, and which young men were in Chipping Common at the time Alice disappeared,' Lucy added.

'Wonderful. Perhaps we could reconvene at, say, The Crown, tomorrow evening?' she asked, thinking it would be nice to have someone else cook for them. Also Miss Busby thought that she might invite the inspector. He had met her and Lucy there before and she suspected the prospect of the landlady's game pie would be much more of a lure than the mere suggestion they have a chat. It was time, she believed, that they had a proper talk.

Lucy was the first to leave, wishing them a pleasant evening and thanking Miss Busby for the meal.

'Do give my regards to your father,' Miss Busby called from the door.

'I suppose he's your errand tomorrow,' Adeline muttered rather ungraciously from the sofa. 'Off for a visit?'

Miss Busby turned to her sharply. 'Not at all. And I rather resent the implication.'

There was silence for a moment. Adeline rubbed lightly at her temples.

'I am sorry, Isabelle,' she conceded, cheeks flushed. 'I don't know what came over me. I am concerned that we don't seem to be getting anywhere, and I have it constantly in my head that Ezekiel could be arrested at any moment.'

'Now, Adeline, we have been through this–'

'Yes, but it's one thing to understand the reasoning behind something, and quite another to stop one's brain fretting all the same. I really am very sorry. I should not have snapped at you. It's quite unforgivable.'

'Don't be ridiculous, it's already forgiven. Now, would you perhaps benefit from a *small* sherry?' she asked, fervently hoping the answer would be 'no' as her bed was calling.

'I shan't now, thank you all the same. It might put me to sleep and I doubt you want me snoring on your sofa.'

Miss Busby smiled. 'We *will* get to the bottom of it, you know. And I want to be sure we have all the information we need to persuade the inspector to act this time. You know what he's like.'

'Yes, utterly useless. Thank you, Isabelle,' she added quietly, 'for helping.'

Miss Busby felt a small flush creep across her own cheeks. 'Goodness, Adeline,' she flustered, 'what are friends for?'

CHAPTER 15

Miss Busby rose later than usual on Wednesday and felt all the better for it. Dr Scholl's powder had soothed the ache in her feet, and a leisurely breakfast in the garden had done the same for her mind. She felt fully restored, and as the morning sun picked out the pretty stocks in her flower beds, her brain began to pick out the pertinent details from all she'd learned the day before.

With Pud and Barnaby fed, she took up her notebook to sit at her desk in the window of the living room and read through all she'd written, pleased to see there was nothing she appeared to have forgotten. From her discussion with Lucy and Adeline the evening before, she added a comment to Alice's entry:

Abandoned at workhouse at birth by unmarried young mother – history repeating?

And under Harrison's Haberdashery she added:

Mrs Harrison on the fundraising committee for the workhouse – irregularities?

Thinking a few moments more, she circled Lady Felicity Spencer's name, before closing the notebook and giving a small, satisfied nod.

'It's beginning to come together, Pud,' she told the cat as he sprang up onto the back of the sofa and began to wash his ridiculously long whiskers. He paused to look at her, one paw held aloft, ginger fur aglow in the sunlight.

Barnaby wandered in from the garden to see what he might be missing. She ruffled his silky ears as he came to lean against her legs.

'It was all rather jumbled at the start. And Adeline is so concerned for her friend she's apt to try and force things,' she continued. 'Oh lord, I am talking to you both as if you could understand.' She thought for a moment, then gave a little shrug. 'Well, I'm quite aware you can't, so I'm not losing my marbles just yet. Besides, it helps to talk things through. Particularly as you two don't interrupt!'

Pudding returned to his grooming, but Barnaby's bright brown eyes remained fixed on his mistress. She thought of Adeline's theory, envisioning Alice returning to Chipping Common after six years to exact vengeance upon Gabriel Travis for dark deeds. Miss Busby, glancing at the calendar on the desk, struggled to imagine the man in such a role. 'We must talk to someone impartial, Barnaby,' she said. 'It's no good taking the word of his friend, however delightful. And I have an idea.'

Barnaby gave a small sigh, realising snacks were unlikely to be involved. Miss Busby crossed to the bookcase in the corner of the room and picked out Edgar Wallace's *The Clue of the New Pin.* She took it to her favourite armchair by the unlit fire and as Barnaby settled at her feet and Pud dozed in the sunshine, she lost herself completely in the final chapters of her book.

An hour or so later, as the clock over her mantelpiece struck 11, Miss Busby, Barnaby, and *The Clue of the New Pin* left the cottage. Barnaby sported his rather dashing tartan collar and matching leash, and Miss Busby had dressed for her outing in complementary colours: a navy blue skirt with a paler blue blouse. She knew Mrs Friedli would approve. A rather stern woman on first encounter, the custodian of Bloxford's mobile library was a delight once you got to know her, and a keen fan of all things Scottish. Were she ever to retire, she often said, it would be to the Highlands. Although given that she was only in her thirties, her plans seemed rather premature.

Mrs Friedli's ex-army grey Ford van stood beside the village green, surrounded by a small cluster of local bibliophiles. Lovingly converted by Mr Friedli and the two Friedli boys, the interior had been stripped, fitted with numerous wooden shelves and filled with several hundred tightly packed volumes. It was a literary wonder on wheels, visiting the Cotswold's more remote villages every month, bringing knowledge, intrigue, and excitement to all.

'Good morning Miss Busby!' Mrs Friedli called cheerily, alighting from the high cab of the van with ease. A tall, athletically built woman dressed in practical brown trousers and white blouse, chestnut hair cut into a neat bob and hazel eyes shining with good humour. 'I was hoping to see you. I have a new Wodehouse on board! It's *A Gentleman of Leisure.*'

'How exciting.' Miss Busby smiled. 'May I exchange him for my Wallace?'

Books swapped and duly stamped, details noted, and with Barnaby fussed and his tartan hues admired, Mrs Friedli turned her attention to the other villagers. Some knew exactly what they were looking for and zeroed in with determination, others came to her for recommendations. Whatever she didn't have on board she noted down and did her best to procure for next time. She was a lifeline for many of the older villagers, her knowledge and enthusiasm supplying them with suitable literary company year-round.

Leaving her to her work, Miss Busby and Barnaby made their way to the bench at the edge of the green. She read a few paragraphs of her new book whilst observing the comings and goings of her neighbours, waiting for the activity around the library to settle. Barnaby entertained himself chasing squirrels around the oak tree.

It was half an hour or so before the village green emptied and the sound of the van door closing could be heard. Mrs Friedli joined her soon afterwards, with her customary flask and two cups. It had become a pleasant habit, as the weather had improved, for the pair to take time to chat before the library departed for its next destination.

Coffee poured and pleasantries exchanged, Miss Busby arrived at the heart of the matter.

'Did Gabriel Travis ever borrow books from you?'

'Aha! The Chipping Common murder! I wondered if you'd mention it. I do hope you are on the case? I was most disappointed to miss all the intrigue at Little Minton last year.'

Miss Busby felt a stab of guilt. It had been an awful business, but murder of any kind seemed to grasp the attention of casual observers like nothing else.

'Oh, it was all terribly unpleasant. And quite sad in the end.'

'Well I should imagine all murders are,' Mrs Friedli pointed out. 'But you were able to work with that Scottish inspector. They say he's awfully handsome.'

'Who does?'

Mrs Friedli laughed. 'Everyone! Well, the ladies, of course.'

'Hmm.' Miss Busby thought of Lucy. She really ought to chivvy the girl along before someone snapped him up. 'He's actually rather difficult,' she said, 'although he means well.'

'Oh, they're all difficult.' Mrs Friedli waved a hand. 'Always a bonus if they look pleasant while they're at it, though.'

Miss Busby laughed. 'Yes, I suppose so.'

Randolf hadn't been difficult in the least, but she knew how lucky she'd been with him. And how terribly unlucky, too, to lose him. Looking down at the book at her side it was hard not to feel a tinge of regret: had Randolf lived, she would no doubt have a grand library of her own. But circumstances were circumstances, and disposition was something else entirely, she reminded herself.

'I'd rather like to meet the inspector,' Mrs Friedli went on. 'Perhaps I could be called upon as a witness, wouldn't that be a scream?' Her eyes twinkled mischievously.

'Does that mean you knew Gabriel Travis, then?' Miss Busby asked, her own eyes brightening. This had been her hope. Eleanor Friedli was fiercely intelligent, a fine judge of character, and famously never forgot a name or a face – which meant no one could ever get away with a late return or a missing book.

'Yes. He was the quiet sort. Didn't come out to the van very often – not much need of a library when you live above a bookshop, after all! But he was keen on poetry, and Mr Melnyk doesn't carry a great deal. Not much call for it, sadly. Keats, I remember, was a favourite.'

'What was he like?'

'Keats? Rather tragic.'

Miss Busby arched an eyebrow.

Mrs Friedli chuckled. 'Travis was painfully shy. Engaging him in anything more than one syllable was like trying to draw blood from a stone. But I judged him to be kind. A decent sort.'

Miss Busby's head tilted in interest. 'How could you tell, if he was so quiet?'

'Oh, the usual way. If anyone dropped something he would hurry to pick it up for them. I remember one of the older ladies once spilled several notes from her purse without noticing, and he gathered them up and ran to return them to her.'

'Ah, I see.' Miss Busby recognised the unspoken – several notes could surely have made all the difference to Travis' situation, but the man had proved himself honest, and trustworthy.

'And what about Alice Albion, did you know her too?'

Mrs Friedli's eyes widened. 'The workhouse girl? Good heavens, has she been found?'

'I'm afraid not.' Miss Busby shook her head.

'Ah, but you suspect involvement?'

'I had heard the two were friends.'

'Yes, she was fond of poetry, too. The romantics, much like Travis. More Byron than Keats, though. Kindred spirits all the same.'

'And did Alice borrow from the library too?'

'Frequently. I remember the bag she carried her books in. So striking! The most beautiful bright, bold colours. I never saw another like it. She had made it herself, taken a simple fabric and worked wonders on it in golden embroidery. I'd always meant to ask if she could make me one, but time rather ran away with me.'

Both women took a sip of coffee. Miss Busby winced at the bitterness; she preferred hers with milk, but drank it to be companionable all the same.

'Did you ever see Alice with any young men, perhaps before the war, or when they were home on leave?' she asked.

'Oh, there'd often be the odd chap not too far off. She was awfully pretty, damn near angelic in the looks department; a tiny little petite thing, but perhaps not the most worldly. Too cloistered, you see. Inevitable I suppose, within the confines of the workhouse.'

'Was there any chap in particular that you can recall?'

'Why do you ask?' Mrs Friedli narrowed her eyes in mock suspicion.

Miss Busby took another sip of coffee before answering carefully, 'I was simply wondering. I had heard she was rather taken with Cameron Spencer.'

'Well, I can't help you there. The Spencers aren't the sort to patronise my little library.'

Miss Busby tried to hide her disappointment, although she felt she should have known. 'Nor Martin Fowler, I presume?'

'The pharmacist? University library sort, I should think, and he's bound to have his own reference books.' She finished her coffee, glanced at her wristwatch, and screwed the lid back onto the flask purposefully. 'I must be getting on, there'll be a riot in Filkins village if I'm late.'

Miss Busby laughed, handing over her cup and rising from the bench. 'I should imagine you'll be quite safe.'

'You haven't met Mrs Lucas. She may be an octogenarian, but she'll be rabid if she doesn't get the next instalment in her series. You can always leave a telephone message for me at the public library in Oxford if you need anything. Especially if the dashing Scot would like to pick my brains.' Her eyes sparkled impishly. 'Lovely to see you, Isabelle.'

'Yes, and you too, Eleanor.' She'd thought to walk into Little Minton, as she needed one or two things from the market, but a far more sensible idea struck her. 'I don't suppose there's any chance of a lift, if it's not too far out of your way?'

'Of course! Hop up! Is your doggie coming too?'

CHAPTER 16

Miss Busby alighted from the cab of the library van outside Lily's Tea Rooms with no small measure of difficulty. Mrs Friedli handed Barnaby down to her before chugging off up the high street, waving out of the window as she went. As Miss Busby turned, she caught sight of Nurse Delaney seated in the window of Lily's, attacking a sausage roll. *Just the person*, she thought, *how fortuitous!*

'Table for one, is it dear?' Maggie asked, hurrying over as the pair came through the door. 'Well, one and a half,' she added, bending to stroke Barnaby.

'Thank you, Maggie, but I wonder if I might join Nurse Delaney, if she doesn't object?'

The stout community nurse turned at the mention of her name, hastily brushing pastry crumbs from her navy uniform. She wore a white cap over grey hair, her blue eyes and round, friendly face shone with welcome.

'Isabelle! Bring more tea will you, Maggie?' she called,

as Miss Busby settled opposite and Barnaby busied himself with crumbs beneath the table.

'And another sausage roll, please,' Miss Busby added.

As the waitress bustled off to oblige, the two women exchanged pleasantries. Nurse Delaney was delighted to hear news of old friends, and Miss Busby was pleased to offer several tips with regard to training young dogs.

'Oh, Duncan doesn't bite, as such,' the nurse insisted. 'He just likes to play. Nips a little, but he's only a puppy. I cleared it all up with young Bobby Miller before he left for Chipping Common.'

'Speaking of which…' Miss Busby seized the opportunity, and as Maggie brought them fresh supplies, the pair discussed the murder at Chipping Common.

'Would it have been terribly difficult, do you think, for someone to fool the police sergeant and ambulance men into thinking it suicide?' Miss Busby asked, thinking of her previous discussion at the tea rooms with Adeline. Nurse Delaney would have far more medical knowhow at her fingertips, and could prove a mine of information.

'Oh I shouldn't think so,' she replied. 'Most people would see the gun and the blood, and draw the same conclusion.'

'Even with medical training?' Miss Busby could see a rural police sergeant missing it, but the ambulance men, she thought, would be a different matter.

The nurse dropped a sugar cube into her tea cup and stirred thoughtfully. 'Training can be somewhat rudimentary, I'm afraid. They may have been young and inexperienced, and are invariably busy, rushing all over the place. They would have ascertained the man was dead, and simply taken him away. The pathologist would carry out a post mortem, but it's up to the coroner to determine the cause of death.'

Miss Busby thought for a moment. 'So the killer would only really have bought himself a little time with such a charade?'

'In effect, yes. I expect he thought he'd done enough to avoid suspicion. Or she, I should think.'

Miss Busby's eyebrows shot up. 'What makes you say that?'

'Well, I would assume poison was involved, and poison is generally considered a woman's weapon.'

'But the vast majority of murderers are male,' Miss Busby countered. 'And what makes you think it was poison?'

The nurse took a sip of tea, and thought for a moment. 'If it has been declared murder, there must be medical evidence,' she reasoned. 'Most poisons leave a trace which can be detected nowadays by chemical tests. Arsenic, for example, is traceable if a body is subjected to a toxicological examination. And the same can be said of strychnine, and various other unpleasant acids.'

Miss Busby sat forward, impressed. She knew Nurse Delaney to be knowledgeable but this was exceeding even her expectations.

'It's a pet interest of mine,' she explained. 'Rather fascinating, actually. Your murderer may have been

KAREN BAUGH MENUHIN & ZOE MARKHAM

quite clever initially,' she went on, 'but they can't be up to date with modern post-mortem methods, or they'd have known they wouldn't get away with it. Either that or they likely assumed they'd done a good enough job for the body to be buried quickly; once it was in the ground, no-one would have known. But something must have sparked the interest of a keen-eyed physician along the way.'

Miss Busby's own interest sparked fiercely, as Nurse Delaney looked down at the silver watch pinned to the front of her uniform and gave a sigh. Waving to Maggie behind the counter, she signalled for the bill. 'I'm sorry, Isabelle, it's wonderful to see you but I must get back to my rounds.' She rose to her feet.

'Yes, of course, don't let me hold you up. And thank you, you've given me something to think about!'

'Now, you mustn't consider me a particular authority on the subject,' the nurse was quick to clarify. 'I've seen a few cases of poisoning over the years, accidental for the most part. But it's always fascinated me how the coroner gets to the bottom of it.'

'Do let me get this,' Miss Busby insisted when Maggie brought the bill. 'It's the least I can do. And could I please have a sausage roll to take out, as well?' she added.

As Maggie went to oblige, she walked the nurse to the door, waving away her objections with one last question. 'Is there nothing else you think it might have been, other than poisoning?'

She considered for a moment. 'They could have found a concealed wound, I suppose. Or perhaps the gunshot wound proved the man couldn't have executed himself. I expect there are all sort of things. I'm only a nurse, after all…'

Miss Busby gave her a wry smile. 'A most knowledgeable and experienced nurse,' she added, thinking the woman could give a few doctors a run for their money.

Nurse Delaney waved away the compliment. 'Poison is the first thing that came to my mind, that's all,' she said. 'Thank you for lunch!'

With the sausage roll carefully wrapped and tucked into her bag, along with the Wodehouse, Miss Busby made a swift visit to the market to order a list of groceries to be delivered to Lavender Cottage. She then dropped into the post office just in time to catch Dennis readying the van for his afternoon deliveries. His face fell when he spotted her striding purposely toward him, but the sausage roll worked its magic, and he tucked in happily as Miss Busby and Barnaby climbed aboard.

'Bloxford is it then, Miss?' he asked in a spray of crumbs.

'Chipping Common, if you wouldn't mind,' she said, handing him the napkin she'd thought to put in her pocket.

'Oh, but Miss, that's miles away! I don't even deliver there!'

'You can drop me at Melnyk's Books,' she went on, waiting a moment for the penny to drop.

'Oo, that's where that man was killed!' he said excitedly, wrestling the van into gear and setting off.

She nodded, a smile on her lips.

'You're never going 'ter see *him*, are you Miss?' His voice dropped in a mix of awe and horror. 'The foreign killer?'

'Don't be silly, Dennis,' she chided. Morbid fascination was one thing – perhaps excusable in the young – baseless accusations quite another. 'Mr Melnyk has not been charged with anything.'

'Everyone in the Dog and Duck says it was him though,' Dennis went on earnestly. 'Some of 'em are saying as that ear trumpet of his is a tiny little concealed pistol, and there ain't really nothin' wrong with his hearin'.'

'Oh, for goodness' sake!'

'I know, Miss, it's daft innit?' He rolled his eyes. 'The landlord says that's rot, and that he keeps a proper pistol under his yam...his yamma...his hat.'

Miss Busby gave a small sigh. 'Yarmulke, Dennis. And you may inform the landlord there isn't room.'

His face fell. 'In't there, Miss?'

'No. Does your mother know you're frequenting the Dog and Duck?'

'Yes, Miss. That is 'ter say, I don't rightly know, Miss.'

Miss Busby shot him a glare.

'No, Miss, she dun't. Sorry, Miss,' he mumbled. Then, softly, 'Please don't tell her, Miss.'

Little Minton's smallest public house, The Dog and Duck was a rather dingy establishment on the outskirts of the town, known for being a haunt of poachers and ne'er-do-wells. Mrs Ogden would box his ears if she knew her son frequented the place.

'I will, if I hear of you drinking in there again. For now, you may make amends by letting any other fools you come across know that the notion is preposterous. And that Inspector McKay will not look kindly upon false accusations from any quarter.'

Dennis kept his eyes on the road, but his cheeks flamed as red as his van. 'Yes, Miss.'

Miss Busby nodded sternly, and the rest of the journey passed in silence until they reached the bookshop. Adeline's Rolls was parked haphazardly outside, and the two could be seen arranging a fresh display of books in the window.

'Thank you, Dennis,' Miss Busby said as she stepped down and let Barnaby out of the van. 'And please don't forget what I told you.'

'I won't Miss,' he promised, eagerly trying to see into the bookshop behind her. She stood firm until he stopped rubbernecking and drove away.

Ezekiel smiled as Miss Busby and Barnaby entered the shop. He looked more alert, Miss Busby thought, as if he had slept well and regained some of his strength.

'Dear lady,' he greeted, extricating himself from the broad window shelf and brushing dust from his trousers. 'I cannot thank you enough. Mrs Fanshawe tells me you are to speak with the inspector tonight, and that the crime is soon to be solved.'

His eyes shone. Miss Busby arched an eyebrow at Adeline.

'I have informed Ezekiel we have gathered fresh information and shall soon be able to clear the Melnyk name once and for all,' Adeline said, turning back to the window to place the final volume amid the display.

'It is the most wonderful news.' Mr Melnyk gave a smile bright enough to rival the spring sunshine streaming through the glass. 'Mrs Fanshawe and I are, how do you say? Making the shop sprucey?'

'Sprucing it up,' Miss Busby supplied automatically, watching Adeline and trying to discern whether she had extracted vital information from the Spencers or was simply awash with overconfidence. Given that her friend wouldn't meet her eye, she suspected the latter.

'Yes! Sprucing it up ready for my customers to return. Soon the dark cloud of suspicion is to be chased away.' He lifted a pile of books from the floor and carried them to the desk, before extracting a feather duster from a drawer. 'Yesterday evening I am cleaning Gabriel's rooms. It is the most harrowing task, but a great relief to know his pain is washed away.' He turned to the nearest shelf and began to attack it with the duster. 'I have cleaned the hurt, and the room is tidy now, airing just as he liked it always to be in the daytime. And with my dear friends bringing his attacker to rights, I know Gabriel is not to be forgotten.' He turned and smiled gratefully at them. 'There is much I will do, also. Gabriel's poems must be copied, and bound, for others to share in. And I am thinking to find an apprentice bookbinder, to learn his trade and fill his most respected shoes. Gabriel, I am quite certain, would think this wonderful.'

Adeline turned, her eyes immediately beginning to well, and Miss Busby began to fret anew over what she had told the man. They had some interesting pieces of information, certainly, but were still a long way from piecing everything together.

'Adeline, might I have a word.' The lack of a question mark was distinctly audible. 'Ezekiel, perhaps we could see Gabriel's rooms whilst the two of us chat, and leave you to your sprucing?'

'Of course! Please, as you wish.' He gestured to the back of the shop where an old wooden staircase, lined with piles of books, led up to Mr Melnyk's flat and Gabriel's rooms in the attic above.

Barnaby took one look at the steps and turned around, trotting off to keep Ezekiel company instead.

CHAPTER 17

Picking their way carefully to the top of the stairs, Miss Busby taking point with Adeline close behind, they found Travis' attic door wide open with a light spring breeze blowing through.

'Adeline, whatever have you told the poor man?' Miss Busby demanded as they were safely out of earshot. 'He appears to be under the impression we are about to solve the murder. Which,' she objected, 'is rather far removed from the truth as I understand it. Unless you discovered something vital in calling on the Spencers?'

Adeline's cheeks flushed, answering Miss Busby's question. 'I simply informed him we have gathered enough information, with help from both the press and the military, to confront the inspector and chivvy him into doing his job properly.'

'Adeline!' Miss Busby exclaimed in outraged astonishment.

'Well,' Adeline huffed, 'Lucy is the press, and Anthony Lannister is our contact in the military. Both are helping us.'

'Yes, but–'

'And we know something untoward was going on at the workhouse, and that Alice's sudden disappearance was never explained, or even properly investigated for that matter. The girl was close to Gabriel Travis, had a thing for Cameron Spencer, and the notion of Ezekiel having anything to do with it is now heavily outweighed by the aforementioned.'

Miss Busby took a deep breath. 'Lucy may be a reporter, and Anthony *was* in the military, but you oughtn't to make it all sound so official. It gives your friend false hope.'

'Isabelle don't *fuss*. We are hot on the trail now, and with the help of our friends things are beginning to move apace. Even the inspector has seen fit to give Ezekiel his key back.'

'Yes, but–'

'And it's no use being so over cautious all the time. Doom and gloom is just as damaging as that which you call "false hope". Did you see how much better Ezekiel looked just now?'

'Yes, but–'

'Good. Now, let's stop bickering and see what Travis' rooms have to tell us.'

Feeling rather affronted by the telling-off, not least because she suspected Adeline had a point, Miss Busby followed her inside a long, narrow room divided in two by heavy red curtains strung from the ceiling. There was a small gap where they didn't quite meet in the middle; it was apparent one half of the room had constituted Travis' living area, the other his workspace.

With sun and fresh air flowing in through two narrow, open windows in the eaves – one on either side of the room – the space felt bright and airy despite the ceiling sloping low and the furnishings being old and worn. The floor was bare wood, uneven in places, with several small rugs strewn about for warmth and comfort. The walls between the ancient joists had been painted daffodil yellow, though they were spotted here and there with small patches of mould and damp.

Gabriel Travis' workspace was nearest the door, a large wooden desk taking up most of the room. A chair was tucked beneath, and on the floor beside it a worn leather tool bag bulged open to reveal all manner of intricate sewing and cutting implements within. Two shelves were fixed to the wall near the desk, one sagging in the middle, heaped with thick notepads, the other holding partially dismantled books apparently waiting to be rebound. A substantial oil lamp and several candles were also placed with them, presumably to allow for delicate work in the evenings.

They stopped by the desk. Dark stains, wet where they'd been scrubbed, covered one part of the surface. More such stains showed on the floorboards below. They stepped respectfully around, neither wanting to refer to the cause, although it gave them both a moment's solemn pause.

Adeline picked up a sheet of paper from a dry corner of the desk, then another. 'Isabelle, look at this.'

Impeccably arranged verses sloped beautifully across the page; poems written in the most immaculate copperplate calligraphy. 'Oh,' she gasped, running a finger along the page. 'Goodness, I haven't seen writing like this since…'

'They are *all* like it,' Adeline announced, searching through the stacks of paper. 'Every single piece written in the same elegant hand!' She looked over at Miss Busby, who had paled noticeably under a shaft of sunlight.

'Isabelle? Whatever is it? Oh, of course. How remiss of me. Here, you must sit down.' She ushered Miss Busby onto a Windsor chair in the corner and laid a hand on her shoulder. 'Randolf had a similar style, didn't he? I am so sorry, I had quite forgotten.' She tried to gently take the paper from Miss Busby's hands, but her grip remained resolute.

'It's really rather beautiful to see it,' she said softly. 'I hadn't expected it, that's all.'

'Nor I. Where on earth would a factory worker have learned such penmanship?' Adeline wondered aloud. She began rummaging in one of the drawers below the desk, coming up with a handful of battered nibs and several half-used bottles of ink.

'I should imagine he taught himself,' Miss Busby reasoned. 'For someone so fond of books and writing, it's perfectly logical.'

'Yes, but Isabelle, *look*.' Adeline gestured to the piles

of paper on the desk, then pulled a notebook down from the shelf to be sure. 'Every single page is covered with the same script. There are no scrappy notes taken or ideas hastily scrawled. It must have taken the man aeons to write everything in this manner!'

Miss Busby took the proffered notebook and glanced through it. 'Calligraphy is actually rather dynamic and flowing,' she explained. 'Once you get the hang of it, it's nowhere near as laborious as it looks. The discipline required, though… you're quite right, it's really rather remarkable.'

For several minutes the pair silently read through original poems, annotated works, and detailed records of books undergoing repair.

'He mentions "The Angel" quite frequently,' Adeline eventually remarked, and read out:

'Upon the poet's quill, grief's ink doth draw,
Verses writ in pain, a heart in stillness sore.
In unseen realms where faded memories cling,
A requiem for the angel, the writer's muse takes wing.'

'Yes, it's very moving.' Miss Busby spoke softly. 'Ezekiel said Travis referred to the muse as his angel. I suppose he may have meant his late wife, or daughter. His writing clearly meant an awful lot to him.'

'He was rather good at it, too. Turns a phrase beautifully here and there. And he was certainly nothing if not thorough,' Adeline observed, placing a set of carefully numbered papers back on the desk with a sigh. 'But this isn't getting us anywhere.'

'Oh, I disagree,' Miss Busby said, rising. 'It has answered one question that has been niggling me from the very beginning.

'Has it? What question?' Adeline looked up in astonishment.

'That of why there was no suicide note.'

'Ah! Because his handwriting would be difficult to forge?'

Miss Busby nodded. 'Not only that, it also proves, to my mind, that Gabriel Travis was murdered.'

Adeline's brow creased. 'How?'

Miss Busby gestured at the desk. 'A man with a mind this ordered and precise wouldn't leave such a significant action undocumented, or such a heavy question unanswered, I'm quite sure of it.'

'Hmm…' Adeline pondered. 'I can see it as an argument, certainly, but it's not actual proof, is it? I mean, you can't imagine someone like McKay picking up on something so subtle.'

'Well, it may have sparked a thought, and given him cause to check further,' Miss Busby reasoned.

Adeline scoffed. 'The man mislaid an entire suspect last year, Isabelle. I shall eat my best summer hat if he has registered a single thought regarding handwriting.'

Miss Busby smiled. 'Well, we'll ask him and see. He may surprise you. Now, let's take a look through here.'

Miss Busby pulled back one half of the curtain and took a step forward, before tripping against something, stumbling, and almost falling to the floor.

'Oh! Ouch!' she called, at the same time as Adeline darted forward and bellowed, 'Isabelle! Are you alright?' as if the blow may have somehow damaged her hearing.

'Yes, I think so.' Miss Busby took her friend's proffered hand and gingerly lifted a foot to feel her ankle. 'I banged it on something hidden behind the curtain. Nothing broken, but I can look forward to a colourful bruise. Oh, and no wonder!' She pulled the curtain back fully to reveal a small, cast-iron heater that she'd knocked over.

'Ah, I was wondering how he kept warm in the winter,' Adeline remarked. 'No gas up here, of course, but the mould on the walls hinted at some form of heat source.'

'Yes.' Miss Busby bent to rub her ankle again, rather surprised Adeline had noticed the damp. 'It's a good thing it's empty,' she said, standing the little heater back up. 'It looks the sort to contain kerosene, or paraffin. It would have made an awful mess otherwise. Poor Ezekiel has had enough to clear up already.'

'I expect he warmed soup and tea on it,' Adeline mused, still staring at the heater. 'He must have been quite self-contained up here. It's rather cosier than I'd imagined.' She ran an eye over the pretty patchwork quilt covering a neatly made bed set alongside the far wall. An old oak bench held colourful blankets and cushions nearby; it all looked remarkably comfortable.

Beside the bed stood a low, round table hosting another oil lamp alongside a metal mug, bowl, plate, and spoon all stacked tidily within one another. A set of three narrow drawers stood opposite, under the eaves, with a wardrobe tucked next to the brick chimney breast coming from below and running up through the roof. She opened the wardrobe: two jackets and four shirts hung in place. They moved to the drawers, which housed trousers and underthings, causing both women's cheeks to flush in tandem.

'Look.' Miss Busby noticed a small photo frame under a pair of thick winter socks. She held it out.

'Oh,' Adeline gasped. 'That must be his wife and child. They're rather beautiful.'

Miss Busby nodded sadly. She found herself wishing Travis had been included, as it would have been nice to put a face to the name.

The photograph was silvered, typical of cheaply developed images. A woman smiling with a curly haired child sitting on her lap. Their clothes were from the turn of the century, their faces timeless.

Miss Busby tucked it back in the drawer, feeling she had trespassed into the dead man's grief. They both remained silent, then sighed.

'He didn't have much in the way of belongings,' Adeline remarked quietly.

'Ezekiel said he lost everything in the fire,' Miss Busby reminded her, picking up the mug and looking inside. Nurse Delaney's theory of poison came back to her; would the police have looked, she wondered. She saw no dark stains, and discerned no bitter odour.

'Yes but he's had years to buy more things since,' Adeline objected, pulling her from her thoughts.

'He lost all his money as well,' Miss Busby pointed out, replacing the mug. Adeline rarely considered that one needed money. It was a mark of someone who'd never been short of it. 'I had the impression that whatever he earned since then had been just enough to keep him fed and clothed.'

'Ezekiel would have paid him appropriately for his work,' Adeline objected.

'Yes, of course. But the room would have been an element of that, and he would have had to pay for his food, materials, and fuel too, of course.' She cast a wry look at the little stove that had attacked her. 'Paper and ink would have been his greatest expense, by the look of it.'

'Yes, I suppose you're right. Oh, but Isabelle! We are quite forgetting the walls!'

'Are we?'

'Yes! We are supposed to be checking for gaps, remember? Our squirrel!'

Miss Busby cast an eye over the adjoining panelled wall. 'I'm no expert, Adeline, but it looks squirrel-proof to me. And human-proof, I'm afraid.'

Adeline ran a hand over the heavy wooden panelling, not yet inclined to admit defeat. 'Our assailant may simply have replaced it after himself. There could be a clever join, or some such. A secret door of sorts. There's one in Jemima's library; you can barely notice it unless you know it's there.'

Miss Busby thought it doubtful.

Adeline determinedly threw her weight against it, succeeding only in hurting her shoulder. She winced, then *harrumphed*.

'We can check with the inspector all the same,' Miss Busby said kindly, before suggesting they return to the shop before either of them picked up further injury.

CHAPTER 18

Halfway down the narrow staircase, Miss Busby paused, struggling a little as her ankle stiffened. Voices could be heard rising from the shop.

'It's Mrs Harrison!' Adeline stage-whispered, peering through the half-open door to be sure. 'Good, we can ask her about the fundraising and irregularities at the workhouse.'

'Who's the gentleman with her?' Miss Busby asked with interest as she reached the bottom of the stairs.

'Mr Harrison, I should imagine. How fortunate. We can ascertain whether he was another one charmed by Alice. Have you got your notebook, Isabelle?'

'The man was practically her father, Adeline,' she chided. 'And no, I didn't bring it today.'

'Why ever not?'

'I didn't have room. Wallace took up most of my bag.'

'Who? Oh, never mind. And anyway, he wasn't practically her anything when Rose took the girl on;

she wasn't even married to him,' she pointed out. 'And men are men, Isabelle. When there is no direct familial link they cannot be trusted to retain their reason where pretty young women are concerned.'

'Adeline, that is nonsense. Did you think that of your own husband?'

'Well, no, but—'

Barnaby gave a small *woof* from the shop, catching sight of them in the doorway and wagging his tail eagerly.

'Ah, my friends!' Mr Melnyk followed the little dog's line of vision and beamed. 'I am blessed with company today! Mr and Mrs Harrison are here also!'

'How lovely,' Miss Busby said, walking into the shop with a slight limp.

'But what has happened, dear lady?' Concern immediately creased Ezekiel's face as he crossed the room and offered an arm in support.

'Oh, it's nothing,' Miss Busby insisted, patting his arm gratefully.

'Just a trip. It happens once you reach a certain age,' Adeline declared.

Miss Busby counted to ten slowly in her head. Adeline was hardly far behind her in that regard, after all.

'I don't believe we've met.' A tall and rather solid woman crossed to meet her, hand outstretched, warm smile in place on brightly painted lips. Her hair was thick and dark, pulled up into a loose bun, several long strands hanging artfully against her neck. She wore a dusky pink dress paired with bright, chunky jewellery that gave her the image of being rather fun. 'I am Rose Harrison, of the haberdasher's next door.'

'Miss Busby,' she replied, shaking hands and smiling in turn. 'I've heard about your expertise from Mrs Fanshawe.'

'Oh, how kind!' She turned her attention to Adeline. 'I've drawn up two dress patterns for you to look at, Mrs Fanshawe. Might you perhaps have time to pop next door and have a look?'

'Yes, certainly.' Adeline nodded and shot a knowing look at Miss Busby. *This*, it said, *shall be our opportunity.*

'Oh, and allow me to introduce my husband, Fraser Harrison.'

Miss Busby found herself fighting to suppress a chuckle as a much shorter, thinner gentleman stepped nervously from behind Rose and muttered, 'Delighted, I'm sure.' He appeared the absolute opposite of his wife in every respect, and she would never have put the two together. The contrast was, unfortunately, almost as amusing as it was fascinating.

Balding, and with a pallid aspect, he looked uncomfortable and out of place in a dark suit and long woollen overcoat ill-suited to the warmth of the afternoon.

'Aren't you absolutely boiling in that?' Adeline, as ever, got straight to the point.

'Oh, Fraser is always cold,' Rose explained. 'He has thin blood, you see.'

Adeline gave him a curious, rather intense stare, which seemed to double his discomfort.

'Mr and Mrs Harrison came to apprise me of the funeral details for the delayed Lady Spencer,' Ezekiel explained.

'Late,' Adeline corrected.

'No… it is not to be until Friday afternoon at three of the clock,' he replied, confused.

'I mean the late Lady Spencer, as opposed to delayed,' she clarified.

'Ah, I am sorry. English is a difficult language for me. So many…how do you say? Idio…?'

'Idiots?' Adeline suggested.

'Idiosyncrasies,' Miss Busby supplied.

'Yes! The latter, thank you!'

'I must be getting back to work,' Mr Harrison mumbled.

'Fraser joined me to pay our respects to the Spencers,' Rose explained.

'I did the very same this morning.' Adeline nodded her approval. Miss Busby remembered they had yet to discuss what had been said.

Adeline continued, 'I must have missed you, who was there?'

'Only Olivia Spencer, and she only came in to take our card of condolence then disappeared again.'

'Ah, I met the daughter, Madeleine. She was rather–' Adeline seemed inclined to go on, but was interrupted.

'I shall see you later, Rose dear. I bid you all good afternoon.' Mr Harrison nodded awkwardly, then turned and left rather hurriedly.

Miss Busby glanced warily at Adeline. Now was not the time to question the retreating Mr Harrison. As Adeline's lips parted to call out to him, she jumped in with, 'Mrs Harrison, would you mind if I looked at the patterns with Mrs Fanshawe? I haven't treated myself to a new dress in an age. I'd be interested to see the latest style.'

'Yes, of course! The more the merrier, Miss Busby. Will your doggie come along too? We've become acquainted.' Barnaby jumped up and put his front paws on Mrs Harrison's knees, requiring his chest to be rubbed.

'Barnaby, down!' said Miss Busby. 'I'm so sorry, he never normally—'

'Oh, it's perfectly fine! I used to have an Irish Wolf-hound, a little terrier won't bother me at all.'

As the group took their leave of Mr Melnyk, Adeline promised she would visit the following day, and her curious eyes didn't leave the back of Mr Harrison's head until they were safely outside.

* * *

'Do sit down.' Rose Harrison waved them towards blue upholstered chairs set around a tidy work table, as Barnaby checked the perimeter of the shop for lost biscuits.

Miss Busby glanced around, the shop was prettily feminine and designed to be practical. Button back chairs in floral fabrics, white cabinets with myriad drawers. Bolts of cloth stacked in a linen cupboard next to a standing mirror with a gold frame, and a curtained dressing room behind the long cutting table obscured the rear. 'I'll leave the "gone away" sign up until we've decided on your design,' Rose said. 'That way we won't be disturbed.'

Miss Busby had smiled at the *Back in 15 minutes* note hung on the shop door. So many people in small towns did the same, and rarely did any of them think to note the time they had left. It had people scratching their heads and wondering whether to wait or not.

Martin Fowler, it seemed, was possessed of no such hesitation. The handsome young pharmacist strolled straight into the shop as the women settled at the table. Barnaby emitted a low growl.

'My jacket needs repairing for the funeral,' he announced. With no time for pleasantries, he dropped a smart black suit jacket on the table. Mrs Harrison leapt to her feet. Adeline arched an eyebrow. Miss Busby flashed her a look: she didn't want her friend to intervene, curious to see for herself how the young man behaved.

The little terrier's growl intensified. Martin looked down at him. 'The pharmaceutical lab in Oxford are always looking for test animals,' he remarked. 'They pay rather well.'

'That won't be necessary, thank you.' Miss Busby's tone was icy, her resolve forgotten in an instant.

'Oh, is he yours?' Martin asked. 'I do beg your pardon. I thought perhaps he was a stray.' He gave Miss Busby a polite bow, leaving her not entirely sure what to make of him. 'There's a rip on the inside pocket, Mrs Harrison. I'll collect it tomorrow morning.'

Rose picked up the jacket and had a look. 'Oh, yes, that won't take a moment. If you want to wait, I could do it–'

'No, thank you. I don't have time. Tomorrow, please.'

'Yes, of course. Do give my best to your mother,' Rose called brightly.

Nodding curtly, the man left as abruptly as he'd arrived.

'Is he always so rude?' Adeline asked, looking daggers at the door.

'Oh, he's always busy, rather than rude,' Rose explained. 'It's been hard for him, since he lost his father. Just he and his mother in such a busy pharmacy. They're very close, and they work wonders as a team. They rather remind me of myself and my Alice, before…'

'Are these the designs?' Adeline asked, hastily moving the jacket aside to reveal the papers beneath. Miss Busby liked to think it was to spare Mrs Harrison upset, rather than in simple excitement at her new frock. 'Oh! They are stunning!' Adeline's genuine delight returned both Miss Busby and Mrs Harrison's attention to the matter at hand. The two dress designs were greatly admired, colour charts were produced and consulted, and both were eventually commissioned as Adeline deemed it quite impossible to choose between them.

Rose Harrison, thrilled with the decision, invited them up to the flat upstairs for coffee and cake to celebrate.

'I'm so pleased you're happy,' she said, carrying coffee pot, cups and saucers, and the usual into the sunny living room on a marquetry tray. 'It can be difficult, bringing a client's vision to life, but I knew those would be perfect for you.' She beamed down at Adeline as she set the tray on the coffee table beside the pink chintz sofa the pair had sunk into. Bustling straight back into the kitchen, she called, 'Pineapple upside down cake or chocolate sponge?'

The chocolate cake took the unanimous vote.

Adeline poured the coffee.

'Don't spill anything,' Miss Busby warned. She hadn't ever been in a room quite so pink, or chintzy, and was surprised to find she rather liked it.

'Really Isabelle, I am quite adept,' Adeline muttered.

'You really do have a wonderful eye, Mrs Harrison,' Miss Busby remarked, taking a plate of cake from their hostess with a graceful nod. 'Your decor is charming.'

'Do call me Rose, and thank you! Pink has always been my favourite colour. Goes with my name, don't you think?' she laughed. 'Fraser isn't keen, of course, you know how men are, so I indulge myself in the flat here. Ditto the cakes – do tuck in.'

'Delicious!' Adeline declared after sampling a mouthful. Miss Busby nodded in agreement. There was nothing quite like homemade chocolate cake.

'I'm delighted you think so. Fraser is on a perpetual

diet,' she sighed. 'It's nice to be able to share a treat with someone.'

'Is that because of his thin blood?' Adeline asked.

Miss Busby thought the question rather rude, but she was curious too, given there was nothing to the man.

'I do tell him he wouldn't be cold all the time if he'd eat a little more. They never listen, though, do they? He has quite a few health issues and is very careful with his diet so as not to exacerbate anything further. My little flat here has become something of an escape from it all.'

'From Fraser?' Adeline pressed, shifting forward in her seat, eyes wide as she attempted to cast Mr Harrison in the role of villain.

'From his bland food and manly decor,' Rose clarified.

'Oh.' Adeline looked disappointed.

'He's an absolute darling,' Rose insisted, 'but it is important to have a space of one's own, isn't it?'

Miss Busby nodded. She would have given anything to share her home with Randolf, but was old enough and wise enough to understand that even the most perfect of gentlemen could irritate given time. The trick, she knew, was to nevertheless appreciate all such moments as a gift. 'Alice must have loved this space too,' she said gently. 'It's perfect for a young lady.'

Rose looked up from her cake in surprise. 'Yes, she did. Cried with delight when I moved her down here from the attic. We chose this wallpaper together. She always loved bright colours and pretty flowers.' Her voice wavered a little. 'Goodness,' she said, clearing her throat, 'it's strange to talk about her again after all this time.'

'Poor Mr Travis' murder has rather churned things up I should imagine; two tragedies in such close proximity,' Miss Busby said.

'Yes, but so many years apart,' Rose replied.

Miss Busby nodded. That was the issue, after all. 'Adeline mentioned you suspected Alice had been led astray?'

'Well, of course. There's no other explanation.' Rose topped up the coffees. 'She was such a kind, sweet girl. She worked hard, and was going to run the haberdashery for me one day. Fraser was looking forward to having me home, although I still would have kept an eye on matters here, of course.'

'Your bolt-hole.' Adeline nodded.

'Yes.' Rose smiled. 'We'd talked about it often, Alice and I. Some wicked young fellow must have put devilry into her head, it's all I can think of.'

CHAPTER 19

Adeline leapt in with both feet. 'There's talk in the town that Alice was soft on Cameron Spencer.'

Rose looked startled.

'Not that we're suggesting Sir Cameron Spencer is any way wicked,' Miss Busby quickly added.

'Well, no,' Adeline conceded. 'But we did wonder if the two of them were close?'

Rose sat quietly for a moment before replying. 'There is always idle talk in small towns, Mrs Fanshawe, particularly amongst the muffin wallopers. But it doesn't mean there's an ounce of truth to what people are saying, or that anyone else should listen to it, let alone repeat it.'

Adeline's cheeks flushed almost the same shade as the wallpaper. As a widow, she didn't qualify as one of said "wallopers" – the expression specifically referring to unmarried women overfond of gossip over cake – but being rather fond of cake and *news*, Miss Busby suspected the expression stung all the same. Adeline opened her mouth to defend herself, but Rose beat her to it.

'And I can imagine what they're saying. That Alice did the same as her mother: got herself into trouble and ran away to take care of it. Well, that's nonsense. Alice was the last person to repeat her mother's mistakes. There's nothing like being abandoned at a workhouse to teach you never to abandon a child of your own.'

'No, I should imagine there isn't,' Miss Busby agreed softly. 'And nor should Adeline.'

'What? Yes. I mean, no. I didn't mean it like that. I simply thought if the two were friends it may have caused some friction in the town.'

'Because Alice was from a workhouse?' Rose's tone remained cold.

'Yes.' Adeline remained oblivious. 'I shouldn't imagine the Spencers would have been keen. In fact, I spoke to Sir Cameron's sister this morning, and she was rather adamant that—'

'Madeleine Spencer has always considered herself a cut above the rest of us,' Rose Harrison cut in. 'Please don't make the mistake of judging the entire town by her standards.'

'Of course.' Miss Busby attempted to defuse the icy chill. She had thought to ask the same regarding Martin Fowler, but couldn't imagine the answer would be any different. The pharmacist's social status wasn't as high as Cameron Spencer's, no matter how proudly he carried himself, but it was far above Alice's all the same.

'This cake really is wonderful, so moist, perhaps you wouldn't mind sharing the recipe?' she asked, taking another bite.

'Certainly. It was my grandmother's,' Rose replied politely before turning back to Adeline. 'Young Cameron is much more pleasant than his sister, and yes, Alice got along with him. She got along with everyone in the town and was civil to all. And where did it get her? Suspicion and nastiness, it seems, nothing more.'

'Oh, not at all,' Miss Busby was quick to interject. 'Mr Melnyk, for one, could not speak more highly of Alice.'

Rose's expression softened. 'Mr Melnyk is a lovely man, and Alice was very fond of him. He and Mr Travis both.'

Miss Busby noted Adeline readying to speak, and silenced her with a sharp look.

'Besides,' Rose continued, 'if her disappearance had been connected to Cameron Spencer, he too would surely have left at the same time. Anyway, he was away at the war when Alice disappeared.'

Miss Busby remembered that the same was true of Martin Fowler.

'Yes, of course,' Adeline huffed. 'I wasn't suggesting–'

'And you really have no idea who it could have been?' Miss Busby asked, sparing Adeline's difficulty. 'You didn't notice anyone acting suspiciously, perhaps, around that time? Someone unusual lurking near the shop, or some upset or concern in Alice?'

Rose sighed. 'If I had, you may rest assured I would have informed the police at the time.'

'Oh I'm sure, it's just sometimes we don't notice things until later, when we stop thinking about them,' Miss Busby continued. 'Does that make sense?'

Rose nodded. 'It does, Miss Busby, thank you. I have racked my brains for six years, I doubt I shall ever stop, but I'm afraid there really is nothing. Alice didn't mention anyone, or anything, troubling her. Although she wouldn't necessarily tell me everything, I'm sure – after all, what youngster would?'

'It must be so upsetting for you, the not knowing.' Miss Busby's heart went out to the woman.

Rose nodded, her lips falling. 'Alice was such a dear she would have given her heart and soul to any who asked, and been entirely at their mercy as a consequence. I did my best to keep her safe but–' Her face crumpled and tears welled in her eyes. She tugged a pink handkerchief from a pocket. 'There was only so much I could do. She was 19, after all, and I wasn't… I'm not…I wasn't even her real mother.'

As Rose dissolved into sobbing tears, Adeline and Miss Busby rallied and moved to comfort her as best they could.

'I always t-told her to be careful with young men, that they weren't to be t-trusted,' she stammered. 'But I couldn't be with her all the time.'

'Of course you couldn't, she was a grown woman,' Adeline insisted. 'And she was extremely fortunate to have you.'

'And you *were* her real mother,' Miss Busby said, taking her hand gently. 'Of course you were.'

'Oh, you are very kind, both of you. Do forgive me, I'm being silly. It all happened so long ago, but I have never stopped grieving for her, or wondering.'

'Please, you must forgive us for bringing the matter up and causing you fresh pain,' Miss Busby said.

'Yes,' Adeline agreed, 'especially after I badgered you about her yesterday.'

'Oh, no, I enjoyed talking to you, Mrs Fanshawe,' Rose insisted. 'It was only when Inspector McKay started asking about her that I found it upsetting.'

Adeline's mouth fell open. She looked rather comical, Miss Busby thought, before realising hers had done the same.

'I find him upsetting too.' Adeline recovered. 'And quite infuriating.'

'When was this?' Miss Busby asked, ignoring Adeline.

'He came to the shop yesterday evening, just before closing time. He was so stern. There wasn't an ounce of warmth to him.'

'There never is,' Adeline concurred. 'I rather–'

'And he was asking about Alice?' Miss Busby pressed.

'Yes. He seemed to imply… well, they choose their words carefully, of course, but, oh, it's too awful.'

'Did he perhaps hint that Alice may have had something to do with Gabriel Travis' murder?' Miss Busby hedged.

Rose nodded glumly. 'I told him it was utter nonsense. She was very fond of Mr Travis, and he was as gentle and kind as she. Neither of them would hurt a fly.'

'We have heard the very same,' Miss Busby assured her.

'And then the inspector started asking about the workhouse, saying it had shut down and asking what I knew about *financial irregularities*.'

'The cheek of the man.' Adeline *tsked*.

It was Miss Busby's turn to flush; she'd been guilty of a similar thought, even though she'd been quick to dismiss it.

'I sent him off with a flea in his ear after that. I had resigned from the fundraising committee long before any of that nonsense. As soon as I married Fraser I stopped all my volunteer work – my shop takes up so much time, I'd have had none left to spend with him otherwise.'

'And that's why you were going to hand the reins of the business to Alice,' Adeline remarked, before asking, 'Did your husband get along with her?' as casually as she could muster.

Miss Busby braced herself for fresh upset, but talk of Mr Harrison only made his wife smile.

'Of course. He adored her, and she him. Like appreciates like, Mrs Fanshawe. I can assure you, the only people you will find who didn't get along with Alice are those with a darkness in their heart that didn't sit comfortably with the light in her own.'

As the pair left the shop, a handwritten copy of the

cake recipe neatly tucked inside Miss Busby's bag, two young women waiting for the shop to open glared in their direction. Miss Busby offered a conciliatory smile, feeling responsible that *Back in 15 minutes* had turned into an hour.

Adeline was oblivious. 'It is high time we talked to McKay,' she declared as Barnaby raced to catch them.

'I'm not so sure,' Miss Busby replied.

Adeline turned to face her. 'Why on earth not? It was your idea to ask him to dine with us this evening.'

'Yes, but that was when I thought we were several steps ahead of him. If he was questioning Rose Harrison about Alice last night, it seems he's keeping up with us rather well. I doubt he'd appreciate us trying to help, in the circumstances.'

'Trying to… Isabelle!' Adeline's face turned a rather ominous shade of puce. 'He doesn't deserve our help, he deserves a stern word or three. He's hounding the wrong people! First poor Ezekiel, and now poor Rose. Who is to be next?'

'Well–'

'You or I, I shouldn't wonder! No, we must head him off at the pass. Come along, there is no time like the present.' And she strode off in the direction of the police station.

'*Oh, Lord,*' Miss Busby muttered under her breath, attaching Barnaby's lead as she hurried to catch up. 'I haven't had a chance to tell you about my chat with the librarian this morning yet, and you haven't told me about your encounter with Madeleine Spencer. We ought to discuss both before–'

'That can wait. Honestly, Isabelle, that poor woman… *hounded* by the man.' She lengthened her stride with fresh purpose.

'We were rather hounding her too,' Miss Busby called as she followed behind.

'That is *entirely* different,' Adeline shot over her shoulder.

'Is it?'

'Yes!' Adeline's exasperation was clear as she turned back once more. 'We were doing it for the good of…' She floundered, arms raised.

'…the case?' Miss Busby finished. 'So is the inspector. He may not be particularly tactful, but that doesn't mean his intentions are poor.'

'It's his *job*.' Adeline was flagging but not ready to admit defeat just yet. 'It's no good excusing him all the time, Isabelle. After all, if he did his job properly we wouldn't have been with Rose to upset her in the first place.'

'He did ask us to stay away,' Miss Busby pointed out.

Adeline's shoulders sagged. Miss Busby realised in that moment Adeline hated to have caused Rose Harrison pain, despite her bluster. Her sudden fierce anger towards the inspector was little more than simple redirection.

'There's no use us going into the station in this state,' Miss Busby reasoned gently. 'Let's go back to Lavender

Cottage. We can telephone the station from there if you still want to talk to him. In the meantime we can compare notes on…Oh! Is that Bobby?'

Adeline turned in the direction of Miss Busby's gaze and saw the figure of Constable Miller approaching on a bicycle at speed.

'Can't stop Miss!' he called as he pedalled past them. 'There's another one been killed!'

'What? Who?' Adeline exclaimed.

Bobby suddenly reversed direction, sped back and braked to a halt beside them. 'Erm, I'd be much obliged if you didn't mention it being me what told you, Miss,' he said, tipping his helmet respectfully to both women before turning and haring off once more.

'Told us what?' Adeline called after him. 'You didn't say who!'

CHAPTER 20

Miss Busby telephoned Lucy the moment they arrived at Lavender Cottage, while Adeline rummaged in the kitchen. Pud's unrelenting chirps and Barnaby's gruff accompaniment left her in no doubt as to what was required. The pair were placated with a saucer of salmon and a dish of chicken scraps, respectively.

'What news?' Adeline asked as Miss Busby finished her call and came through. They had speculated on Bobby Miller's dramatic declaration all the way back from Chipping Common, but were still none the wiser as to who was dead.

'Lucy hasn't heard of any murders, so it's a mystery to her too. Nothing has been reported to the paper. And she agrees we ought not to bother the inspector for the moment,' Miss Busby said. 'She'll join us for dinner at The Crown in an hour or so. Anthony and Richard will tag along. It's their chef's night off.'

'Good. I could eat a horse.'

'We have just had chocolate cake!'

'Yes, it gets the digestion in the mood. But what did she make of Bobby Miller's news?' she asked.

'She thought it intriguing, and worrying, of course.' Miss Busby's tone was stern. 'But she added that we ought not to speculate.'

Adeline huffed. 'Not much of a newshound, is she. I'd have thought she'd be tearing off on the hunt for an exclusive.'

'I rather think she learned her lesson last December. Flying off half-cocked can do more harm than good, if you recall.'

'But it's strange Isabelle,' Adeline fretted. 'I mean if a fresh murder has taken place, then *someone* has found the body and called the police, and the ambulance most likely. That sort of news travels in the blink of an eye. And yet we haven't heard a dickie bird.'

Miss Busby thought she had a point; the silence was almost unsettling. 'We can't ask around or we risk dropping Bobby in trouble.' Her tone brooked no argument. 'Don't forget, *we* wouldn't even know about it if he hadn't told us.'

That gave Adeline pause. They knew it didn't involve Ezekiel, as they'd halted for a quick look through the bookshop window en route home to Bloxford. With their friend safe, there didn't seem any tearing sense of urgency. 'In that case, tell me what you learned this morning,' she said.

'I think it would be better to discuss everything with Lucy later. It'll save us going over it all twice.'

'We should update your notes, at least,' Adeline decided. 'Shall I fetch your notebook?'

'It's on the davenport. Let's go through, the evening light in the living room is perfect. Did you notice Harrison's Haberdashery wasn't locked?' Miss Busby settled at the desk and flicked through the pages. 'Here.' She tapped her pencil beneath a note. '*Other two shop attics used for storage. All Fowler windows secured, as are the shop doors.* Yet we walked straight in with Mrs Harrison.'

'She may lock up at night,' Adeline pointed out, reading over her shoulder. 'I would have thought it likely, as both her immediate neighbours do the same.'

'Yes, cloth and thread can't be as valuable as the medicines at Fowler's, and Rose has no reason to fear attack like Ezekiel, but she would be terribly out of pocket if her stock were stolen,' Miss Busby mused. 'But if we are looking for a point of entry, Harrison's is the obvious choice. We should look for evidence of a break-in.'

'And we need to get into Rose's attic,' Adeline declared. 'I should have thought of it while we were there. She rather derailed me, becoming so upset.'

'We can add that to our list for next time. Although, we ought to be gentler with the poor woman.'

'Isabelle!' Adeline proclaimed eagerly, making Miss Busby jump. 'If the shop isn't locked we could look there tonight! And if it is locked, our question will be answered all the same.'

Miss Busby turned and looked up at her friend. 'We are not cat burglars, Adeline,' she said tartly.

'Of course not, but we could learn all we needed without upsetting Rose further,' she reasoned.

Miss Busby was silent for a moment, waiting for Adeline to perhaps smile and insist she'd been joking.

She did not.

'Adeline, you can't possibly be serious.'

'Why not?'

'Well, never mind the ethics of it,' she flustered, thinking it ought to be obvious, 'what if we were seen?'

'Whoever broke in to murder Gabriel Travis wasn't seen,' she noted. 'And we could wear black. I've a rather nice dress which would–'

'Adeline, *really*.' Miss Busby shook her head in disbelief. 'We will call in and *ask* Rose tomorrow.'

'It's that adjoining wall, Isabelle,' Adeline continued determinedly. 'It has to be. Are you sure we oughtn't–'

'Quite sure.' Miss Busby turned her attention back to her notes. Under *Harrison's Haberdashery* she added that Rose had stopped volunteering at the workhouse after getting married, and beneath this noted, *Old clothes? Rag and bone?*

'Rag and Bone what?' Adeline asked, peering over her shoulder.

'I bumped into the Rag and Bone man in Chipping Common yesterday. Well, Barnaby did at least.'

'That's hardly noteworthy,' Adeline remarked. 'There are plenty of them around.'

'Yes, I know, but sales from rags and scraps cropped up in the workhouse irregularities you mentioned.'

'Well it would hardly have been the same man.' Adeline *tsked*. 'Really, Isabelle, you are fixating on the strangest intricacies when the question of access is far more pressing. And I haven't told you about my visit to Hale Court yet, or what was said.'

'Oh yes.' Miss Busby closed her notebook and set it on the desk. 'We can discuss it this evening. I must just freshen up a little before we leave.'

'Ahh, of course. Sir Richard will be joining us...' Bright mischief returned to Adeline's eyes.

Miss Busby fixed her with an iron stare. 'Perhaps you'd like to clear the tea things,' she suggested, heading for the stairs. 'And I'm sure Barnaby would appreciate a turn around the green before we go.'

* * *

Adeline parked the Rolls beside Sir Richard's Austin Twenty some thirty minutes later. Miss Busby checked her wristwatch. She had exchanged her blouse for a cream twin set and simple jacket with a single string of pearls.

'It doesn't do a man any harm to wait,' Adeline said pointedly. As Miss Busby alighted, she strode towards the heavy front door of Little Minton's largest, and most genteel, public house. Built in honey-coloured Cotswold stone, The Crown sported two overflowing hanging baskets either side of the door; filled with sweet woodruff, mint, lemon balm, oregano, and chives, the herbs were as practical as they were pretty. Taking a moment to smell the mint, Miss Busby followed Adeline inside and found Richard and Lucy at a large table laid for five in the far corner.

'Isabelle!' Sir Richard Lannister rose with the aid of his stick and kissed her hand gallantly. Impeccably dressed in a smart linen suit and tie, he made her glad she had thought to change for dinner. 'I hope you don't mind me tagging along?' he asked. 'I rather rattle in the house when the offspring are absent.'

'Not at all, it's always a pleasure to see you.' Miss Busby found her hand creeping up to check her hair was in place. She distinctly heard a most unladylike snort from Adeline's vicinity.

'I've dispatched Anthony to the bar and suggested he order you a sweet sherry.'

'Thank you,' Miss Busby replied.

'Lucy mentioned you've had a long day. And she said there's talk of another death! Nothing has been reported to the paper. We're all agog for more news.' He pulled out a chair for her and saw her comfortably settled.

Adeline cleared her throat.

'Mrs Fanshawe, where are my manners! Good evening.' He offered a courteous bow and pulled out a second chair. 'What can we get you to drink?'

'Most kind,' she smiled graciously. 'A sweet sherry would–'

'Lemonade for Mrs Fanshawe. She is driving, and

will need her wits about her,' Miss Busby cut in, as Richard waved a hand to Anthony at the bar.

Adeline gave her a hard stare.

Drinks ordered, Anthony ambled over, his dress as casual as his demeanour. Blue slacks paired with a blue and white striped shirt, no tie. His dark hair fell rather longer than it ought to over his ears, but his wide smile drew the eye away.

'Hallo Miss B, Mrs F,' he called. 'I hear our body count is rising.'

Lucy groaned from her seat. 'I swore my father and brother to secrecy, Miss Busby. Not that you might think it.'

'Sorry, was I shouting? I don't realise, sometimes. It's from the shelling,' he explained as he sat down.

'So you still don't know who it is, either?' Miss Busby asked.

'No, we hoped you would,' Lucy replied.

Miss Busby shook her head. 'The news will be out soon enough, I suppose.'

'I'm astonished it isn't already,' Adeline said, eyeing her lemonade with a frown.

'So, who do we suspect?' Anthony leaned across the table, a mischievous spark in his eyes.

Miss Busby smiled. The young man was utterly charming. 'Murderer, or victim?' she threw back, a spark of her own igniting.

Adeline bristled. 'Well, there's a fine thing. When *I* speculate–'

'Here we are, then.' The landlady, Mrs Harbottle, appeared with a tray of drinks. 'There's vegetable soup and the special's steak and ale pie with green beans and mash.'

Lucy and Miss Busby chose the soup, the others plumped for the pie. The landlady bustled off, maintaining the air of being rushed off her feet even though the pub was quiet that evening.

'You don't suppose the constable could have been referring to Lady Felicity Spencer?' Anthony asked.

'Hardly,' Richard said. 'Everyone knows she's dead.'

'Yes, but everyone thinks she died because she was ill. And ancient,' Anthony countered.

Adeline bristled.

'Apologies, I meant no disrespect, Mrs F,' he added hastily. 'Lucy, you said the constable mentioned another one had *been killed*?'

'Yes,' Lucy answered, looking to Miss Busby, who nodded.

'Could refer to circumstances discovered after the fact, I should say,' Anthony went on. 'Just like the poet fellow.'

Miss Busby paused, a small sherry halfway to her lips. 'I hadn't thought of it like that,' she admitted, rather impressed. 'Although I had thought it a remarkable coincidence, two deaths in quick succession.'

'This inspector of yours may have found the same whatever-it-was in Lady Spencer's case, and reached the same conclusion.'

Richard beamed at his son with pride. 'You'd make a decent detective yourself!'

'He'd make a darn sight better job of it than that—'

'I imagine the skills are somewhat interchangeable,' Miss Busby cut across Adeline while reaching into her bag for her notebook. She wasn't entirely convinced of the idea, not being able to imagine who would want to murder a penniless poet *and* a moneyed matriarch. It could still be nothing more than a coincidence but it warranted consideration all the same. She added the question to her notes, then moved on to their chat with Mrs Harrison. 'Rose mentioned Cameron Spencer was away soldiering at the time Alice disappeared,' she said. 'Does that fit with what you were able to find out, Lucy?'

'Yes, I checked the records. His battalion didn't get any leave at all over Christmas.'

'Could he have come back unofficially?'

Anthony laughed. 'I'm afraid, not, Miss B. It's not like playing truant from school!'

CHAPTER 21

'Tell Miss Busby what you told me about Martin, Anthony,' Lucy prompted.

'Oh, yes. I forgot about him when you first mentioned Chipping Common. Bit of a rogue by all accounts, if it's the same chap. Hung around with Cameron a fair bit. Handsome sort.'

Richard spluttered into his stout.

'Not to me,' Anthony laughed. 'But it's why I remember him. And why half of the girls in Belgium do too I shouldn't wonder. He was very popular among the ladies.'

'Anthony, that's enough of that,' Richard scolded.

'Martin is rather striking, I agree,' Miss Busby confirmed, waving Richard's objection away. 'If rather abrupt in his manner. But his mother was adamant he wouldn't have had anything to do with Alice.'

'Oh, mothers always are,' Adeline said dismissively. 'Rose Harrison was just the same in defence of Alice.'

'It's the age, I'm afraid,' Lucy said. 'The youngsters, I

mean, not the mothers. Caught between two states, if you will. Old enough to get themselves into trouble–'

'And die on the battlefield,' Anthony pointed out solemnly.

'Yes, but still young enough to seem like children in their parents' eyes,' Richard concluded.

Adeline considered a moment. 'Madeleine Spencer is little more than a girl herself, yet she was equally protective of Cameron.'

'Adeline paid her respects to the Spencer family at Hayle Court this morning,' Miss Busby explained.

'Do tell!' Anthony leaned forward as all eyes turned keenly now to Adeline, who suddenly sparkled.

'Well, I went at the appropriate "visiting hour" although there weren't many there, despite the elaborate mourning wreath hung on the door. All the Spencers save Madeleine were too distraught at the loss of their matriarch to receive,' she began with aplomb, enjoying being the centre of attention.

Miss Busby recalled Mrs Olivia Spencer's fierce stare in the church the previous day, alongside her daughter's announcement that she was unable to speak. She attempted to attribute both to grief. It was rather a stretch.

'I was shown into the drawing room,' Adeline continued with a wave of the hands. 'Absolutely beautiful decor, mirrors duly covered in the Victorian style, and all the clocks were stopped – but no refreshments!' She widened her eyes at that. 'I suspect young Madeleine was rather overwhelmed,' she added graciously. 'I offered my sincere condolences, naturally, explaining that I played bridge with Lady Felicity some years ago, and often ran into her at the opera. In truth, I had always found her to be rather difficult, but naturally didn't say so, given the circumstances.'

Lucy gave a light laugh.

'They say people improve with age,' Anthony remarked. 'And never more so than when they die – then they positively augment.'

Miss Busby smiled into her sherry.

'Madeleine thanked me, naturally,' Adeline continued. 'And she passed me a beautifully handwritten invitation with details of Friday's service. It was the most luxurious sort–'

'And did you manage to ask about Alice?' Miss Busby nudged her along.

'I was coming to that, thank you, Isabelle.' Adeline sniffed, then took a moment to sip her drink. 'I asked how her brother, Sir Cameron, was keeping, and then rather casually threw in that Chipping Common seems to attract mystery. I added that I understood he'd got on well with the girl who had disappeared. Miss Spencer was then spurred into something of a minor tirade.' She raised her brows meaningfully.

'Ah, takes after her grandmother,' Richard observed. 'Formidable woman!'

'What did she say?' Lucy asked, taking a small notebook and pencil of her own from a pocket rather cleverly hidden in her skirt.

A born reporter, Miss Busby thought.

'She said that there was no *getting on well* about it, rather that Alice had hounded Cameron following his kindness, as she put it, in acknowledging *the stray's* existence.'

'Steady on,' Anthony objected. 'What an awful phrase.'

'How strange, that's exactly how Mrs Fowler referred to the girl,' Miss Busby commented. 'As a workhouse stray.'

'The Spencers are an old family,' Richard said, as if this excused it. 'Traditional sort.'

'Well, so are we,' Anthony replied. 'And neither Lucy nor I would be so crass. Besides, Cameron talked about the girl with respect.'

'It does seem the young men treated Alice with more respect than the young women,' Miss Busby observed, and told them about the girl in the post office. 'I suspect the antipathy came from jealousy. Alice was said to have been rather beautiful.'

Anthony's smile returned. '*Divine*, Cameron said, if I recall. Petite, too, and rather delicate.'

'Anthony, you couldn't recall Alice's name,' Lucy pointed out. 'What if Cameron had been talking about someone else?'

He shrugged rather good-naturedly, Miss Busby thought, given the accusation.

'I'm quite sure I recall Cameron being the opposite of the likes of Fowler when it came to talking about girls. Martin, for example, would more likely have said–'

'Thank you, Anthony,' Richard interjected sternly.

'We really ought to talk to both of them,' Miss Busby said, noting it down.

'Yes, straight to the horses' mouths,' Adeline agreed. 'Madeline was *convinced* Alice had designs on her brother,' she went on, drawing attention back to herself. 'Said she'd caught the girl "hanging around the grounds" more than once, and had to send the staff out to shoo her away.'

'But why was she so concerned?' Miss Busby asked. 'If it had been his mother, or grandmother ordering the shooing, that would be more understandable.'

'Typical baby sister, by the sound of it.' Anthony inclined his head in Lucy's direction. 'Fussed over endlessly by the parents and thinking themselves the ruler of the roost. Happens a lot.'

Lucy gave him a swift kick under the table.

'Why so interested in Alice though, Miss B?' Anthony asked, rubbing his shin. 'I thought this was all about the poet. Madeleine Spencer is hardly likely to have shot him.'

'I wondered the same,' Richard confessed. 'Although the missing girl is interesting, of course.'

'They both make good stories,' Lucy said. 'I think local readers will put the two together and link them. The more we can find out, the better.'

'Yes, but is all this good for *you*, Isabelle?' Richard asked, concern etched on his features. 'This detecting must be awfully wearing.'

Miss Busby had certainly found herself feeling tired

of late, and the issue had rather taken over, but she was loath to admit it. 'It's just a few questions in order to help Mr Melnyk,' she said.

'Isn't he off the hook now, though?' Lucy asked.

'Being *off the hook* is hardly the same as having one's name cleared,' Adeline objected.

'Things might all change when news of this other murder breaks,' Anthony said. 'Even if it wasn't old Lady Felicity who was done in, it'll be a whole new can of worms either way.'

'You see?' Adeline huffed. 'All this supposition, and if we had simply gone straight to the station as soon as we heard—'

'We should still be none the wiser, because they wouldn't have answered our questions,' Miss Busby insisted. 'Patience, Adeline.'

'Ah, patience indeed,' Sir Richard declared as Mrs Harbottle approached with piled plates. 'No talk of murder over dinner, that is an absolute rule of mine. Good lord, those look wonderful!'

Miss Busby sighed contentedly. Mrs Harbottle had outdone herself: the soup of leeks, peas, new potatoes, and spinach had been cooked together and seasoned with dill and parsley. Warm crusty rolls and salted butter had been the perfect accompaniment, along with good friends and a welcome break from missing girls and dead poets.

Richard pushed aside his empty plate and sat back, hands resting happily on his stomach. 'Wonderful,' he proclaimed. 'We must do this more often. Perhaps I should give Chef two nights a week off. He doesn't hold with pies, I'm afraid.'

'Do they do pudding?' Anthony asked, looking hopefully to the bar. 'I'll go and ask.'

'He's a bottomless pit,' Lucy said. 'Shall we have coffee?'

'You should, Lucy, as I've decided you're driving us home,' Richard said. 'I'll have a digestif. What would you like, Isabelle?'

'Coffee please,' Miss Busby said.

'You will be awake all night. We are not as young as we once were. Have a hot cocoa. And one for me, please,' Adeline added.

'I'll go.' Lucy sprang up and went to join her brother.

'If you'll excuse me, I shall just be a moment.' Adeline got up too and made her way to the Ladies.

'Alone at last!' Richard quipped, a gleam in his eyes.

Miss Busby gave him a smile before beginning to stack the plates neatly on the table.

'I really do worry that you're taking on unnecessary strain with this murder business,' he said. 'I'm sure Mrs Fanshawe is perfectly capable of looking after her friend's interests without you.'

'Perhaps, but Mr Melnyk has become my friend too,' Miss Busby replied.

'Well tomorrow you can contact this inspector chap of yours, tell him everything you and Mrs Fanshawe have dug up, and then be done with the whole business. He gets paid to do this, you know,' Richard chided.

Miss Busby sat up sharply. 'Or perhaps the inspector will welcome our help.' It was unlikely, she thought, but he might need it and that was almost the same thing in the long-run. 'Either way, I shall decide for myself,' she declared, sounding just like the school teacher she had been.

Richard's face fell. 'Oh, yes of course, I wasn't suggesting…'

Miss Busby felt that he had indeed been suggesting, and she wished he wouldn't. She had come to manage her own affairs quite nicely over the years, and didn't appreciate anyone else thinking they had a say in them.

'I'm having jam roly poly with custard,' Anthony announced happily, retaking his seat before darting a concerned look between the pair of them.

'Everything alright?'

'Yes, thank you.' Miss Busby smiled. She felt rather proud of herself, she realised, for making her point.

'I'll bring your coffee and cocoas in a moment.' Mrs Harbottle appeared along with Adeline. Richard's discomfort was swallowed up in a rush of the table being cleared, Adeline deciding that she, too, would like pudding and custard, and Lucy wavering but ultimately holding firm.

Mr Harbottle, a tall and muscular fellow with a thick moustache and distinct look of disapproval, appeared with Richard's digestif and a small glass filled with a violent yellowish-green liquid.

'Good Lord, what on earth is that?' Adeline asked, eyes wide.

'Absinthe, that's mine, thank you.' Anthony grinned as the glass was placed in front of him. Mr Harbottle muttered something under his breath as he left.

'Abswhat? Sin?' Adeline asked. 'It certainly looks ungodly.'

Anthony laughed. 'It's wormwood and anise, essentially. I grew rather fond of it in Belgium. It's banned over there, of course. And in France, Switzerland, America too, now. But where there's a will.' He smiled and took a sip.

'Why is it banned?' Adeline's confusion intensified.

'Wormwood…' Miss Busby mused, her brain shifting into high gear. 'It can be poisonous in high enough doses.'

'Then why on earth is Mrs Harbottle selling it?' Adeline demanded.

'It's very popular in Oxford,' Lucy said. 'I expect they keep it in for the students. Oscar Wilde used to drink it.'

'Is it poisonous or not?' Adeline looked from Lucy to Anthony, brows almost comically creased.

'Wormwood can be, absinthe isn't, but that's no good reason to drink it.' Richard's tone was stern. 'We are enjoying a quiet meal with friends, Anthony, not a drunken carousal with your army chums.'

'I'm only having one.' He smiled and lifted his glass.

'Isabelle, have you heard of this drink?' Adeline asked. She turned to Miss Busby, who seemed lost in thought.

'Oh, Adeline!' She came to. 'I was going to tell you at Melnyk's, and then you mentioned Travis' belongings and I forgot all about it!' She raised a hand to her forehead in disbelief. Had Richard been right, she wondered? Was it all getting too much for her? *No, of course not.* There had simply been so much discussed over the past three days, that was all. Anyone could miss a detail.

'Forgot about what?' Adeline pressed.

'The poison.'

Anthony darted a concerned look into his now empty glass.

Adeline took a sharp breath. 'I thought we had just ascertained–'

'I had lunch with Nurse Delaney, and she thinks Travis may have been poisoned,' Miss Busby explained.

'With absinthe?' Anthony coughed.

'No, with…well, I'm not entirely sure, but it would show on a post-mortem. She thinks they might have found a substance, and discovered it was murder dressed as suicide.'

'Aha! And I imagine they have now detected the same in Lady Felicity's case,' Anthony declared. 'And of course, as we all know, poison is a *woman*'s weapon!'

Silence fell for a moment, before Adeline gasped, 'Madeleine!'

CHAPTER 22

Miss Busby jumped at the sharp knock on the front door. Looking up from her book to the clock on the mantel, she saw that it wasn't yet 9 o'clock. She had only just finished her breakfast and settled down on the sofa with the latest Wodehouse minutes before.

'Really, Adeline,' she complained, opening the door as she bent to brush away a piece of lint that had caught her eye on her maroon skirt. 'I know you're keen, but I was rather hoping—'

'Good morning, Miss Busby.'

The deep Scots lilt stopped her in her tracks, and she looked up to see the tall figure of Inspector Alastair McKay on her doorstep. Clad in his customary dark suit, his expression stern, the sun illuminating his fiery red hair from behind rendered him quite the imposing figure.

Oh Lord, she thought. *Now I shall be in trouble.*

'Good morning, Inspector. What a surprise. Do forgive me, I was expecting Mrs Fanshawe.'

'Aye, I'm sure you were. I hear the pair of you've been indulging in a fair amount of *detecting*, in spite of my advice.'

Miss Busby bristled at his emphasis on the word. It saddened her to think that the respect, possibly even friendship, that had grown between them last year with the apprehension of Vernon Potter's murderer had so soon been replaced by the distrust he had shown when they first met. It was as if all her assistance with the case had been struck from his memory.

'And we hear you have been indulging in rather a lot of *suspecting*,' she parried. She had no desire to antagonise the man, but she certainly would not stand back and let him get away with any unpleasantness scot-free.

Scot-free, she thought with a smile. *Adeline would appreciate that one.*

'Suspicion is my profession, Miss Busby,' Inspector McKay reasoned. 'Traditionally followed by detecting. And detecting,' he went on, lifting himself up onto his toes for a moment, as if to highlight his importance, 'is far more difficult when civilians persist in muddying the waters.'

Pud did the same thing, Miss Busby thought as she watched the inspector: when feeling threatened by Barnaby he would rise up onto his tiptoes and arch his back. Barnaby would have no truck with it, and neither would she.

'As a retiree, Inspector,' she said, 'I enjoy a fondness for my neighbours and a keen interest in local affairs.

This enjoyment is far more difficult to attain when your professional suspicions persist in muddying the waters.'

'*Hum*,' he managed, after a rather drawn-out pause.

'Indeed,' said Miss Busby. 'As with most things, you'll find it works both ways.' Nodding curtly, she fought her naturally hospitable urge to ask him in with a brisk, 'Was there anything else?'

When he had declined her invitation on the Monday she'd heard of Travis' death, it had stung her a little. She'd felt the two of them had shared a spark of warmth last Christmas Eve, and although she would never admit it to Adeline, his recent coldness had pained her.

The inspector seemed to soften under her stare. 'I wonder if you have a moment to talk,' he said politely.

Miss Busby's shoulders dropped a little; she hadn't realised she'd become quite so tense, and her heart felt lighter as she ushered him inside. The man had a difficult job to do, she reminded herself, and his manner was naturally gruff. There was no use taking it personally.

'Coffee?' she asked, as Barnaby trotted over.

The inspector nodded, then took a step back as Barnaby issued forth a low rumble.

'You kept the wee dog, I see,' he muttered.

'Yes, but he can only see Mrs Fellows when Matron isn't about.' Miss Busby went through to the kitchen, calling over her shoulder, 'Do sit down, Inspector. Barnaby, *leave*.'

When she returned she saw that Pudding had settled

into the inspector's lap on the sofa. The ginger tom's engine-like purr seemed to have soothed him further into a better mood, and she caught him looking down fondly as he scratched behind the cat's ears.

'I see you have made a friend.' Miss Busby's blue eyes warmed as she set the tray down on the coffee table.

'One of your animals likes me, at least.'

'Oh, I think it's more a matter of whether or not you like them,' she pointed out.

He eyed the Jack Russell sitting ramrod straight on the rug, and lowered his brows in mock fierceness as the dog steadily returned his gaze with a low rumble in his chest.

'I understand the police force in the north are starting to use dogs to help their officers,' she offered in defence of her canine companion. 'Terriers, even. They have wonderful noses.'

'I couldn't say,' he replied and gave up trying to out-stare the dog.

Coffee poured, shortbread fingers neatly waiting on a pretty plate – his favourite biscuits, she recalled – Miss Busby sat back in her armchair and looked expectantly at her visitor.

It didn't take long. He leaned carefully across the cat, stirred two sugars into his cup, and announced, 'We have uncovered another murder in Chipping Common.'

'Goodness!' Miss Busby affected surprise and even remembered to clutch her pearls. 'Who?'

'Alice Albion.'

Her affected surprise became genuine and she dropped her hand. Whilst she hadn't been entirely sold on Anthony's theory regarding Lady Felicity Spencer, it had seemed plausible and well-reasoned nonetheless.

'You know about Alice, of course,' he went on, studying her expression carefully.

'Yes, I've met her adoptive mother, Mrs Harrison. I assume you've broken the news to her, she must be heartbroken. What happened to the poor girl? And how do you know it was murder?'

The inspector leaned forward. 'I thought to ask you the same; I wondered if you'd be a step ahead of me.'

'Oh, but I'm only a *civilian*, Inspector,' she countered with faux modesty, noting that he hadn't answered her question.

He had the grace to fidget in his seat, causing Pudding to turn and glare. Miss Busby took a sip of her coffee and a moment to think. A faint, half-formed suspicion – so nebulous she hadn't yet discussed it with anyone – began to coalesce.

'You were fortunate in your detecting endeavours last year,' the inspector conceded, 'but it doesn't do to push your luck.'

'Ah.' She put her cup and saucer down on the table. 'I was beginning to think you'd forgotten.'

'Of course not,' he said softly.

Miss Busby eyed him thoughtfully. 'We worked rather well together, didn't we? In solving the murder at Little Minton.'

'Ye-es,' he agreed hesitantly. 'After a fashion.'

'And we learned a great deal.'

'Yes, we learned the identity of Potter's murderer.' He was on firmer ground here.

As far as Miss Busby was concerned they had learned a great deal more. How people would talk at length to a friend or neighbour when they wouldn't offer more than a word or two to a police officer. How things often weren't as they appeared, and how it was no use approaching matters with blinkers on and refusing help from any quarter.

'And yet the moment you heard I'd spoken to Ezekiel Melnyk you felt compelled to rush to Bloxford and warn me off.'

'You had been fraternising with a suspected murderer and I was concerned for your safety.' His green eyes widened in indignation. 'I thought I had made that clear.'

'*Fraternising*? What a ridiculous word. And I am perfectly capable of taking care of myself, Inspector. Besides, if the risk had already been run, why not at least ask what Mr Melnyk had told me? That was a missed opportunity on your part. Shortbread finger?'

'I– yes, thank you.' He took a biscuit from the proffered plate, thrown somewhat, before regrouping. 'Sergeant Heaton told me Melnyk was friends with Mrs Fanshawe,' he continued, mid-biscuit.

'That's true.' Miss Busby nodded.

'And that Mrs Fanshawe had been most…' He searched for the word. 'Adamant in his defence at the station.'

'Yes, I should imagine so.'

'Well, there you are then.'

'Am I?' Miss Busby didn't follow.

'It seemed to me you were far more likely to be concerned with helping your friend than assisting the investigation,' he explained, taking a final bite of the biscuit.

'Ah, I see. You imagine I have become devoid of moral fibre.' Miss Busby's eyebrows arched.

The inspector choked on his shortbread.

'That's not what I—'

'I do want to help Adeline, of course,' Miss Busby agreed. 'But only in terms of finding the truth. Not *a* truth, palatable to my friends, but *the* truth, Inspector. I had hoped you knew me well enough by now to understand that.'

He looked down at the cat and began stroking him under the chin, clearing his throat awkwardly. 'Yes. I do.' He raised his eyes to meet hers. 'Finding the truth is my job, as much as you feel it your purpose. In my case there is, in addition, a great deal of pressure from above.'

'Well, perhaps the same could be said of me,' Miss Busby suggested with a glance towards the blue sky outside the window.

'Is that why you were seen in St. Mary's Church with Melnyk?'

Miss Busby smiled. 'Perhaps. I see you are rather well informed. The vicar?'

The inspector shook his head. 'Mrs Spencer.'

A spark fired in Miss Busby's mind. Was it possible the woman had something against her? To her knowledge they'd never even spoken. No, surely it had to be her imagination.

'Well, the question is where does all this leave us, Inspector?' she asked. 'Ought we to search for the truth together, as we did last Christmas, or work against each other for no discernible reason?'

He smiled at her phrasing. 'I suppose there's only one answer to that.' He eyed the plate of shortbread hopefully before committing.

'Do please help yourself,' she insisted.

'Together, then, I should say,' he said as he reached for a biscuit.

'Excellent.' Miss Busby smiled as she finished her coffee and sat forward in the chair, hands folded neatly in her lap, eyes bright and eager. 'Now, what *exactly* did you discover yesterday?'

'The skeletal remains of Alice Albion in the Spencer family mausoleum.'

'Oh.' Miss Busby sat back in her chair, mind racing. *Of all the places...* 'Goodness me. How terrible. I assume she'd been there for some time?'

'It would appear so,' he replied drily.

'How do you know it's Alice?'

'The pathologist can tell the sex and approximate age from the skeleton,' he explained. 'Which is enough for an educated guess in the circumstances. Dental records will confirm it.'

'Not too many missing persons in Chipping Common or the environs, I suppose,' Miss Busby suggested.

'No, although the victim could have come from anywhere. Fortunately for us she was left in her clothes, several scraps of which remain. Mrs Harrison has been able to verify the blouse was Alice's.'

'Oh Lord, what an awful thing for her to have to do.' Miss Busby's heart went out to the woman. 'But what makes you certain it was murder?' she asked again.

'She was hardly likely to have crawled into the mausoleum of her own accord to die.'

'No, of course.' Miss Busby ignored his tone. 'But perhaps she had arranged to meet someone, and become trapped. It could have been a tragic accident. When was the mausoleum last opened?'

'I'm curious as to why you took such an interest in Alice,' the inspector said. Miss Busby noted his evasion of the question.

'Well, you did say you suspected I'd be a step ahead.' She took a sip of her coffee. 'It's only natural,' she reasoned before he could object. 'Travis was murdered next door to where a girl disappeared without a trace. Any enquiring mind would wonder at a connection.'

'Even after six years?'

'When you get to my age, Inspector, six years is no time at all.'

He appeared unconvinced. 'I'm sure I needn't remind you this is a very serious matter. We are now dealing with two victims.'

'Just like last time,' Miss Busby mused. Part of her wanted to add that perhaps he oughtn't to have waited for the second body before coming to her, but it wouldn't help matters.

'Yes, well, at least there's nothing inflammatory in the local press this time,' he huffed.

'Oh, Lucy fries bigger fish these days,' Miss Busby said, 'although she has taken an interest all the same. Along with her brother, Anthony Lannister.'

'Lannister? I thought her name was Weasley?'

'Wesley.' Miss Busby frowned at him. 'She used to use her mother's name when reporting, but now writes as herself.'

The inspector pulled a notebook from his jacket pocket. 'Anthony Lannister was at the front with Cameron Spencer,' he read.

'Yes, they were in the same battalion. As was Martin Fowler.'

The inspector's head shot up. 'The Ox and Bucks. You have been thorough. Why didn't you come to me with this information sooner?'

'You made it quite clear you didn't want my help. Besides, we were waiting until we were sure of several points. We were in fact on our way to see you yesterday,' she said, 'when...'

'When what?'

'Something cropped up.' She felt her cheeks flush, and then remembered she wasn't the only one holding back. She hastened to switch tack. 'How did you know Travis had been murdered?'

'We have our ways,' he replied cagily.

Miss Busby was in no mood for games. 'He was poisoned, I imagine.'

The inspector's expression remained inscrutable. Miss Busby rose to the challenge.

'I suspect the sergeant and the ambulance men missed it because of the clever staging, but the pathologist would have noted some small subtlety that escaped them.' She was unclear on the details past this point, but it appeared she had done enough to convince him.

'Aye,' he conceded, a mixture of annoyance and admiration in his expression. 'Travis' lips were cherry red when he arrived at the morgue. A clear sign of carbon monoxide poisoning, or possible cyanide toxicity.'

Miss Busby sat back, her mind lighting up as the pieces began to click together.

'Cyanide would be picked up in a toxicological examination,' she said, remembering Nurse Delaney's words. Miss Busby made a mental note to buy the nurse a pastry next time she saw her.

'It would.' The inspector nodded, looking rather impressed. 'And as there was no sign of it in this case, we believe carbon monoxide is to blame.'

CHAPTER 23

'The kerosene heater in the attic!' Miss Busby proclaimed, her ankle throbbing at the thought. 'It would have given off fumes. If the windows and the door were closed as usual, and it was left on for a long time...'

'You've been in Mr Travis' rooms?' the inspector asked with a tired air.

'Yes, but only after you returned the key to Ezekiel. He said the room was "airing and tidy now, just as he liked it in the daytime." When Adeline and I first spoke to him he said Travis always shut his door and windows at night in the warmer months.' It was all starting to come together now.

'And did he say why?'

'Yes, because of the moths. They might eat the paper if they got in.'

The inspector looked up in disbelief. 'So the man risked poisoning himself every night? He doesn't sound the brightest spark.'

'His poetry was everything to him,' Miss Busby

explained. 'And he didn't light the heater after dark and he wouldn't have needed it at all in the warmer months, when moths would have been an issue.'

The inspector made a note in his book with one hand, then reached for a third biscuit. Barnaby, no longer able to bear it, gave in and trotted over, his love of shortbread outweighing his distrust of the man in possession of it.

The inspector laughed. 'I don't think so, laddie.'

'You have a lot to learn about making alliances,' Miss Busby chided with a wry smile. She took the last biscuit and shared it with the small dog. 'But if Travis were killed by carbon monoxide poisoning, why the charade with the gun?' she asked, puzzling over it. 'I'm sure you could kill yourself just as effectively, and rather more peacefully, with the fumes if desired.'

'Not in this case. The heater in the attic was small. Even if it was fully fuelled it wouldn't have been enough to kill a grown man.'

'Then why... Ah, it would have been enough to subdue him, of course.' Miss Busby cottoned on. 'So someone must have broken in when he was asleep, lit the heater and let the gas do its work.'

'It's a bit more complicated than that. They would have had to leave the room, to ensure they weren't also affected. Which again points to Melnyk as the only reasonable suspect, unless we are to believe someone broke in twice.'

'Or unless that someone had a gas mask.' Miss Busby was thinking aloud.

The inspector sighed. 'Have you been reading detective novels again?'

'Yes, but that's not the point. Gas masks were used at the front, and plenty of young men in the area served.'

He sighed. 'I suppose so.'

'And have you considered squirrels?' she asked, before remembering he wouldn't have the faintest idea what she was talking about. This was the problem with coming together late in the investigation. You tended to forget who you had spoken to about what.

'Squirrels?' The inspector's brow creased in confusion. Barnaby, being familiar with the word, flew to the front window in a frenzy of barking. Despite Miss Busby's stern admonition, he refused to give up. Pudding rose from McKay's lap and left the room in disgust.

'Oh, he won't stop now, he hasn't been out this morning.' Miss Busby raised her voice over the yapping. 'Would you excuse us for a moment?'

The inspector nodded, still looking confused.

As Miss Busby rose to open the front door for the determined animal, she saw her notebook on the desk and crossed to pass it to the inspector. 'I've kept my notes up to date,' she said. 'Why don't you read through them while Barnaby and I attend to matters. Then we can continue our discussion from the same page.'

Taking Barnaby's lead from the hook by the door, Miss Busby hurried him out into the morning sunshine. He made straight for the chestnut tree opposite, home to a family of red squirrels who frequently tormented him by running up and down the front path when he could only look on through the window. After several excited circuits of the tree, he gave up when no rodents were forthcoming and walked back to his mistress with a dejected air.

'Try the hedgerows,' she said, bending to ruffle his ears. 'I'm sure you'll find a vole or two.'

'Oo' you talkin' to, Miss?'

'Good Lord! Not again, Dennis!' Miss Busby clutched her chest in fright at the young postman's sudden appearance.

'Sorry, Miss, I couldn't see the dog from 'ere. Innit beautiful?'

Emerging from behind the inspector's grey Alvis, Dennis ran a hand lovingly along the sleek bonnet.

'It's pleasant enough, I suppose. But where's your post van?' she asked, looking around. Dennis was in his uniform but minus his usual transport.

'I'm on that today Miss,' he muttered, throwing a dark look towards a rusty bicycle propped against the cherry tree at the end of the lane.

'Why?' Miss Busby noticed the post bag was missing from Dennis' shoulder.

'There was an accident earlier this mornin,' he said mournfully. 'It weren't my fault, but the van copped it. Came right round the bend on the wrong side of the road, she did in the middle of Little Minton. There's some people as shouldn't be allowed behind the wheel, if you ask me.'

'Oh, dear.' Miss Busby had a terrible feeling she knew what was coming.

'It was your friend, Miss, the one with the enormous Rolls Royce she leaves parked funny all over the place.'

Miss Busby's stomach began to churn. She was constantly having to remind Adeline to pay attention to the road, and had feared something like this would happen ever since James died. 'Is Mrs Fanshawe alright?' she asked, her voice small and distant. She didn't know what she would do without Adeline, however bossy and frustrating she could be at times. Friends saw through all that sort of thing.

'*She's* fine, Miss. Didn't get nothin' but a bad mood from it all. The Rolls took a batterin' though. And my van, well, you oughter see it Miss, it'd break your heart, the whole–'

'Why on earth didn't she telephone me?' The panic was beginning to fade into a feeling of annoyance. Surely Adeline would have known how worried she'd be if she heard the news from someone else.

'She was goin' to, Miss, but she 'phoned the Chipping Common garage first, from the post office an' all, even after she jus' about killed the post van, which is some cheek if you ask me. And then Sergeant Brierly came out of the police station to see what was goin' on, an' he looked at it an' said as how it was her fault and she oughter be more careful.' He paused to take a breath, before ploughing on, 'Well, she got angry at that, an' they argued right up until Mr Doggett came all the way from Chipping Common garage in his truck, an' then he said as how he's never fixed a Rolls before an' she got cross all over again an' said she'd better go back with him in the truck to make sure he knew what he was doin'.'

Miss Busby couldn't help but smile at that. Adeline knew which end of the car to point forwards, but otherwise gave the impression the rest of it was none of her concern. 'She must have known I'd be worried, though,' she said. It was still rather a wrench that Adeline had prioritised the car.

'Oh yes, Miss, she shouted at me that I had to come an' tell you that you wasn't to worry an' that she'd be seeing Mr Melnyk...' He thought for a moment '...an' Mrs Harrison while she was out that way, an' that p'raps Sir Richard might bring you over later. An' I've only just got here 'cos I had to ride the old post bike an' the bloomin' chain keeps coming off. It wants puttin' in a museum,' he muttered.

'Why didn't you just telephone me from the post office?'

'Oh.' Dennis scratched at his dark curls. 'I never thought of that. What with everyone shoutin' an' all.'

Miss Busby bit back a smile. 'Exactly where did the accident happen?'

'Right in the High Street, Miss, as you come off the big bend by the war memorial. She nearly took that out, an' all,' he muttered.

'But what would Mrs Fanshawe have been doing there so early?'

'Gettin' cakes from Lilly's, Miss. Mrs Trounce came out with a big bag full for her while she was shoutin' at the sergeant.'

'Ah, that explains it. Well, thank you for letting me know, Dennis. And I am sorry to hear about your van. How will you manage the post?'

He gave a long-suffering sigh and pointed to the bike. 'On that, Miss. I oughter get back, it's going 'ter take forever.'

'At least the weather is nice,' she offered as consolation.

'I s'pose. But Miss, why's the inspector here?' His gaze was drawn to the Alvis once more, before he turned wide eyes to her. 'Is it because of the accident? Only I can tell him what happened–'

'It's nothing you need to worry about. Off you go, Dennis.' And then, because he looked so dejected, she added, 'Go to Lilly's Tea Rooms and ask Mrs Trounce for an iced bun. Tell her she may put it on my account.'

'Oh, thanks, Miss! I will! Bye Miss!'

As boy and bicycle rode off unsteadily into the distance, Miss Busby returned her attention to Barnaby. Having cut through to the fields at the back of the cottages to do what needed to be done, he was slowly returning, nose to the ground. Calling him to heel, the pair walked back into the cottage to find the inspector pouring fresh coffee from the pot.

'Your notes are well taken, Miss Busby,' he said with solemn approval.

She smiled as she sat down, Barnaby wandering contentedly back to the rug for a snooze. *High praise indeed!* 'Did you find anything useful?'

'I found something interesting,' he said. *'Who would want to murder both a penniless poet and a moneyed matriarch?'* He arched a quizzical eyebrow.

'Ah.' Miss Busby had forgotten she'd noted that particular suspicion down. It was rather poetic of her, though, she thought.

'I assume by matriarch you're referring to Lady Felicity Spencer?' he asked.

'Yes.'

'So you suspect she was also murdered?' A second brow joined the first, giving him a rather cynical look of disapproval.

'Oh, not really.' She gave a delicate shrug. 'It just seemed rather a coincidence.'

'Hmm, yes. I thought the same to begin with,' he admitted. 'But I checked with her doctor. Lady Spencer had been ill for several months, and her death was anticipated. I didn't see any need to look further.'

'Yes, and I believe her illness was common knowledge within the town?'

'I don't think much escapes any of them,' he agreed. 'Do you mind if I take your notes to the station? I would like to have Constable Miller copy and cross-reference them.'

'Not at all.' She considered a moment. 'Would you mind in turn giving me a lift to Chipping Common? Adeline has…been detained.'

The inspector's expression turned stern. 'I still do not believe it is either advisable or safe to spend time with Mr Melnyk, however harmless he may appear. That's another of the lessons we learned last December, is it not? Appearances can be extremely deceptive.'

'It is.' Miss Busby gave a sad sigh. It had been a hard lesson to learn, and one she often found herself trying to forget. 'I shall be careful, Inspector. I would like to see Mrs Harrison, though, and offer my condolences.'

He considered a moment, then nodded, rising and carrying the coffee tray through to the kitchen for Miss Busby. *What a difference,* she thought, *from the manner in which he had arrived not forty minutes since.* For a brief, guilty moment she caught herself wondering if Adeline's accident hadn't been something of a blessing in disguise. If her friend had been at the cottage when the inspector called, she suspected things would have played out rather differently.

'I shall just be a moment,' she called, heading upstairs to check her hair and select a cardigan. 'Will Barnaby be alright in your car?'

'No!' the inspector shouted categorically from the kitchen.

'You had better leave the back door ajar for him, then,' she called down, not knowing how long they would be.

CHAPTER 24

Guiding the grey Alvis expertly through the bends, dips, and sharp turns of the roads winding through the Cotswold countryside, the inspector left Miss Busby free to think. She took a moment to revel in the view. Even after a lifetime in the area, the beauty of her surroundings still warmed her heart. The thought that murderous intentions could surface in such tranquil surroundings, however, was a sobering one.

If it was common knowledge Lady Felicity Spencer didn't have long to live, she reasoned, the same would be true of the fact that the Spencer family mausoleum would soon be opening. Whoever had left Alice Albion inside all those years ago would have known their crime was about to be discovered. Assuming Alice's killer still lived locally, that is. And was still alive. Of course, if it was the same person who had murdered Gabriel Travis, they must be.

'Squirrels.' Inspector McKay interrupted her thoughts. Miss Busby turned sharply, as if one were nearby.

'You asked earlier if I had considered squirrels,' he prompted.

'Oh, yes, I'd forgotten.' Miss Busby proceeded to tell him about Mary Fellows' squirrel, and the gaps in the loft spaces.

'The panelling was sound and firm, I checked it myself.'

'Did you check the other attics?'

'Well.' He cleared his throat. 'Not yet. There were no visible gaps in Travis' room.' The engine laboured. He shifted gear, looking rather uncomfortable. Miss Busby let the silence draw on and work its magic. 'As the party wall in the attic looked undisturbed,' he eventually added, 'I didn't see a need to probe further.'

'Hmm. But perhaps you will do so now?'

'Because you are still convinced Melnyk is a gentleman and therefore innocent?' The inspector turned briefly to shoot her a look of disapproval.

'Because Harrison's Haberdashery is next door, and unlike Melnyk's Books, I don't believe Rose Harrison's shop would be difficult to break into – that's assuming she is actually in the habit of locking the premises.'

The inspector looked back to the road, where a short, squat omnibus was taking up a good deal of space ahead.

'Our murderer, therefore,' Miss Busby continued, 'may well have used Harrison's as a point of access.'

'Just the one murderer, is it?' he muttered, pulling out carefully to overtake as the red and yellow bus struggled slowly up the hill. Miss Busby looked up and spotted Enid Montgomery in one of the windows. She smiled and waved as the Alvis pulled ahead. 'That's the new community bus,' she explained. 'Spring Meadows have provided it, but they pick up residents of a certain age from all over Little Minton, and once a week there's an outing.'

'A very slow outing, by the looks of it,' he said.

'I should imagine that's half the fun. And yes, I think just the one murderer for both deaths, don't you?' She rested her hands neatly in her lap as the rooftops and chimneys of Chipping Common came into view.

'Two murders six years apart? Once someone gets a taste for murder they don't tend to wait so long before striking again,' the inspector commented, pulling aside to let the rubbish cart pass. Market day was in full flow as the car crawled along the busy high street. The Tolsey, now filled with stalls selling meat, cheese, bread, and vegetables drew people from all over the town like a magnet in the bright morning sunshine.

'Yes,' Miss Busby replied thoughtfully. 'I should imagine whoever murdered Alice didn't have much of a taste for it at all.'

'A reluctant killer?' he asked, turning to her. 'He can't have been that reluctant if he did it twice. Put a fair amount of effort in, too, in the second instance. What do you see as motive?' he asked.

'Oh, love, I should think.'

'Aye. And that's exactly why we don't have lady detectives,' he scoffed.

'I beg your pardon?' Miss Busby's eyes grew as icy as her tone as she turned in her seat to offer the full force of her stare.

'Well…' He fidgeted under her gaze. 'Murder tends to come down to one of two things: money, or lust. Cruel, dangerous things men recognise far more easily. *Love,* as women think of it, rarely comes into the equation.'

She kept her gaze fixed on him, her tone arctic. 'Tell me, Inspector, when you found Gabriel Travis, what was clutched in his hand?'

'Melnyk's gun.'

Miss Busby's nostrils flared slightly as she took a fortifying breath. 'In the other hand?' she asked, tight-lipped.

'A poem to his so-called *Angel of Hayle Court Road.*'

'Alice Albion?'

The inspector's eyes widened before he nodded. 'How did you know?'

'Oh, we are rather good with poetry, Inspector. And emotions. Humanity's gentler side which women recognise far more easily…'

He frowned, then doubled down with, 'There's nothing gentle about a man of Travis' age writing such things about a girl young enough to be his daughter.'

'Ah, but there you are. I believe that's exactly how he saw Alice. As the daughter he lost in the fire.'

'With respect, Miss Busby, you haven't seen the poem in question.' The inspector eased the car off the crowded street and pulled to a stop outside the police station.

She tilted her head slightly, and smiled. 'You are quite right, although I've seen others. You must show it to me, and we'll see which of us has the more suitable temperament for interpretation.' Without waiting for the inspector to either agree, or open the car door for her, she dismounted and stalked into the station.

Entering a bright reception area with several chairs neatly arranged, and eye-catching posters on the walls urging visitors to 'Join the Special Constabulary!' Miss Busby saw a young constable glance up from behind the counter. Thin and wiry, with a haircut so severe as to look almost painful, he appeared entirely disinterested until the inspector's boots sounded on the tiles behind her.

'Sir!' He shot rather comically to attention.

'Where's Miller?' McKay asked.

'Up at Hayle Court with Sergeant Heaton, sir. Asking staff about the–'

'Thank you, Constable Garthwaite.' The inspector swung the counter top open and ushered Miss Busby through to the back, where three doors led off an impeccably clean corridor. Having had a rather eventful morning at Little Minton Station last year, she suspected one would lead to an office, one to an interview room, and one to a cell.

The inspector opened the first door onto a neat office with lino-covered floor, a polished oak desk with two cushioned visitors' chairs in front of it. Opposite was a cast-iron fireplace, its mantel supporting a clock and two small ferns sitting on lace doilies. The frosted window was framed by red gingham curtains and matching pelmet.

'Oh, this is nice!' Miss Busby exclaimed.

The inspector sighed. 'Sergeant Heaton's wife looks after the station. She got rather carried away with the decor, apparently. Please, sit down.'

Miss Busby made herself comfortable while he opened the top drawer of the desk and handed over a sheet of paper. Rather than the beautiful copperplate hand she was expecting, the lettering on the paper was hurriedly scrawled. She looked up in enquiry.

'Constable Garthwaite copied it. The original is official evidence,' the inspector explained, taking the seat behind the desk. 'Gabriel Travis had rather remarkable handwriting,' he continued. Leaning back in the chair, he stretched his arms behind his head. 'Which is presumably why no suicide note was forged and added to the scene.'

She nodded in approval and cast her eye over the first verse. It was easy to see why he might think the poet's relationship with Alice untoward, but of course the inspector didn't have children. *Neither do I, for that matter*, she reminded herself. Although having taught for so long it often felt as though she'd had an endless supply of them.

She read aloud:

'An angel sent from heaven, pure and sweet,
lending wings to my words.
They take flight and soar to you, my star above,
my muse, my dear, my Alice,'

The inspector grimaced.

Miss Busby scanned the rest of the poem, before proclaiming it, 'all rather innocent.'

'Innocent?' he huffed. 'There's a line about "buds and plucking" that I'm sure the man had no business writing.' The tips of his ears turned almost the same shade as the curtains.

Miss Busby found the line in question. 'That's simply a reference to spring. You're awfully cynical, Inspector. Oh,' she went on before he could object, 'he may have written this recently? I wonder what made him think of Alice again after all this time.'

'The fact that her body was about to be discovered and he'd soon be for the noose, I shouldn't wonder. It reads as if he knows she's dead, after all.'

How awful it must be, Miss Busby thought, *to see cruel, dark things above all else*. 'Not necessarily, he could have thought of her as an angel on earth, and *star above* doesn't have to be literal. It's a poem, after all. Besides, someone popping up at that exact time to kill him would have been rather a coincidence, don't you think?'

'Not if he confessed.' Inspector McKay stood and began to pace the room. 'Travis would likely have heard that Lady Spencer was worsening. He may have fallen into a panic, written about the girl, perhaps showed the poem to his only friend, Melnyk, and confessed his terrible crime.'

'Why?'

The inspector stopped, surprised. 'To ease his conscience, or maybe to ask for help in moving the skeleton before it could be discovered.'

'And Mr Melnyk was so thoroughly disgusted he shot Travis? After first gassing him?' Miss Busby asked, disbelief clear in her tone.

The inspector resumed pacing. 'Travis may have been in the process of gassing himself, and Melnyk simply lost patience and finished the job. It was his gun, after all.'

Miss Busby shook her head. 'Ezekiel is patience personified, and speaks so warmly and fondly of Travis he would have to be one of the finest actors in the country.'

'You can't take people at face value,' the inspector reminded her. 'Your local knowledge proved invaluable in Little Minton,' he conceded, 'but Melnyk is far from local. We know nothing of his past other than what he chooses to tell us. And the man is obsessed with books.'

Miss Busby frowned. 'What on earth does that have to do with anything?'

'Stories. Fiction. He surrounds himself with them. What's to say he doesn't fabricate a few of his own?'

'Oh, really Inspector, I suspect we all tell ourselves a story or two from time to time.' Miss Busby gave a disappointed shake of her head. She had encountered McKay's distrust of fiction the previous year, and held no truck with it. 'You must employ a modicum of common sense,' she chided. 'Why would Ezekiel not go straight to the police rather than implicating himself in the whole business?'

'He may have been obsessed with the girl too.' The inspector shrugged his broad shoulders. 'The pair may have been co-conspirators, and turned on each other under the pressure of impending discovery.'

'In which case, why would Ezekiel now risk his own life in defending Gabriel Travis' honour?'

He was silent a moment, before taking the poem back and digging into his pockets for her notebook.

'I'll ask Miller to copy these when he's back, and then return them to you. Thank you, Miss Busby. I do appreciate your time.'

She smiled at his attempted dismissal, and caught sight of a note left on his desk as he replaced the copy of the poem in the drawer. 'Not at all. Shall we check the attic, just to be sure?'

'I shall check the attic, when I have the time.'

'There's no time like the present. I should look from Harrison's side, if I were you. We can go together. I'd like to talk to Rose, and I'm sure your visit will be less distressing for her if there's a friendly face present.'

Miss Busby hadn't been able to read the entirety of the message, but the words "Chief Inspector Long", "Oxford Station", and "Progress report" had been clear.

With the body count doubled, he must now be feeling the pressure. 'I won't go upstairs, or get in your way. I'll simply sit with Rose,' she clarified.

He considered her for a moment, brow furrowed. 'Aye, very well then,' he eventually conceded with a weary air.

When the pair entered the Haberdashery, Mrs Harrison was nowhere to be seen. The bell above the shop failed to summon her, but voices, and sobs, could be heard from the flat above.

'She didn't turn the "closed" sign,' Miss Busby pointed out. 'Should we go up?'

'Mrs Harrison?' the inspector called. 'It's the police.'

'And Miss Busby,' she called.

When they reached the first floor, they found the door to the flat closed. The inspector rapped authoritatively, and a slightly dishevelled Adeline opened the door, eyes widening as she spotted Miss Busby. 'I shan't be a moment, Rose,' she called over her shoulder, before closing the door discreetly behind her. 'We were right all along, Isabelle! The bounder got in through the attic just like your squirrel. Only with a bit more ingenuity in this instance.' She turned to the inspector and her expression hardened. 'You, young man,' she went on before he could object, 'have failed to investigate the neighbouring attic. One of the panels can be removed! You have accused an impeccable man of an abhorrent crime with absolutely no cause. And mark my words, I shall have your badge for it.'

CHAPTER 25

After decades in the classroom Miss Busby was well seasoned in resolving conflict. Adeline herself once noted that had Jacob and Esau been in her charge, the whole issue would have been dealt with in a matter of minutes.

'No one is taking anyone's badge,' Miss Busby said firmly before the inspector could retaliate. 'Adeline, Inspector McKay is here to investigate the attic for himself. Inspector,' she went on, sensing him bristling as she spoke, 'you must forgive Mrs Fanshawe's abrupt manner. She was involved in a motorcar accident this morning and is not herself.'

The pair huffed. They were very alike, Miss Busby thought, as she took both a literal and metaphorical step back to allow the inspector to take control.

He took a breath. 'I sincerely hope, Mrs Fanshawe, that you have not disturbed any evidence in the course of your snooping.'

Miss Busby sighed and slowly closed her eyes.

'Snooping, is it? Well, *I* would have hoped,' Adeline shot back, 'not to have had to *snoop*, had you done your job in the first instance.'

The door to the flat opened and a teary-eyed Rose Harrison peered out. 'Has something else happened?' she asked. 'Oh, I don't think I could bear it.'

Miss Busby raised her eyebrows pointedly at her companions, before turning to Mrs Harrison and saying softly, 'Rose, I was so sorry to hear about Alice. I wanted to come and see how you were. The inspector has come to look upstairs. Mrs Fanshawe was just bringing him up to date.'

Inspector McKay rose up onto his toes, elevating himself above Adeline, who cut quite the imposing figure in her heels. 'I will go straight up, Mrs Harrison, if it's convenient. I may need to bring my sergeant and constable across too.'

'Yes, of course.' She sniffed and nodded. 'Anything to help find the monster who... Oh!' Dissolving into fresh sobs, she simply waved him up.

Adeline darted after him. 'I shall show you—'

'No, thank you. This is a police matter now,' he threw over his shoulder.

'Well, *really*,' Adeline exhaled in disgust.

Miss Busby laid a comforting hand on Rose's arm, directing her back inside. 'We'll sit with you, Rose, while the police do their work. You oughtn't to be alone.'

'Oh, you are kind, thank you. It's all been such a shock. To think...Mrs Fanshawe said the murderer must have been inside…' She shuddered. 'It's too awful.'

'Well, we must let the inspector decide, and perhaps shouldn't worry too much until we know for certain,' Miss Busby said, looking over her shoulder and narrowing her eyes at Adeline, who remained glaring up after the inspector, oblivious. 'Perhaps some sweet tea, for the shock.' Having settled Rose on the sofa, she popped back out to the hall and hissed, '*Adeline!*'

'Hmm?' Her eyes were fixed on the staircase.

'Come and help me with the tea.'

'I don't want any tea, Isabelle. We are forever drinking tea when there are things to be done. I should much rather—'

'The tea is for Rose, and you can tell me what you found in the attic while we make it,' she hissed.

'Oh! Yes, good idea.'

Adeline bustled through to the kitchen and fussed with the kettle and teapot.

'I was worried when Dennis told me about the accident,' Miss Busby scolded. 'Have you seen a doctor?'

'No. I wasn't hurt, simply inconvenienced. That young whippersnapper with the post van needs to learn how to manage a vehicle. And I told him to tell you there was no cause for concern. Biscuits, Rose?' she called through to the living room, before Miss Busby could comment.

'Second cupboard from the left,' came the shaky response.

Adeline fetched a handful while Miss Busby procured a plate. Heavy footsteps thudded down the stairs, before the faint tinkle of the shop bell could just about be heard.

'I wonder if he'll think to flip the sign,' Miss Busby mused.

'I should very much doubt it. Why did you bring him?' she asked accusingly.

'He came to Lavender Cottage this morning and we had a long chat. I lent him my notes.'

Adeline *tsked*. 'He ought to have made his own. Did he tell you about the bones? Poor Rose was distraught when I arrived.'

Miss Busby nodded. 'It seems we were rather off the mark regarding the second murder.'

Adeline waved a hand dismissively. 'We have far more important things to consider now. Come with me.' She suddenly turned and made a dash for the stairs, shouting, 'Shan't be a moment, Rose!' over her shoulder.

'Where are we going?' Miss Busby whispered.

'To show you the panelling while he's out!'

Miss Busby followed Adeline into the attic, a dusty place with boxes shoved haphazardly away from the panelling dividing the two attics.

'Here for all to see.' Adeline indicated a narrow panel at the end of the attic. 'See how these nails have been driven into each corner, and bent over to form hooks? They can be twisted aside to free the panel. I did it myself.' She was quite triumphant, despite talking in a hushed tones.

Miss Busby reached for one of the nails and found it turned easily. 'It looks as though this is very old.'

'Yes, I suppose the attics were used to house servants once upon a time. But look here.' She pointed. 'There's a knot hole. Our murderer could have spied on poor Gabriel through there.'

'Oh, Adeline, well done!' Miss Busby knelt to look through it, and saw nothing but shadow. 'Why didn't we see this from the other side?'

'The bench seat is there, covered in cushions. It's behind one of them.'

Miss Busby pushed her finger through and felt soft fabric. 'Ah yes.'

The bell tinkled from the shop door opening downstairs.

'Quickly,' Adeline said, and they both rushed back downstairs, barely making it to the flat before the inspector and two other policemen thudded up the stairs.

They caught their breath before carrying on making the tea.

'When I went up earlier,' Adeline explained while waiting for the kettle to boil, 'the attic was filled with boxes and trunks. Most of them were thick with dust, but I saw that the dust appeared to have been disturbed in places, so I pulled a few out of the way.'

Miss Busby found herself impressed.

'I realised immediately that our enterprising murderer, our squirrel, if you will, had removed one of the panels to gain access to Travis' rooms.'

'Yes.' Her earlier conversation with the Inspector came back to mind. 'And once inside, he was able to subdue him. It was done with carbon monoxide.'

'What?' Adeline took the whistling kettle from the stove and poured water into the teapot.

'The inspector told me Gabriel had cherry red lips when he was found. He had been rendered unconscious by carbon monoxide before he was shot. Or rather, before he was set into his chair and his death made to look like suicide.' She spoke quietly while arranging a cup and saucer on a tray.

'Good heavens.' Adeline stopped stirring the teapot and gazed at her for a few moments. 'The kerosene heater!' she exclaimed, making the connection.

Miss Busby nodded. 'It certainly looks that way.'

'Well, he's clever, whoever he is! I think they ought to do a post mortem on Felicity Spencer, too, the way things are going.'

'The inspector doesn't think it necessary, given her ill health.'

'Oh, well, if *the inspector*—'

'Adeline, you really must try to be less abrasive with him. He is doing his best. Besides, Lady Spencer's death must have been more of an inconvenience to our murderer than anything else. The longer she lived, the longer the crime would have lain undiscovered. Killing her would have served no purpose.'

'Well…' Adeline's brows furrowed as she considered. 'What if someone killed her precisely *to* uncover the bones?' She brushed dust from the sleeve of her navy and red dress. 'And I am not abrasive, Isabelle. I simply say it as it is.'

Miss Busby decided against arguing the point. 'What happened before you found the panelling this morning?'

'Yes, I am getting to that,' Adeline explained as she filled the milk jug. 'Once I was confident Mr Doggett was fully aware of what needs to be done to the car, I came to ask Rose whether she locks the shop at night, and she said she does. But it's such an easy thing to forget that I thought I ought to look upstairs all the same, and–'

'Wasn't she awfully upset?' Miss Busby asked, hoping Adeline had at least been gentle.

'Yes, of course she was. It took her an age to tell me what had happened, but we got there in the end. Don't give me that look, Isabelle, the poor woman wants to know who killed Alice, she considered the girl her daughter. Anyway, she was perfectly happy for me to go up to the attic. Tea cosy, Rose?' she shouted, making Miss Busby jump.

'In the drawer. Shall I come and help?' came the rather tearful response.

'No, no, we're almost there,' Adeline shouted, then dropped her voice. 'Isabelle, there's a bag of cakes on the side from Lily's Tea Rooms. We may as well share them out. Help me find a bigger plate.'

'Right,' Miss Busby said, arranging the cakes delicately, 'let's take Rose her tea before it's stone cold.'

'What's that terrible noise?' Adeline asked with a start, as an engine laboured outside and several bangs and clashes followed.

Miss Busby listened. 'It's the rubbish cart. We saw it earlier. It must be dustbin day for Chipping Common.'

'Awful racket,' Adeline complained as she went into the sitting room. 'Tea, Rose!'

Rose woke with a start as Miss Busby placed the tray on the table. 'Oh, I'm so sorry, I must have dozed off for a moment. I didn't sleep much last night, not after the inspector told me what had been found.'

'Of course, the news must have been a dreadful shock.' Miss Busby laid a sympathetic hand on her arm before sitting down.

'Yes…and no,' she replied, rubbing a hand over tired eyes. 'Oh, I liked to pretend to myself that Alice had started a new life somewhere, and was doing rather well at it, but of course when so much time passed without a word… Well, I knew. I think we all knew, really.' She took a deep breath. 'I suppose it's good to have it confirmed, after all. Does that sound terrible?'

'Of course not. It's dreadfully sad, but it makes perfect sense,' Miss Busby assured her.

'The hardest thing is realising she was so close for all these years, and we had no inkling.' A small sob escaped her lips.

'Thank goodness you had Mr Harrison with you when you found out,' Miss Busby said. 'I assume he was home at the time?'

'Oh, yes, and he is a comfort, bless him. But...'

Adeline poured the tea and dropped three sugars into Rose's cup. 'But he's a man, and they don't really understand, do they?' she finished, so gently as to surprise Miss Busby.

'No, they don't.' Rose smiled as she took the cup and nodded her thanks. 'He loved Alice, of course, everyone did, but he never quite saw her as his child in the same way I did. Which is only to be expected. We weren't married when I adopted her, you see, and he's rather more...how can I put it without making him sound awful? Rather more conservative than I am, perhaps.'

'He would have been against the adoption, then?' Adeline pressed, dangerous determination flashing in her eyes.

Rose took a sip of tea and considered. 'Not against it, as such, but he wouldn't have thought it wise. A risk, perhaps. But of course he didn't know Alice as I did.'

'You came to know her when volunteering at the workhouse?' Miss Busby pressed, realising she'd never thought to ask before.

Adeline reached for a cake, then passed the plate to Rose, who declined with a waved of a hand.

'I caught my skirt on a nail one afternoon when I visited to discuss a fundraiser, and they sent Alice to me, to effect a repair. Well, she did such a good job that I went back to thank her the next time, with a small gift of a new set of needles. From then on, each time

I went to the workhouse we would talk. Such a lovely girl, really. A kind heart.' Her eyes began to water once more.

Footsteps thumped down the stairs, making Rose jump.

'They'll be dusting for fingerprints, I imagine,' Miss Busby said. 'Inspector McKay will soon have the culprit now.'

Adeline scoffed, then recovered herself, brushing crumbs from her ample chest. 'Yes, the net will be closing in. You mustn't worry.'

'It's just so awful to think of whoever it was, creeping about the place.' Rose shivered. 'Once in a while I'll bring some patterns up here and work on them until quite late, particularly if Fraser is working in London. What if I'd been here when the murderer came in?'

'You mustn't think like that,' Adeline chivvied. 'You may thank the Lord you weren't, which is all one can do.'

'I so rarely go up to the attic now,' Rose explained. 'I do a stock-take once a year, and Fraser helps me with the boxes up there and anything that needs bringing down. It's mostly just old fabrics out of style now, and things I can't bear to part with.'

'You really mustn't trouble yourself,' Miss Busby insisted. 'It may be that the police have the culprit's fingerprints as we speak. Would it be a good idea for you to go home, I wonder?' she suggested. 'I'm surprised you came in today at all, under the circumstances.'

'Oh, I'd rather be busy. No good sitting around the house on my own while Fraser's at the office. But thank you, Miss Busby,' she said. 'You have been a great comfort.'

Adeline cleared her throat.

'And you too, of course, Mrs Fanshawe,' Rose added.

A familiar, sharp knock rapped on the door. Miss Busby stood to open it as Rose dabbed at her eyes.

'Inspector,' she said, taking in his grave expression.

'We need Mrs Harrison to come to the station and have her fingerprints taken, for elimination purposes. And Mrs Fanshawe,' he said, with just a hint of a gleam in his eye.

'What?' Adeline squawked from the sofa, before marching to the door to object. 'I will certainly not have my fingerprints taken like some common criminal!'

'Don't be silly, Adeline. I had mine taken last year,' Miss Busby pointed out. 'I shall leave you to it, Inspector.' She turned back to say her goodbyes to Mrs Harrison and insisting she must telephone if there's anything she needs. 'Adeline, I'll meet you at the Tolsey after you've been printed,' she said, hiding a smile as she left the flat.

'Now, wait just a minute, I–'

'Good day, Inspector.'

'Good day, Miss Busby,' he replied, amusement lifting his tone.

CHAPTER 26

As Miss Busby left Harrison's, the rubbish cart was just pulling away. One of the men was diligently carrying two empty dustbins around the back of the building. 'Aft'noon, Miss,' he said.

Dustbins… A distant bell rang in Miss Busby's memory. Ezekiel had mentioned the back door of Harrison's opening onto an alley where dustbins were stored, and with everything else that was coming to light she had quite forgotten. Glancing around to make sure no one was watching, lest she appear furtive, she crept around to the back for a look.

The alley was wider than average, bound by a high wall which surrounded the local allotments. Harrison's was indeed the only shop with a back door, and a quick rattle of the handle confirmed it was firmly bolted. The small back window, however, was wide open. And directly beneath it stood a sturdy metal dustbin which would provide a boost were anyone so inclined. It would not be too difficult to lean in from there and unbolt the door. Having seen all she needed, Miss Busby left the alley swiftly; the smell of freshly disturbed rubbish was distinctly unpleasant.

As she rounded the building, something at Doggett's Garage opposite caught her eye: a display of kerosene bottles stacked haphazardly outside the workshop. Crossing the road, she went for a closer look.

'Help you, Miss?' a grease-stained young lad asked, wiping his hands on a rag.

'Is Mr Doggett available?'

'Not really Miss. He's under there.' The lad pointed to the interior, where Adeline's Rolls was parked. Miss Busby observed a pair of blue overall-clad legs protruding from beneath.

'If that's Herself again, Kevin, tell her I'm going as fast as I can and interrupting won't make me go no faster,' a grumpy voice called from beneath the car.

Kevin looked at Miss Busby, who gave a shake of her head.

'It 'int,' he shouted back. 'It's another 'un.'

The overalls grunted, but weren't forthcoming.

'Perhaps you could help me,' Miss Busby tried asking the young lad. 'Did you know Mr Gabriel Travis, from Melnyk's Books, opposite?'

'Him as what was shot? Yeah, I did Miss. Strange, that was, an' now there's talk—'

Miss Busby interrupted before the lad became too garrulous. 'Did he buy kerosene from here?'

'No Miss, he hardly never come out. Mr Melnyk bought kerosene though. Are you wantin' some?'

'No, thank you, but I wonder… might you be able to remember anyone who purchased more than usual recently? Perhaps someone who wouldn't normally buy it?'

He scratched his head. 'I don't think so, Miss. I'd ask Mr Doggett,' he nodded toward the man in overalls under the car, 'but he int' in the best o' moods presently. Mr Melnyk bought his usual last week, though,' he went on slowly, as if faced with a difficult problem in his schoolbook. 'Every Friday after work, reg'lar as clockwork, the foreign gentleman is. And there's the vicar,' he counted off on his fingers, 'and Mrs Huggins from the school, and Mrs Fowler, Mr Harrison, and Mrs Sheppard at the post office. They all buy it reg'lar, too.'

'That's very helpful, thank you,' Miss Busby replied. 'How is the motor car coming along?' she asked quietly.

'It's a mess, Miss. She bashed it up good and proper.'

'Oh, dear. Well, these things are sent to try us.'

Leaving the friendly young lad and the grumpy overalls behind, Miss Busby headed for the busy Tolsey building. She wandered about, examining the tempting goods displayed on the market stalls until a familiar red and gold yarmulke came into view. 'Dear lady, I thought it was you! How are you enjoying our market?'

'Ezekiel, how lovely to see you. It's rather impressive; much busier than the market at Little Minton.'

'I can recommend the breads, and the cheeses. There is a most delicious double Gloucester made with chives that is, how do you say? Deathly?'

Miss Busby thought for a moment, then suggested, 'To die for?'

'Yes. To die for! Such a strange expression. If something is good, one should wish to live for it, no?'

He tried to smile but his face was uncharacteristically mournful, and Miss Busby realised that he, too, would have just learned of Alice's demise.

'I am so sorry, Ezekiel, about Alice,' she said. 'It must have been an awful shock. Are you taking a break from the bookshop?' She turned aside as a group of women with baskets over their arms jostled past.

Ezekiel cupped a hand to his ear, then extracted the ear trumpet. 'It is hard for me, I am sorry – there are many voices.'

'Shall we move to the green?' She spoke clearly so he would also be able to read her lips.

Ezekiel nodded, tucked the trumpet away again and took her arm. They headed towards a vacant bench overlooking the pretty green. With so many people out and about it seemed sad no one had the time to sit and enjoy the view, but of course most of them had work to return to, or family to care for. *I only have Pud and Barnaby,* she thought. Then, scolding herself, *but I have my friends, and my health, and that is as much as anyone could wish for.*

'Are you taking a break?' she asked again.

He nodded sadly. 'The news of Alice is most awful. But, dear lady, it has been six years. I think, deep in my heart, I am always knowing she is no more. Alice would never leave us otherwise.'

'Mrs Harrison said much the same. The poor woman is distraught.'

'Of course. For a mother, no matter what the head says, hope in the heart never leaves, I am sure of it.'

'Do you think Gabriel would have been sad?' she asked, not quite sure why the idea popped into her head.

'Oh, he would be heartbroken, of course, but he knew too, I think. Six years, dear lady…who stays away from their loved ones for so long?'

She sighed. 'Yes, of course. I am sure you are quite right.'

'The police are there now, once again looking at his rooms, another reason for me to come away,' Ezekiel continued, sitting beside her and relaxing into the quiet of the open space, the market now a dull buzz in the background. 'I have left a note on the door to say I will soon return to the shop. It does not seem right, to sell books while this awful occasion is happening.'

'Did they tell you what they found at Harrison's?' Miss Busby asked.

'Before I came here, the inspector did show me the hole in Gabriel's room where the murderer watched, and then the panel where he sneaked in.' He shook his head sadly. 'It is an awful thing, but for me it is also a relief – that they can now see it is someone else who is doing this. But I feel most terrible for this relief, because my friend is dead no matter what. And it is my home where this is happening.'

'You mustn't feel bad,' Miss Busby insisted. 'Anyone would feel relief in your situation, I'm sure. It doesn't lessen your grief, and you are not responsible for the evil of others. If anything, you too are a victim.'

'I think the inspector is distrusting me still,' he confessed. 'Even with the finding of the entrance, the gun used to kill was my own. I am lending it to no one, and telling no one of its place. Except for Gabriel, in case the shop is ever attacked.'

Miss Busby thought for a moment. 'Might you have mentioned it to Alice?'

He looked at her in surprise. 'Never. A girl should not know of such things. It saddens me you would think it.'

'Oh, since the war I find girls have become a little different. Young nurses cared for soldiers with terrible gunshot wounds, and many girls worked in the munitions factories. Guns aren't nearly such a foreign concept to them nowadays.'

'Then that is a great shame.'

'Perhaps…'

Miss Busby sat in thought for a moment. *What if Travis told Alice?* she wondered, not liking to upset Ezekiel again by asking – and besides, she thought, how would he know?

It all comes down to who had access to the cash drawer, she mused, *and he has already admitted to not keeping it locked.* Anyone might have stumbled across it whilst looking to steal money, although surely such an incident would have been noted and reported? Her brain fizzed, fingers itching for her notebook. She hoped the inspector would return it to her quickly.

'You say you didn't need to lock the cash drawer, because you lock the shop at night,' she said, casting her mind back to the earlier conversation. 'But the shop is unlocked now?' He nodded. 'Is this something that may have happened prior to Travis' death?' she pressed.

'My home is filled with police, dear lady. It is safe. I have no concern today in leaving the shop open. Before Travis is killed, this does not happen.'

The word "safe" rang in Miss Busby's ears. 'Do you keep a safe for valuables on the premises?' she asked.

He shook his head. 'Many customers pay on account, most often with cheques. I carry these and the cash to the bank each week. There is no need for more than my drawer. I am rich in my friends and my peaceful life here, but not in my pocketbook,' he concluded with a wry smile.

Miss Busby's blue eyes shone with warmth as she placed a hand on his arm. 'We are rich in similar ways, and must never forget how fortunate we are. And you mustn't let the inspector upset you,' she continued. 'He distrusts everyone. I found it jarring at first but am becoming quite used to it.'

'Isabelle!' The unmistakable boom of Adeline's voice rang across the green as she strode towards them.

'Ah, where there is one of you, the other is soon to follow!' Ezekiel smiled and rose to his feet, greeting her warmly as she approached.

'Dear Ezekiel, isn't it the most wonderful news?'

Miss Busby winced. 'The panelling, Adeline,' she clarified. 'Poor Ezekiel has had two items of news today, and the other is not so wonderful.'

'Oh. Yes.' Adeline flushed. 'I am so sorry, Ezekiel. You must forgive me.'

Miss Busby saw his discomfort return as he nodded curtly and said, 'The inspector is most clever in his discovery.'

'Clever my eye!' Adeline exclaimed. '*I* discovered the attic route this morning!'

His eyes widened. 'Then it is to you I owe my thanks, as always.' He bowed graciously, taking her hand and kissing it, before looking more closely at her black-stained hands in confusion.

'The ink. It gets everywhere, I'm afraid,' she said.

'They surely have not taken your fingers too, dear lady?'

Miss Busby smiled. His speech patterns were so endearing.

'I have had to be eliminated from enquiries. Ridiculous, of course. But also rather fun, as it turns out. It tickled!'

Miss Busby's smile turned to laughter at how quickly Adeline's emotions could switch.

As the church bell struck one o'clock in the distance, Ezekiel glanced back towards the market.

'Dear ladies, it has been a delight, but I must return to the shop. Hesitating at the cheese stall, I think, now it has quietened a little.'

'Isabelle, we must be going, too,' Adeline insisted. 'Enid is waiting.'

'Enid?'

'Yes! Didn't you see the omnibus on the high street?' she accused. 'Enid has a table at The Bridge, and they can surely squeeze us in if we're quick. We can enjoy lunch before collecting the car.'

'Very well,' Miss Busby agreed, then halted. 'Oh, that reminds me! Ezekiel?' she called. He turned, tilting his head to one side in polite enquiry. 'Do you recall when you last purchased kerosene for Mr Travis?'

'On Friday,' he replied without hesitation. 'Always Friday after work I am buying more fuel.'

'Even when the weather is clement?' Miss Busby queried.

Ezekiel smiled. 'I am, how do you say? A person of habituals?'

'Creature of habit,' Adeline corrected automatically. 'But why would Travis need fuel when the weather is warm?'

'He would make tea, and sometimes to warm soup and so forth in his rooms in the daytime.'

'I thought he took his lunch with you?'

'Some days, yes.' Ezekiel nodded. 'Other days his

work consumed him greatly. I would take food up for him to warm when his muse permitted.'

Miss Busby remembered her earlier discussion of moths and windows with the inspector. 'And he would always close the windows at night, you say, at this time of the year?'

Ezekiel gave a sad smile. 'Always,' he confirmed.

'Didn't the kerosene fumes affect him?' Miss Busby pressed.

'He would not use the heater at night, dear lady. Following the tragedy of the fire at his home he was always most careful. If he used it in the daytime, he would open the window just a little. But it was never lit at night, when he may have fallen asleep and the flame could have escaped its confines.'

'Ah, of course.' Miss Busby nodded, relieved that it all now made sense. She would have to tell the inspector. 'Thank you, Ezekiel. Will we see you tomorrow, at the funeral?'

'I had hoped so, but Miss Spencer forgot to issue an invitation when I paid my respects, and I would not like to intrude. Such sorrow.' He bowed and touched his yarmulke respectfully, then wended his way to the market.

Adeline tried to chivvy Miss Busby along towards the High Street, but she was deep in thought.

'What is it?' Adeline asked.

'The kerosene heater.' She had stopped, and was frowning. 'The murderer must have left it burning all night – Gabriel certainly wouldn't have done so, and there's no way a week's worth of fuel could have been consumed otherwise. No one would have used the heater since Mr Travis died, and it was empty when I hit my ankle on it.'

'Yes, but we already know the murderer used the heater, Isabelle. What difference does it make whether it was full or not?'

'Whoever broke into Travis' rooms must have known the heater would be fully fuelled that night. The whole plan would have failed if there weren't enough fuel to produce the fumes to subdue him.'

'He may simply have been rather fortunate,' Adeline suggested.

'No, I think he was a clever chap who wouldn't leave something like that to chance. He would have known Ezekiel's habits, which also fits with him knowing of the existence and whereabouts of Ezekiel's gun. It must have been someone local, and not far away. Adeline...' She lowered her voice. 'We must be careful.'

'We are always careful.' Adeline remained unperturbed. 'The question is, *why?*'

'So that we are not next,' Miss Busby answered hoarsely, feeling rather unsafe in her detecting for the first time.

'I mean, *why* would the murderer have gone to all the trouble of such an elaborate charade with the gas and the gun,' Adeline clarified with a rather disappointed look. 'But as you have so much faith in the inspector,' she sighed, 'I'm sure he'll solve the mystery. Now come along. The sandwiches and cakes at The Bridge Tea Rooms are supposed to be second to none, and if we don't hurry, *none* is precisely what we'll get.'

Finding her friend's dogged determination and complete inability to feel fear somewhat heartening, Miss Busby asked drily, 'I thought you didn't want to drink tea when there are things to be done?'

'I don't.' Adeline held her head high as she strode across the road. 'I shall drink coffee.'

CHAPTER 27

Twice the size of Lily's, The Bridge Tea Rooms were completely full – an inevitable consequence of market day combined with bright spring sunshine. An extra chair was procured from the back by a smart young waitress, who converted Enid's table for two into snug seating for three.

'Sandwiches and cakes all round?' the girl asked, laying extra cutlery on the table.

'What are the cooked options?' Adeline settled her substantial frame into the small space.

'Fried haddock with potatoes, or cheese and leek pie. It's on the board, Miss.' The waitress pulled a pad and pencil from the pocket of her starched white apron.

'And today's sandwiches?' Adeline asked, oblivious to the girl's tone.

'Cucumber and dill with cream cheese, ham and mustard, salmon and prawn, egg and cress,' she rattled off, before pre-empting, 'and the cakes are–'

'We will have the sandwiches for three, please,' Enid interjected. 'And a large pot of tea.'

Adeline bristled. 'I may have wanted the haddock.'

'There's hardly room on the table,' Enid pointed out as she shuffled her chair sideways, the sunlight catching auburn streaks in her white hair. Dressed in a silver-grey blouse and black skirt, she looked trim and smart and more like her usual self.

Adeline looked longingly at the larger tables in the centre of the room, all of which were occupied. 'Well,' she huffed in response, 'regardless, I would like coffee with my sandwiches.'

The waitress duly took note and hurried off.

Miss Busby looked about with interest. The walls were papered in pretty, paisley design, and each table boasted a thick white cloth and plushly upholstered chairs in a rich, dark plum. Elegant gilded lights above each table sparkled in sunshine dancing through the tall windows. Exotic plants with arcing fronds were clustered in each corner of the room, and the luxuriously thick, green carpet felt soft and welcome beneath her feet.

'This is lovely, Enid,' Miss Busby remarked.

'I usually come here with Mary on market day for a treat, but she was feeling unwell this morning.'

'Oh, I'm sorry to hear that.' Miss Busby's brow furrowed in concern. 'I do hope it's nothing serious.'

'The doctor said he will call this afternoon,' Enid replied.

'Would you give her our love, and tell her she was right about the squirrel?' Miss Busby asked.

'The squirrel?' Enid's brows rose. 'I certainly will. It

seems I have some news to catch up with? I am so glad you found me, Adeline. In more ways than one.' She shot a marked glance through the window beside them.

On the other side of the road, looking mournfully towards them, was the gaunt figure of a well-dressed, elderly gentleman.

Adeline brightened immediately. 'Your Mr Waterhouse,' she remarked with a mischievous smile. 'I recognise him from Spring Meadows.'

'He is not *my* Mr Waterhouse.' Enid narrowed her eyes at Adeline as Miss Busby peered through the glass for a better look. Seeing her gaze, the gentleman turned and continued walking.

'He must have thought Mary not being with you a gift, and planned to join you,' Adeline said. 'What fun!'

'You have a strange idea of fun,' Enid remarked.

'And you can see that he was a handsome chap,' Adeline expanded.

'Not anymore.' Enid was not to be drawn.

'Expensive looking suit, too,' Adeline continued, undeterred. 'You could do worse.'

Miss Busby winced.

'I could do a great deal better, if I were so inclined,' Enid replied tartly, then turned her attention to Miss Busby. 'What about this squirrel, Isabelle? Have you solved the murder?'

'I'm afraid there are two murders now,' Miss Busby said, the busy chatter all around them dispersing any fear of being overheard.

'Was Lady Felicity Spencer bumped off too?' Enid asked in surprise. 'I read the obituary in the newspaper, but assumed her infirmity had simply got the better of her.'

'That remains to be seen,' Adeline muttered, before Miss Busby asked,

'Were the two of you friends?'

'Not in the least, but we used to move in the same circles.'

'Tell her about the *bones*, Isabelle,' Adeline insisted, keen to move matters along.

Miss Busby winced. 'Bones sound rather disrespectful, don't you think? As if the poor girl has been reduced to nothing.'

'I hardly think she'll mind.' Adeline waved the objection aside impatiently.

'No, but I think I do,' Miss Busby said rather sternly.

'Oh, very well. The skeleton, then, is that better?'

'Marginally, I suppose.' Miss Busby sighed, and told Enid how poor Alice's remains had been found in the Spencer family mausoleum.

Enid listened intently, as Adeline threw in the odd embellishment for good measure.

'Poor Alice, so now three deaths, including Lady Felicity. You seem to be a magnet for them, Isabelle,' Enid remarked upon completion of the tale.

'Tea for two.' The young waitress had reappeared in time to hear part of the conversation, and looked at them warily.

'Thank you.' Miss Busby smiled brightly, hoping to convey she wasn't in the least bit sinister but fearing she was only achieving the opposite.

'And one coffee.' The girl set the drinks down abruptly and hurried away.

'Richard Lannister commented about there being three deaths too,' Miss Busby said. 'I am beginning to find it rather unfair. Lady Spencer had been ill for a long time, and Alice has been dead for years.'

'No one is *blaming* you, Isabelle,' Enid pointed out. 'But how close are you to solving it? All three deaths are connected, I take it?'

'I am convinced Lady Spencer was killed so the tomb would be opened and Alice's skeleton would be found,' Adeline pronounced, adding sugar to her coffee. 'Travis was gassed before being shot…' She went on to explain about the carbon monoxide. 'And I shall eat my hat if Felicity wasn't gassed in the very same way.'

'Is that the same summer hat you will eat if Inspector McKay noticed Travis' handwriting?' Miss Busby asked.

'I have more than one hat, Isabelle.' Adeline was not amused.

'Good, because you'll need to eat that one. I completely forgot to tell you about the poem.'

Adeline and Enid leaned forward as Miss Busby told them about *The Angel of Hayle Court Road*, the poem found clutched in Travis' hands upon his death. And the fact that McKay had, indeed, noted Travis' unusual handwriting.

'Well, you have certainly had a busy week,' Enid said, as a different waitress set a pretty three-tier plate filled with delicate finger sandwiches in the centre of the table. Enid thanked her, saying, 'You must have frightened the young one off, Isabelle,' as she left.

Miss Busby opened her mouth to object.

'Your poet was framed,' Enid declared before she had the chance.

'Framed?' Adeline raised her brows.

'A phrase from a book I read,' Enid explained. 'It means a set-up, or something.' She took one of each sandwich to place them on her plate before continuing. 'It is the only possible explanation for the complicated tableau left by the murderer.'

'Yes, I believe you're right,' Miss Busby agreed, sighing as she stirred the pot.

'Do you? You never said!' Adeline looked aggrieved. 'A set-up for what?'

'The murder of Alice Albion,' Miss Busby and Enid answered in tandem.

'It has felt like a rather tricky jigsaw puzzle in my head,' Miss Busby confessed. 'One with significant missing pieces until now.'

'The skeleton, and the poem?' Enid suggested.

Miss Busby nodded.

Adeline, feeling rather left behind, reached for a ham and mustard. 'Well it would have been nice had you mentioned it to me. Ezekiel is my friend, after all. And I hold no truck with jigsaws. I don't see the appeal.'

'You need a certain sort of brain,' said Enid. 'And a lot of patience. Try the prawn and salmon, Isabelle, they are delicious.'

Complying, Miss Busby agreed. *Pud would like these*, she thought.

'This is all very well, but why frame the poet?' Adeline asked, unconvinced.

'Convenience,' Enid replied. 'He has no one to stand up for him in death.'

'He has Ezekiel,' Adeline objected.

'Ezekiel is a foreign gentleman, and–'

'Enid, I thought better of you.' Adeline glared across the table.

'–people in small towns often have small minds. They can be suspicious of foreigners, his support of the poet would count for little.' Enid finished. 'And Travis was virtually a recluse and known to be fond of the girl, some would say over fond. He is the perfect scapegoat.'

Miss Busby thought for a moment, discreetly slipping half of the sandwich into her bag to take home for Pud. 'Ezekiel has been accepted rather fondly into the community,' she said. 'I haven't seen evidence of any ill will towards him.'

Enid gave a small shrug. 'Then perhaps your murderer had some issue with Travis, and attempting to stage his death as suicide was simply killing two birds with one stone.'

'He is not *my* murderer!' Miss Busby insisted.

'And Ezekiel is adamant no one could have taken issue with Travis,' Adeline added. 'He wasn't the sort.'

'We don't always know everything about our friends,' Enid pointed out.

'No,' Miss Busby conceded, 'but I should imagine when you live in such close proximity, issues of any note would be difficult to hide. Ezekiel naturally knew Travis' traits and habits extremely well. He knew how tidy the man was, for example. And yet when he discovered the crime scene, he mentioned there were papers strewn all over the desk and floor. That has been puzzling me.'

'The murderer rifled through his papers to find a suitable candidate,' Enid said. 'A poem most likely to implicate Travis.'

Adeline sat back in her chair and considered. 'He must have known he would find something suitable among Travis' works, otherwise what would he have done?'

'Yes, he couldn't forge a poem for the same reason he couldn't forge a suicide note. That's a good point, Adeline,' Miss Busby said. 'He must have known how much Travis thought of the girl to be confident such a personal poem existed.' Miss Busby thought for a moment, then said, 'I'm sure Mrs Fowler mentioned that Travis and Alice wrote poetry together.'

'How on earth would she know that?' Adeline asked.

'Something Martin told her, if I recall. I can't remember her exact phrasing, only the impression that she found the whole thing rather distasteful.'

'Well, there you are then. Martin knew about the poetry,' Adeline remarked.

'As did his mother,' Enid pointed out. 'But the rifled desk suggests a rush.' She poured fresh tea. 'If the murderer had easy access to the rooms via the panelling, he could surely have found a suitable poem prior to the deed, and been better prepared.'

'Ah, but we know Travis didn't leave his rooms often,' Adeline said, spurred on by her friend's praise.

'Except to visit Ezekiel at lunchtimes,' Miss Busby remembered.

'Yes, but in those instances he would only have been downstairs. Were someone to move aside the panelling, and the bench seat, then rifle through his desk, I'm sure Travis would have heard.'

'Why didn't he hear the murderer enter his rooms that night?' Enid asked. 'And why is no one eating the egg and cress? They're extremely good. I shall finish them all myself if you're not careful.'

'He must have been asleep.' Miss Busby took one without thinking. 'The murderer could have looked through the knothole in the wood to be sure.'

'But the cushion was in front of the hole,' Adeline said.

'He only had to poke through and knock it over, then replace it before he pulled the bench seat back when he left.'

'It sounds to me,' Enid said, 'as if the whole thing was rushed. Well thought out, in essence, but simple mistakes have been made which could have been avoided with more careful planning.'

'What would have caused him to rush?' Adeline asked, taking the last egg and cress. 'Lady Spencer has been ill for months. He has had plenty of time to prepare for the eventuality.'

'Perhaps we are looking for someone who has been away recently,' Miss Busby mused.

'Or perhaps our murderer had a different scapegoat in mind,' Enid said. 'He may have had to change his plans at the last minute. There are any number of reasons, and I doubt we shall guess them all.' She dabbed her mouth with a napkin and set her plate aside. 'We must stick to the facts. We are looking for someone who knew Travis was close to Alice, and who knew Ezekiel kept a gun on the premises, *and* who had access to Harrison's, *and* who was in Chipping Common six years ago.'

'It's the gun that's troubling. Ezekiel insists Travis was the only one who knew about it.'

'And Travis could have told just about anyone else. We are back to guessing,' Enid reminded her.

'He hardly spoke to anyone,' Adeline said. 'There can't be many people he would confide in.'

'Unless he confided in Alice,' Miss Busby suggested, thinking back to Ezekiel's earlier horror at the notion of her knowing.

'Ah, now, an *educated* guess.' Enid's eyes flashed brightly. 'We know they were close. Now, who was *Alice* close to whom she may have told in turn?'

'Cameron Spencer,' Miss Busby said quietly.

'I was rather thinking of someone closer to home…'

Adeline got there first. 'Enid, *really*, you can't possibly think Rose Harrison would do such a thing. To her own daughter!'

'She wasn't her daughter, Adeline.' Enid remained resolute.

'As good as!'

'I am simply playing devil's advocate,' Enid continued, spreading her hands in a gesture of innocence. 'Mrs Harrison was possessed of both the means and the opportunity to carry out both murders.'

'That is preposterous–'

'But what would her motive be?' Miss Busby asked, cutting Adeline's histrionics off.

'In the case of Gabriel Travis – to get herself off the hook for Alice Albion's murder,' Enid explained. 'And in Alice's case, it could have been anything. Youngsters of a certain *inbetween* age have tested the patience of their parents throughout history. Mrs Harrison certainly wouldn't have been the first to succumb. Nor will she be the last.'

'Are we all finished, then?' The older waitress reappeared and began to clear the plates. 'Fresh pot of tea, is it?'

'No, thank you, that was quite sufficient,' Miss Busby replied.

'I should like another coffee,' Adeline said pointedly.

'Right you are. Back in a jiffy.' The waitress went off.

'Mrs Harrison ticks all our boxes,' Enid said, still deep in thought. 'She knew Travis well enough to be aware of his movements, not to mention she had access to a view of his rooms through the knot hole. She knows of Mr Melnyk's habits, too, and that he is hard of hearing.'

'As do the vast majority of Chipping Common,' Adeline was quick to clarify.

'This would have given her confidence in taking the shot.' Enid wasn't listening. 'In addition, she knew Travis was fond of Alice. This in itself may have aggrieved her. In loco parentis she may have found his attention untoward and felt it her duty to avenge.'

'You are contradicting yourself, Enid.' Adeline's sudden smile was shark-like. 'If she cared enough for Alice to be angry over untoward attention, she would hardly have killed the girl herself. Nor would she have waited six years for retribution.'

'She was protecting her own interests at this point, don't forget,' Enid pointed out. 'It may have been the extra push she needed to justify the act.'

'Tenuous, at best,' Adeline huffed.

'It all comes back to the gun,' Miss Busby said in the frustrated silence that followed.

The cakes arrived, along with Adeline's coffee. Petit fours, fondant fancies, Viennese whirls and cherry bakewells would usually have prompted exclamations of delight, but all three women remained deep in thought for several moments.

'Men talk about guns,' Adeline announced, reaching triumphantly for a fondant fancy.

Miss Busby looked up with a frown.

'They do,' Adeline insisted. 'And they know things about panelling, and fuel, and such.'

Enid took a cherry bakewell and looked at Adeline with interest. 'What are you getting at?'

'You were almost there, Enid,' Adeline conceded, with a hint of a smirk. 'But it wasn't *Mrs* Harrison, it was *Mr* Harrison,' she proclaimed with the air of judge, jury, and executioner. 'Isabelle, much as it pains me to say it, we must visit your inspector post-haste.'

CHAPTER 28

Enid insisted on paying for lunch. She was also rather late to take the bus back to Spring Meadows, and they accompanied her hurriedly to where the bus waited, leaving her looking distinctly uncomfortable as Mr Waterhouse arrived almost on cue.

'I should have thought Enid would find it rather nice to have a gentleman companion,' Adeline said as she and Miss Busby walked towards the police station. 'I do miss my James so.'

Miss Busby thought of Adeline's teasing regarding her own friendship with Sir Richard Lannister, but bit her tongue. 'Enid knows her own mind, Adeline,' she cautioned gently. 'We mustn't meddle.'

Adeline huffed. 'I'm not meddling. I am simply taking an interest.'

'What will we do if your car isn't fixed?' Miss Busby asked, to distract her.

Adeline raised an eyebrow. 'I shall make sure it is.'

As they rounded the corner and approached the

station, they saw Bobby Miller wheeling his bicycle around to the front.

'Afternoon,' he said, doffing his helmet. Lowering his voice, he added, 'Have you heard about the skeleton?'

Miss Busby nodded. 'The inspector told me. I didn't say a word about your comment,' she assured him.

'Thanks, Miss. Everyone'll know soon enough. News as big as that'll spread like wildfire.'

'Come *on*, Isabelle,' Adeline said, eyes shining as she marched into the station, head held high.

'Miss Busby.' Bobby detained her for a moment's quiet word of warning. 'The Oxford chief isn't very happy,' he whispered. 'You could hear him shouting down the telephone at Inspector McKay, and now he isn't in the best 'o moods.'

'Oh dear.' *Just like Mr Doggett*, she thought. It was ironic that women had a reputation for moodiness when men were equally, if not more, given to the same. 'Thank you, Bobby.'

Miss Busby entered the station to find Adeline remonstrating with the crop haired Constable Garthwaite, who was leaning on the long wooden countertop with a long face.

'I can't let you through,' he said glumly, before making an attempt to pull his shoulders back and look professional. 'The inspector is not to be disturbed.'

'He will want to see us,' Adeline announced regally, rapping on the countertop to make her point. 'You must fetch him.'

A look of obstinacy spread over the constable's lean features, just as the inspector opened the door behind him and glared out in their direction.

'Mrs Fanshawe, I thought I heard your voice. You have saved me the trouble of coming to find you.'

'You see?' Adeline shot an imperious look at the young constable.

Miss Busby, however, felt a sinking feeling.

'We have been unable to find any fingerprints at Harrison's other than yours. It is my assumption that you have therefore destroyed vital evidence, and as such I have a good mind to arrest you for–'

'Nonsense, Inspector,' Adeline said imperiously. 'I have uncovered your murderer. Shall we go through?'

Inspector McKay ushered them into the office with a growled warning. 'If I find you are wasting my time, Mrs Fanshawe…'

'I do not waste time, Inspector. Quite the reverse.'

'Well then. You had better sit down,' he said gruffly.

They each took one of the cushioned chairs in front of the desk. The red gingham curtains were brightly lit by the sunshine falling through the window behind, and had it not been for the inspector's stern presence they would have felt themselves anywhere but in a police station.

'As you know,' Adeline began, 'I have been tireless in defence of Mr Melnyk since you cruelly and falsely accused him of murder.'

When no objection came from the inspector, Miss

Busby wondered just how severe his telling-off must have been. Near fatal, surely, if he was willing to clutch at an Adeline-shaped straw.

'And today, with the help of my friends,' Adeline continued graciously, 'I believe I have uncovered the true culprit…' She paused, for dramatic effect. '…Your murderer is Mr Fraser Harrison, Inspector. In both instances.'

Miss Busby braced herself, half expecting the inspector to march Adeline directly to the cells. She had most certainly not been expecting him to look at first surprised, and then rather impressed.

'Mr Harrison is already of interest to the investigation,' he replied carefully.

'I should think so. He ought to be your primary suspect.'

The inspector reached for his notebook.

'For what reason?'

'It's obvious. The man had motive, means, and opportunity.'

'Ah, are you another reader of crime novels, Mrs Fanshawe?' he asked, eyes narrowing.

'Not in the least,' she assured him. 'But I am possessed of a brain, Inspector. And this is not my first investigation.'

Miss Busby stifled a smile. However imperious and abrupt she could be, Adeline certainly knew how to turn a phrase.

'Mrs Harrison herself admits her husband thought the adoption of Alice Albion *unwise*,' Adeline continued. 'And that he did not see Alice in the same parental manner as she did.'

'That's maybe understandable,' the inspector countered, 'as they were not married at the time of Alice's adoption.'

'Immaterial.' Adeline dismissed the objection. 'He knew Alice was part of Rose's family when he married her, and should have accepted her as such. And having met the man myself yesterday I must say he is a most shifty and suspicious individual.'

'Mere disapproval of the girl is not a motive, Mrs Fanshawe,' the inspector said, looking up from his notepad. 'And we are unable to apprehend suspects simply because they look *shifty*.'

'Aha! So you *do* deem him a suspect?'

Miss Busby watched the exchange in fascination. She'd expected a tetchy argument at best, but the pair were discussing the case in an almost amicable manner.

'What makes you think Mr Harrison could be responsible for both deaths?' The inspector avoided the question.

Adeline sighed dramatically, as if it were perfectly obvious. 'I have already said. He is of the sort to deem Alice a *stray*, as we have heard others within the town label her. Her social status would have been an embarrassment to him. In other words, Inspector, she would not have been a welcome addition to his family.'

'And yet he married Mrs Harrison all the same.'

Adeline bristled. 'I am not privy to the man's every

thought. But yesterday at Melnyk's Books I witnessed him acting in a most nervous and awkward fashion. He was pallid and evasive; the very picture of a man wracked with guilt.'

'Miss Busby?' The inspector looked to her for the first time for confirmation.

'He did seem rather uncomfortable,' she admitted.

'And Mrs Harrison told us he often helped her bring boxes down from the attic,' Adeline continued. 'He could therefore easily have made the modifications to the panelling, or used existing modifications to his own ends.'

The inspector made a note.

'I'm not sure Rose said *often*,' Miss Busby pointed out.

'It was implied.' Adeline remained undeterred. 'She would have needed stored items from the attic regularly enough. And Mr Harrison is clearly familiar with Melnyk's Books, too. He was quite at home there yesterday when we saw him.'

'And this was when he looked uncomfortable?' the inspector asked, one fiery red brow arched as he looked between the two women.

'Yes.' Adeline was unperturbed. 'A man can look both at home and uncomfortable simultaneously, although it may well take a woman to see it.'

Bravo, Miss Busby thought. Whilst she wasn't entirely convinced Mr Harrison was the culprit, she was impressed by the manner in which Adeline was fighting her corner.

'What I'm most interested in, Mrs Fanshawe, is how you think Mr Harrison came to be in possession of Mr Melnyk's gun?' The inspector switched tack.

'Men talk about guns, Inspector. Lord knows why, but they do.'

'Mr Melnyk remained very clear he wasn't in the habit of discussing the weapon,' he stated.

'He may simply have mentioned it in passing, years ago perhaps, and forgotten. Mr Harrison was clearly able to access the premises, locks or no locks, and the cash drawer would have been no obstacle. And he knew about Ezekiel's weak hearing, of course. Rose and Mr Melnyk were friends, Mr Harrison could easily have wrested anything he needed to know from her in order to commit the foul deed. Oh!' She raised a hand to her mouth in horror. 'Poor Rose! She will be *destroyed* when she finds out.'

Adeline's emotions were genuine, Miss Busby knew, although there was often a note of drama in the expressing of them.

The inspector took a long breath and looked down at his notes.

'Well?' Adeline demanded.

'Thank you, Mrs Fanshawe, your information has been most enlightening,' he concluded, rising to his feet. 'I would, however, remind you to please leave the investigation to me from hereon in. As I stated, you have left fingerprints in the Harrison's attic, and potentially deprived us of vital evidence.'

'Oh for goodness' sake, Inspector, I–' Adeline attempted to argue.

'I am prepared to overlook it this time, as I genuinely believe you were trying to help,' McKay conceded with a rare grace.

Miss Busby realised her mouth had dropped open in surprise. She hastily closed it.

'Yes, well, that is to say… Good.' Adeline was clearly equally surprised, and rather flustered.

'Miss Busby.' McKay turned to her. 'Is there anything you would like to add whilst you and Mrs Fanshawe are here?'

'Tell him about the kerosene, Isabelle,' Adeline prompted, before she had a chance to think.

'Oh, yes. Yesterday I hit my shin on the small kerosene heater I mentioned to you, the one in Mr Travis' rooms. I noted at the time it was empty. Ezekiel has just now told me he was in the habit of purchasing kerosene for Travis every Friday after work.'

The inspector looked down at his notebook thoughtfully. 'And you mentioned Mr Travis was in the habit of keeping his windows closed at night at this time of year.'

Miss Busby nodded.

'*Hm.* Burning the entire reservoir of kerosene in an unventilated room would certainly have been sufficient to knock a man out.'

'You see?' Adeline's voice grew in excitement. 'Rose would have known Ezekiel's habits, and quite possibly mentioned it to her husband in all innocence. He picked his moment with care. Fraser Harrison is your man, Inspector. Mark my words.'

He looked carefully at Miss Busby. 'You don't seem convinced,' he observed.

'Well, it's very possible, of course. But it's the dustbins that worry me, I'm afraid.'

* * *

'You might have told me, Isabelle,' Adeline huffed as they made their way out of the station and back towards Doggett's Garage several minutes later.

'I only noticed it myself when I left Harrison's this morning,' she offered in her defence. 'Much in the same way as you discovering the issue with the panelling.'

'Miss Busby?'

The pair turned to see Inspector McKay in the doorway, her leather notebook held out in front of him.

'Oh, I'd quite forgotten! I shan't be a moment, Adeline.' She hurried back to take it from him. 'Thank you, Inspector. I do hope it was helpful.'

'Aye, you have been,' he answered, and she looked up in surprise at his phrasing. The young Scot cleared his throat. 'My mother used to say *I'm no as green as I am cabbage lookin'*.'

'Did she?'

He nodded.

Miss Busby felt rather lost.

'It means, in essence, you could never tell her anything,' he explained. 'And my father says I'm the same, more often than not.'

'Oh, well, I should think we all can be, in our own way.'

'Perhaps.' He cleared his throat once more, clearly struggling with something he wanted to say. Miss Busby didn't know how best to help him, so she simply offered an encouraging smile. 'It's her birthday today,' he finally said, looking down at his hands for a moment. 'It made me think of her.'

She began to understand. 'And so you wanted to listen?' she asked softly.

'In a way, aye. That's not to say that your friend should have trampled all over my evidence,' he added, sounding much more like himself for a moment.

'When will you next see her, do you think?' Miss Busby asked.

'Not yet a while. But I telephoned the home this morning. She didn't recognise my voice.'

'Oh, I can't even begin to imagine how difficult that must be,' she said, thinking what a cruel disease Alzheimer's was.

'No, well. She also used to say *whit's fur ye'll no go by ye.*'

Miss Busby took a moment to translate. 'Be it good or bad, I suppose.'

He nodded. 'Well, good afternoon, Miss Busby.'

'Good afternoon, Inspector.'

CHAPTER 29

'That went rather well, I thought, and now you will need to add to your notes,' Adeline said as Miss Busby rejoined her en route to the garage. 'It's all starting to move fast now, isn't it?' There was an excitement in her voice that Miss Busby wasn't sure she shared.

'I keep forgetting what I have and haven't told you,' she admitted. 'The dustbins…my suspicions about why Travis was murdered…even the poem. I do hope it isn't my age beginning to tell.'

'Of course it isn't. It is small towns with secrets. It takes two of us to get to the bottom of everything – three, if you include the inspector,' she added, with less reluctance than usual. 'It's all a muddle to start with, then it comes together in a rush. Anyone would forget bits and pieces along the way.'

Miss Busby smiled. 'Thank you, Adeline,' she said quietly.

'He took us *seriously*, Isabelle,' she added, a note of pride ringing in her voice.

Miss Busby smiled. 'Yes, he did.' She considered explaining why, but decided it was a private matter. She was pleased to see the pair finally thawing to one another though, whatever the reason.

'Of course,' Adeline added as they crossed the road, 'had he not been so pig-headed and done so from the start, we should already be much further along.' Adeline caught sight of the overalls protruding from beneath her car. 'Ah, Mr Doggett!' she boomed.

A bang and a muffled cry greeted them in return, before Mr Doggett rolled himself out from under the vehicle and climbed to his feet, rubbing his head. He was tall and rather solid, not the type you would expect to find fitting himself under cars. Late forties, perhaps, his hair was beginning to show flecks of grey, but his thick beard and moustache were black.

'Mrs Fanshawe,' he exclaimed angrily, 'hasn't anyone ever told you it's dangerous to–'

'Is it ready?' Adeline asked, walking around the car to inspect the damage. 'It certainly doesn't look ready,' she huffed, turning back to him, brows furrowed in displeasure.

'You crunched her good and proper,' he admonished. 'You'll need to take her to Oxford Garage for a new wheel arch. There's only so much I can do in terms of beating out dents. And that wasn't so much a dent as a–'

'The sun was low in the sky, Mr Doggett,' Adeline said, no hint of warmth in her own tone. 'What would you have me do? Drive only in the dark?' She raised her eyebrows. 'And you have left greasy fingerprints on the bodywork. If you cannot make the car look better than this, what on earth have you been doing all morning?'

'Making her safe for you to drive, which is what counts.' Mr Doggett gave her a stern look in response. Miss Busby thought him exceptionally brave. 'You clipped the axle on the chassis. I've welded it back for you, and if that don't suit, you can take your car elsewhere.' His bushy brows drew together.

Adeline's bombast withered. 'Oh. In that case, very well, Mr Doggett. Thank you. I…If you could drive her over to the bookshop for me once the marks have been cleaned, I would much appreciate it.'

There was a moment's silence, before Mr Doggett nodded curtly, then turned to shout over his shoulder. 'Kevin, job for you.' Turning back to Adeline, he added, 'The young lad'll get her shining again.'

'Thank you, Mr Doggett, and please send the bill,' Adeline said contritely, then turned and walked with head lowered towards Melnyk's Books.

Miss Busby offered an apologetic smile and made to follow, when Kevin came rushing over, calling, 'Miss! Wait!'

She turned.

'Mr Doggett, sir,' he said, 'this is the lady what was askin' earlier 'bout who buys their kerosene from us. I told her the reg'lars, but then you said as how Mrs Fowler bought extra last week, an' how you thought it were odd 'cos she don't normally spend a penny more'n she has to, and—'

'Kevin.' Mr Doggett's tone was sharp. 'I don't recall saying anything of the sort.' The flush above his whiskers suggested otherwise.

'But—!'

'You'll want your cloth, a bucket of soapy water, and plenty of elbow grease. Quick smart, now. Mrs Fanshawe's waiting for her car.'

'Yes sir,' he muttered glumly, shoulders drooping as he sloped off to fetch what was needed.

'I am from Bloxford, Mr Doggett,' Miss Busby reassured him, her tone conspiratorial. 'And barely acquainted with Mrs Fowler, but I would not repeat anything told to me in confidence. I am simply a friend of Mr Melnyk's, and—'

'Of Mr Melnyk's? Well *that's* alright then,' he said, whiskers twitching in relief. 'There's been too much talk against him, and he's a good sort.' He leaned a bit closer and lowered his voice. 'Mrs Fowler bought two lots of kerosene last week, her usual amount on Monday, then the same again on Thursday. I told the lad it was unusual, you see. Might of got a bit carried away with my wording, admittedly, but he shouldn't have repeated it.'

Miss Busby smiled. 'It takes them a while to learn.'

Mr Doggett gave a throaty chuckle. 'If they ever do! Mrs Fowler can be right rude at times. Accused me of short-changing her once. As if I'd ever do such a thing.'

'Goodness, how unpleasant. I quite understand. But I wonder what she could have needed extra fuel for at this time of year,' Miss Busby mused.

'Probably for that son of hers,' he said, wiping his hands clean on a rag and walking Miss Busby towards the road.

She stopped short. 'Martin? In what way?'

'He mixes powders and potions, him being a fully qualified pharmacist, as she never tires of telling everyone. I expect he has to heat some of them.'

'Yes, of course. Thank you, Mr Doggett.' Miss Busby took her leave. Crossing the road to join Adeline, she wondered what reason there could have been for Martin Fowler to heat more potions last week than any other. If, indeed, any of them needed heating in the first place. And surely his workspace in the flat above had a gas connection?

Adeline was chatting to Ezekiel when Miss Busby entered the bookshop. She didn't feel ready to share the news of the Fowlers and the kerosene, not being entirely sure yet how important it was. She headed straight for the shelves instead, thinking to choose a book for Mary to cheer her up as Enid had said she wasn't feeling well. As she did so, the bell over the door jangled once more, and she turned to see a tall, handsome young man enter the shop. He had dark-brown hair and the same arresting green eyes as Madeleine Spencer.

'Cameron, my dear boy.' Ezekiel confirmed it as he hurried to greet the young man. 'Sir Cameron, I should say!'

'No, you shouldn't. I've already said, Mr Melnyk, it makes me sound far too old. Cameron is fine.'

'As you wish, of course. But how are you? How is your family? Oh, but it is the most foolish question to ask. You are all suffering. I understand. What can I do for you?'

'Actually, it's what I can do for you, Mr Melnyk,' he said, in a warm, rich voice. Miss Busby found herself quite captivated by him. She blushed as she realised she could certainly see how Alice may have felt the same. 'I believe my sister forgot to give you this when you called to pay your respects. Do forgive her, she's finding the responsibility of it all rather difficult. I should have stayed to help out, but I couldn't face it either, I'm afraid.' He held out a piece of card; surely Ezekiel's invite to the funeral. 'Sorry it's late, but I didn't want you to feel as if you weren't welcome.'

'Such a kind boy, to think of it at all. Thank you.' Ezekiel smiled as he took the card, and shook the young man's hand vigorously.

Cameron smiled in return, before looking across to see Miss Busby staring directly at him.

'Oh!' she flustered, turning back to the shelves, then realising she must look extremely rude, and turning back to him. 'I'm so sorry, I didn't mean to stare. I was miles away.'

'Dear lady, of course! You do not know each other,' Ezekiel said. 'This is Miss Busby. She is solving the murder of Gabriel Travis, and perhaps our dearest Alice, too.'

The young man's eyes flashed darkly, and Miss Busby felt momentarily threatened, before he quickly fixed his smile back in place and nodded politely.

'And Miss Busby,' Ezekiel went on, 'this is Sir Cameron Spencer.'

'I'm pleased to meet you, Miss Busby.' She noticed he was happy for the honorific to remain in place. 'What a fascinating hobby you have – solving murders.' There, again, was the flash of darkness that made her feel uncomfortable. 'Tell me, do you have anyone in the frame?'

'Oh, well, I'm really not—'

'We have an idea.' Adeline's voice made Miss Busby jump. She'd quite forgotten her friend was there.

'Ah, and Mrs Fanshawe!' Ezekiel announced happily. 'Three of my most favourite people, now all knowing one another. I shall make tea!'

'Delighted, Mrs Fanshawe.' Cameron offered a courtly bow. 'But I'm afraid I really can't stay, Mr Melnyk. There's still a great deal to do before tomorrow.'

'And yet you are taking the time to come to see me. It is most wonderful, thank you.' Mr Melnyk shook his hand once more.

'Absolutely no trouble. I'd love to hear who you ladies think responsible, but of course I'm sure the police have matters in hand.'

Adeline *harrumphed*, while Miss Busby gave a curt nod and Ezekiel saw the young man out of the shop.

'Well, what do you make of that?' Adeline asked, crossing to stand beside her.

'I'm not sure,' Miss Busby confessed. 'It was nice of him to pass along the invitation.' And extremely unpleasant of Madeleine to have *forgotten*, she thought.

'Hmm, I suppose,' Adeline conceded. 'He didn't seem thrilled with the idea of us investigating though, did he?'

'No,' Miss Busby agreed, and then realised, 'But Adeline, I don't have an invitation!'

'No matter. I do, and you are my guest,' Adeline asserted, unconcerned.

'Now, Miss Busby, what can I do for you?' Ezekiel asked, crossing the shop floor and smiling with his customary warmth – amplified, no doubt, by Adeline suggesting to him she had uncovered the murderer. 'Are you looking for anything in particular?'

'Actually,' she said, her thoughts returning to Mary, 'I'm looking for something for an exceptionally well-read friend, and would welcome your advice.'

'Of course! What does the lady like most to read?' Ezekiel asked happily.

'A little bit of everything,' she replied, 'hence my struggle. Although she has recently mentioned enjoying an Edgar Allan Poe story.'

'Ah, the darker side of the American romantics! Please, come!' He directed her towards the rear of the shop, searched along a shelf for a book then thrust a small leather bound volume into her hands. '*The*

Piazza Tales,' he exclaimed with a sort of infectious reverence. 'Here are collected short stories from Mr Melville. Inside rests one entitled *Bartleby the Scrivener.* Most Poe-like, I am happy to assure you! And should your friend not like it, which I cannot possibly envisage, she may of course exchange it.'

'That's most kind, thank you.' Miss Busby took the book.

'It is nothing after all you are doing for me.' He bowed graciously. 'Although, dear lady, as I am just telling Mrs Fanshawe,' he looked around to ensure there was no one else in the shop, 'I do not think Mr Harrison is doing this terrible thing. He is a good man. He reads Jules Verne. I find it impossible to think someone who reads delightful adventure stories can do such a thing.'

Miss Busby smiled at the endless generosity of his spirit, and considered. Was there any possible correlation, she wondered, between chosen reading matter and general criminal inclination? She doubted it, of course, but thought it would be a fascinating topic to dive into…

'Verne had a powerful imagination,' Adeline interjected, crossing to them and pulling her from her thoughts. 'And so did our murderer.' She took the book from Miss Busby and glanced at it, wrinkling her nose on seeing Melville's name. '*Ugh.* I cannot stand that endless whale tome of his.'

Ezekiel opened his mouth to object, but the jingle of the shop bell once more caused all three to turn.

CHAPTER 30

Rose Harrison entered Melnyk's Books with a determined smile on her face which wavered and crumpled the moment she locked eyes with the bookseller.

Ezekiel rushed across and took her hands, murmuring soft condolences. Miss Busby gently pulled Adeline aside. 'You mustn't go asking anything about Mr Harrison,' she whispered. 'Leave it to the inspector. We have upset the poor woman enough for one day.'

'We shall be far more delicate about it than he will, I'm sure,' Adeline objected.

'It will come easier with a professional touch,' Miss Busby insisted. 'Come on.' She deftly manoeuvred Adeline towards the door. 'We can wait for your car outside.'

'Oh, please don't leave on my account,' Rose called, catching sight of their movement. 'I just wondered if I might exchange a ten shilling note for coins, Mr Melnyk?' She sniffed, and rubbed delicately at her eyes. 'I hadn't thought to go to the bank with everything going on.'

KAREN BAUGH MENUHIN & ZOE MARKHAM

'Of course! Please, exchange for the coins you are in need of, it is as always,' he said, gesturing to the desk before turning to straighten a row of books that had fallen askew.

Miss Busby and Adeline watched in open-mouthed astonishment as Rose Harrison crossed to the back of the shop, walked around the desk, and opened the cash drawer to rummage inside.

'Isabelle!' Adeline breathed.

'Good Lord,' Miss Busby replied, eyes wide. The bell jingled behind them again, but neither woman took their eyes off the cash drawer.

'*Och*, well now, that's interesting…' Both ladies startled and turned at the soft Scottish lilt behind them.

'Inspector!' Adeline hissed eagerly. 'That's how he got the gun, do you see? He must have–'

Inspector McKay held up a finger for silence, watching as Rose withdrew a handful of coins.

'Thank you so much, Ezekiel, I shall– Oh, Inspector,' she said in surprise, straightening up and seeing the three of them watching her.

'Mrs Harrison.' McKay nodded politely. 'I was just next door and must have missed you. I wondered if I might have a word?'

'Yes, of course. I am on my way back now. Thank you, Ezekiel. You are so kind, as always.'

'It is nothing,' he said, the bookshelf looking immaculate once more. 'And please, if there is any more I can do to help, you know where I am to be found.'

As Rose and the inspector left, Miss Busby could feel Adeline's barely contained triumph swelling, before the throaty purr of her Rolls outside distracted her.

'Ah! I shan't be a moment, Isabelle. I must see if the greasy marks are all gone.'

'Ezekiel,' Miss Busby said softly as Adeline rushed out, 'do you often let people change notes in that manner?'

His brow creased in puzzlement. 'My neighbours, yes, of course. It is a considerable walk to the bank. They do the same for me, if I have occasion to ask. We are brothers and sisters in shopkeeping!'

'I see.' She wondered how it could be that he hadn't made the connection, although the inspector would surely quiz him on the matter soon enough. Glancing out of the window, she saw Adeline accepting possession of her clean, but rather mangled-looking car.

Ezekiel followed her gaze. '*Oy!*' he exhaled in surprise. 'What is happened to Mrs Fanshawe's motor vehicle?'

Miss Busby explained about the accident, and a trip to Oxford being required to have it returned to normal.

'Thank goodness Mrs Fanshawe is still normal,' he said earnestly. 'And not crumpled also.'

'Yes,' Miss Busby agreed, thinking she must remember to tell Adeline his exact words.

Adeline popped her head back through the door and called, 'I will drive over to Oxford now, Isabelle. James would hate to see the car looking like this. Shall I take you home first?'

'I need to pay for Mary's book, and I might drop into Fowler's for a tonic while I'm here. I've been feeling rather tired lately. You head off, I'll find my own way home.'

'As you wish. I will pick you up at two tomorrow for the funeral. We will see you there, Ezekiel.' She beamed at him. 'Whereupon I fully anticipate all suspicion to be lifted from your shoulders!'

'Now, Adeline,' Miss Busby cautioned, 'we don't–'

But she was gone.

Ezekiel patted Miss Busby's hand. 'It is understood, dear lady. These things take time. Mrs Fanshawe does not have…how do you say? The skill of waiting?'

'Patience,' Miss Busby supplied.

He nodded. 'Just so. For me, suspicion or no suspicion is no matter. What is important is that a terrible man is brought to justice. I am afraid,' he bowed his head, as if he were letting her down somehow, 'I am quite sure Mr Harrison is not a terrible man.'

'The inspector will get to the bottom of it,' she said. 'He is awash with patience, in professional matters,' she qualified, 'and diligent to boot. Now, how much is the book?'

'There is no charge,' Ezekiel said.

'Oh, no, that is too much.' Miss Busby stepped forward towards the desk. A glance around the otherwise empty shop stiffened her resolve. 'I insist.'

After a short verbal tussle, and with Mary's book paid for and beautifully wrapped – 'a gift, yes? We must make it pretty!' – Miss Busby left for Fowler's, only to find the *closed* sign hung and the door locked.

'Miss Busby! Are you not feeling well?' a familiar voice called from across the street, and she turned to see Lucy hurrying towards her.

Dressed in a smart burgundy blouse with a black skirt and cardigan, her dark hair pulled back loosely from her shoulders, concern creased the young woman's features as she approached.

'Lucy! What a lovely surprise! I am quite well, thank you. I have found myself dozing off in cars this week like an old woman, and thought a Sanatogen tonic might do the trick.'

'I often doze if someone else is driving,' Lucy said. 'It's the rumble of the engine, and the road. And you're not old.'

Miss Busby smiled. 'I am, but you're very kind. And perhaps you're right, the vibrations are rather soothing.'

'Odd that they're shut on market day,' Lucy remarked, looking at the sign.

'Yes. And not even a *back in five minutes* note. A late lunch, perhaps. No matter. But what are you doing in Chipping Common?'

'Looking for you,' Lucy said. 'There's something I need to tell you. Shall we go to Lavender Cottage? We can talk there. It's rather delicate.'

Miss Busby's eyes widened. 'Is it? How intriguing. And yes, that would be nice, if you're not too busy?'

'I've been in Oxford all morning,' Lucy said, taking

Miss Busby's arm and walking back towards the high street, 'trying to get to the bottom of a silly spat between the Operatic Society and the AmDram Club. Scripts and scores at dawn. I can't face the thought of writing about it yet, it's all too silly. But when I got back to the office, I had a message–'

The door of Harrison's opened as they walked past, and the inspector stepped into the street right in front of them.

'Oh! Inspector McKay, good afternoon,' Lucy said, her cheeks flushing prettily.

'Hmm?' The inspector looked up, annoyed, and then confused. It took him a moment to place her. 'Ah… Miss Weasley, good afternoon,' he managed, as recognition dawned.

'Wesley,' Miss Busby corrected.

'Actually I go by Lannister now,' Lucy admitted. 'The cat's out of the bag on that front.'

'I see. Right. Well, good afternoon, Miss Lannister.'

Miss Busby smiled into the rather awkward pause that followed.

'I do hope you are well?' Lucy offered, at the exact same time as the inspector said, 'If you'll excuse me, I must—'

'Oh, of course,' Lucy replied, just as he in turn said, 'Yes, very well, thank you.'

Miss Busby stifled a laugh. Amidst all the aching sadness of the last few days, watching the pair of them was a better tonic than Fowler's could have provided.

'Well, yes, I must–'

Miss Busby shot him a Look.

'Erm, I hope you are well, also?' he asked, looking every bit the fish out of water.

'Yes. Very. Thank you.'

'Good. Then I shall…' He waved a hand towards the back of the buildings, and strode off.

Lucy blinked after him.

'He's had a busy morning,' Miss Busby explained. 'I'll tell you all about it on the way. It will keep me awake.'

Lucy risked a quick glance back over her shoulder, before saying, 'I don't think you need to worry about that today!'

As the red Sunbeam sports car came into view, its top down and paintwork gleaming, Miss Busby laughed, and felt lighter somehow than she had in days.

CHAPTER 31

As they left Chipping Common, the undulating Cotswold hills spread out before them, Miss Busby felt her shoulders loosen, the countryside as much a tonic as the young woman beside her.

'I have a terrible feeling your father may have been right last night,' she confessed.

'Right about what?'

'About detecting putting a strain on me. Perhaps I'm a little too old for it, after all.'

'Just because you've been feeling a bit tired?' Lucy shook her head. 'I shouldn't take any notice if I were you. Daddy nods off all the time, and still refuses to retire properly. It's a bit rich of him to say anything, if you ask me.'

Miss Busby considered. 'Yes, I suppose it is, really.' *Just another example*, she thought, *of the rules being different for men than for women.*

'Unless you *want* to stop detecting, that is. Do you?' Lucy looked at her passenger earnestly.

Miss Busby gazed out of the window and contemplated the matter in silence.

'I thought you enjoyed it?' Lucy prompted. 'You're awfully good at it.'

Miss Busby smiled at the compliment. 'I suppose I do, rather. It's given me something of a new lease of life. But I don't really think of it as *detecting*. That's what the inspector does. I just take an interest. I talk to people, and try to help them.'

'Something the inspector struggles with,' Lucy commented wryly.

Miss Busby smiled. 'It does my brain good, having puzzles to solve. I might need to slow down at times, perhaps, but I see no reason to stop.'

'Well, that's alright then.' Lucy beamed across at her, returning her eyes to the road just in time to see a pheasant amble from the verge into their path. She swerved, and Miss Busby was relieved to turn and see the creature in one piece, utterly unconcerned.

'Brainless articles,' Lucy muttered. 'Daddy always tells me not to move for them. It's dangerous. He says if I hit one I ought to bring it home for Chef. But I can't stand the thought of it. I always think, what if it has a family?'

Miss Busby smiled. 'Yes. And they're rather handsome, if completely dim.'

'Actually, that's what I wanted to talk to you about,' Lucy said.

'Pheasants?'

'No, articles. News articles, I mean.'

'Ah. The *Oxford News* will be writing about the murders now, I imagine?'

'Yes. You know about the skeleton, I take it? Our mystery victim uncovered.'

Miss Busby nodded as Lucy took the turning towards Little Minton. 'The inspector told me this morning.' She went on to explain all they had discussed, linking the carbon monoxide poisoning to the kerosene sales from the garage Mr Doggett had mentioned, and adding Adeline's dramatic discovery in the Harrison's attic as well as her insistence that Mr Harrison was responsible, along with Rose changing notes for coins in the cash drawer.

'You have been busy! All that in one morning would be enough to make anyone tired!'

'Yes, I suppose it would.' Miss Busby felt worlds better. It had been a sinister thought, she realised, the idea of age catching up with her. It was nice to think she may have the better of it for a while yet.

They were driving through the high street and making their way up the lane to Bloxford when Miss Busby remembered.

'But what was it you wanted to tell me?' she asked.

'Shall we wait until we're inside? It's the sort of thing that might go better with a cup of tea.'

'It must be serious, then.' Miss Busby tilted her head in concern. 'It's not your father, is it?'

'Oh, no! He's fine! I'm sorry, I should've said.'

Miss Busby felt the sudden weight that had descended on her chest lift as swiftly as it had landed, the severity of it rather taking her by surprise.

'In that case,' she said, Adeline's earlier words regarding tea coming back to her, 'shall we treat ourselves and try it with a small glass of sherry?'

* * *

Barnaby was beside himself with excitement at his mistress's return, dancing eagerly around her knees on his back legs.

'Yes, I have missed you too,' Miss Busby assured him, as Lucy laughed delightedly.

'He's spritely for his age, isn't he?' she said.

'I feed him a lot of oily fish. It's good for his joints,' Miss Busby said, as Pud padded down the stairs to see what all the noise was about. 'That reminds me.' She fished in her bag for the salmon and prawn sandwich for Pud, took it through into the kitchen, and fetched two sausages from the cold shelf in the pantry for Barnaby. Having filled each of their bowls, she poured two sweet sherries and took them through to the sitting room.

'They're only very small,' she pointed out, handing a glass to Lucy. 'But if you'd rather something else?'

'No, that'll be fine, thank you. Daddy's the only one who fusses about it.'

Barnaby made light work of his meal and flew back to his mistress's heels before she'd even sat down.

'It was the inspector's fault,' she told him, bending to ruffle his ears. 'He didn't want you in his car, otherwise you could have come with us.'

'Ah, now that sounds more like him,' Lucy said, sitting on the sofa and curling her legs beneath her.

Miss Busby looked over and raised a brow.

'Well, he seemed almost human today for a moment,' Lucy explained.

Miss Busby smiled. 'It takes a bit of getting used to, doesn't it?'

She laughed. 'It does rather.'

'It's his mother's birthday today. I think her illness is taking a toll on him. He was even nice to Adeline.'

'Oh, yes, of course,' Lucy said. 'I'd forgotten. It must be awful for him. At least Mummy's illness was quick. We were lucky in that respect, I suppose.'

'I think it's awful either way. Losing a mother,' Miss Busby said. 'I doubt there can be a greater sadness.'

'Except perhaps losing a child,' Lucy suggested quietly.

The pair sat in silence for a moment, before Miss Busby gathered herself and said, 'Now, we are indoors, and I have a drink. What is it you want to tell me?'

'Oh, dear. It feels worse somehow, given what we've just said. It's the skeleton, you see.' She took a sip of sherry, before putting her glass on the little side table. 'It wasn't just Alice.'

Miss Busby put down her own glass, as yet untouched. Her heart sank as her brain made the connection, before Lucy confirmed:

'The coroner found the remains of a baby, I'm afraid. In utero.'

Miss Busby closed her eyes. 'The poor child.' She felt the weight of helplessness and sorrow descend. 'Both of them. Dear lord. Both just children. Oh, Lucy, how on earth could anyone be so cruel?'

Lucy hopped up from the sofa and took her hand. 'I know, it's terrible. But it gives our murderer motive, don't you think?'

'I'm not sure I *can* think, at the moment. Three murders, now.' She looked over at her glass. 'Would you mind pouring me a brandy? There's a bottle in the cupboard. I wouldn't normally, but I don't think sherry is quite up to the task.'

With the fire dancing merrily in the grate – Lucy having lit it more for light against the darkness of the news than anything else – and a small glass of brandy duly consumed for the shock, Miss Busby gathered her thoughts. Having glanced up to the little cross on the wall above the doorway and said a silent prayer for child and mother alike, questions now began to dance in her mind.

'How did you find out?' she asked, then, rather more urgently, 'does the inspector know?'

'He'll know first thing in the morning when he gets the report. It was a tip-off from one of the juniors at the coroner's office. It must have come to me because they still had my details from the last time, with Vernon Potter in Little Minton.'

'Oh, yes. It must feel rather like a cloud that follows you.' Miss Busby sighed sadly. 'I expect you rue the day you followed me to Lily's Tea Rooms last year.'

'Of course I don't! I was chasing that story before we met, remember. And it's all just part of the job,' Lucy said, working hard, Miss Busby suspected, to lift the gloom. 'Although you made it more than that,' she added quietly.

Miss Busby looked up with a grateful twitch of her lips.

'It was lucky, really, because I was able to take the information straight to Daddy. If it had gone to anyone else, the story would have been in the paper tomorrow morning, and that would have been awful for Mrs Harrison. We talked it through, and he thought it better to give the police more time to tell her before the news comes out.'

Miss Busby looked up in surprise. 'That's very good of him. I should have thought such a dramatic exclusive would be rather a coup.'

'It still will be, just on Saturday rather than Friday. Daddy's not a monster, you know,' she added.

'Of course. I didn't mean to imply…'

Lucy waved the thought away.

Miss Busby rose to her feet to clear the glasses. Barnaby looked up eagerly. 'I ought to take him for a walk.'

'Do you feel like it?' Lucy asked.

'Not really.'

'Perhaps let him potter round the garden for a while?' she suggested.

'Good idea.' Miss Busby opened the back door, then returned to her seat. 'I suppose the killer did know about the baby?' she mused.

Lucy grimaced. 'I should imagine so. It's probably why they did it, don't you think? Poor Alice must have been taken advantage of, and then killed so the culprit didn't have to face the consequences.'

'And the murderer panicked when he realised the bones would be discovered,' Miss Busby added. 'The bones of both of them.' Her voice caught on the last.

'Would you rather I hadn't told you?' Lucy asked, looking distressed at the thought.

Miss Busby plumped for a white lie to spare her feelings. 'No, not at all. Besides, I would have found out eventually,' she reasoned. She looked into the flames for a moment, then asked, 'Why *did* you tell me, though?'

'It got me thinking,' Lucy said, as Barnaby stomped back into the room looking cheated. He jumped up onto the sofa beside her and she rubbed his chest. 'About how you solved the Potter murder when everyone was gathered together.'

'That wasn't just me,' she protested, trying not to let the weight of Lucy's expectation settle too firmly on her shoulders.

'You were the force majeure, Miss B.' Miss Busby smiled at Lucy's use of her brother's name for her. 'And with the funeral being tomorrow, I thought perhaps this way you might have a better chance of doing the same.'

'Adeline is convinced she has already solved the case,' Miss Busby pointed out.

'She doesn't know about the baby, though.'

'No, but I have a horrible feeling it would only fuel her suspicions.'

Lucy looked aghast. 'Surely not?'

'She has it in her head that all men can be fiends where pretty girls are concerned,' Miss Busby said with a sigh. 'Particularly when they are vulnerable.'

'I suppose, really, she's not *too* far wrong,' Lucy conceded. 'And Mr Harrison and Alice weren't technically related, after all.'

Miss Busby wondered, with a heavy heart, if she were the only one left who didn't think such dark thoughts of people.

CHAPTER 32

'Do you imagine the murderer will be at the funeral?' Miss Busby said.

'I should think so,' Lucy said. 'He must be local, after all.'

Miss Busby nodded. 'I suppose Cameron Spencer is firmly in the frame now. With Alice having been keen on him.'

'Perhaps, but Anthony is convinced he's not the sort.'

'As is Ezekiel. He seems very fond of the young gentleman. Although Ezekiel seems fond of most people. He certainly sees the good in everyone.'

'An admirable trait,' Lucy noted.

'Yes, but I suspect it could also be rather dangerous. I met the young man myself this morning, just briefly.'

'What did you make of him?'

'He's very handsome. Remarkable eyes. Just the sort of chap they put on the cover of romance serials.'

'The sort any young girl would have fallen for, then.'

Miss Busby nodded sadly. 'I found him rather sharp,'

KAREN BAUGH MENUHIN & ZOE MARKHAM

she added. 'Something in his manner. Although he was awfully polite with it.'

'And of course with him having easy access to the mausoleum, it all points directly to him, I suppose.' Lucy sighed.

'Oh, that's an excellent point.' Miss Busby sat straighter in her chair. 'Cameron would have had access to the keys to the mausoleum. He could have moved the skeleton at any time.'

'Well, yes…' Lucy's brow crinkled in confusion. 'And he could have hidden her body there at any time.'

'Perhaps, but he certainly wouldn't have needed to kill to explain the discovery of the bones. Moving them would have been far simpler. And how would he have got hold of Ezekiel's gun?'

Lucy thought for a moment. 'We don't know when the gun went missing. If Alice found out about it somehow, she may have mentioned it to him.'

'But he was fighting abroad when Alice went missing,' Miss Busby reminded her.

'He might have paid someone else to kill her. That sort of thing does happen. Particularly if you aren't short of money, like the Spencers.'

Miss Busby rubbed her temples. 'It's all guesswork, that's the trouble.' She gave a frustrated sigh. 'What do we know for certain?

She rose to add a log to the fire. It was easier to think, she felt, when one moved about.

'Well, I checked the parish records, and the last time

the mausoleum was opened was February 1918, when Sir Everard Spencer died – he was Lady Felicity's husband. That was the other thing I wanted to tell you.'

'Ah, excellent.' Miss Busby felt on firmer ground here. Postulating was all well and good, but facts and dates made her feel much more in control. As if she were back in the classroom, showing her pupils how to use the information they were given in an equation to find the number they *weren't* given. 'I suspected his death would have been the most recent, but now we know for certain. So,' she went on, replacing the poker after chivvying the flames, 'that was several weeks after Alice went missing. Oh, and of course it would have been when Cameron inherited the title.'

'Yes, I suppose so.'

'Are you hungry, Lucy?'

Lucy looked up, thrown off track by the question. 'Oh, erm, yes, I am a little.'

'Shall I make us a sandwich?' Miss Busby's brain was revving up, and fuel was required. 'There are some cold cuts in the pantry.'

'Let me.' Lucy jumped up to oblige. Barnaby trotted eagerly after her into the kitchen, licking his lips in anticipation. 'Do you think the culprit killed her straight away? Or perhaps lured her off somewhere first, promising to look after her?' she called through to Miss Busby, who was pulling the curtains closed in the sitting room and lighting the little oil lamp by her chair.

It had a safe, cosy feel which fought off the darkness of their chatter.

'There's mustard in the cupboard. And some Battenberg, too, for afterwards if you'd like,' she called, settling back into her chair and stretching out her legs before the fire. 'He may have kept her hidden away somewhere until he came up with a plan to dispose of her for good, although I think it unlikely she would have been alive for long. She seemed so close to Rose, I'm sure she would have found a way to get a message to her.'

'What about the money missing from the till?' Lucy called amidst the cheery clatter of plates.

'Yes, that's puzzling. Cameron certainly wouldn't have needed it, even if he had been home, and nor would Mr Harrison. But we are back to guesswork.'

Lucy came back in with a neat ham sandwich on thick buttered bread. She placed the plate on the table beside Miss Busby, as a small whine emanated from the kitchen.

'Could Barnaby have a slice of meat?'

'Yes.' Miss Busby smiled. 'And bring a small piece for Pud, too.'

Lucy ducked back in and returned with her sandwich and two excitable animals in tow. They were each given their own dishes beside the fire.

'Whoever it was,' Lucy pondered between bites, 'surely it would have been easier for them to break into the mausoleum and move the body than to stage a whole new murder.'

'I'm not sure,' Miss Busby replied. 'I would imagine it's well secured, and items such as lockpicks aren't easy to procure. I wonder,' she went on, 'do you think you could check Cameron and Martin's leave records again?'

Lucy's eyebrows rose. 'I could, but I'm certain they didn't get leave at Christmas.'

'Oh, I don't doubt it, I just wondered if you might check a little further back. And, in fact, forward. I suppose Cameron would have been allowed to come home for the funeral?'

'I expect so.' Lucy nodded. 'But why further back?'

Miss Busby's cheeks flushed. 'Well…given that Alice was pregnant when she died…'

'Ah, of course.' Lucy spared her further blushes. 'I'll check first thing in the morning.'

They finished their sandwiches in thoughtful silence, before Lucy put the kettle on for tea and sliced the Battenberg.

'There are so many variables and unknowns, I suppose the only way we'll get to the bottom of it all is if we can somehow wrest a confession,' she declared, setting down the tea tray. 'That's why I thought if you have all the facts, then at the funeral tomorrow when everyone's gathered together, you might be able to work your magic.'

'Oh, I'm flattered, Lucy, but I'm not sure there's much I can do,' Miss Busby cautioned, stirring the pot. 'Everyone will be grieving.'

'A lot of them will be gawking,' Lucy pointed out.

Miss Busby felt her cheeks flush again.

'Oh! I didn't mean… I just meant…' Lucy trailed off, struggling.

'No, you're quite right. I didn't know Lady Spencer. But perhaps it would be kinder to say a lot of us will be *paying our respects*. Either way, I can hardly go about asking awkward questions in the chapel.'

'There'll be a reception afterwards,' Lucy said, adding, 'and isn't Mrs Fanshawe going with you?' with a wry smile.

Miss Busby laughed. 'Yes, she is. That's a good point.' And she poured the tea, feeling much better.

The pair switched to the subject of the dance Lucy was planning at Lannister House for her father's birthday, and the gloom lifted from Lavender Cottage as talk turned to dresses and music, food and drink, and all thoughts of murder and mausoleums fell aside. They passed a pleasant hour or so in a much brighter mood, before Lucy glanced up at the clock and groaned.

'I ought to go. If I don't finish that article about the Operatic Society and the AmDram crowd they'll both start attacking me instead of each other.' She stood. 'Don't get up, I'll see myself out. Have a restful evening, and I'll see you at the funeral tomorrow.'

'Are all three of you going?' Miss Busby asked.

'Yes. You should come back with us afterwards,' Lucy offered. 'Stay for dinner. Unless you need to talk to the inspector, of course.'

'Perhaps he could come too,' Miss Busby hazarded, a gleam of mischief in her eye.

'Oh. Yes. I'm sure. That is, if he'd like.'

Miss Busby laughed. 'Would you mind passing me my bag? I ought to bring my notes up to date with all that's happened. And then I will rest for the evening, I promise.'

After Lucy had left, it took another half hour of careful thought and precise commentary before she was satisfied. The heartbreaking news of the baby made sense of why Alice was killed, and the prospect of the skeleton being found made sense of why Travis was killed. Now all she had to do was find the link between the two.

Setting the notebook to one side, she sank back into the cushions. Pud sprang onto her lap, and the engine-like purr of the ginger tom soothed her busy mind. She had just drifted into a light doze when the shrill peal of the telephone rang out from the hall.

'Miss Busby?'

'Inspector.' Her heart began to race, as if he knew Lucy had shared her secret and was angry she hadn't rushed to Chipping Common to tell him.

'I'm sorry to disturb you, but I thought this less invasive than calling on you at this hour.'

'Not at all,' she answered, her mouth dry. Having just regained the inspector's trust, her mind raced ahead for possible explanations as to why she had now betrayed it.

'When you left Harrison's this afternoon, and looked at the–'

'Oh wait! Mabel!' Miss Busby swiftly interjected.

'I have already informed the operator it is an offence to listen in to police matters,' he reassured her. 'Did anyone see you looking around the back of Harrison's?'

'No,' she answered, surprised. 'I made sure no one was watching, as I felt rather foolish.'

'And you are absolutely sure the downstairs window was open at the time?'

'Yes, of course. Why?'

'Because sometime between then, and my speaking to Mrs Harrison, somebody returned and closed the window from the outside.'

'Are you sure?'

He let out a sigh which crackled and popped across the wires. 'Yes, I'm quite sure. I checked the window with Mrs Harrison myself. It was closed, but unlatched. I have had my officers dust the outside of the window for fingerprints, to no avail.'

'So someone climbed up onto the bin and pushed it shut, presumably wearing gloves.'

'They may simply have used a sleeve or handkerchief. It would look less suspicious than gloves at this time of year.'

Miss Busby had a sudden image of Mrs Olivia Spencer in her long black gloves but dismissed it as fancy. She racked her brain. 'I distinctly remember looking around first, as I felt a bit furtive. There was no one. Could it have blown shut?'

'There was not a lick of wind this afternoon,' he said rather curtly.

She had known this, of course, but the slight possibility had seemed more attractive than the alternative. 'Oh dear.'

'Miss Busby, it may be no more than coincidence, but I suspect the murderer saw you snooping—'

'That infernal word again, Inspector. I was merely looking.'

'Regardless, they may have seen you and realised their mistake. Mrs Harrison insists that the window is habitually closed, but is unable to recall when she last checked.'

'So it could have been open since last weekend,' Miss Busby followed. 'That's how he got in, he leaned in to unbolt the door. And he forgot to close the window when he left.' She thought for a moment. 'Isn't that rather odd, that someone would arrange such an intricate tableau, but forget such a simple matter?'

'Not at all. It's how we catch the majority of criminals.'

'Yes, I suppose you're right. Well, the net is certainly closing in, Inspector.'

'Aye,' he agreed. 'We now know for certain our murderer is in the area, and I have my officers out on patrol accordingly. They're asking questions – delicately, so as not to cause concern.'

'I should imagine it's too late for that,' Miss Busby murmured.

A hint of cynicism darkened the inspector's tone. 'The man has killed a workhouse waif and a penniless poet. I doubt the majority of Chipping Common feel themselves in any danger.'

'Perhaps,' Miss Busby said, rather sharply, 'but that doesn't mean they don't care. Concern isn't a matter purely for oneself, after all.'

'*Hum*, well.' He cleared his throat. 'As I said, they are being delicate.'

Miss Busby wondered just how delicate young Bobby Miller would be, before admonishing herself. He was a diligent young man who took pride in his work, and she knew he would do his best, even if he occasionally got a little swept up in the excitement.

'I have an experienced officer on his way over from Oxford, too,' the inspector added, as if reading her mind. 'The net is closing in, as you say. What concerns me is who is being caught within it. This is a nasty individual, Miss Busby, who goes to great lengths to cover his tracks.'

'Yes.' Miss Busby understood. She felt small, and afraid, and this annoyed her greatly. Adeline would not be concerned in her position. She would be off to Chipping Common post-haste to see which vantage points offered a view of the dustbins, and who might have seen her friend looking there that afternoon. 'But I am not Adeline,' she murmured.

'What was that?'

'Oh, nothing.' She fiddled with the telephone cord nervously.

'I really do think, Miss Busby,' he continued, 'that

this is the point at which I must insist you stop sn–, looking.'

'Yes. And I think this is the point at which I shall respectfully comply,' she answered gravely. 'Although, I shall be at the funeral tomorrow, of course.'

'That's fine,' he conceded. 'I will be there too. As will Sergeant Heaton, two local constables, and at least one Oxford officer.'

'You expect the murderer to attend, then?' she asked.

There was a pause on the line before he answered, 'I should think it very likely, yes. But that is not an invitation for you to attempt to identify him. Please, Miss Busby, stay close to your friends, and resist the urge to…wander.'

'I will. Thank you, Inspector.'

'Not at all. Good evening.'

CHAPTER 33

After a night of disturbed sleep and unsettling dreams, Miss Busby rose early and made herself a strong pot of coffee. Boiling three eggs, she sat at her wooden table outside, snuggly wrapped in a woollen shawl over her old blue dress, and let her garden work its magic. Pud and Barnaby had a mashed egg each. Miss Busby enjoyed toast and buttered soldiers with hers while watching the house martins and swifts dance in the sky above.

Once refreshed, and dressed in a neat grey skirt with a charcoal-coloured blouse sufficiently solemn for a funeral, she fetched Barnaby's lead from the hall. They walked around the green and across to the orchard at the rear of the cottages. Mary's back garden, she noticed, was becoming woefully overgrown. 'I hope new owners are found soon, Barnaby,' she said, as the terrier's bright eyes looked up at her. 'Your mistress's heart would break at the sight of those weeds.'

They were home in time for the post, and Miss

Busby used the leftover Battenberg to entice Dennis into giving her a lift to Little Minton. She was pleased to see the post van back in commission.

'They put new paint on it an' all, looks good dunnit Miss?' He beamed.

'It certainly does.' She smiled, thinking that perhaps Adeline had done the boy a favour in the long run.

She visited the butcher for some fresh cuts of meat, and the general stores for milk and butter, as well as some of her favourite tea, before popping into Lily's for a coffee and a chat with Maggie. She was feeling altogether more like her old self by the time she sat on the wooden bench outside the post office, taking in the sunshine and waiting for Dennis to drive her and her groceries home.

The sound of slowly clopping hooves in the distance pulled her from her daydreams, and she looked up to see the Rag and Bone man advancing down the road. *He must be doing all the small towns and villages out this way this week*, she thought, not having seen him in Little Minton for some time.

'Raaaaag n' bo-ohne!' the old man called, the tattered flag on the back of his cart fluttering, the faded colours a contrast to the dull greys and browns of his ill-fitting clothes. No doors opened to offer anything, and Miss Busby felt sorry for the man.

'Mornin' Miss,' he called, doffing his cap as he drew near, his hobnailed boots ringing on the road. 'No dog today?' he asked, pulling the horse to a stop.

Miss Busby was surprised he recognised her, and smiled up at him.

'He's at home, in Bloxford. Will you call there later? I have an old jacket and skirt I could leave out for you.'

'We might make it up that way. Depends on how Robbie here feels.' He patted the horse's neck. 'He's slowin' down a bit these days. Mind, we both are. It takes us longer to get about.'

'I shall leave them at the gate in case,' she said.

He tapped his fingers to his cap and moved off. As the cart passed, Miss Busby noticed a flash of something catch the sun. A thin line of neat embroidery in gold thread was worked across part of the makeshift flag, where pieces of different fabrics had been sewn together. She peered more closely at the material, and a memory danced in her brain. She called after him.

'Excuse me, your flag at the back, the embroidery is very eye-catching. I don't suppose you remember where you got it?' She realised as she asked that it was a ridiculous question. The man would collect material from all over the county, of course he wouldn't remember.

He laughed, and she was about to apologise for her foolishness when he said, 'My lucky flag, that is. Got 'er round the back o' the shops in Chippin' Common, years ago it were. Left out for me by the bins, all in a big sack.'

Miss Busby's mind sparked and shone just like the gold thread. 'Which shops? The haberdashery, perhaps?'

'Aye, that row down by the garage. The haberdasher uses all her scraps in her work I should imagine, an' the bookstore don't give no paper away. Her at the pharm'cy wouldn't give 'yer the time o' day, never mind nothin' else, so I dunno who put it out, but I never had a haul like it before,' he continued. 'There was a few coins bundled up inside this 'un.' He nodded to the flag. 'I kept 'er for luck, but it ain't never happened again since!' He doffed his cap, smiling at the memory. 'Gee up, Robbie!'

* * *

Dennis had to call her name three times when he came out of the post office.

'Are you sure you're alright, Miss?' he said, having driven her back. 'I'll carry the bags into the kitchen for you.' He opened the van door to let her alight, then went through the cottage as she trailed along behind. 'You in't your normal self, Miss,' he pressed. 'You look like you've seen a ghost.'

'I'm fine, thank you Dennis.' She had recovered her senses on the drive, but her mind was still tumbling. Of course the murderer wouldn't have left a bag of the victim's clothes out for anyone to find; it was far more likely, she reasoned, that Mrs Harrison had donated Alice's remaining clothes. She had simply got carried away following Mr Doggett's information regarding the kerosene. 'Oh, and there's a quarter of Black Jacks and a small bar of Fruit and Nut in there for you, for your trouble.'

'Oo, thanks, Miss!' He grinned. 'I'll unpack it for you, shall I? It 'int no trouble at all!'

Once her shopping was put away and Dennis had gone off, happily chewing the sweets, Miss Busby spent some time tidying and cleaning her cottage. She hadn't realised how far behind she was with her chores, and suspected the relatively disordered state of things hadn't helped her usually neat and ordered mind.

With everything shipshape and Bristol fashion once more, she sat in the garden under the shade of the mulberry tree and went through her notes for what she hoped would be the final time.

Who could have been watching the alley behind Harrison's yesterday?

The answer, of course, was just about anyone. Market day was the busiest day for the town, and anybody could have been passing, even if she hadn't spotted them at that precise moment. The thought that the murderer was in such close proximity yesterday, however, was a chilling one.

As far as immediate neighbours were concerned, any of them could have been watching from a back window. As Ezekiel was the one who'd told her about the alley in the first place, he was hardly likely to have snuck out and shut the window. The pharmacy had been closed when she'd looked in the afternoon, meaning it was unlikely the Fowlers had been in the building. Mrs Harrison could have seen her, but of course it would have been far easier for her to close the window from the inside. And the same for Mr Harrison, she reasoned, thinking ahead to what would inevitably be Adeline's suggestion when she heard.

Check when Fowlers closed on Thursday, and why she noted beneath. Then, *Clothes left outside several years ago, including material embroidered in similar style to one of Alice's bags. Did Rose donate to Rag and Bone man?*

But what about the coins, she thought. Had they simply been left in the bundle by mistake? She added, *Coins?* then, with her notebook tucked safely into her handbag, went into the kitchen and prepared a light, early lunch of pate and toast, before settling down on the sofa with her Wodehouse and waiting for Adeline to arrive.

The ring of the telephone, harsh and insistent in the silence of the little cottage, woke Miss Busby with a start. Glancing at the clock on the mantel, she saw it was a little after one; she must have dozed off after lunch.

'Miss Busby!' Lucy's voice was breathless, and Miss Busby found herself fully awake, all senses tingling, before remembering Mabel.

'Mabel, if you are listening, please stop,' she said sharply.

'I wasn't Miss,' came the voice, then the sound of a clunk on the line as she switched herself off.

'Lucy, please go ahead.'

'I'm in the office and can't leave yet, but I expect you'll want to see Inspector McKay before the funeral, and you ought to know: I've checked the dates, and Cameron Spencer did indeed come back for the funeral in February 1918.'

Miss Busby reached for the pen and paper she kept by the telephone and made a note.

'And that's not all!' Lucy lowered her voice, as if trying to curb her excitement. 'Martin Fowler came back with him.'

'Did he?' Miss Busby looked down at the telephone in astonishment. 'Why?'

'Well, I did a bit more digging – quite a lot, in fact, I was at the records office for hours, and, Miss Busby, they are related! The pair are second cousins!'

Miss Busby felt her eyes widen. *Oh, the eyes*! she thought. *Of course*. Both had the most startling green eyes.

'And did one or the other also come back prior to Alice's disappearance?' Miss Busby pressed.

'Both! In early October 1917. It wasn't official leave, you see. The grandfather, Sir Everard Spencer, was at death's door, or so they thought. Cameron was his heir, and Martin was close enough family to be granted compassionate leave. They both returned home, but the grandfather rallied, so they went back to Belgium to rejoin the war. Sir Everard hung on until February 1918, and that's when they opened the mausoleum up to bury him.'

She ran the mental calculations, and sighed. 'Oh, Lord.'

'I know. It makes it all even trickier, doesn't it? I thought you should know as soon as possible. I'll see you later on. Good luck, Miss Busby!'

Replacing the receiver, her mind racing, Miss Busby hurried to the front window hoping to catch sight of Dennis, but the post van was nowhere to be seen. With no time to lose, she picked the receiver straight back up and put a call through to Adeline, asking her to come as quickly as possible.

'Why didn't you just telephone the police station if you're so eager to speak to the inspector,' Adeline asked, breathless on the front step in a sleek black dress paired with an eye-catching, jet-black rhinestone choker and matching earrings. 'I risked my new wheel arch several times getting here this fast. And I would have preferred more time to do my hair.' She patted her perfectly coiffed hair, silver strands catching the early afternoon sun.

'It looks lovely,' Miss Busby said, fetching her bag and a light jacket from the hall.

'Which?' Adeline asked.

'Hmm? Oh, both,' she replied absently, then focused sharply. 'It would have been no use telephoning, Inspector McKay will be running here, there and everywhere this morning. Barnaby, *stay*. Dennis will let you out when he comes with the afternoon post,' she told the little terrier. 'He might even take you for a drive.' She stuck her hastily penned note to the front door for the young postman, and set off towards the Rolls.

Adeline's jaw dropped progressively further as she drove them towards Chipping Common and Miss Busby told her about the baby, the leave dates, and the fact that Cameron and Martin were related.

'Well, the latter is hardly surprising,' Adeline said, recovering herself somewhat. 'Most of the well-to-do families in Oxfordshire are interconnected. There are only so many suitable matches to be formed within the county, after all. No one wants to risk bringing bad blood into the line.'

Miss Busby opened her mouth to reply, then fell silent as a fresh barrage of thoughts assaulted her brain.

'The baby *is* shocking, of course,' Adeline went on. 'Although perhaps also not a surprise. We did wonder, after all, if the whole thing might have been a case of history repeating itself.'

'Hmm?' Miss Busby tried to pay attention as the whole case seemed to unfold and reveal itself in her mind.

'Good Lord, Isabelle, do keep up. Alice's mother abandoned her in shame at the workhouse. Which looks like a divine act of mercy compared to what happened to the poor girl's own baby. '

They were approaching Chipping Common and Miss Busby suggested they stop at the police station first. 'Someone will be there to direct us,' she said, looking down at her wristwatch. 'We have just over an hour until the funeral, and I really must speak to the inspector before then.'

'Yes, about Mr Harrison.' Adeline nodded as she steered the Rolls down the high street.

'Mr Harrison?' Miss Busby looked across in surprise.

'The father of the baby, of course.'

Miss Busby blinked. In her excitement, she'd quite forgotten Adeline's fixation with the man. 'No, Adeline, it wasn't him,' she said.

Adeline drew the car to an abrupt halt. 'Of course it was him. Isn't that exactly what we have just been saying? He took advantage of the girl, realised his mistake in getting a child upon her, and erased that mistake before Rose found out. Why?' she asked, eyes wide. 'Who do you think it was?'

Miss Busby took up her jacket and bag as she got out of the car.

'There's no time. I'll explain when we're all together.'

CHAPTER 34

Their dash down the path to the station was brought to a halt by the sobbing figure of Mrs Harrison just inside the door.

'Oh, Rose, whatever is it?' Miss Busby hurried to place a comforting hand on her shoulder.

'It's a-awful,' she cried. 'They have Fraser!' She covered her face with a pink handkerchief, as Adeline directed a triumphant look Miss Busby's way.

'There,' Adeline whispered. 'What did I tell you?'

'No, this is wrong,' Miss Busby murmured. 'Look after Rose, Adeline. I will be back in a moment.' She gently manoeuvred the weeping woman toward Adeline, and hurried to the front desk.

Constable Bobby Miller, seeing her advancing, straightened up and crossed his arms over his chest.

'Now Miss Busby, Inspector McKay isn't–'

'Tell him I know about the baby,' she said quietly but firmly. 'And more besides. I really must speak to him.'

The lad's eyes widened, before he made a visible effort to strengthen his resolve.

'Miss, I can't–'

'Please just tell him, Bobby. Quickly. If he doesn't want to talk to me I promise I shall leave.'

Adeline's booming attempts at consolation rang out in the small reception area: 'I knew it, Rose dear, I just knew it. Now, you are not to blame yourself…'

The sound of Mrs Harrison's weeping intensified.

'And I shall take Mrs Fanshawe and Mrs Harrison away with me,' Miss Busby added, deftly.

The young constable wavered.

Miss Busby arched an eyebrow.

'I'll just be a minute,' he sighed, ducking through to the back.

Miss Busby returned to Adeline and Mrs Harrison. 'You mustn't concern yourself so, Rose. It wasn't Fraser. I'm certain of it, but I need to talk to the inspector. Adeline, why don't you take Rose home for a hot, sweet tea? I'll join you as soon as I can.'

'What? Isabelle, no! I want to talk to the inspector, too,' Adeline huffed, indignant.

'Yes, and so do I!' Rose blew her nose into her hankie.

'I know, but there's very little time before the funeral, and I've promised to explain.'

'Now look,' Adeline objected. 'I started this whole investigation, and I don't see why–'

'Miss Busby?' Bobby Miller had returned.

'Yes?' All three women turned to him expectantly.

'He'll see you. But only you. And quickly, mind.'

'Adeline please let me do this,' Miss Busby urged her.

'Oh, very well.' Adeline gave her most put-upon sigh. 'Come along Rose. Isabelle will explain everything,' she shot her friend a glare, adding, 'very shortly.'

'Miss Busby?' Inspector McKay had appeared from the back. He looked tired, rather harassed, and not in the least happy to see her. 'I really don't have long.'

Once safely ensconced in the bright and cheery office, Miss Busby launched into an explanation before the inspector could remind her he'd asked her to leave matters alone not 24 hours before.

'There was a tip-off to the local paper, about the baby,' she began.

The inspector's mouth hung open a moment, before he lowered his head into his hands with a soft groan. 'And I didnae think the day could get any worse.'

Miss Busby remembered noting last year that his accent became more pronounced when he was under pressure.

'It's alright,' she said kindly. 'It went to Lucy, and she has ensured the story won't be in the newspaper until tomorrow.'

The inspector looked up. 'Has she? Why would she do that?'

'To allow you to inform Mrs Harrison, and because she wants the murderer caught as much as any of us, Inspector. And she's also a very kind young woman.'

She gave him a pointed look. The pale freckles on his cheeks disappeared beneath a flush.

'Well, that's decent of her. We are aware of the baby, and I've acted accordingly.'

'By bringing Mr Harrison in for questioning,' Miss Busby said, a knowing look on her face.

He sighed. 'You are one step ahead yet again, I suppose?' he asked, watching her carefully.

'Well, no. Two perhaps.' She smiled, and waved a hand amicably before he could object. 'I'm just trying to lighten the tone, although it really isn't a light matter. I apologise, Inspector, but I believe I know who the culprit is, and it is not Mr Harrison.'

The inspector sat back in his chair, steepling his fingers and resting his chin on them. 'We have been here before, Miss Busby.'

'Yes, it seems so. Although we are at a different police station, this time. And I am, I suspect, only moments ahead of you, so you shouldn't reproach yourself.'

He laughed, despite himself. Miss Busby realised things weren't like last year at all. The relationship between them had improved, despite a shaky start, and she decided she was very pleased that he was still a feature in her life.

'Mr Harrison was at his offices in London all day yesterday,' he explained. 'With plenty of witnesses, and so couldn't have been in Chipping Common to see you in the alley, or shut the downstairs window of Harrison's. I have just told Sergeant Heaton to let him go.'

'It was perfectly reasonable to suspect him,' Miss Busby offered in consolation. 'As Adeline's theories go, it was rather sound.'

'You never quite believed it, though.'

'Not entirely. There's so much about this business that relates to motherhood, you see. I couldn't get the notion out of my head.'

'In what respect?' he asked.

She looked at the clock above the fireplace. 'It's almost time for the funeral. I need to be certain, but I wanted to warn you, before the funeral takes place: please have your officers keep a careful eye on the two young men. I have been fearful the culprit may attempt to leave the country.'

'Miss Busby, really. Martin Fowler and Sir Cameron Spencer are the obvious suspects, but both were away at war at the time of Alice's disappearance. I have confirmed this myself with the war office records.'

'Yes, but both of them were here for the funeral of Sir Everard Spencer in February 1918.'

There was a pause, before the inspector's expression grew dark once more.

'I would have telephoned the information, if I thought Mabel could be trusted.'

The inspector reached for his notebook. 'Both of them came back, you say?'

'Yes, you see, they are second cousins.'

The inspector looked up once more, brows creased.

'Again, I have only recently found out. But it's why

they both would have been granted compassionate leave.'

'And how, exactly, did you find this out?' he asked.

She told him quickly what Lucy had discovered, including their return in October 1917 and the reason why.

'Very well. But please tell me how you imagine either man could possibly be the killer when both were in Belgium at the time of Alice's disappearance in December.'

'Oh, I don't imagine any such thing.'

'What?'

Miss Busby briefly outlined her suspicions.

'Ah,' he murmured, as she concluded. 'I see.'

'It is awful to think of, isn't it?' She sighed.

'Murder always is,' he agreed, rising to his feet. 'But some murders are certainly harder to think of than others.'

Miss Busby hurried to Harrison's Haberdashery to find Rose upstairs in the pretty flat. She was looking brighter. Her husband sat next to her on the sofa and was patently furious. Adeline sat apart from the pair, looking none too pleased herself.

'Oh, Miss Busby! Thank you!' Rose cried, and stood to rush over and take her hands. 'That awful inspector had the nerve to suggest…oh, it's too dreadful!'

'You mustn't give it a moment's thought,' Miss Busby said softly. 'It's his job to think dreadful things and imagine everyone capable of them. He once even thought me nefarious, you know.' She smiled over at Mr Harrison as if to offer comfort, but his eyes remained cold and angry, and he was even paler than usual.

'It is hard to imagine that man "capable" of catching a killer,' Fraser Harrison said quietly.

Adeline gave a small snort from the corner. Miss Busby shot her a look.

'Fraser has recently begun to play golf with the police commissioner,' Rose said. 'I expect you'll say something, won't you dear? It's terrible, what that inspector was implying.'

'He did more than imply, Rose, he accused me of the most terrible acts,' he said softly. 'I will certainly say something, you may rest assured. I was fond of the girl. I could never have harmed her.'

'It's his role to investigate without fear or favour. He must get to the bottom of it,' Miss Busby said in as kindly a tone as she could muster, 'but we ought to be going if we're to be on time for the funeral. Adeline?'

Adeline nodded and made for the door, before Rose stopped them both. 'Miss Busby, what were you going to tell us? What did you need to speak to that awful man about?'

Miss Busby glanced at Fraser Harrison and realised she didn't dare risk dropping the inspector into any more trouble. If the commissioner were to hear of an elderly lady solving the case before the inspector, goodness only knew what he'd think. 'Oh, just to tell him it couldn't have been Mr Harrison, of course.' Adeline was about to object, so she hurried on with, 'Rose, may I ask what you did with the clothes Alice left behind when she went missing?'

Mr Harrison came over and reached awkwardly to put an arm around his wife's shoulder. 'I think my wife has been through enough today. We both have.'

'No, darling, it's fine.' She patted his hand and turned back to Miss Busby. 'I kept them for a long while, of course, hoping…but on the third anniversary of her disappearance I cut them into pieces for a patchwork quilt. To remember her by, you see.'

'Oh, how lovely. And I expect you popped the leftover pieces out for the rag and bone man?' Miss Busby pressed gently.

'Goodness, no. I couldn't bear to throw away anything of Alice in such a manner. I used every scrap of material. I made two quilts. One for myself, and one for Mr Travis.'

Miss Busby remembered the pretty patchwork quilt they'd seen in his room.

'When I curl up beneath it,' Rose went on, 'it's as if the dear girl is still nearby. And I suspect poor Mr Travis felt the same. He had nothing left of his own daughter. Everything was lost in the fire. And now he is gone too.'

CHAPTER 35

'Why are you so obsessed with the rag and bone man?' Adeline asked as she steered the Rolls towards Hayle Court.

'I'm not obsessed, although I did have the strangest encounter with him in Little Minton.' Miss Busby went on to explain, and Adeline's eyes grew wider as she laid out her theory of how and why Alice Albion, and consequently Gabriel Travis, had met their respective deaths.

'Well I wish you'd said something sooner, rather than letting me hare off thinking it was Fraser Harrison,' Adeline complained as they turned to enter the imposing gates and long driveway to Hayle Court.

Miss Busby wasn't entirely listening, her mind still whirring. She did however notice the front lawns were immaculate but devoid of trees or shrubs. As neat and tidy as it was, it all looked rather soulless.

'Besides,' Adeline was still rattling on, 'I seem to remember you agreeing with me that Fraser Harrison was shifty.'

'I said he looked uncomfortable,' Miss Busby countered. 'It was you who used the word shifty. But it was certainly an avenue the inspector had to explore. Although I admit, he could have done it a little more discreetly.'

'And you are quite sure this time?' Adeline went on, as if Mr Harrison's guilt hadn't been her own idea. 'What proof do we have?'

'That's the trouble,' Miss Busby sighed. 'Nothing concrete, I'm afraid. But there's the panelling, the kerosene, the rag and bone man, and now the baby, of course.'

'All circumstantial,' Adeline cautioned as she abandoned, rather than parked, the Rolls in the spacious area outside the imposing mansion: a Georgian house built of red brick with sash windows and a stone portico over the glossy front door.

'Yes, although enough, I think, to wrest a confession, if we are clever about it.' Miss Busby climbed out and looked around. The gravelled drive was crammed with gleaming motorcars, and liveried staff hurried about checking invitations and directing mourners in hushed, respectful tones.

'Well, you are endlessly clever Isabelle, there is no doubt about that,' Adeline proclaimed as she disembarked. 'Barring the odd false start, of course,' she qualified, before a footman approached.

Adeline wafted her invitation under his nose. He bowed and indicated they follow the winding path around the back of the house.

The rear gardens were far prettier; the scent of wisteria and magnolia drifting in the faint breeze. Miss Busby glanced over at the house, smartly stark with French windows, a terrace, and handsome bronze urns filled with tumbling flowers in pastel colours.

'I've always thought Mrs Fowler rather unpleasant,' Adeline confided quietly, as other mourners in groups of twos and threes became visible further along the path.

Miss Busby gave a little smile. Adeline was wonderful at such nuances after the fact.

'And Martin Fowler?'

'I can't say as I've ever spoken to him. But he has a hard look about him.'

'Yes,' Miss Busby mused. 'Something in those green eyes…'

They walked beneath a belt of trees, weeping willow, beach and elm, and turned towards the pretty family chapel. The day was warm and bright, the grounds pleasant despite the sadness of the occasion and the pall of murder hanging over the town. Birds still sang, the sun still shone, and the surrounding fields and the winding River Glyme still looked beautiful in the distance.

'We are a little early,' Adeline said as they reached the high hedge surrounding the chapel and graveyard. Black-clad relatives and townsfolk had gathered quietly near the iron gate leading into the chapel yard. They let themselves in and closed it behind them. 'We ought to have stopped for Ezekiel, if we'd thought of it.'

'I'm sure Rose will bring him,' Miss Busby said, standing on her tiptoes to see over those already present. The chapel was much older than the mansion, stone built under a steep slate roof, windows tall and narrow with pointed arches and plain glass. There was no steeple, just a simple tower housing a bell which rang mournfully, one bass bong marking the minutes. The iron-studded door stood closed; nobody approached it, the crowd keeping a respectful distance.

Bobby Miller was standing smartly to attention on one side of the carved entrance. He glanced over and gave her the faintest nod, the polished shield on his helmet gleaming in the afternoon sun. She nodded discreetly back, then looked across at the other young constable, recognising him as Garthwaite from the local station. There was no sign of the inspector, or his Oxford colleague – although, if the colleague wasn't in uniform she wouldn't know him from Adam.

Miss Busby glanced across to the family mausoleum, tall and proud amid old gravestones, presumably memorials to family retainers and lesser mortals. The grass had been scythed short, the gravel path leading to it neatly raked. The building was half sunken into the ground; a miniature version of the chapel itself, although lacking windows and tower. Stone steps led down to its door, which was also closed, and also made of iron-studded oak. She noted the large handle and elaborate key hole; there were faint scratches on the metal and dark smudges on the door itself.

These were the only signs of the recent drama. She thought of the opening of its door in readiness to receive the recently deceased Lady Felicity Spencer. The shock of finding skeletal remains among the mouldering coffins. The frantic panic of the household, the police being summoned and their rush through the streets to the spot. Then their quiet picking over the bones and painstaking search for evidence. And finally the gathering up and carrying away of poor Alice and her unborn babe.

After several more moments the bell fell silent and sombre organ music could be heard. The chapel door swung open, and the vicar emerged to solemnly usher the waiting mourners inside.

The Spencer family were already seated at the front of the chapel, the coffin on a bier placed before the simple altar. Flowers and wreaths of white lilies were placed alongside, their heavy scent suffusing the space. Each of the family was distinctly recognisable from the rear. Cameron's tall figure elegantly clad in a black suit, Olivia's dramatic black crepe and trailing veil, and Madeleine's slim figure and bowed silken head.

'Let's sit at the back,' Adeline suggested in hushed tones, then bustled into the furthermost, and indeed shortest, pew nearest the door. 'This way we can see everyone coming in without having to crane our necks.'

Miss Busby followed, crossing herself before dropping to the kneeler for a moment of private prayer. Lucy's comment regarding "gawkers" lay on her mind, and she expelled it by commending Lady Spencer's soul to heaven, before sitting down. There was no reason, she thought, why one couldn't mourn and observe at the same time.

The chapel filled steadily. Miss Busby hardly recognised anyone until Rose and Fraser Harrison arrived with Ezekiel in tow. They had all changed into sombre clothing, Ezekiel had even found a black velvet yarmulke.

Richard Lannister entered on Lucy's arm for support. He had foregone his stick for the occasion; Miss Busby knew how much he hated being dependent on it. *'It doesn't go with any of my smarter suits,'* he would say, as if to disguise how much his infirmity bothered him. His limp was heavy, and her heart went out to him. Anthony Lannister brought up the rear, spotting her and waving, gesturing ahead with a grimace of regret that there wasn't room for all of them on the same pew. Miss Busby was still watching them settle when Adeline gasped beside her.

'Isabelle!' she hissed. 'The Fowlers!'

Miss Busby turned to see Mrs Fowler enter, stiffly upright with one hand resting imperiously on Martin's arm. Martin looked stern, the black of his suit and tie setting his green eyes ablaze. His hair was neatly trimmed, and he walked tall and proud to the very front of the chapel, where he and his mother took a seat beside the Spencers.

'I thought you said they were only second cousins?'

Adeline whispered. 'I should have thought second row, at the very most.'

'Ah, but you are a step behind.' Both Adeline and Isabelle jumped before recognising the figure who had taken a seat beside them whilst their attention was focused ahead.

'Enid! How did you get here?' Miss Busby was the first to recover.

'Good Lord, you scared me half to death!' Adeline added, earning several stern looks from mourners in the row in front.

'I telephoned Lavender Cottage, but there was no answer, so I summoned a taxi,' she explained in hushed tones.

'Did you?' Adeline's eyes widened, impressed. 'But why? And how did you manage without an invitation?'

'I raised my chin and walked with purpose,' she explained, as if it were obvious. 'And I came because I thought you ought to know that Martin Fowler's engagement to Madeleine Spencer is to be announced at the reception.'

Adeline's sharp intake of breath was covered by the sound of the organ as the opening hymn commenced the service. Miss Busby's thoughts fizzed excitedly before finally beginning to settle. *Here*, she thought, *was the final piece of the puzzle.*

As the vicar began a eulogy in praise of Lady Felicity Spencer's poise and grace, Miss Busby dwelt on the ambition and cunning of those around her. As he touched on Felicity's devotion to God, she considered the hand of the devil at play in Chipping Common. And as Sir Cameron Spencer rose to read Psalm 23, the final verse resonated so soundly it felt almost as if it were a confirmation from the very heavens:

'You prepare a table before me
   in the presence of my enemies…'

Just as the killer prepared the desk, finding the right poem and placing the gun in Travis' hand.

'You anoint my head with oil;
   my cup overflows…'

Just as Travis' heater was filled with oil the night of his murder.

'Surely your goodness and love will follow me
   all the days of my life,
   and I will dwell in the house of the Lord forever.'

Just as the guilty would dwell, cell-bound, at His Majesty's pleasure until such time as justice was fully served.

Miss Busby patiently waited for the readings to end, prayers to be offered, and the final hymn to begin before whispering to Enid, 'How did you find out about the engagement?'

'Jilly told me,' she replied, Adeline straining to

hear beside them. 'She spoke to one of Olivia's maids at the market in Little Minton this morning, who happened to mention that the Fowlers were up at the house most of yesterday, making the necessary arrangements.'

So that was why the pharmacy had been closed, Miss Busby thought.

'Then Jilly announced there was a whole new hullabaloo in Chipping Common regarding the baby's bones. Everybody is talking about it. I thought back to our chat at The Bridge, and pondered it all whilst enjoying my lunch, and it suddenly became no great leap to put it all together.'

Miss Busby was surprised news had travelled so swiftly, although domestic staff, she knew, had their own network which could rival British Intelligence.

'You have competition, Isabelle!' Adeline stage-whispered, a gleam in her eye. 'Two Sherlocks!'

'I could not even begin to compete,' she said softly, turning to Enid. 'You are a marvel, Enid. I suspected as much: it's all about ambition and envy, and Adeline, when you mentioned that there are only so many suitable matches to be found within the county, I was almost sure of it. I suppose second cousins rarely give pause, in consideration of a suitable match.'

'Am I a marvel too, then?' Adeline asked.

Miss Busby nodded. 'I should say so. Our erstwhile Watson.' She patted her friend's hand.

'Oh, well, thank you.' Adeline smiled and puffed

out her ample chest with pride. 'I like to think I have learned a thing or two in my time.'

'Now we have confirmation, it is time to act. 'We must find Inspector McKay,' Miss Busby urged, as the final chords of *Dear Lord and Father of Mankind* rang out.

They had to wait some time. The coffin was carried out with due solemnity, the family and mourners following. The lilies and wreaths were taken from the chapel and placed either side of the path to the mausoleum. More prayers ensued. Finally the coffin was carried into the tomb and the crowd were left to make their way back towards the house for the formal repast.

Miss Busby spotted Inspector McKay standing at a distance among the gravestones. He came down to meet her and the two ladies.

'I take it you've noticed nobody has fled the country?' he asked wryly.

'Yes. Why would they, when they are convinced they've got away with it? Is there somewhere we can talk, quickly?' she asked, as the mourners drifted away.

McKay looked over at the mausoleum, its door still standing open. For one terrible moment Miss Busby feared he was going to usher them inside.

'Follow me,' he said, leading them instead to a pretty garden pavilion just beyond the chapel yard hedge. It was built in octagonal shape and shielded from view behind thick, fragrant rose bushes. Inside offered comfortable, padded seating on white wicker chairs, which Enid was pleased to take advantage of.

'Is someone watching the suspects, Inspector?' Miss Busby asked, making herself comfortable.

The inspector nodded. 'Sergeant Heaton and the Oxford inspector, they're both out of uniform,' he explained. 'Although I'm still awaiting a more detailed explanation.' He arched a brow at Miss Busby.

'Yes, well, I had to be sure. Now that I am, I will explain. Then you can make your arrests, and no one will be any the wiser that it was us who told you. It will help, you see, when Mr Harrison complains to the police commissioner about you,' she added kindly.

CHAPTER 36

'Complains to the police commissioner about what?' A deep furrow appeared between the inspector's brows.

'Never mind that for now,' Miss Busby said. 'Here is what I believe happened: Alice Albion, pretty, naive young thing as she was, fell in love with Cameron Spencer,' she explained. 'Cameron liked the girl, and was kind to her, but being of a strict and traditional family could offer no more. Particularly as he was due to inherit the title,' she added, waiting while the inspector reached into his jacket pocket for his notebook. 'Martin Fowler, however–' She broke off as Madeleine Spencer marched in through the door.

'What do you think you are doing?' she shrieked, her fine-boned face red with fury. Martin Fowler was behind her. 'This is a solemn family occasion and we emerge to find policemen standing outside our private chapel door as though we are common criminals. And now you are skulking in here. How dare you!'

'I'm reporting you for this outrage.' Martin added

his own shrill bluster to that of his putative fiancée. 'I'll have your badge.'

There was quite the queue forming, Miss Busby thought, *for the poor inspector's credentials.*

'What's going on?' Cameron Spencer stepped in, followed by Mrs Fowler, her lips pursed in indignation.

They had all sat in silent shock. McKay was the first to recover. 'There's a good reason we're here, Mr Fowler. And you are party to it.'

'What?' Martin Fowler's green eyes rounded, then narrowed. 'What are you insinuating?'

His mother advanced. 'My son is party to nothing whatsoever, you ignorant man. He is about to announce his engagement to Miss Spencer, and we have no time for this nonsense. You must remove yourself from these grounds and take your lackeys with you.'

Cameron Spencer was less agitated, seeming confused and uncomfortable in equal measure. He shoved his hands deep in his pockets. 'I don't know what this is all about, but this is neither the time or place, Inspector,' he said, then glanced with open curiosity at the ladies.

'I'm afraid it is the very time and place, Sir Cameron. We're here to disclose the killer of Gabriel Travis and Alice Albion.' Miss Busby spoke quietly and calmly.

Mrs Fowler sneered. 'How utterly risible. You have been poking your nose around town searching for gossip, and now you're giving yourself ridiculous airs to excuse your behaviour.'

'I want you all to leave now.' Madeleine Spencer spoke sharply. 'Right now!' Miss Busby quite expected her to stamp her foot.

'Don't you want to know who killed them?' Miss Busby continued, unperturbed. She'd dealt with childish behaviour like Madeleine's for many years in the classroom, after all. 'The culprit is right here, among us.'

'You mean *culprits*, Isabelle,' Adeline corrected.

Silence followed for an instant as the words sank in.

'I will not stand here and be insulted by some interfering busybody,' Mrs Fowler snapped. 'Martin, we are leaving.' She turned toward the glass door, half open in the light breeze.

'No you're not.' McKay was on his feet. 'You're all staying here until you've heard us out.'

Miss Busby felt a quick swell of pride at his use of *us*.

He strode to the door before they could move, put his head outside and whistled loudly. A moment later both constables came running up.

'Sir?' Bobby Miller asked, Constable Garthwaite by his side.

'Stand guard by this door,' McKay ordered.

'Righto, sir.' Bobby saluted, as did Garthwaite, then they positioned themselves to face the garden.

McKay walked back to the centre of the space. 'Now, let's hear Miss Busby out, shall we?'

She suddenly felt a little overwhelmed. Adeline had been sitting with her mouth open; Enid was watching with a smile playing on her lips. They both turned to her now with a nod of encouragement.

'Very well,' she said, taking a deep breath. 'It is my belief that one of the killers took cruel advantage of Alice's heartbreak to impose himself upon her when he returned to Chipping Common on leave in October 1917.'

'Who took advantage?' Madeleine demanded. 'What on earth are you talking about?'

Miss Busby held a hand up. 'I'm coming to that. Alice had been in love with you, Cameron, hadn't she? And you were fond of the girl, but you told her you couldn't ever offer marriage. It would be met with opposition by your family. You may even have been disowned?'

Cameron watched her. A strand of dark hair slipped out of place. He swept it back, then nodded. 'Yes, I'm afraid that is what happened. We had become close, but poor Alice didn't quite grasp it could never be anything more.'

Madeline clasped a hand to her mouth in horror.

'But I never took advantage of her,' he continued. 'Alice was a sweet girl. We were both young, but we knew not to overstep the bounds.'

'What did you think when you heard she'd disappeared?' Miss Busby asked.

He sighed. 'I was truly sorry, but I thought she'd simply run away to escape her disappointment.' He leaned against a post holding the roof of the pavilion up.

'Disappointment is hardly the word,' Mrs Fowler snorted. 'All her machinations were for nothing. She thought she could snare you, Cameron, and become the next Lady Spencer. A workhouse brat, of all people. She ran off with her tail between her legs when she failed. And good riddance.'

'That's a despicable lie and you know it.' Enid couldn't keep quiet. 'Alice didn't run anywhere. The poor girl was murdered.'

'Who on earth are you?' Mrs Fowler retorted. 'Not that it matters. You are quite as unhinged as your interfering friend. Of course she ran. And when she realised she was with child, she returned to confront the father: that disgusting, sneaking Travis person. And he killed her.'

'Exactly,' Madeline cut in. 'It wasn't Cameron's child. It's obvious she had been playing around with someone. And that old man was obsessed with her, everyone knew it.'

'Cameron.' Miss Busby looked to him. 'Could the child have been yours?'

'How *dare*—'

Cameron held up a hand to silence his sister's high-pitched objection.

'It's alright, Maddie.' His handsome face had fallen, his sadness clearly visible. 'I give you my word, Miss Busby, Inspector.' He glanced between them. 'The baby was not mine.'

'You were very close to her, Cameron,' Miss Busby continued quietly. 'She must have talked to you about

Gabriel. Do you believe he could possibly have been the father of her child?'

'No, I do not,' he said firmly. 'I knew him too, we sometimes talked together about books and poetry. He was a gentle soul. He regarded Alice as a daughter.'

All eyes turned to Mrs Fowler, whose sharp cheeks reddened. She couldn't support her awful accusations in the light of Cameron's plain statement.

'Well, it was Melnyk then,' she blustered. 'Those foreigners can never be trusted.' She folded her arms under her thin chest.

'It is not my mother's job to uncover the killer,' Martin drawled. 'This really is the most preposterous—'

'Do you know who killed Alice?' McKay asked Cameron, ignoring Martin.

He shook his head. 'I don't, Inspector. I can't make any sense of it.'

'Oh for heaven's sake, Cameron.' Madeleine spoke sharply to her brother. 'You could never see it. Half the boys in the town were soft on her. It was obviously one of them. Mama always said you shouldn't consort with a workhouse stray and she was right, look what's happened. Alice was nothing but a guttersnipe with no sense of right or wrong. You have had a lucky escape.'

Cameron looked at his feet as Mrs Fowler smirked in triumph.

'Come along, Mother, these people can't keep us here.' Martin Fowler held a hand to reach for the door. 'Madeleine, after you.'

'Not so fast,' McKay called out. 'This isn't finished yet.'

'Yes, it is. Good day, *Inspector*.'

'You were the father of the child, weren't you, Mr Fowler,' Miss Busby said, stopping him in his tracks.

He swung around with rage in his eyes, which he quelled almost instantly. 'That is a slanderous lie,' he stated in a voice coldly controlled. 'I do hope you have a competent solicitor, Miss Busby.'

Cameron slowly looked up, staring at the man who was soon to become his brother-in-law.

'How dare you,' Mrs Fowler hissed. 'How dare you make such a filthy accusation against my son.'

'It's alright, Mother. I was in Belgium when she died,' Martin said with a sneer. 'As any competent police officer would know.'

'And how do you know when she died?' Miss Busby asked, rising to her feet the better to face him.

The sneer died on his lips. 'I…you said…'

'You said she ran away,' Miss Busby continued. 'So did your mother. So did everyone. But she didn't run away, did she? You know she didn't, because you know who killed her.'

His eyes flicked to his mother's. Hers widened and she took an involuntary step backwards.

'You killed Alice Albion, Mrs Fowler,' Inspector McKay accused. 'And we're going to prove it.'

'You killed her because your son was the father of her child,' Miss Busby added, then found she felt rather faint and sat back down. 'And you couldn't bear him to be saddled with a girl of no standing.'

'No, no!' Mrs Fowler shrieked. 'Martin would never touch her, she was nothing, a nobody, a common foundling!'

'Damn you, Martin.' Cameron spoke quietly, slowly, before suddenly shouting, 'Damn you to hell!' All eyes turned to him in astonishment. 'It was you. Of course it was you, it's so obvious now.' His voice fell, as he rubbed at his temples. 'I never imagined… but I remember the way you looked at her, and I remember how self-satisfied you were at the end of our October leave. I was cut up because I'd told Alice we had no future together, and you were swaggering about the place even more than usual.' His eyes flashed with fury. 'What did you do? Did you take advantage, or did you force yourself on her?' he shouted and advanced on Martin.

'Shut up Cameron, you don't know what you're talking about,' Martin yelled, taking a step back. 'I didn't kill her.'

'No, but you disposed of her body.' Miss Busby had to say it, although her head was spinning with the awfulness of it all. 'You put Alice's body in the Spencers' mausoleum after Sir Everard's funeral.'

Madeleine shrieked and put her hand over her mouth once more. Nobody took any notice.

Cameron's eyes narrowed, his breathing growing ragged in the ensuing quiet. 'You came to see me,' he said slowly, glaring at Martin. 'The evening of the funeral. You parked your van by the chapel. I thought it was strange. The mausoleum hadn't been locked yet because the flowers had just been placed inside.' He rubbed at his temples again, as if loosening the memory. 'You'd asked me about it that morning, you even offered to come down and lock the door with me.' He raised a hand, stepping forward and shoving Martin in the shoulder. 'You'd just dumped her body in there, hadn't you? Alice was innocent, and pure, and you – you *devil* What did you do to her?' he bellowed. 'Tell me what you did to her.'

'Don't you lay another finger on him,' Mrs Fowler dashed forward to protect her beloved son, throwing herself in front of him. 'Leave him alone. It wasn't him.'

'No, it was you, Mrs Fowler.' McKay stepped forward, ready to separate them. 'You killed Alice and hid her body until Martin returned home to help you dispose of it.'

'Don't say anything, Ma,' Martin said, his voice weak and shaky now. 'Not one more word. They can't prove anything, and they know it.'

'You're both under arrest,' McKay said, then put his fingers together and whistled loudly.

Bobby Miller and Constable Garthwaite ran through the door. 'Handcuff them both.' He pointed to mother and son.

It didn't take a moment. Everybody was dazed by the speed of it all. Within a few minutes, the Fowlers had been marched out and through the garden, escorted by the police officers.

Madeleine burst into horrified sobs, and Cameron helped her back to the house, almost as shaken as she was.

The three ladies sat in the ensuing silence.

'Isabelle,' Adeline broke the silence. 'That was magnificent!'

CHAPTER 37

'Excellent, Isabelle.' Enid added her voice. 'But you must be quite wrung out.'

Miss Busby slumped back in the wicker chair, feeling utterly drained.

'I have brandy in my handbag,' Enid added. 'If you're in need of a tot?'

'Brandy?' Miss Busby sat up. 'Enid you really shouldn't be carrying brandy about with you.'

'I'll have some,' Adeline said.

'No, Adeline, you are driving us home,' Miss Busby said quite sharply.

'Oh we were only teasing.' Adeline smiled. 'And it's brought some colour back to your face.'

Miss Busby smiled wanly, then sighed. 'That was a rather unfortunate interruption.'

'Nonsense.' Enid was dismissive. 'Cameron Spencer was the key to all of this. He knew Alice and, Gabriel Travis, and Martin, and what had been said and done. It worked out perfectly, Isabelle, however traumatic it was.'

'And I think Madeleine Spencer has seen the light too,' Adeline added. 'But I'm still rather bemused by some of it, Isabelle.'

The door opened at that moment and Ezekiel peered in nervously, confusion on his face. 'My dear friends, there is much consternation. The police have escorted away the Fowlers, and the young lady came into the repast with many tears and much shrieking. I heard your name mentioned, Miss Busby, and the garden pavilion. I was most concerned for you, thinking there is something amiss.'

'Nothing is amiss. All is, in fact, righted. The Fowlers are the guilty party,' Enid announced with some satisfaction.

Ezekiel looked even more confused.

'Do sit down.' Adeline patted the chair next to her. 'Isabelle is about to explain all.'

'Ah, then I shall be most happy to do so,' he replied and settled in the chair.

'And you must also tell us, Isabelle,' Enid added, 'what possible proof will convict those murderers after all this time.'

All Miss Busby really wanted was a cup of hot, sweet tea, but she gathered her thoughts nevertheless. 'Well, I cannot offer you evidence,' she began. 'Other than the bones of the poor child, of course. But I believe we can deduce exactly what happened by logic.'

'Aha!' Enid interjected. '"Crime is common. Logic is rare. Therefore, it is upon the logic rather than upon the crime that you should dwell." Sir Arthur Conan Doyle, writing in *The Adventure of the Copper Beeches*.'

'Yes indeed.' Ezekiel nodded, looking at Enid with respect. 'It is always such joy to meet a fellow reader of Conan Doyle. But I do not believe we have been introduced.'

'Mrs Montgomery,' Enid said with a gracious nod. 'And you are Ezekiel Melnyk of course.'

He bowed, and smiled.

Adeline looked confused. 'Yes, but what's all this about copper beeches?'

'It's a quote, Adeline. And Enid and Mr Conan Doyle are quite correct,' Miss Busby went on earnestly. 'Without evidence we can only go by reason.'

'Ah. Very well, then. Reason away.'

Miss Busby smiled. 'When I first suggested to Mrs Fowler that Mrs Spencer wouldn't be pleased to find her son spending time with such a girl, she replied, few mothers would. It got me thinking. Not only about Cameron and Martin, but also about motherhood in general. There are few things a mother won't do to protect her child. But who could Alice turn to, in her time of need? Her own mother having abandoned her.'

'Rose, of course,' Adeline objected.

'Not necessarily,' Enid said with a sad shake of her head. 'A mother's love is unconditional. Can the same be said for a mother who didn't give birth to her child?'

'Of course it can,' Adeline admonished. 'Rose adored the girl.'

'No one doubts that for a moment,' Miss Busby assured her. 'But it is, perhaps, a different sort of relationship. The poor girl would have carried the weight of her birth mother's mistake on her shoulders for many years, and I expect she felt immense shame over what happened with Martin. Going to Rose must have felt so difficult, with both of them knowing the mistakes of her past. Alice may have been rather naïve, but she wasn't stupid. She would have been furious with herself, I'm sure.'

Adeline thought for a moment. 'And so, given Martin's absence, the only person she felt she could turn to was Mrs Fowler.'

'Who, of course,' Enid chimed in, 'was the absolute last person in whom she should have confided. The very notion of Martin associating with a workhouse girl would have near killed her. So she killed the girl instead.'

'Good Lord, Enid. You needn't be so blunt,' Adeline objected.

'I think, after all we've been through this afternoon, there's no point trying to sugar coat it,' Miss Busby said with a sigh.

'Being in possession of a pharmacy, it was only too easy for Mrs Fowler to remove the threat facing her son, by killing the girl. Perhaps a hefty dose of a sedative, no doubt concealed in a cup of tea offered to calm and soothe.'

'Forgive me, for I am a little confused,' Ezekiel said quietly. 'Am I to understand this baby everyone is talking of, was fathered by Martin Fowler?'

'Yes, I'm afraid so,' Miss Busby replied, realising he had missed the most important part of the revelation. 'The young pharmacist took advantage.'

Ezekiel hung his head. 'So very sad,' he muttered, wiping a tear from his eye when he looked up once more. 'But after six years, how can there be proof of this?'

'We can only follow the narrative and hope to arrive at some evidence,' Miss Busby said. 'And so we move on to disposing of the body, which would not have been so straightforward.'

'Due to the time of year.' Enid nodded, keeping pace with Miss Busby.

'Yes, the ground would have been frozen, making digging difficult.' Miss Busby continued. 'The attic, similarly, would have been icy cold, and a reasonable place to store a body. The police must search the pharmacy attic, there may be a trunk or hiding place under the eaves. Alice was only a slip of a thing, by all accounts.'

'And then, after making this most unforgivable deed, Mrs Fowler pretended a robbery at Harrison's?' Ezekiel was catching up quickly.

'Yes,' Miss Busby answered. 'We witnessed Rose come into your shop,' she reminded him, 'taking change from the cash drawer without a thought. Mrs Fowler could have easily done the same at the haberdashery, and taken extra. Or simply helped herself when the shop was empty. And hurrying up to the flat to remove some of Alice's possessions would surely not have been difficult.'

'This is very possible,' Ezekiel agreed, sadness in his eyes at how easily it was done.

'And of course Martin could have procured your gun in the same manner,' Miss Busby continued, 'When Martin returned for Sir Everard Spencer's funeral in February 1918, Mrs Fowler would have had to tell him what she'd done. The body in the attic would, at that point, have soon become a problem. With the internment of Sir Everard in the mausoleum, it would have been easy for Martin to carry the body in his van and hide it in there. Cameron confirmed as much just before the Fowlers were taken away. He saw Martin there just before the tomb was locked.'

'Did he? Oh, the poor boy. Such sorrow.' Ezekiel frowned. 'But why did Martin not simply bury her in the woods?'

Miss Busby had already considered this. 'It is rarely that simple. As we said, the ground would still have been hard, and the countryside is never quite vacant; there is always someone about. On top of which I suspect it is beneath Martin Fowler's dignity to dig holes in the ground.'

'He was an officer in the war, was he not?' Adeline added. 'They're not the digging type.'

'He was.' Ezekiel sighed. 'A man of importance, and trust. And arrogance also, yes. But what of my poor friend, Gabriel Travis?'

'A simple scapegoat, I'm afraid, as Enid first recognised,' Miss Busby replied, with a nod of acknowledgement to her companion. 'With the impending demise of Lady Spencer, the Fowlers knew Alice would be discovered. It was common knowledge Travis had been fond of her, Mrs Fowler herself told me as much, and I believe there is an evil streak in Martin Fowler such that he revelled in the opportunity to punish the poor man twice.'

'Punish him for what?' Ezekiel asked.

'For what he perceived as improper designs. The police thought the same when they read the poem Martin had forced into Travis' hands.'

Ezekiel bowed his head, muttering something softly in a language none of them understood.

'We know Travis loved Alice like a daughter, Ezekiel,' Adeline said kindly.

They waited until he composed himself. 'How did he die?' he asked quietly. 'His real death, not as it was painted.'

'His heater was lit and the fumes overcame him,' Miss Busby explained in a gentle tone. 'He would not have known anything. It would have been just like going to sleep.'

'And we know it was the Fowlers,' Adeline added, 'because Mrs Fowler bought extra kerosene the day before Travis was gassed with it, didn't she Isabelle?'

Miss Busby winced at the phrasing, but nodded. 'Twice her usual amount for the week.'

'Have you offered this information to the police?' Ezekiel asked.

Miss Busby wasn't entirely sure at this point what she had told Inspector McKay. Her mind was unsettled by the awful confrontation with the Spencers and Fowlers. 'I believe so. I will speak to the inspector later. I must also mention the rag and bone man,' she added. 'If they can track him down. I don't know the man's name, but his horse is called Robbie.'

'What on earth for?' Enid raised her brows

'Because he recalls collecting items from outside the shops years ago, one of which resembles a bag Mrs Friedli, the mobile librarian, described Alice having made.'

'Are you sure of this, Isabelle?' Adeline quizzed her. 'I doubt anyone would be foolish enough to leave evidence like that out for others to find.'

'People make mistakes,' Enid pointed out. 'Particularly when they have done wrong. Panic often pushes reason aside.'

'And the inspector did mention,' Miss Busby added, 'that simple mistakes are how they catch the majority of criminals. Besides, it's not as if the rag and bone man would have known what he had. I should think he wouldn't normally have given the sack a second glance until he sold the contents on. And by then it would have been too late. Mere chance must have intervened.'

'Mrs Fowler may have put the sack out the moment she heard his call,' Adeline considered. 'It could have been very carefully done. Regardless, if the police find the item, and confirm where it was found, they will have the Fowler woman bang to rights!'

'I doubt she's the type to confess,' Enid said. 'The entitled ones rarely are. Not unless they feel there is something to be gained from it.'

Miss Busby thought for a moment. 'She may confess to save Martin. She has done worse for the boy, after all.'

'There's no saving him,' Enid said dourly. 'He condemned himself by his own words. *"I was in Belgium when she died,"* he said, and Isabelle, you recognised his mistake immediately. A heartbeat before I did, even. *"How do you know when she died?", you asked.* And he will hang for that mistake.'

'I am not sure such a simple statement will be enough,' Miss Busby noted. 'He can merely say he was misunderstood. No, it is the evidence, however scattered and inconsequential it may appear. When it is combined with the narrative, I'm certain it will bring about their downfall.'

CHAPTER 38

They all left the pavilion together. Ezekiel explained he would like a moment to himself in the graveyard, and then he would walk home. Before he parted he offered a sweeping bow and took Adeline's hand. 'You are my dearest of friends. I am the richest man of all, to know you.'

Adeline was momentarily lost for words, although she soon found them again. 'Oh how very kind, but it was Isabelle who did the detecting.'

'Whereas you, Adeline, were the driving force,' Enid interjected.

'Indeed, each of you have brought me peace. I am most thankful,' Ezekiel said solemnly.

They wished him god bless then retraced their route along the winding path, intent on avoiding the mansion and the no doubt confused and disrupted gathering within.

'Miss B!' Anthony spotted her as they were crossing the drive towards the Rolls. He had just stepped down from the front door. 'Are you making an escape? So are we. It's all rather falling apart inside. The family rushed off and we waited around, making polite conversation, then gave up.'

She saw Richard and Lucy weaving between the cars towards them.

'Ah, I'm sorry to hear that, but there has been rather an unfortunate incident,' she replied.

'You have been sleuthing! Your name was mentioned. You are becoming quite the detective in your own right.' His tease held an underlying seriousness. 'The police have disappeared, and so have the pharmacists.' He was handsome in his smart black suit and tie, his hair neatly combed and usual rumpled manner disguised.

'Well, it was rather eventful.' She was beginning to feel relieved that her part in proceedings was over. She'd felt a weight of not only expectation this time, but also responsibility. Alice and her unborn child, as well as her adoptive mother, all deserved justice as much as poor, Gabriel Travis. 'The inspector now has the task of convicting the guilty, and I don't envy him that.'

'Well, that's what the fellow gets paid for, don't forget. You've done more than enough of his work for him. Are you still coming back with us for dinner?' He lowered his voice. 'Our article about the baby is coming out tomorrow, and I know Lucy wants to talk to you about the final details.'

'Yes, that would be lovely, although I'm afraid the news about the baby is all over town.'

'We're used to the close-knit places beating us to the news, but the larger conurbations won't have heard about it yet.' He sounded unconcerned.

A thought struck her. 'May I bring my friends to dinner?'

'Of course. The more the merrier!'

Adeline and Enid would enjoy Chef's efforts, she knew, and would also eagerly disclose all they had just discussed. *It will give me a much needed break and some time with Richard to puzzle over a crossword rather than unhappy murder*, she thought.

'Miss Busby, I wondered where you'd got to!' Lucy appeared at her side. Her black dress looked stylish paired with silver jewellery, her hair held back with a matching clasp. 'We couldn't find you after the service.'

'Hello, Lucy. We were with the inspector. It's all rather come to a head – with a little help from Adeline and Mrs Montgomery.'

'You solved it?' Lucy asked quietly, eyes shining eagerly. 'I knew you would.'

'It was very much a joint effort.' Miss Busby smiled across at Adeline and Enid, who were in close conversation with Richard.

A flash of bright light from the house caused them to turn and look up. Olivia Spencer was standing at an upstairs window; her jewellery had caught the sun.

'Oh, if looks could kill,' Lucy said.

Miss Busby raised her brows in question.

'Mrs Spencer has had her eye on Daddy for ages,'

she explained. 'She kept coming to parties at the paper until he stopped going. He's not keen, says she never stops talking about herself. She's even been known to hunt him down at the theatre until you started going along with him. That rather put her nose out of joint.' She gave Miss Busby a mischievous smile.

'Ahh.' Comprehension dawned. 'I wondered why she'd looked daggers at me the first time I met her.'

'Should we head for home, do you think?' Lucy grinned.

'I think it would be a good idea.

They all walked slowly to their cars. Miss Busby glanced back at the house as she climbed into the Rolls. Mrs Spencer had vanished from sight.

They arrived at Lannister House after stopping to pick up Barnaby and feed Pud, who was most put out at his supper being late.

Miss Busby settled with Richard out on the terrace, sherry in hand.

'Anthony and Lucy are quite comfortably gathered in the library with your friends, talking murder,' he said.

Miss Busby nodded. 'Adeline and Enid will enjoy helping out. I think I would prefer to talk about other things, if you don't mind. It's all been rather…' She hesitated, not wanting to admit how much Mrs Fowler's actions had upset her. She'd always thought she'd have children with Randolf, and it was one of the great regrets of her life that they'd been robbed of the opportunity. Thinking of poor Alice going to Mrs Fowler for help in her time of need made her feel wretched. 'Hectic,' she concluded, vaguely.

'We can talk of whatever you choose.' He turned to raise his glass. She saw his slight wince at the movement. 'Chef is preparing something special, and we shall put our feet up and be spoiled for the evening. How does that sound?'

'Rather lovely,' she said, with a smile. 'But speaking of putting your feet up, why haven't you been using your stick? And don't give me that nonsense about it not going with your suit,' she added before he had the chance. 'I know you think it makes you look old. Well, you are old, Richard, and so am I. And we are fortunate to have reached this age when so many others haven't. You ought to parade it like a badge of honour.'

He laughed. 'You really are exceedingly wise, Isabelle. I see why Adeline comes to you with her mysteries.'

'Well, you might also see that you remember what I said. Don't think that flattering me will put it out of my mind.'

Following a light dinner of ratatouille, one of Chef's favourite childhood dishes, Enid retired to the library for a nap with Barnaby, where Dawkins lit the fire for them both. Adeline sat at the table in the drawing room with Anthony and Lucy, playing whist.

Miss Busby retired back to the rear courtyard with Richard, and both sat on his favourite bench beneath the rose arbour, wrestling several tricky crossword clues whilst enjoying the last rays of the setting sun. She glanced up as the crunch of tyres on gravel could be heard from the front of the house. Several minutes later Inspector McKay was shown through.

Barnaby's excited yipping soon filled the house. The little terrier scurried out to investigate, and Lucy, Anthony and Adeline weren't far behind. Enid, it appeared, slept on.

'Ah, the Scottish Inspector! Delighted to meet you. Your reputation has preceded you.' Richard greeted him amiably.

McKay gave a formal bow and they then shook hands. 'I hope my reputation hasn't suffered too greatly.'

'I'm a newspaperman, I've long since learned to make my own mind up. Now, sit down," Richard went on. 'No need to stand on ceremony here.'

'Thank you, Sir Richard.' He took a wooden seat opposite the bench, the sun seeming to set his red hair aflame. Adeline came to sit next to him, whilst Lucy and Anthony leaned against the heavy outdoor table, and Barnaby jumped up into Miss Busby's lap.

'How did you know where to find me, Inspector?' she asked.

'I'm a detective,' he replied, with a rare hint of humour.

'So you are. What news?' she pressed.

'Mrs Fowler has confessed to the murder of Alice Albion,' he answered, his usual grave manner returning.

Miss Busby let out a breath she didn't realise she'd been holding. She had no doubt as to the woman's guilt, but hadn't been sure how the inspector would fare in attempting a confession.

'In addition to the murder of Gabriel Travis,' he added. Miss Busby looked surprised.

'Surely that was Martin?' she asked.

'Aye. But the woman is determined to spare her son. It seems getting him an education, profession, and a suitable marriage was her life's work, and Madeleine Spencer was quite the coup. Mrs Fowler is not ready to throw that all away without a fight. The cloth from the rag and bone man may yet condemn her, but she's determined to spare her golden boy.'

'That's quite some sacrifice,' Lucy said, a note of what sounded like admiration in her tone. 'However misguided,' she added hastily.

The inspector nodded. 'Motherhood,' he said. 'You thought it was at the heart of all this, Miss Busby, and you were right.'

Richard looked to her, pride evident on his face.

Anthony asked, 'You'll get the bounder though, won't you, Inspector?'

'That's a rather kind word for him,' Lucy admonished.

'I can't call him what I really think of him, not with Miss B present,' Anthony quipped.

'Chief Inspector Long from Oxford is bringing Cameron Spencer in to help with our enquiries,' the inspector said. 'We think with his witness account we might just have enough to convict him.' He nodded to

Miss Busby. 'As you thought, we also found a gas mask in his rooms at home.'

Lucy gasped. 'So he was able to stay in Travis' rooms while the poor man succumbed to the fumes. How awful!'

The inspector nodded. 'It was well thought out, the mask would have disguised him if he'd been disturbed in the act. We have officers searching the attic at the pharmacy, and the panelling between Harrison's and Melnyk's is being thoroughly examined again. Martin Fowler won't get away with it,' he concluded, his voice filled with determination.

'Well, jolly well done, both of you,' Richard said, raising his glass in salute. 'Anthony, fetch our guest a drink, would you?'

'Not whilst I'm on duty, thank you, sir,' the inspector replied.

'Ever the professional, eh? Admirable!' He smiled, then narrowed his eyes and gave the inspector a curious look. 'Are you married, young man?' he asked, with a glance at Lucy that made her blush.

'What about the window?' Miss Busby asked, jumping to her rescue. 'It's been niggling me since we left Chipping Common. If Martin and his mother were at the Spencers' yesterday, who shut the window at the back of Harrison's?'

'One of the household staff at Hayle Court told Constable Miller that Martin left for an hour or so soon after lunch,' McKay explained. 'Apparently he had a delivery needing attention. He may have spotted you from somewhere.'

'Ah. Well, that explains it then. And of course, he's rather slimmer and more agile than his mother. Mrs Fowler could never have leaned in through such a small window.'

Inspector McKay nodded. 'Aye. And it was the only point of access.' He rose to his feet. 'I ought to get back. There's much to do, but I wanted you to be the first to know.'

'Thank you, Inspector.' Miss Busby smiled up at him.

'Quick question, old boy,' Anthony said. 'Tomorrow's article is about to hurtle off to print – you're happy for us to add in the Fowler woman's admission, I take it? Make you look quite the hero, I should think, solving a case six years old alongside one in less than a week.'

'You may mention it in Alice Albion's case,' the inspector replied. 'But please remember our enquiries are ongoing in the case of the murder of Gabriel Travis.'

'Righto.' Anthony nodded amicably. 'Say no more.'

'You'd best get onto that now, Anthony. We are cutting it rather fine as it is. You didn't mention if you were married, Inspector?' Richard pressed.

Lucy groaned. 'Come on, I'll show you out.'

'Thank you,' McKay mumbled.

Miss Busby cleared her throat meaningfully.

'Oh, yes.' He took up the prompt. 'And thank you for holding back the article, Miss Lannister. It was a kindness and it helped to give us time to act.'

'Not at all,' Lucy said graciously. 'We're on the same side, after all.

Richard's face shone with further mischief. 'Yes, teamwork, that's the key. Do you dance, Inspector?'

He blinked, surprised. 'Erm, yes, a little.'

Richard nodded. 'Thought as much. Great dancers, the Scots. You must come to my birthday celebration next month. Lucy has hired a band.'

'Oh, *ahem,*' McKay cleared his throat awkwardly. 'That's very kind, but—'

'We need more young people to show us older fellows exactly how one dances to jazz. Could be a disaster, otherwise. Seven pm sharp, Inspector, on the 11th June. We shall look forward to seeing you.'

Miss Busby chuckled as the young pair left. 'You know he isn't married,' she chided softly.

'Yes, I just thought the pair of them could use a little nudge in the right direction.'

'Oh, he always needs a nudge, that one,' Adeline sniffed.

Miss Busby couldn't help but agree.

'Only one clue left to solve now, Isabelle, and then we may declare all operations a success,' Richard said.

'Which clue? What did I miss?'

'Twelve down.' He rustled the newspaper in his lap. '*Hands up for an early lunch.* Four letters. Any thoughts?'

A considered pause ensued, before Miss Busby declared, 'Noon, I should think.'

EPILOGUE

'He looks rather dashing,' Adeline said, taking a seat to catch her breath.

'Who?' Miss Busby asked. She had been resting at one of several round tables dotted about the lawn, each covered in a soft white cloth and graced with a small vase containing a single rose.

'Richard, of course.'

'Oh, yes. Lucy bought him the cane. It makes him look awfully smart.'

Sir Richard Lannister held court in the middle of the dance floor that had been laid outside for the occasion. His guests twirled and spun to music played by the American four-piece band, surrounded by the sloping beauty of the idyllic, grounds. Dressed in white linen and supported by the new, silver-topped black cane, he gave it an occasional twirl whenever they looked his way, chuckling each time.

'His arthritis seems to have improved a little,' Miss Busby said. 'Enid asked Jilly to have a word with Chef, and between them they've put him on a new diet which is thought to help.'

'Jemima says some London doctors are suggesting gold injections may treat the disease,' Adeline remarked.

Miss Busby nodded. 'I have heard they are being used for tuberculosis as well. Richard isn't fond of needles, though.'

Adeline *tsked*. 'Men. They will happily go off to fight wars, but a visit to the doctor terrifies them.'

Miss Busby smiled.

'Lucy said her father intends to make an *announcement* this evening,' Adeline continued, imbuing the word with all manner of suggestion.

'Yes, I believe so.' Miss Busby turned in her seat to look at her friend. Her long dress was cut cleverly to flatter a fuller figure, the red silk soft and forgiving. Fine gold embroidery at the neck drew the eyes. 'That dress really is awfully pretty, Adeline. Rose did a wonderful job.'

'Yes, she said she was thinking of Alice when she made the final touches.' Adeline gently smoothed the fabric. 'There's a short jacket to go with it, for cooler evenings, but I have decided I shall warm myself by dancing, tonight. When will your new frock be ready?' she asked.

'Another week or so yet. Rose is awfully busy.'

'Yes, I can imagine.' Adeline sniffed. 'Besides, I have always liked that blouse on you.'

A soft cream silk, it was a firm favourite of Miss Busby's for any social occasion, paired with a navy skirt and her favourite pearls.

'I'm not awfully keen on this music,' Miss Busby confessed. The band playing enthusiastically by the ornamental pond were clearly accomplished, but she found the overall sound rather discordant.

'One must embrace change, Isabelle. Jazz is all the rage in London now. Take a leaf out of Enid's book,' Adeline said with a smile, nodding to their friend. Spurred on by several sweet sherries, Enid was gliding across the dance floor with Mr Waterhouse in tow, her stick forgotten for the moment.

'Yes, whatever happened there, do you know?' Miss Busby asked. Between chatting to the others, she hadn't yet had much chance to talk to Enid.

'He joined her weekly tarot reading group, at Spring Meadows. I believe it was Mary's suggestion.'

'Oh, how clever of Mary.' Miss Busby smiled. Enid was surprisingly passionate about the cards. 'Is she any better? I must take Barnaby to see her soon.'

Adeline nodded. 'She has rallied, by all accounts. She insists she is better at Spring Meadows than at the hospital. They have respected her choice, although there has been the rather stark suggestion that she ensure her affairs are in order.'

'I do hope they are wrong,' Miss Busby said. 'She has defied the odds before.'

They watched the couple for a few moments in silence.

'All Mr Waterhouse had to do to was feign interest in the tarot,' Adeline went on, 'and Enid began to look rather more kindly upon him.'

'I should imagine that interest grew more genuine once Enid displayed her skill in interpreting the cards,' Miss Busby said, remembering how her friend had surprised her with her insight last Christmas.

Adeline shot her a disappointed look. 'It is all codswallop, Isabelle.'

'Perhaps. Perhaps not. *There are more things in heaven and earth*, Adeline, *than are dreamt of in your philosophy.*'

'Tosh,' Adeline scoffed. 'But where matters of the heart are concerned, one must make allowances. Speaking of which…'

She directed her gaze to Lucy Lannister, who looked beautiful in a russet-coloured silk dress, her hair curled and styled. She was dancing with the tall, flame-haired Scot. He was dressed simply but elegantly in black trousers with a crisp white shirt and a tie almost the same shade as Lucy's dress. Without his detecting overcoat, notebook and pencil, and customary frown, he looked younger, and happier.

'It's rather lovely, isn't it?' Miss Busby said, following her gaze. 'It's funny to think they were so at odds with one another just a few short months ago.'

'Yes, but he's at odds with everyone, initially,' Adeline replied. 'He scrubs up well, though, and the rough edges smooth out after a couple of brandies.'

Alcohol had flowed rather freely all evening. Richard was insistent everyone enjoy themselves, and it seemed impolite to refuse his hospitality. Besides, Miss Busby reasoned, they all deserved a treat.

As the music came to a close and the band announced a short break, Richard crossed the lawn to join them.

'I'm going to have to insist you give me the next dance, Isabelle,' he said, easing himself down into the chair opposite. 'It is my birthday, after all.' He waved to Lucy and the inspector, who came over to join them. Enid and Mr Waterhouse, Miss Busby noted with a smile, went to take a turn around the pond. *A shared interest can work such wonders*, she thought.

Dawkins appeared beside the table with a selection of fresh drinks. Miss Busby, having found her head spinning somewhat when she had danced with Anthony earlier, selected an orange juice.

'Did Daddy tell you about the poems, Miss Busby?' Lucy asked.

'No?' She looked to Richard, who clapped a hand to his forehead.

'Forgive me, Isabelle! My head is full of music! But it was your idea, Lucy, and the honour should be yours.' He nodded reverently to his daughter, who laughed.

'We are going to publish a selection of Mr Travis' poems in the paper, in the Arts and Culture supplement. Mr Melnyk is helping us choose the best candidates.'

'Oh! How wonderful!' Miss Busby was touched at the gesture.

'We'll publish a note about the shared memorial service for him and Alice Albion, too. Mr Melnyk will be doing a reading. You'll be there, won't you?'

'Of course,' Miss Busby said. 'It will be lovely to see Rose and Ezekiel again.'

'Now that Martin Fowler has been charged with murder, it seems the right time to honour them both,' Adeline said, having had a hand in proceedings.

The inspector sat a little straighter in his chair, pride adding a glow to his already sun-warmed cheeks.

'Will you be able to attend, Inspector?' Miss Busby asked.

'Aye, Mrs Fanshawe was kind enough to arrange it for a Sunday, when I won't be working.'

Miss Busby braced for a possible sarcastic remark from Adeline, but none was forthcoming. Had a truce been reached, she wondered.

'Perfect. You can accompany Lucy,' Richard said with a smile. 'Anthony will have more than enough to do.'

'More than enough of what?' Lucy asked.

'Ah, yes, perhaps it's time,' Richard said, rising to his feet and flicking his glass loudly to attract the attention of all his guests.

'Ladies and gentlemen,' he said, his voice ringing with the confidence and self-assuredness of a man who was master of all he surveyed. 'If I may have your attention for a moment.' Silence fell, and all eyes turned to him. 'Firstly, thank you for helping me celebrate my birthday in style!' He lifted his cane, to much applause. 'Lucy has made a wonderful job of the arrangements, and I can't tell you how happy it makes me to have so many dear friends close by.' He looked down at Miss Busby, who smiled shyly, before suddenly finding her orange juice rather compelling. She could feel Adeline sliding further forward in her seat, eager to find out what was coming. 'With great age,' he went on, to scattered laughter, 'comes a certain wisdom. The wisdom to know what one is and isn't capable of, and to recognise when the time is right. And it is with happiness, rather than the reluctance I've felt prior, that I today officially hand over ownership of the *Oxford News* to my son, Anthony.'

Miss Busby shot a glance at Lucy, who kept her head down and applauded along with the others.

'Congratulations, Anthony!' Richard shouted, raising his glass. Anthony, several tables away, stood and manfully took a bow, seeming to struggle a little with the attention.

'Now, whilst Anthony is a top-rate chap,' Richard continued, 'I think it's fair to say he is not, by any stretch of the imagination, a born reporter. Unlike my wonderful daughter, Lucy.'

Lucy looked up in surprise.

'Stand up, Lucy!' Richard urged. 'You are one of the most gifted, natural-born reporters I have ever encountered, and with this in mind, I would like you to run the paper alongside Anthony as Editor-in-Chief.'

Miss Busby broke into a huge smile as she applauded, mouthing '*Well done*!' to the beaming Lucy opposite.

'Bravo!' The distinctive Scots accent rang out, and Miss Busby smiled even wider.

'And one final thing,' Richard called, as the congratulations died down. 'With this in mind, I have decided to leave Lannister House to my wonderful offspring, and take a smaller place for my own.'

Lucy looked more startled than ever. 'I shan't be far away,' he said, catching sight of her expression. 'But a rather wonderful new friend of mine, Mrs Enid Montgomery, is selling a place in Little Minton that suits me perfectly.'

The Grange, Miss Busby thought, as startled as Lucy had looked. She searched for her friend in the crowd, and found her smiling beside Mr Waterhouse, by the rose bushes. The sale would be an immense relief to Enid, as the fees at Spring Meadows were not inconsiderable.

'Miss Busby!' Her name rang out among the guests, startling her out of her reverie.

'Yes?'

Richard laughed, then ducked down to explain. 'A toast. I was saying how fortuitous the move is, as it will bring me closer to my dear friend and gifted sleuth, Miss Busby!'

'Oh. Goodness.' She looked around nervously, raising her glass in acknowledgement.

The band started up again in the distance, and as the buzz of movement and chatter began, Richard held out his hand to her. 'May I have this dance?'

As the pair made their way to the dance floor, past the flickering oil lamps that had been hung around the grounds, Richard asked quietly, 'You don't mind, do you? I didn't want to say anything until it was all arranged.'

'No, of course not. Enid must be thrilled.' Miss Busby did mind a little, she thought, that Enid hadn't given her a single hint.

'I swore Mrs Montgomery to secrecy,' he said, as if somehow reading her mind. 'Until it was signed and sealed.'

She laughed. 'I'm not sure I quite understand, though,' she confessed, as they found some space on the floor and began to move to the music. 'Aren't you comfortable here?'

'Oh, hugely. But Anthony will be looking for a wife before I know it, and Lucy…' He looked off to where she sat, deep in discussion with the handsome inspector. 'I thought it better to give them some space. They're such wonderful children. Well, not children anymore of course, but they always will be to me.'

Miss Busby sighed. *This is not the time to dwell on regrets*, she thought, as the music picked up pace. 'But why The Grange?' she asked, distracting herself.

'Well, it's much smaller, of course. Bit more manageable with my gammy leg. And it's out of the way. Oxford is a young man's city. I feel more ready for the gentle quiet of the countryside.'

'Not always so gentle…' she warned.

'Oh, I know! The murders! But I shall be perfectly

safe, living in close proximity to such an accomplished sleuth!'

'Richard, really,' she chided. 'I simply helped a friend, that's all.'

He laughed. 'I'm only teasing. And besides, we might have an adventure or two along the way, Isabelle. It has been glorious, these last few months, to have a friend such as yourself.'

'Yes,' she said, 'I have enjoyed it too, but…'

'What is it?' He looked at her, concern creasing his features.

'Oh, it's just… I hope you understand that I will always think of Randolf as my husband, even though he was taken from me before we wed.'

He smiled down at her. 'Of course you will. And I am the very same with my own dear late wife. That's one of the reasons we get on so well, I think, don't you?'

Relief eased the ache in Miss Busby's shoulders. 'Yes, well, that and the fact that you can't finish one of those new crosswords without my help.'

Richard laughed. 'I've told Anthony we need to take on our mystery setter permanently.'

'You still don't know who he is?'

'We only know him as *The Saint*. It's all very intriguing. Difficult to hire the chap when we don't know who he is, though. Perhaps I should set you on the case!'

Miss Busby smiled, and with her friends around her she began to relax into the music. Jazz, she decided, perhaps wasn't quite so bad after all.

I do hope you have enjoyed this book. If you'd like to leave a review, I'd be very grateful.

Would you like to take a look at the Readers Club website? As a member of the Readers Club, you'll receive the FREE short story, 'Heathcliff Lennox – France 1918' , which you can listen to in audio version or read as an ebook.

There's also access to the 'World of Lennox' page, where you can view portraits of Lennox, Swift, Greggs, Foggy, Tubbs, Persi and Tommy Jenkins. There are 'inspirations' for the books, plus occasional newsletters with updates and free giveaways.

You can find the Readers Club, and more, at *https://karenmenuhin.com/*

You can also *follow me on Amazon* for immediate updates on new releases and of course, all the many deals and offers Amazon runs on the books in the series.

* * *

Here's the full **Heathcliff Lennox** series list and **Miss Busby** so far, more are on the way. All the ebooks are on Amazon. Print books can be found on Amazon and online through your favourite book stores.

Book 1: *Murder at Melrose Court*
Book 2: *The Black Cat Murders*
Book 3: *The Curse of Braeburn Castle*
Book 4: *Death in Damascus*

Book 5: *The Monks Hood Murders*
Book 6: *The Tomb of the Chatelaine*
Book 7: *The Mystery of Montague Morgan*
Book 8: *The Birdcage Murders*
Book 9: *A Wreath of Red Roses*
Book 10: *Murder at Ashton Steeple*
Book 11: *The Belvedere Murders*
Book 12: *The Twelve Saints of Christmas* – ready for
   pre-order now. Available mid 2024

AMAZING AUDIBLE

And there are Audio versions read by Sam Dewhurst-Phillips, who is superb. He 'acts' all the voices – it's just as if listening to a radio play. Corrie James reads Miss Busby beautifully, and really brings the lady and all her friends alive.

Audible books can be found on Amazon, Audible and Apple Books.

There is also the **Miss Busby** series. So far there are only two books, but more are in the pipeline.

Miss Busby Investigates, Book 1: *Murder at Little
   Minton*
Miss Busby Investigates, Book 2: *Death of a Penniless
   Poet*
Miss Busby Investigates, Book 3: *The Lord of Cold
   Compton* ready for pre-order early in the new year.

A LITTLE ABOUT KAREN BAUGH MENUHIN

1920s, Cozy crime, Traditional Detectives, Downton Abbey – I love them! Along with my family, my dog and my cat.

At 60 I decided to write, I don't know why but suddenly the stories came pouring out, along with the characters. Eccentric Uncles, stalwart butlers, idiosyncratic servants, machinating Countesses, and the hapless Major Heathcliff Lennox. A whole world built itself upon the page and I just followed along.

Now, some years later I have reached number 1 in the USA and sold over a million books. It's been a huge surprise, and goes to show that it's never too late to try something new.

I grew up in the military, often on RAF bases but preferring to be in the countryside when we could. I adore whodunnits, art and history of any description.

I have two amazing sons – Jonathan and Sam Baugh, and his wife, Wendy, and five grandchildren, Charlie, Joshua, Isabella-Rose, Scarlett and Hugo.

I am married to Krov, my wonderful husband, who is a retired film maker and eldest son of the violinist, Yehudi Menuhin. We live in the Cotswolds.

For more information you can contact me via my email address,

karenmenuhinauthor@littledogpublishing.com

Karen Baugh Menuhin is a member of The Crime Writers Association, The Author's Guild and The Society of Author's.

* * *

ABOUT CO-AUTHOR ZOE MARKHAM

I'm an ex-teacher living in West Oxfordshire with my teenage son and our Jack Russell terrier. I'm fortunate enough to edit fiction for a living, and have had three Young Adult novels published. Miss Busby is my first foray into both adult fiction and the 1920s!

Printed in Great Britain
by Amazon

48440647R00229